The
Morning
Star

Also by Robert Aitken

The Morning Star

New and Selected Zen Writings

Robert Aitken

SHOEMAKER S&H HOARD, *Publishers*

WASHINGTON, DC

The drawings of Makkōhō and Zazen positions on pages 64 and 66 are by Andrew Thomas.

Some of these writings have appeared in slightly different forms, or in excerpts, in the following journals: *Avaloka: A Journal of Traditional Religion and Culture; The International Journal of Transpersonal Studies; Kenyon Review; Mind, Moon, Circle; News from Kaimu; Parabola; Shambhala Sun; Tricycle; Turning Wheel;* and *The Wallace Stevens Journal.* Further acknowledgments can be found on page 287.

Library of Congress Cataloging-in-Publication Data
Aitken, Robert, 1917–
  The morning star : new and selected Zen writings / Robert Aitken.
    p. cm.
  ISBN 1-59376-001-9
  1. Spiritual life—Zen Buddhism. 2. Zen Buddhism—Doctrines.
  I. Title.
BQ9288 .A355 2003
294.3'444—dc22   2003014108

Text and cover design by Amy Evans McClure
Printed in the United States of America

 SHOEMAKER & HOARD, *Publishers*
A Division of the Avalon Publishing Group
Distributed by Publishers Group West

10 9 8 7 6 5 4 3 2 1

For
Nelson Foster

Contents

Reflections

When the mind is like a hall in which thought is like a voice speaking, the voice is always that of some one else.

Wallace Stevens, "Adagia"

Acknowledgments

R. H. Blyth opened the door of Zen for me. My teachers Nyogen Senzaki, Sōen Nakagawa, Haku'un Yasutani, and finally my primary master Kōun Yamada set me firmly on the path. Anne Hopkins Aitken, Nelson Foster, and Jack Shoemaker gave me consistent encouragement, support, and practical assistance through the years of composing most of the pieces in this collection. Gillian Coote, editor of *Mind Moon Circle*, Susan Moon, editor of *Turning Wheel,* and Robert Tindall, editor of *Blind Donkey*, prompted me to compose journal articles.

In addition to friends acknowledged in the various books represented here, I received good ideas, significant assistance, and encouragement from Thomas Aitken, Lewis Hyde, Arnold Kotler, Amy Evans McClure, Gregory Mello, Daniel Mintie, Unzan Harry Pfennig, Samuel Shapiro, Victoria Shoemaker, John Thomas, Arthur Versluis, Edward Walters, and Gray Zeitz. I want especially to thank my editor, Trish Hoard. Her vision of the best possible book and her talent and patience in following through kept me ever faithful to my own intentions.

In previous books, I acknowledged the tireless secretaries and other helpers who assisted me with editing and research. To that roster I wish to add Janice Brown, Gloria Coffey, Kristine Kubat, and Nil Özbek.

References

Thirty years ago, under the guidance of the late Yamada Kōun Rōshi, I translated the cases that make up the four principal collections studied in his school, the Sanbōkyōdan, which we also use in the Diamond Sangha. Those drafts form the basis of translations of many cases I have used in this book, and are cited by initials and case numbers. For comparisons, see the following:

(BCR) The Blue Cliff Record (Pi-yen lu, Chinese; *Hekiganshū* or *Hekiganroku,* Japanese); Thomas and J. C. Cleary, *The Blue Cliff Record* (Boston: Shambhala Publications, 1992)

(BS) The Book of Serenity (Ts'ung-jung lu, C; *Shōyōroku,* J)); Thomas Cleary, *Book of Serenity* (Hudson, N.Y.: Lindisfarne Books, 1990)

(GB) The Gateless Barrier (Wu-men kuan, C; *Mumonkan,* J); Zenkei Shibayama, *The Gateless Barrier: Zen Comments on the Mumonkan,* translated by Sumiko Kudo (Boston: Shambhala Publications, 2000)

(TL) The Transmission of the Light (Denkōroku, J); Francis Dojun Cook, *The Record of Transmitting the Light: Zen Master Keizan's Denkoroku* (Boston: Wisdom Publications, 2002)

The other translations in this book are mine, for the most part—made from original texts with a check against other translations. The

Genjōkōan, Bendōwa, and other writings of Dōgen Kigen are mostly from his collection, the *Shōbōgenzō.* See Gudo Nishimura and Chodo Cross, *Master Dogen's Shobogenzo,* 4 vols. (Woking, Surrey/ London: Windbell Publications, 1994–1999). *The Transmission of the Lamp* is the *Ching-te Chu'an-teng lu* (*Keitoku Dentōroku*), published in 1004, a treasury of sayings and doings of over 600 earlier masters. See Andy Ferguson, *Zen's Chinese Heritage: The Masters and Their Teachings* (Boston: Wisdom Publications, 2000).

Taking the Path Anew

My first book on Zen practice, *Taking the Path of Zen,* was a compilation of introductory talks I gave in Hawai'i at the Maui Zendo and the Koko An Zendo during the 1970s, which I then revised for publication in 1982. Over the two decades since, my views have become clearer, so refinements continue.

I remember reading in the memoirs of Walter De La Mare how impressed he was on looking over what he had written forty years earlier: "What a clever fellow I was!" he exclaimed. Well, I don't have that response when I read my old writings. I find more affinity with R. H. Blyth, who once remarked to me, "I've reached the point where I can say, 'What a fool I was three weeks ago!'"

De La Mare probably did not revise his old words. W. S. Merwin mentions in the foreword to his *Selected Poems* that he hadn't changed his earlier poems in the least, since in some respects he is not the person he was when he wrote them. I was reading Merwin's poetry in *The Nation* some fifty years ago, and it was fine work. I wouldn't change it either.

However, I write about the Buddha Dharma. My early writings might have interest for a scholar pursuing a history of North American Zen, but my purpose in publishing this selection is not simply to resurrect my archives, but to set forth Zen in the truest way I can at this present moment. Thus I have revised some of my old writings a bit, some more than just a bit. I'm confident that in time my successors will correct my present views as their own understanding deepens.

Taking the Path of Zen remains a straightforward presentation of the practice: its rationale, method, attitudes, key terminology, etymology, and everyday application—with cautions about pitfalls. Some of it is out-of-date (for example, the training-center functions of the Maui Zendo and the Koko An Zendo have been assumed by the Pālolo Zen Center), but I don't disagree with the main points, and I continue to recommend it to inquirers. However, "Taking the Path Anew" is what I am always doing, as all teachers have done.

> Ta-mei asked Ma-tsu (709–788), "What is Buddha?"
> Ma-tsu said, "This very mind is Buddha."
> Later another monk asked Ma-tsu, "What is Buddha?"
> Ma-tsu said, "Not mind, not Buddha."
>   (GB-30, 33)

Over the years, I have been fascinated by stories of the Buddha's enlightenment, and the words he used to sum up his realization. In the millennia since his time, the chronicle and the précis have changed radically with the evolution of the religious views of his followers in widely diverse cultures, particularly those of India and China. I shall muse in this essay how the major changes in the story reflect worldviews of Mahāyāna and Zen Buddhism, and, by implication at least, how they reflect my own views, now that I've retired from an active teaching career.

The Classical accounts of the Buddha's enlightenment place him under a Bodhi tree, after a pilgrimage that involved study with leading teachers of mind control, and then a period of ascetic practices. He took up focused meditation and, passing through a succession of inner conditions, discerned that *duhkha* (an anguished sense of lack) is everywhere.[1] He gained insight into the cycle of karma in which sentient beings are ensnared. People seek permanence, accumulation, and power to smother their well-founded suspicion that nothing abides. These efforts don't work, and anguish is the inevitable outcome. Liberation from this misery comes when it is crystal clear that essence, soul, and self are delusions, and that, for better or for worse, everything is contingent on everything else. The whole of Buddhism begins with this teaching, formulated by the Buddha as the Four Noble Truths:

1. An anguished sense of lack is everywhere.
2. The source of this anguished sense of lack is our desire for permanent existence for ourselves and our loved ones, and our desire to prove ourselves free of others and superior to them.
3. Liberation from this anguish comes with the profound realization that we live only briefly, that we are reliant on one another, and that we have no essential substance.
4. Attainment of this liberation is the Eightfold Path: Right Views, Right Resolve, Right Speech, Right Conduct, Right Livelihood, Right Endeavor, Right Recollection, and Right *Samādhi*, focused meditation.

The Four Noble Truths are called "noble" because they present the vocation of deepest wisdom and boundless compassion. Each of the steps on the Eightfold Path is correct because, beginning with Right Views, they are in keeping with reality. By following this path, we not only enable liberation for ourselves, but for everyone and everything. We set the scene, so to speak, for universal happiness.

The use of the term "path" can be misleading, for the eight steps really form a loop, beginning and ending with the wisdom of Right Views. Right Resolve is *bodhichitta*, literally "the thought of enlightenment," the determination to realize the truths of inexorable ephemerality and interdependence in this multi-centered world. Ethical speech, conduct, and livelihood follow upon a wise understanding of how things are, and rigorous endeavor, recollection, and exacting meditation enhance and clarify the original wisdom. And it is more than a loop; it's a feedback system, with each step clarifying each other step. With Right Livelihood, my views are enhanced. With Right Recollection, my resolve is enhanced. The diagram would be a kind of wheel, with lines from each point across to every other point.

The teaching of Right Speech sets forth a vitally important path in itself, carrying over and enriching the maxims of Gentle Speech in earlier Hinduism. It is the way of the healing truth, of avoiding slander, gossip, and malicious words, which cause disunion. Right Speech is not harsh or frivolous, but is appropriate, cogent, and instructive. It encourages others and displays patience with the slow-witted and uninformed.

Right Conduct is sometimes narrowly interpreted simply as the avoidance of killing, theft, and sexual promiscuity, but in everyday practice it follows the guidelines for Right Speech. It brings the beings of the world together, and helps to clear the way for them to realize their true nature, by direct action and by virtuous example.

Right Livelihood is likewise narrowly defined in Classical texts as avoiding particular occupations that, almost by definition, tend to harm others, such as swindling, fabricating and trading in lethal weapons, producing and selling liquor or drugs, butchering, and so on. By extension one can find harmful implications in a broad range of modern occupations. An attorney, for example, can be involved either in pernicious mischief or in community organization that works for social betterment and is clearly "Right." On the other hand, there is not much ethical range in the manufacture and sale of weaponry, or in some other "Wrong" livelihoods.

Right Endeavor is the practice of Right Resolve, and is the zeal of earnest students, their perseverance, ardor, and unfaltering effort. The imperative of *bodhichitta*, the passion for realization, plays out in Right Endeavor, sweeping everything else off the path.

Right Recollection is sometimes rendered "Right Mindfulness," and both terms are to the point of practicing awareness of who and what we are and can be, who and what our fellow beings are and can be. Grieving over the death of a spouse or parent, one regrets not practicing Right Mindfulness in days that are now unhappily past. It is a poignant reminder that as we neglect the reality of our transience and interrelationships, we neglect our chance to realize our precious heritage as human beings.

Right Samādhi is the practice of *samatha* (quieting the mind) and *vipassanā* (insight) designed to enable Right Views and the other steps on the path, first taught in Classical Buddhism, and taught today in South and Southeast Asia.

❖❖❖

The legend of the Buddha's early life recounts his departure from home and family at age twenty-eight or so, to search for spiritual understanding. He studied with leading masters of yoga of his time, then left them for a solitary practice in the forest. After a stint of asceticism, he took up focused meditation beneath a pipal tree (a species later called the Bodhi tree, the tree of enlightenment), and in time he passed through stages of spiritual understanding and found liberation in his realization that the self and soul are false concepts. He formulated the Four Noble Truths as his first teaching of the way to this liberation.

This legend undergirds the teachings of Classical Buddhism, which prevailed for about 500 years and continues to evolve in modern schools of the Theravāda, or "Way of the Elders," in South and Southeast Asia, and in centers today throughout the Western Hemisphere. The Mahāyāna or "Great Vehicle" arose at about the beginning of the Common Era and is quite different in doctrine, but still traceable to expressions of understanding found in the Buddha's own sermons.

Both Theravāda and Mahāyāna traditions set forth the practice and experience of liberation from false views of an enduring self or soul, but they differ in approach and emphasis. The Theravāda way is traditionally monastic (though most Western Theravāda centers are made up of lay members). The individual Theravāda student reaches out to others in loving-kindness, and thus encourages selflessness in the world. The Mahāyāna way began as monastic and a certain monastic tradition continues. However, lay responsibility for Buddhist practice is clearly evident in many of its sects, both East and West. A great variety of teachings are found in the Mahāyāna, including the Zen view that the many beings are no other than oneself. Empathy with others becomes suffering *as* others.

Along with the other innovations found in the Mahāyāna, the story of the Buddha's realization beneath the Bodhi tree underwent a profound change. Style shifted from the discursive of South Asian culture to the presentational and metaphorical of East Asia. Content too shifted, as points of emphasis formed a pattern of teaching in keeping with Mahāyāna endeavor to practice in organic and dynamic accord with the world.

In inimitable Chinese matter-of-fact style, here is Ta-hui Tsung-kao, a twelfth-century Lin-chi (Rinzai) master, addressing his assembly (from an account in *The Transmission of the Lamp*):

> When old Shākyamuni was at the foot of the Mountain of True Awakening, he lifted his head, saw the morning star, and suddenly awakened to the Tao. Thereupon he said with surprise, "How strange! All the many beings are endowed with the wisdom and virtue of the Tathāgata, yet simply because of their delusions and preoccupations, they cannot bear witness to their endowment."

"Tathāgata" is another name for Buddha, the one who "thus comes." Ta-hui's words established the version of the Buddha's enlightenment story taught in the Lin-chi school of Ch'an, and now in the Rinzai school of Zen, and in the early Ts'ao-tung or Sōtō school version as well.

This story did not spring fully developed in Chinese Buddhism. As the broadly inclusive views of the Mahāyāna became established, the earlier account of his personal stages of meditation was dropped and circumstantial details were added—that his realization came at dawn, that it came on his glimpse of the morning star—and then with the translation and reformulation of the *Avatamsaka Sūtra* as the *Hua-yen ching* in the seventh century we find a stunningly elaborate account of the wisdom he attained, which is no other than the wisdom inherent in all beings. Finally, with the peak of Ch'an development in the twelfth century, the quintessentially Zen kind of encapsulation of the legend was set forth by Ta-hui.

Though in wording the Zen version of the Buddha's realization differs sharply from the Classical account, it is clear that the distinction is a matter of emphasis. The actual turning point of the Buddha's great attainment is omitted from the Classical account, but is central to the Zen story. Character formation and practice are stressed in the Classical legend. They are omitted in the Zen version, but are stressed in the rigors of monastic training. These subtle differences manifest cultural attitudes of India and China, and play out to the present day in Theravāda and Zen centers, noticeably in rhetorical styles. Here, for example, the bandit in the Classical *Angulimāla Sutta* addresses the Buddha in verse, and the Buddha responds:

"While you were walking, recluse, you tell me you have stopped;
But now, when I have stopped, you say I have not stopped.
I ask you now, O recluse, about the meaning:
How is it that you have stopped and I have not?"

"Angulimāla, I have stopped forever,
I abstain from violence towards living beings;
But you have no restraint towards things that live:
That is why I have stopped and you have not."[2]

The Buddha explains his metaphor of "stopping," and thus, together
with Angulimāla, we are persuaded by reason. Contrast with the traditional style of Zen:

> As Yün-yen was sweeping the grounds, Tao-wu said, "You are very
> busy."
>   Yün-yen said, "You should know that there is someone who isn't
> busy."
>   Tao-wu said, "Is that so? You mean there's a second moon?"
>   Yün-yen held up his broom and asked, "Which moon is this?"
>
>   (BS-21)

With metaphors of busy and not busy and the moon, Tao-wu and
his younger brother lightly toss the wicker ball of the Dharma back
and forth, and the reader or listener is left with seeing into the poetry. We are persuaded by metaphor. With metaphor comes humor,
and one can imagine how they grinned at each other. I found to my
surprise in my formal Zen practice in Japan that the *teishō*, or
Dharma talk of the Zen master, can be marked by giggles and occasionally even outright laughter from the monks, even though they
are constrained to be earnest at such times while "listening to the
very words of the Buddha."

It seems, however, that while the movement of the Dharma from
India to China tended to accompany a shift from the discursive to
the metaphorical, important exceptions tend to prove the general-
ization. For example, the *Vimalakīrti Sūtra*, composed in India after
the rise of the Mahāyāna, is metaphorical from beginning to end,
and is full of humor, some of it hilarious. The monumental
Avatamsaka Sūtra too is metaphor. The Sanskrit originals of both of
these sūtras are lost, and we are dependent on Chinese and Tibetan

translations for our judgments. It is nonetheless apparent that evolution in religion as well as conversion to a new culture played a role in the change.

Moreover, the discerning student will find what might be considered a Mahāyāna perspective in the teachings of certain teachers of Theravāda. Here, for example, is a passage from the writings of the Bhikkhu Buddhadāsa, whose followers form an important part of contemporary Thai Buddhism:

> The entire cosmos is a cooperative. The sun, the moon, and the stars live together as a cooperative. The same is true for humans, animals, and the soil. Our bodily parts function as a cooperative. When we realize that the world is a mutually interdependent, cooperative enterprise, that human beings are all mutual friends in the process of birth, old age, suffering, and death, then we can build a noble, even a heavenly environment. If our lives are not based on this truth then we shall all perish.[3]

This cosmic vision of interdependence and its pertinent implications for people today is Mahāyāna in its vast scope and its use of simile, if not metaphor, but it is nonetheless rooted firmly in the Classical account of the Buddha's fundamental teaching, that human misery is rooted in pernicious self-centeredness.

The modern schools of Theravāda and Mahāyāna emerged from Classical Buddhism because there are people disposed toward the two different views. As my first Zen friend, R. H. Blyth, used to say in the sexist rhetoric of the 1940s, "There is a man for every religion, and a religion for every man." As a Zen Buddhist, I find myself in the Mahāyāna camp, and in the Zen camp of the Mahāyāna. I focus my attention there.

The Zen camp is set up in the domain of folklore and metaphor. When scholars point out that internal evidence tends to belie the tradition that Hui-neng, the Sixth Ancestor, was illiterate, then folklore can challenge historical fact. Dostoyevsky's Father Zossima is a fictional personage, but he has changed many lives. The legend that Hui-neng was illiterate is likewise profoundly instructive. It is in keeping with the Four Statements of Bodhidharma, which are also apocryphal:

1. A special transmission outside the sūtras
2. Not founded on words or letters
3. Directly pointing to the human mind
4. Seeing into true nature and attaining Buddhahood

Br'er Rabbit didn't *really* taunt Br'er Fox, "Born and bred in the briar patch!" but the child takes the story to heart. The adult student of Zen takes the folklore of the Buddha and his successors to heart as well.

What can we learn from this folklore? The Buddha Way itself. The entire Zen story is folklore. If it could be shown that the Buddha never lived, it wouldn't matter a smidgen. There is nothing to believe, and I say that as a believer. Wallace Stevens remarked in his "Adagia":

> The final belief is to believe in a fiction, which you know to be a fiction, there being nothing else. The exquisite truth is to know that it is a fiction and that you believe in it willingly.[4]

I'm not condemning the disciplines of translation, history, metaphysics, hermeneutics, and theology. They provide invaluable texts and enrich our practice, but our practice is not grounded in scholarship. In fact, the morning star folk-story continues to unfold. A century or so after Ta-hui's account of the Buddha's realization, Dōgen Kigen offered his version in his *Hotsumujōshin*, which is widely quoted today:

> When the bright star appeared, the Buddha Shākyamuni said, "Intimately together, I and the great Earth have at this same moment attained the Tao."

You can see why Theravāda followers of Classical Buddhism will sometimes say that Zen is not Buddhism. Over centuries and across cultural lines, doctors of the Dharma refined the old diagnoses and adjusted styles of treatment. Shākyamuni is reenvisioned and words traditionally ascribed to him are totally changed. The opaque from the past becomes transparent for the present time and culture.

Incidentally, I do not wish to imply that Zen Buddhism awaited Dōgen's words to establish its inclusive views. The views were long since established, and the world of Zen simply awaited Dōgen to reformulate the Buddha's words accordingly. I also do not wish to imply that Dōgen's version was somehow wiser or deeper than that of Ta-hui. Both formulated important aspects of the great matter.

Though the terms "sentient beings" and "all beings" (*shujō*) are not included in Dōgen's version, most translators shoehorn them in. Rightfully, I think, Gudo Nishijima and Chodo Cross, for example, translate the passage: "When the bright star appeared, I together with the Earth and all sentient beings, simultaneously realized the truth."[5] All are the Sangha, a treasure of Buddhism, in which we take refuge. "Sangha" derives from an Indic root meaning "aggregate," a conjunction or collection of particles—bits of gravel, for example, which can be crushed together for the construction of roads. Originally, and to this day in some contexts, "Sangha" has referred simply to the priesthood, and with that meaning, taking refuge in the Sangha is simply an expression of fealty to the community of monks.

The Mahāyāna understanding seems to me to be truer to etymology: All particles form the Sangha, and together they are consonant. Indeed, one particle contains all particles. "Sangha" in East Asian languages, *sō* in Sino-Japanese, for example, can also mean just one monk. Here is Matsuo Bashō, seventeenth-century founder of the school of haiku that bears his name:

> Drinking his morning tea
> the monk is at peace
> chrysanthemums

Asa cha nomu	Morning tea drinks
sō shizuka nari	monk peaceful is
kiku no hana	chrysanthemum flowers

Though the line "the monk is at peace" has been criticized, probably because it is seen to be prosaic, the poem is useful for our purposes. Not only does it illustrate the use of *sō* as the individual monk, but his peace on taking tea in the context of the chrysanthemums pervades the poem, and it pervades everyone on reading it. That is Sangha. The whole universe is there with Bashō, experiencing his experience of the monk's experience.

Ordinary individual laypeople are also the Sangha, embodying the cooperative community of the world—past, present, and future. Here is Tao-ch'ang Ming-pien, a twelfth-century Lin-chi master:

> A monk asked Tao-ch'ang, "What is 'Sangha'?"
> Tao-ch'ang said, "An old woman selling fans shades herself from the sun with her hand."[6]

The old woman selling fans at a wayside stand shields herself from the sun with her hand rather than with her handiwork, and we empathize—we identify with her together in the great aggregate across the world and the centuries. At the moment she lifts her hand, all beings shield themselves. This is, one might say, the experiential proof of Bell's Theorem, that anything that happens to a single particle anywhere happens to all other particles everywhere at the same moment and in the same way. Bell's Theorem is a complex hypothesis, grounded in concepts of advanced physics and justified by elaborate experiments, which some scientists regard with suspicion. They would become even more suspicious if they realized that Tao-ch'ang intends to say that the moment the old woman raised her hand is the very moment he presented her experience before his monks, and to his successors in our own time. This is mutually dependent arising, and is reflected in many Zen stories:

> A monk asked Chao-chou, the great T'ang period master, "Has the newborn infant the sixth sense?"
> Chao-chou said, "Tossing a ball on a swift current."
> The monk went to T'ou-tzu and asked, "What does 'Tossing a ball on a swift current' mean?"
> T'ou-tzu said, "Moment by moment it never stops flowing."
> (BCR-80)

However you may understand Chao-chou and T'ou-tzu here, it is clear that they occupied a common ground. Commenting on this case in *The Blue Cliff Record*, Yüan-wu remarks, "The practice of these ancients, Chao-chou and T'ou-tzu, was so thoroughgoing that they answered as one." The insightful student can join their team in a cogent presentation before the master on a day chronologically remote and at a place on the other side of the world.

Here is a case from *The Transmission of the Lamp* that illustrates the same point:

When Teng Ying-feng was about to leave Ma-tsu, the Ancestor asked him, "Where are you going?"

Ying-feng said, "To Shih-t'ou."

The Ancestor said, "Shih-t'ou's path is slippery."

Ying-feng said, "I will use my own skills to deal with the situation as it presents itself." Then he left.

As soon as he arrived in front of Shih-t'ou, he walked around the Ch'an seat once, struck his staff on the ground, and asked, "What is the meaning?"

Shih-t'ou said, "Heavens! Heavens!" Ying-feng was left speechless.

He returned to the Ancestor and reported what had happened. The Ancestor said, "Go back and see him again. When he says, 'Heavens! Heavens!' you make a deep sigh twice."

Ying-feng went back to Shih-t'ou and asked the same question as before. Shih-t'ou made a deep sigh twice. Ying-feng was left speechless again. He returned to the Ancestor and related what happened.

The Ancestor said, "I told you Shih-t'ou's path was slippery."

Ma-tsu and Shih-t'ou were contemporaneous masters in the ninth century whose successors developed the separate lines of Lin-chi and Ts'ao-tung. They conspired—breathed together—to bring the monk around. Like Chao-chou and T'ou-tzu, they were a Sangha within the broad monastery of Chinese Buddhism, a monastery now greatly enlarged with you and me involved, working together—cells giving life to cells in the vast universal organism.

This is *Pratītya samutpāda*, "mutually dependent arising," a term sometimes rendered as "mutual interdependence," though that translation lacks the active dynamic of "arising" or "coming into being." It is the other side of emptiness, so to speak. With the essential absence of soul and self, the great community manifests. Beings appear in their uniqueness without pith or permanence, and the whole magnificent system is their raison d'être. People, animals, and plants embody it as unique individuals.

This also from *The Transmission of the Lamp*:

Ch'ang-sha Ch'ing-ts'en, a ninth-century master, addressed his assembly and said, "If I were to raise the purport of the Dharma, grass would sprout up ten feet high in this hall. But I can't refrain from saying this to you brothers: The entire universe is the eye of a monk; the entire universe is the complete body of a monk; the entire universe is within your own luminance. In the entire universe there is no being that is not yourself. . . ."

A monk asked, "What is the eye of a monk?"

Ch'ang-sha said, "You must go far to get out of it. . . . You cannot get out of it even if you become a Buddha or an Ancestral Teacher, or if you transmigrate through the six paths [of hells, hungry ghosts, malevolent spirits, animals, humans, and devas]."

Ch'ang-sha's words about the eye of his brothers are one of the plainest presentations in Zen literature of the world as a hologram: the very eye of the observer is the boundless center. Two generations later, the master Hsüeh-feng checked the understanding of his monks by asking, "The entire universe is the single eye of a monk; where will you people go to defecate?" (BCR-5). In the record of Chao-chou, we find the point nailed home:

Chao-chou asked a newly arrived monk, "Where have you come from?"

The monk said, "From Hsüeh-feng."

Chao-chou asked, "What is Hsüeh-feng saying these days?"

The monk said, "The Master is saying, 'The entire universe is the eye of a monk, where will you people go to defecate?'"

Chao-chou said, "When you return there, take along this mattock."

You live in your all-inclusive universe as you stand up, sit down, and go to the toilet. There is actually only one dimension—in the whole universe there is no being that is not yourself: the bombers and the hapless peasants they bomb, the lumber executives and the old-growth forests they chop down, your spouse and kids tooling around with you in your SUV, and the innumerable who cannot afford a bicycle. Peasants and redwoods are not "out there." Compassionately, Ch'ang-sha and Chao-chou evoke the Buddha's fundamental teaching of living and dying together in a dynamic network of mutual interaction. Bombs destroy the bombers. Chain saws level the mansions. SUVs poison the air and exhaust the oil reserves, and those of us still with feet are reduced to walking. You cannot get out of the boundless dimension that you center, the plural "you," of course, but the one responsible is singular.

Children know about the limitless extent of their presence. In one of my earliest memories, perhaps a memory of a memory, I am being dried off after a bath, and am fascinated by the can of baby powder. A blue can, as I recall. The decoration includes an oval picture of a baby, holding the same can of baby powder. On that little can is a tiny picture of a baby, holding a can of baby powder. There is a little squiggle on the picture within the picture which I know is the same baby holding his can. "His" can, because I also know that the baby in those progressively inward pictures is myself. Later, as a boy of eight or nine, I had similar experiences in a barbershop, seeing myself on my chair, the mirrored walls projecting me deeper and deeper, lost only as the images blurred together deep in the distance.

Depths beyond depths. In 1984, I was invited to Europe for talks and meetings. Anne Aitken and I flew over the Pole in broad daylight, and as Anne on her inner seat read her book and napped, I watched from my window as lakes in the snowy terrain reflected the sun. The sun shone up at me from beneath the lakes. The frozen landscape was no more than a transparent film laid between sun above and sun beneath. The sun beneath was there from the beginning, and only momentarily disclosed itself through the transparent water as we zoomed by above. "These reflections," Thoreau remarked about his visit to a pond near Walden, "suggest that the sky underlies the hills as well as overlies above them, and in another sense than in appearance"[7]—and in settings other than ponds and the sky as well. I am reminded that woodblock prints of Japan are called *ukiyoe*, "pictures of the floating world" of human affairs.

It is your eye and mine, free from the conventional, that contains depths within depths—depths all the way down. I think Thoreau would have resonated with the experience of Sudhana, told in Book Three of the *Hua-yen ching*. He had visited fifty teachers and then met Maitreya, the Buddha still to be born in each of us, who guided him to his tower. On entering it:

> He saw the tower immensely vast and wide, hundreds of thousands
> of leagues wide, as measureless as the sky, as vast as all of space,
> adorned with countless attributes; countless canopies, banners,
> pennants, jewels, garlands of pearls and gems, moons and half-
> moons, multicolored streamers, jewel nets, gold nets, strings of

jewels, jewels on golden threads, sweetly ringing bells and nets of chimes, flowers showering. . . . Also inside the great tower he saw hundreds of thousands of other towers similarly arrayed; he saw those towers as infinitely vast as space, evenly arrayed in all directions, yet these towers were not mixed up with each other, each being distinct while appearing reflected in each and every other object of all the other towers.[8]

The sūtra goes on to recount how Sudhana found himself in all the towers, and in each of them he viewed an infinite variety of miraculous scenes. For many pages we are treated to immeasurable arrays: assemblies of Buddhas; circles of Bodhisattvas; congregations of disciples; defiled lands; pure lands; worlds in the cosmic net of Indra; subtle worlds; gross worlds; worlds of hells, animals, and ghosts; and worlds of celestials and humans.

The point here is inclusion, and the joy of Sudhana, and the joy of each of us with the bliss of the Sambhogakāya Buddha, the incarnation of intimate embodiment. The self is forgotten after a long pilgrimage, and one finds a containment of all towers, *as* all towers —of all beings *as* all beings.

This is the setting of the Bodhisattva Imperative to deny full and complete realization for oneself until all beings are realized. Fifty teachers conspired to bring Sudhana to Maitreya, who disclosed the pagoda of inner within inner. Maitreya then referred Sudhana back to Mañjushrī, Sudhana's first teacher, where he realized that his entry to his pilgrimage was no other than its goal. Mañjushrī then referred him on to Samantabhadra, whose vows as the Bodhisattva of Great Action for the realization of all beings became his own, fulfilled in their fulfilling.

This Third Book of the *Hua-yen ching* is our inspiration, yet its lofty imagery must not obscure its ground. There is something natural and essential involved here, the symbiosis of spirochetes in the gut of a termite that enables it to digest wood, the symbiosis that enables fungi, aphids, and leeches to survive. Indeed it is the inner within inner that is life itself, that creates life itself, a point reflected in Buddhadāsa's disquisition about community.

Each life is responsible to its constituency, a responsibility that is expressed in the action of the bee, for example, in inverse proportion to its self-consciousness, or so we judge. The human being is, it seems, far more aware and, at least when immature, far weaker in responsibility. Yet we must practice the kind of one-pointed focus that inspires a bee, in order to fulfill our vows.

> Yün-yen asked Tao-wu, "How does the Bodhisattva of Great Compassion use all those many hands and eyes?"
>
> Tao-wu said, "It is like reaching behind your head for your pillow in the middle of the night."
>
> (BCR-89)

In the person of the pilgrim Sudhana, the Bodhisattva Kuan-yin, the Incarnation of Great Mercy and Compassion, takes a long circuitous pilgrimage, from Mañjushrī to Mañjushrī, to reach the place where great action is so totally integrated that it is as unconscious as reaching behind one's head for a pillow, or, in the case of the bee, unconscious in sacrificing the self for the hive. I find it intriguing that Christian anarchists in Chiapas call themselves "The Bees" (*Las Abejas*).

Other possible analogies thus spring to mind. Competitive farmers and small shopkeepers in the French village of Le Chambon awaken to the plight of their fellows, and conspire to hide and ultimately liberate thousands of Jews in imminent danger of deportation to death camps. Concerned citizens come together in little Base Communities in the Philippines, which in turn network to aid in the overthrow of the despot Marcos. The imperative, set forth by Peter Kropotkin as *Mutual Aid* more than a hundred years ago, is by no means exclusively Buddhist.

I imagine how Kropotkin might have valued the eloquent archetypes of Mahāyāna Buddhism. The Net of Indra, a glorious metaphor found in *Hua-yen* commentaries, presents the universe and its beings as a great, multi-dimensional net, in which each point is a jewel, perfectly reflecting, and indeed including, all other jewels. Taken with the Buddha Shākyamuni's teaching of mutually dependent arising, the Bodhisattva Imperative kicks in. All beings are saved in daily-life reality.

Just as everyone inherently has the wisdom and virtue of the Tathāgata, so the Net of Indra, by whatever name, has been in place since the beginningless beginning. The question then arises: "How does networking operate?" It is a matter of conscious attunement, it seems. The Catholic Worker movement in the United States is a network that has no formal organization. There is no executive director, no head office, no official publication. Yet there are CW houses in most major cities, as well as CW farms scattered across the country. Visit one of these homes or farms in New York, and you will meet people who hold views that resonate to an uncanny degree with their counterparts in California. They call themselves anarchists, and I sense they mean that they occupy a common ground and that without formal appurtenances are nonetheless in good communication.

This common ground is the consonance of all the aggregate beings, human and non-human, within the confines of the great temple of the cosmos. Everything is involved in the Net of Indra, and with one touch, everything moves.

A well-known story in *The Transmission of the Lamp* helps to clarify this point. Hsüeh-feng and Yen-t'ou were on pilgrimage together. Fellow disciples of Te-shan Hsüan-chien, these two monks were intimate friends, Hsüeh-feng the older, but Yen-t'ou the wiser:

> The two monks stayed overnight at the village of Tortoise Mountain, where they were snowbound for several days. Yen-t'ou spent much of his time sleeping, but Hsüeh-feng sat up all day and for most of each night focusing himself in his formal practice. During one of his waking moments Yen-t'ou said, "What are you doing, sitting there all day long like a stone figure by the road?"
>
> Hsüeh-feng pointed to his chest and said, "I am not yet peaceful here."
>
> Yen-t'ou said, "What kinds of experiences have you had in the past? Tell me, and I will examine them for you."
>
> Hsüeh-feng then related a series of insights he experienced with his various teachers, and at the close of each story, Yen-t'ou had a sarcastic comment. Finally, Yen-t'ou shouted, and exclaimed, "Don't you know that what enters from the gate cannot be the treasure of the house? If you want to propagate the Great Teaching, it must flow point by point from within your own breast to cover Heaven

and Earth. Only then will it be the action of someone with spiritual power."

At that instant, Hsüeh-feng suddenly had realization and cried loudly, "Today, for the first time, Tortoise Mountain has become enlightened!"

The very bushes and grasses, the very trees and rice fields of Tortoise Mountain, became enlightened with Yen-t'ou's cogent admonition. Hsüeh-feng's experience on hearing Yen-t'ou's shout and then his definitive words was exactly in accord with the Buddha's realization as Dōgen understood it: "I and the great Earth have at the same moment attained the Tao." In the *Hotsumujōshin*, Dōgen goes on to say:

> The body-mind of the Buddha's truth is grass, trees, tiles, and pebbles; it is wind, rain, water, and fire. The mind is established when you work together with them so that the Buddha's truth is realized.

Hsüeh-feng's realization that Tortoise Mountain attained the way was a great experience, but it had a long lead. Actualizing grass, trees, tiles, and pebbles as the body-mind comes with a huge amount of practice. As a young student, reading through *kenshō* stories in the essays of D. T. Suzuki, I found myself in fields of beautiful, exotic flowers. It was only later that I learned that each flower was nurtured in dirt and had deep roots—and that I could not begin to flower for myself until I had tasted the muck and descended the depths. Nonetheless it was the inspiration of the flowers that carried me through—the kind of inspiration set forth so lyrically by John Masefield at the end of his narrative poem "The Everlasting Mercy":

> O lily springing clean,
> O lily bursting white,
> Dear lily of delight,
> Spring to my heart agen
> That I may flower to men.[9]

This is the inspiration of Zen students. Without the flowers and memories of them, the bone bending of formal zazen practice, the sleep deprivation in sesshin, the Zen seclusion, the discomforts of ritualized meals, and the rigor of the schedule would simply be yogic heroics. The presence of Hsüeh-feng's teachers in his memory, the promise implicit in their teaching, and the sweet intimations he experienced under their guidance inspired him to sit in zazen all day every day when he and his companion were snowed in at Tortoise Mountain. He had worked hard in his practice, for more than twenty years, it seems. Yen-t'ou kindly showed him the importance of making the points of his old teachers his own, and how he could not otherwise expound the Dharma for the world. Finally he was able to hear Yen-t'ou's reproof. Similarly, Dōgen braved a dangerous ocean voyage in a frail thirteenth-century Japanese ship to practice in a foreign language and culture, and to sweat blood in his effort to realize the great matter, and all great teachers have stories of equivalent endeavor.

The importance of practice cannot be overemphasized. Hsüeh-feng, Dōgen, you, and I are endowed with the wisdom and virtue of the Tathāgata, but visit a nursery school and notice how often the teachers are obliged to separate their little charges and admonish them to be decent to one another. Purity and equanimity may be there from the beginning, but it takes work to clarify it for oneself. The Bees of Chiapas offer analogies as they train together to find a ground for non-violent resistance to oppression. Catholic Workers pray, study, and practice in the trenches of poverty on their way of perfection. Here is a Zen story of realizing inherent purity, which is, of course, the same as the equanimity and harmony set forth in so many colors and forms in the ancestral teaching:

> The fiftieth ancestor was the Priest T'ien-t'ung Ju-ching (Tendō Nyojō, 1163–1228). One day his teacher Hsüeh-tou asked him, "How can you purify what has never been defiled?"
>
> The Master spent more than a year working on this question. Suddenly he realized the point, and exclaimed, "I have seen into what has never been defiled!"
>
> (TL-50)

He had it from the beginning, but it wasn't at all clear. T'ien-t'ung went on to be a great master in the Ts'ao-tung school of Ch'an, and the teacher of Dōgen Kigen.

❖❖❖

Lin-chi had the same view of wisdom and virtue intrinsic to human beings, which then must be brought to a level of understanding by practice with a good teacher. Once he reminisced with his students about his early study of the *vinaya*, the classical moral teachings, the sūtras, and the treatises, and his decision finally to set them aside, and seek the Way through Zen practice:

> I encountered an excellent friend and teacher, and then my Dharma eye at last became keen and bright, and for the first time I could judge the old priests of the world and tell who was crooked and who was straight. But this understanding was not with me when my mother gave birth to me. I had to probe and polish and undergo experiences until one morning I could see clearly for myself.

Indeed, "No man is born wise," as Don Quixote said. I get quite exercised by the Rousseauian view of human nature that can be found in some Zen settings. This is the notion that we are born enlightened, and that somehow family influences and bad schooling divert us into delusion. If we just sit quietly and let thoughts and feelings die down, then our true nature will manifest of itself. This is a fundamental error. It's not that easy and it's not self-taught.

"Probing and polishing" are the way of zazen, under the guidance of a good teacher. Closely defined, zazen is the seated practice of focusing upon and attunement with a single matter. In chapters of *Taking the Path of Zen* that I include in this volume, I set forth the methods and rationale of this practice, but I offer just my own perspective. You will want to read about the perspectives of our great ancestors. Six books are right at hand as I work: Hee-Jin Kim's *Dōgen Kigen: Mystical Realist;* Isshū Miura and Ruth Fuller Sasaki's *Zen Dust;* Arthur Braverman's *Mud and Water: The Collected Teachings of Zen Master Bassui;* Burton Watson's *The Zen Teachings of Master Lin-chi;* Urs App's *Master Unmen;* and Norman Waddell's *The Essential Teachings of Zen Master Hakuin.* What expression of Zen makes the most sense to you? The old teachers were each of them individual personalities, and their sayings and doings reflected their uniqueness. At any given point in your practice you will find affinity with some and not so much with others. Those who seem to speak directly to you are the ones you can study most productively.

I have heard that some Western teachers urge their students not to read. This is an egregious error in a number of respects. First, it has no basis in tradition. Zen monks I have come to respect over the years are learned people, who not only keep up with writing in their field, but who read broadly otherwise. When I first began my practice, I could find only the writings of D. T. Suzuki, the booklets of Nyogen Senzaki—later collected in *Zen Flesh, Zen Bones*—and some incidental ephemera. I devoured them all. Today there are hundreds of cogent translations, commentaries, surveys, and references. Let your library angel guide you.

In addition, the admonition not to read is an error because of our cultural situation. Zen Buddhism is even now part of the air of Japan. A teacher there will not have to simplify much when addressing a lay audience. It is different here in the Western Hemisphere. As a beginner in Zen practice, I heard D. T. Suzuki address an academic audience at the University of Hawai'i, back in the summer of 1949. Listening to him, I felt that he was weaving a tapestry in a pattern I trusted was altogether congruous. But I was sitting on the other side of the frame, and the threads came poking through in a seemingly random manner that was completely incoherent for me. This kind of response to a presentation of Zen is one the average Western newcomer knows very well. Thus it is important to read about Zen to get a good sense of its tapestry.

It is also important to learn about its context. Excellent studies of Confucianism and Taoism are appearing these days, and these should be included in your reading, for after all, Ch'an and Zen emerged from the sea of Chinese culture. Without a pretty good sense of the cultural background of the old teachers, Zen becomes just a kind of Western cult, like Theosophy, with only faint echoes of the original.

Another point is that powerful old words come with reading. I deplore the way the vocabulary of Zen is dumbed down in some English texts. The Dharma becomes simply teaching; *samādhi* becomes "trance"; *bodhisattva* becomes "enlightening being"—and so on. The rich ambiguity and associational virtues of the terms are lost, the message of the ancestors is diverted and diminished, and our practice is impoverished. The great early translators of Indian texts into Chinese, Kumarajiva, Tao-an, and Hsüang-tsan recognized that many Sanskrit and Pali words were simply untranslatable because they had no equivalent in Chinese, or because they had many meanings and a rendering of just one of them as an equivalent would devitalize the Dharma. We must take their findings to heart in our own situation.

I suppose there are eighty or ninety Sino-Japanese, Sino-Korean, or Sino-Vietnamese terms that the English-speaking students learn in the course of preliminary Zen study, depending on the ethnic origin of their particular practice. In addition there are Sanskrit or Pali expressions to learn, and a significant number of terms that are specialized English translations, and thus have special English usages— lack, anguish, emptiness, mutually dependent arising, and so on.

It is not a heavy burden to learn these terms. The diligent student of a foreign language learns a hundred new words a week. New Irish Christians learned that many Latin words and more, and Indonesian Muslims face the same challenge with Arabic liturgical language. In the misguided imperative to make Zen accessible, the teacher who reduces Zen with a kindergarten vocabulary is guiding students into a kind of blancmange in which nothing is distinct.

Pronunciation is a mark of fidelity. I sometimes hear "Buda" in place of "Buddha," and "sessheen" in place of "sesshin." Pronounce the old words faithfully, The "h" in "Buddha" is sounded, and with that one hears the etymology, "the enlightened one." "Sesshin" is, by its ideographs, *setsu* and *shin*. The two are elided to give emphasis to the first syllable. The ambiguous meanings of *setsu*, "to touch," "to receive," and "to convey," are thus retained, and *shin*, "the mind," is not obscured. By being precise you evoke the old masters and their intent here and now.

Still, Dōgen, for one among our enlightened ancestors, would say that something is missing. It is important to be familiar with the tapestry. It is important to be conversant with the silent way of Te-shan and his stick, and with the generous way of Chao-chou— accommodating himself to each student who appeared. It is fundamental to the study to know the words and their pronunciation. But beyond this essential kind of background, how do I get at the meaning? Dōgen said that mind is established when you work together with grass, trees, tiles, and pebbles so that the Buddha's truth is realized. How does that happen? In a celebrated passage in his *Genjōkōan*, he presents the challenge:

> Mustering body and mind, we see things. Mustering body and mind we hear sounds, thereby we understand them intimately. However, it is not like a reflection in a mirror, nor like the moon in the water. As one side is illuminated, the other side is dark.

There is only the song of the thrush and the sighing of wind through the casuarina trees. Dōgen sets forth an experience complementary to the universe as the eye of the monk, and a step deeper than my vision of the floating world as the sun glittered from beneath an arctic lake. Beheld most intimately, the lovely lily springs clean in the void. Heard most personally, the Melodious Laughing Thrush astonishes the silence. It is as though the experience were its own source.

Muck and roots make these pretty flowers of realization possible. Practice, practice—authentic practice with cogent guidance! "Authentic practice" is Dōgen Zenji's expression, and appears in his *Bendōwa*, an essay he composed very early in his teaching career. He appended a series of questions to the published form of the essay, probably asked one evening after he had delivered it as a teishō. One of the questions relates to the teachings and doctrines of other schools, the Lotus School, the Avatamsaka School, the Esoteric School. The monk then asks, "Which aspect of the practice you mention makes you recommend it over the practices of other schools?" Dōgen replies:

> In the Buddha's house, we do not discuss superiority or inferiority of doctrine; nor do we concern ourselves with the depth or shallowness of teachings, but only with the authenticity or inauthenticity of practice.

For Dōgen, "authentic practice" identified the foundation of the Way, and he is clear about that foundation. From the *Bendōwa* again:

> The Buddha Shākyamuni and the Venerable Mahākāshyapa lived by practice that was grounded in realization. The Great Master Bodhidharma and the venerated Hui-neng were likewise guided by practice grounded in realization. There is no exception in the way the Buddha Dharma has been kept alive.

These words narrate what went before, and have set the tone for countless monks, nuns, and lay students after, down through the centuries to our own time. Just as Right Samādhi leads directly to Right Views, back at the beginning of the Eightfold Path, and the Path then loops around to deeper zazen and clearer views, so the ground of realization makes authentic practice possible, which loops around to the source of the source, and there are sources all the way down.

Lots of people call themselves Buddhist; they avoid meat, subscribe to *Tricycle* and *Shambhala Sun*, decorate their homes with scrolls and images, and have "Free Tibet" bumper-stickers on their cars. Not enough, I'm thinking. Dōgen Zenji also calls for consistent, hard work at fundamentals. This from his *Fukanzazengi*:

> Sitting fixedly, think without thoughts. How do you think without thoughts? Non-thinking. This is the essential art of zazen. Zazen is not the practice of *dhyāna*: it is simply the Dharma gate of ease and joy. It is the practice and verification of ultimate bodhi.

Difficult to understand, difficult to do. *Dhyāna* became *Ch'an* which became *Zen* in etymological history, yet Dōgen says that seated Zen is not dhyāna. By this I think he is distinguishing method from experience. Non-thinking is *shikantaza*, the ground of all zazen. Sōtō or Rinzai, it is the truly authentic practice. From *The Transmission of the Lamp*:

> A monk asked Yüeh-shan, "What must I think in zazen?"
> Yüeh-shan said, "Think non-thinking."
> The monk asked, "How can I think non-thinking?"
> Yüeh-shan said, "Non-thinking."

Yüeh-shan is the master who did zazen as a presentation of the Dharma when he had promised to give a Dharma talk:

> The head monk followed him back to his room and protested, "You promised to give a Dharma talk, how is it that you said not a word?" Yüeh-shan said, "For sūtras there are sūtra specialists. For commentaries, there are commentary specialists. Why do you wonder at this old monk?"
>
> (BS-7)

Don't suppose that Yüeh-shan is simply sitting quietly. Dōgen warns against "stopping thoughts in abysmal quietude." You will find this phrase in his *Zazenshin*, where he also remarks:

> There is somebody in non-thinking; the somebody maintains my self. Even though it is I that sits adamantly in zazen, this is not a matter of thinking. It is the totality of the unmoving zazen itself.

If you miss Dōgen's point, your questioning spirit can betray you and ask, "Who is that somebody?" Sometimes a Zen student will ask "Who am I?" as a kōan. A mistake, for Dōgen goes on to say,

> If the unmoving zazen is as it is, how can it think of itself as an object? Therefore, the unmoving zazen is not measured by Buddhas, by phenomena, by enlightenment, or by any comprehension.

Grounded! There is authentic practice! "Somebody" is the act. "Who am I?" is an abstract query. Some North American teachers assign "Who am I?" as a kōan, and I have worked with students who come to me in desperation as the walls close in on them with this futile practice. "To study the self is to forget the self," as Dōgen says in the *Genjōkōan*. Completely! So how can one grasp and let go of something simultaneously?

"To forget the self," Dōgen continues, "is to be confirmed by the myriad things" in mutually dependent arising, during zazen or on the street, an experience not possible by trying to reify a theoretical notion. It is the thrush! the siren! the sound of clappers in the dōjō! It is the fragrance of incense! the sudden appearance of a pear tree in full bloom! When your practice is ripened and you have forgotten yourself, you can be confirmed by a footstep in the dark. The ideograph *shō*, which I render as "confirmed," is found also in the compound *inka shōmei*, the seal of confirmed transmission that is conveyed to the new master as an enlightened successor of the Buddha. You receive transmission from the thrush.

Thus we must liberate ourselves from our heads, and step into the dimension that includes the many beings of the universe. "Who hears that sound?" asked the fourteenth-century master Bassui Tokushō.[10] Sometimes a student will say, "I hear it," or "Nobody hears it." Won't do. Interrogative and affirmative drop away in a single imperative.

Here is a story from *The Transmission of the Lamp* about Kuei-tsung, an heir of Ma-tsu, and thus an early ninth-century figure:

> A monk said to Kuei-tsung, "Is there no expedient gate through which you can help me to enter?"
> The Master said, "The power of Kuan-yin's sublime wisdom can save the world from suffering."
> The monk asked, "What is the power of Kuan-yin's sublime wisdom?"
> The Master struck the lid of the three-legged incense pot three times and said, "Do you hear that?"
> The monk said, "I heard it."
> The Master said, "Why didn't I hear it?" The monk was speechless, so the Master took his staff and got down from his seat.

Time to move on! A vase drops to the floor, smashed to smithereens. Did you hear that? What did Kuei-tsung mean when he implied that he couldn't? Kuan-yin can hear. Who is Kuan-yin? Literally, "The One Who Hears Sounds." Get literal. Who hears? Kuei-tsung again:

> Kuei-tsung entered the hall and addressed the monks saying, "I want to speak about Ch'an. All of you, gather around."
> The monks gathered closely around Kuei-tsung. He then said, "Look at Kuan-yin's practice, responding well in all the various circumstances."
> A monk asked, "What is Kuan-yin's practice?"
> The Master then snapped his fingers and said, "Do all of you hear it?"

The monks said, "We hear it."

The Master said, "What is this pack of fools looking for here?" and he took his staff and drove them out with blows. Laughing loudly he returned to his quarters.

Here is still another provocative story about hearing, this one with P'an-shan, also a disciple of Ma-tsu, and thus a brother monk of Kuei-tsung:

As the Master was walking through a marketplace, he heard a customer who was buying some pork say to the butcher, "Cut me a pound of the fine stuff."

The butcher put down his cleaver, folded his arms and said, "Inspector, which isn't fine?" At this the Master had some insight.

Again one day when he had gone out of the monastery, he saw people mourning, singing and ringing bells. "The red disk inevitably sinks into the west. / We don't know where the ghost will go," they were singing. Inside an enclosure, a filial son was crying "Alas! Alas!" The Master's body and mind leaped. He returned and told Ma-tsu about it. Ma-tsu gave him his seal of approval.[11]

The Buddha said, "Now I see that all beings are the Tathāgata." P'an-shan could say, "Now I see that all beings are chanting the Tathāgata's words." Veneration to Kuan-yin!

The way of Kuan-yin continues endlessly. It is not a matter of a weekend workshop. My teacher, Yamada Kōun Rōshi, told me that Bassui's directive "Who hears!" was his ongoing practice after he completed his formal study. He was then in his seventies and it was the theme he breathed in intervals between exterior demands. Bassui lived long ago in medieval Japan but he is still our master teacher:

You should know that the voices of frogs and worms, the sound of wind and raindrops, all speak the wonderful language of the Dharma, and that birds in flight, swimming fish, floating clouds all turn the Dharma Wheel.[12]

"Dharma" has many meanings, including "phenomena" and "teaching." Phenomena *are* teachings. This is not merely a Zen notion. Here is a passage from the *Ts'ai-ken t'an*, a Ming-period collection of little homilies from a variety of Chinese religious sources:

The chattering of birds and the humming of insects are secrets im-
parted to the heart-mind. There is not a petal of a flower or a blade
of grass that does not configure the Way.[13]

Indeed we find the same kind of understanding among the desert
fathers of very early Christianity:

> A certain philosopher asked St. Anthony: "Father, how can you be
> so happy when you are deprived of the consolation of books?"
>   Anthony replied, "My book, O philosopher, is the nature of
> created things, and any time I want to read the words of God, the
> book is before me."[14]

The Duke in Shakespeare's *As You Like It* remarks,

> And this our life, exempt from public haunt,
> finds tongues in trees, books in the running brooks.
> Sermons in stones, and good in everything.

"Public haunt" refers to the Duke's life before he was exiled to his
present rural setting. He is now exempt from his former busy life
and busy mind, and the tongues and books and sermons of the natural world have a chance. When you are naked of preoccupations
you are open to the disclosures of the world, and the Dharma by
whatever name comes forth from the other, and reveals our inclusion of them. The Sung dynasty poet Su Tung-p'o presented the following verse to his master to attest to his realization:

> The sound of the valley stream is the long, broad tongue;
> The form of the mountains—isn't that the pure, clear body?
> In the course of the night—eighty-four thousand *gāthās*—
> Tomorrow, how could I explain them to anyone else?
>   (BCR-37)

A long, broad tongue is one of the traditional thirty-two marks of
the Buddha, and the pure and clear body is the body of the Dharma.
Eighty-four thousand little verses, each of them summing up an aspect of the teaching, come forth in the night, beyond explanation.
Created things present the words of God for St. Anthony, the sounds
of the valley stream and the form of the mountains present the teachings of the Buddha for Su Tung-p'o. The point is the same, only the

expression differs. T'ao Ch'ien (365–427) avoids any link to formal religion, and so is closer to the truth of the commons, and indeed to the realm of poetry:

> Plucking chrysanthemums along the east fence;
> Gazing in silence at the Southern Hills,
> The birds flying home in pairs
> Through the soft mountain air of dusk—
> In these things there is a deep meaning
> But when we try to express it,
> We suddenly forget the words.[15]

Indeed, "tomorrow, how could I explain them to anyone else?" Gazing in silence—exempt from public haunt, body and mind can drop away, we can be open to the teachings of hills and birds. This is not exactly nature mysticism of the sort practiced by Druids and ancient Slavs, for whom certain trees had healing powers and for whom (like traditional American people) certain places on the Earth were "power spots" that helped induce particular states of consciousness. Rather it is teaching by beings through one's skin, including the specialized skin of eyes, ears, nose, tongue, and brain, that prompts a dropped-away body and mind.

In any case the sole self is not the point. "Who is hearing that sound?" should not lead to the question, "Who is asking 'Who is hearing?'" That leads to "Who is asking who is asking 'Who is hearing?'"—again, such questions just take you around in circles until "palsy shakes a few, sad, last gray hairs." Wrong road!

Self-preoccupation does not give the wind and the stars and the trees a chance to make their case. Neither does the romantic cast of mind, so prevalent in Chinese poetry. Li-po is a prime example:

> Athwart the yellow clouds of sunset, seeking their nests under the
> city wall,
> The crows fly homeward. Caw! Caw! Caw! they cry among the
> branches.
> At her loom sits weaving silk brocade, one like the Lady of Ch'in-
> ch'üan;
> Their voices come to her through the window with its curtains
> misty-blue.

She stays the shuttle; grieving, she thinks of her distant lord;
In the lonely, empty room, her tears fall like rain.[16]

Even T'ao Ch'ien was self-preoccupied sometimes, worried about his health and his career, finding solace in wine, but he never smothered the caw of the crows with romance. "Caw! Caw! Caw!" That would have been the message of any poem he might have titled "Crows Cawing at Nightfall." *Be clear about this.*

Zen falls at the plain end of the poetical spectrum, where we find a number of masters who were also accomplished poets. Here are two poetical cases from the record of Ta-lung Chih-hung, a relatively obscure figure. We only know that he lived deep in mountains of what is now Hunan province, probably in the ninth century, and that he was part of a far-flung community of teachers who were descended from Te-shan Hsüan-chien. He is remembered with just a few stories, but they offer a vivid sense of his character and realization. The first case goes like this:

> A monk asked Ta-lung: "The body of form perishes. What is the eternal Dharma body?"
> Ta-lung said, "The mountain flowers bloom like brocade; the river between the hills is blue as indigo."
>
> (BCR-82)

I find the monk's question about the eternal Dharma body to be a little coarse, and rather abstract. After all, is there any such thing as an eternal Dharma body? Ta-lung called the question into question, and showed the true world of the Dharma, with the ephemeral as the real and the beautiful.

The other case featuring a poetical response from Ta-lung is found in *The Transmission of the Lamp:*

> A monk asked Ta-lung, "What is the 'minutely subtle'?"
> Ta-lung said, "The breeze brings the voice of the water close to my pillow; the moon carries the shadow of the mountain near to my couch."

The monk who asked about the "minutely subtle" would probably not find noetic significance in Li-po's simile of a lady weeping about her distant lord. I imagine that he was an old-timer in the practice, in tune with a subtle teacher. He was also creative and unconventional. I do not find his term, "minutely subtle," *wei-miao* (J. *mimyō*), in other kōan collections, though it certainly is current in other Ch'an and Zen literature, and is the familiar "minutely subtle" in our gāthā "On Opening the Dharma":

> The Dharma, incomparably profound and minutely subtle,
> is rarely encountered, even in hundreds of thousands of millions
>   of kalpas;
> we now can see it, listen to it, accept and hold it;
> may we completely realize the Tathāgata's true meaning.

This gāthā is attributed to the Empress Wu Tse-t'ien, who reigned from 685 to 704 and was a patron of the Hua-yen school of Buddhism. It has been recited in all Chinese Buddhist schools down through the centuries, and is today the gāthā that precedes the master's *teishō*, or Dharma presentation, in both the Sōtō and Rinzai Zen traditions. It seems likely that it was recited in Ta-lung's monastery, and the monk picked out the term for his inquiry, while his colleagues simply repeated the words by rote. "Minutely subtle" would be a metaphor for the Dharma that at the same time identifies its nature. Thus the monk would be asking, "What is this 'minutely subtle' Dharma?"

Miura Isshū and Ruth Sasaki translate *wei-miao* as "the mysterious."[17] This is all right, but it carries an occult overtone. D. T. Suzuki translates it as "exquisite."[18] This too is all right, but it's a bit dainty. The Dharma is of this world and of the earth earthy, of the air airy, of the rain wet. "Minutely subtle" is the literal translation of *wei-miao*, and when in doubt that's the kind of translation I choose.

I imagine that the monk sensed what the "minutely subtle" might be, but wanted his teacher's view. His question was intimate, and Ta-lung's response presents the movement of intimacy. "The wind brings... The moon carries...." I daresay that his words did not seem a non sequitur to the monk, whereas Ta-lung's response to the question about the eternal Dharma probably seemed to come out of left field for the monk in the earlier story. Yet poetical teachers can in time bring forth the poetry in their students and, of course, in students to come.

The ore is refined from the crude to the subtle and beyond, from grim certainty to good-humored insecurity, and most of all from isolation to intimacy. When this refinement is our focus, exploitive teachers and exploitive systems are seen for what they are, and rejected, and the daily misunderstandings and disagreements that seem so important in the moment will fade away. It is the shadow of the mountain coming closer and yet closer as the moon sets at midnight that lifts us from the sole self. It's the ten thousand things of the boundless self that advance and confirm you and me. Here's another example from Chinese poetry of nature advancing to the quiet listener:

> A cricket chirps and is silent;
> The guttering lamp sinks and flares up again.
> Outside the window, evening rain is heard.
> It is the banana plant that speaks of it first.[19]

First the sound of pattering on the banana leaves, then on the roof. Nearer and nearer, more and more intimate. Intimacy is the message. David Hinton quotes an otherwise untranslated poem of T'ao Ch'ien:

> Vast and majestic, the mountains embrace your shadow,
> broad and deep, rivers harbor your voice.[20]

T'ao Ch'ien sums up the true nature of self as the mountains and rivers in two profoundly beautiful lines, long before Bodhidharma, and even longer before the *Avatamsaka Sūtra* was translated as the *Hua-yen*. Dōgen's memorable passage in the *Genjōkōan*, cited in part earlier, is almost bald by comparison:

> To study the Buddha Way is to study the self. To study the self is to
> forget the self. To forget the self is to be confirmed by the myriad
> things. To be confirmed by the myriad things is to cast off the body

and mind of the self as well as those of others. Even traces of realization are wiped away, and life with traceless realization is maintained forever and ever.

Dōgen puts T'ao Ch'ien's lines into the context of practice: the self as the agent of realization, the confirmation of the agent by mountains and rivers, the great dropping away that makes this confirmation possible—for the agent and for all agents, and the maintenance of this realization for all time—with every element of this practice coincident with all other elements, each step containing all other steps.

Notice that Dōgen does not deny the self. Just forget it, that's all. But forgetting the self is a matter of being actualized by mountains and rivers and the myriad other things. It is not a matter of walking around in self-denial.

"No-self" refers to a peak experience, and then to the understanding of how that experience plays out in daily life. The peak experience is, in effect, T'ao Ch'ien's realization, and an affirmation of the words of Ch'ang-sha about the eye of the monk:

> What the Buddha means by the self is precisely the whole universe.
> Thus, whether one is aware of it or not, there is no universe that
> is not the self.

These are Dōgen's words in his *Yuibutsu Yōbutsu*. How is the self the whole universe? Chao-chou brings the matter down to earth:

> A monk asked Chao-chou, "What is the self?"
> Chao-chou said, "Well, do you see the oak tree in the garden?"

This is clearly an echo of Chao-chou's response to another monk who asked about the reason Bodhidharma came from the West. "Oak tree in the front garden!" (GB-37). However, here the point is the self. What is the self? Well, how about the oak tree? Do you think your skin binds you? How about your family and friends? Cast off body and mind, and the oak tree will confirm you.

I'm referencing Dōgen's *Genjōkōan* here of course. The old master goes on to say that all traces of realization are wiped away. Nothing remains. And this no-trace is continued endlessly.

> A monk asked Chao-chou, "In the Kalpa of Emptiness, is there still
> someone cultivating practice?"
>   Chao-chou asked, "What do you call the Kalpa of Emptiness?"
>   The monk said, "Where not a single thing exists."
>   Chao-chou said, "Only that can be called true cultivation."[21]

Only that can be called authentic practice! Buddhas, phenomena, enlightenment—self-nature, lotus land, nirvana, even the *samādhi* of self-fulfilling activity—there are so many Buddhist concepts, notions, and archetypes, and all are traces that disappear in true cultivation, in authentic practice.

For Dōgen, writing in *Gyōji*, authentic practice was a matter of sitting erect in zazen, but it was also in activity, unremitting activity, the pilgrimage of life. Usually the pilgrimage is not special, a realized practice at home, on the job, at the temple, in the community. Sometimes it is overtly a journey, and can present the contours of practice, realization, and application clearly for the rest of us.

The poet Bashō chose the difficult way of actual pilgrimage, traveling on foot to sacred and historical places, setting forth the poetry of his journey, and of the people and the events it evoked. We are not all poets, but we can discover the poetry of our lives, and Zen is poetry. Bashō showed the bowl in the face of the conventions of his time, sleeping rough, eating irregularly, probably shortening his life. But he lives on in creative moments that inspire us today, across the world and across the centuries:

> Coming along the mountain path,
> I find something endearing
> about violets.

Bashō wrote this poem in 1685, a year before his milestone "Old Pond" poem, and eleven years before his vivid haiku tracing his experience on a similar pilgrimage when the sun came up.

> In the scent of plum blossoms
> pop! the sun appears—
> the mountain path[22]

Bashō's verse about violets appearing is softer in its movement from absorption to realization than those later poems, but nonetheless it is as incisively true as the movement was for the Buddha, from zazen to the twinkle of the morning star through leaves of the Bodhi tree.

There were the violets before Bashō, *there* were his disciples awaiting the Buddha in Benares. *There* are your spouse and kids awaiting your return from sesshin. *There* is the Nevada Test Site, awaiting your presentation of the bowl. In the midst of his rigorous pilgrimage, in three brief segments in a seventeen-syllable poem, Bashō sets forth authentic practice: total absorption on the path, the sudden realization of a natural, inviting phenomenon, and the intimate response.

As Zen students you sit with your feet in your lap as best you can, and maintain your focus in that position, not always comfortable. Authentic practice is not a way of dodging around and making things easy for yourself. It is the Middle Way of the true pilgrimage through all the difficult things your path encounters. That is the way that can rightfully be called the Tao.

The *Ts'ai-ken t'an* includes this entry, one I never tire of quoting:

> If treacherous talk is constantly in your ears, and unwanted thoughts are constantly in your mind, you can turn these about and use them as whetstones to enhance your practice. If every word that came to your ears were agreeable, and all things in your mind were pleasant, then your whole life would be poisoned and wasted.[23]

A nasty boss and a hostile work environment can be whetstones to enhance your practice. Misunderstandings and illness in the family can temper your spirit. However, many people take up zazen in order to escape from treacherous talk and unwanted thoughts. Some even ask me for a referral to a monastery in Japan. I'm usually able to persuade them of the vanity of their aspiration. Many monasteries, in Japan at any rate, are hotbeds of gossip, intrigue, and one-upmanship, all in the Japanese language in a homogeneous setting that makes foreigners truly foreign. You think you have distractions at home? Try a Japanese monastery!

So here we are, lay students for the most part, with spouse or partner, perhaps with children, and job. "Lay practice" seems like an oxymoron. I find myself frequently saying that our task is to leave home without leaving home. In other words, to find the way of practice where we are, as we are. Yet formal Zen practice is very rigorous and takes a lot of time and actually involves some separation from the household, for you can't do zazen easily in a room full of children. So how do we work it out?

Monks have problems with gossip, intrigue, and one-upmanship in their monasteries, and laymen and -women have problems integrating practice with workaday life. Surely authentic practice is a matter of doing right by fellow monks and the world outside the monastery, and it's a matter of laypeople doing right by the kids, the spouse or partner, the organism of family, the organism of community, the organism of the culture.

There seem to be two worlds, one the everyday life of the monastery or the lay home, and the other the life of committed practice, but they are essentially one.

For guidance on the path of realizing this fundamental union, we can turn to the Ten *Pāramitās*, or "Perfections." Quintessentially Mahāyāna practice, and thus Zen practice, these are paradigms of views, conduct, speech, and practice transmuted from earlier Classical Buddhist models. Like their antecedents, they are not carved in stone, but rather they form lights on our path. Or it might better be said that it is we who cast light on the Pāramitās, illuminating their truths with our noble conduct and practice. They clearly echo the steps on the Eightfold Path, and offer amplification and emphasis in keeping with Mahāyāna views as well. By title the Ten Pāramitās are: Giving, Morality, Forbearance, Zeal, Focused Meditation, Wisdom, Compassionate Means, Aspiration, Spiritual Power, and Knowledge. Like the Eightfold Path, the Ten Pāramitās are a feedback system, with Wisdom informing the way of Giving, Knowledge giving contours to Wisdom, and so on.

The Pāramitā of Morality is a prime example of one that informs all others. In Sanskrit, "Morality" is *Shīla*, a term that literally means "cool and peaceful," implying a life that is free from false notions of permanence and domination of others. Shīla is the rationale of the *vinaya*, the detailed rules of the Buddhist community. The *vinaya* is the foundation of Buddhism as a religion of conduct, and many of the great personages in our tradition began their study here.

The Classical code of Shīla was developed from earlier Indian and Persian precepts, and consisted of five injunctions: not to kill, not to steal, not to misuse sex, not to speak falsely, and not to give or take drink or drugs. Known as the *Pañchashīla*, these five basic precepts are accepted by monks, nuns, laymen, and laywomen in all schools of Buddhism. With the rise of the Mahāyāna, five additional precepts were added: not to speak of the faults of others, not to praise the self while abusing others, not to spare the Dharma assets, not to indulge in anger, and not to defame the Three Treasures.[24]

Zen Buddhist ritual and monastic practice acknowledge the importance of the precepts, and the advanced student takes them up as kōans. Over and over we find sharp reminders that we are living in this world with other beings.

> A monk asked T'ou-tzu, "All sounds are the sounds of Buddha—right or wrong?"
> T'ou-tzu said, "Right."
> The monk said, "Your Reverence, doesn't your ass hole make farting sounds?" T'ou-tzu then hit him.
> Again the monk said, "Coarse words or subtle talk, all returns to the primary meaning—right or wrong?"
> T'ou-tzu said, "Right."
> The monk said, "Then can I call Your Reverence a donkey?"
> T'ou-tzu hit him again.
>
> (BCR-79)

In the dimension of primary meaning all sounds are the sounds of the Buddha and all talk illuminates his teaching. This is the vast and fathomless *Dharmakāya*, the empty and undifferentiated Buddha body. It inspires us at each moment. but nobody lives there, just as nobody lives exclusively in the worlds of harmony or individuality. The monk delivered a couple of cheap doctrinal shots and got his comeuppance.

The ceremony of accepting the precepts that is designed for laymen and -women, known in Japanese centers as *Jukai*, and the ordination ceremony, called *Tokudō*, involves the postulant personally at every step, and has the most ancient roots. In preparation for Jukai, the lay student sews a *rakusu*, a biblike garment that is metaphorically the Buddha's robe, and in preparation for Tokudō, the new monk or nun sews an *o-kesa*, a larger and more formal representation of the original robe. In the course of the ceremony they don their new garments to acknowledge the Buddha as their teacher. This ritual derives from the practice of the earliest novice monks and nuns, who walked naked to the village dump, salvaged scraps of discarded cloth, bleached them, dyed them, and sewed them together to form a simple robe, a garment that has evolved into the rakusu and o-kesa. Those postulants disrobed themselves of their old ways of acquisition and personal concern, and donned the new way of ultimate poverty at the dump of the town, inspiring their successors, clerical and lay, down through the ages, to follow their path of renunciation and inspiration.

The colors of the rakusu and o-kesa are traditionally blue, yellow, red, black, or purple, but according to Dōgen in *Kesa Kudoku*, these are secondary colors, for the saffron robe of Shākyamuni was intended to be flesh-color, the color of the human skin, the ultimate vestment of the human being, which even in his community would probably have varied from pink to black.

In any case, the rakusu and o-kesa are robes of liberation that we as men and women who are totally naked of all preoccupations wear to confirm our intimacy with the teachings of one who was as clear as the sky on a sunny day—and our intimacy with the teachings of his enlightened successors. We bow in veneration to these marvelous doctors of the human condition, casting away everything as we touch forehead to floor while lifting our hands.

> I wear the robe of liberation,
> the formless field of benefaction,
> the teachings of the Tathāgata,
> saving all the many beings.

Students, lay and ordained, recite this "Verse of the Kesa" from Dōgen's *Den E* each time they put on the rakusu or kesa. Thus we invest in the teachings of the Buddha, as our own. Dōgen reminisced in *Den E* about this daily practice of investment by a monk he once practiced with:

> During my stay in Sung China, making effort on the long platform, I saw that my neighbor every morning at the time of releasing the stillness, would lift up his kesa and place it on his head; then, holding his palms together in veneration, would silently recite the "Verse of the Kesa." At that time, there arose in me a feeling I had never before experienced. My body was overfilled with joy, and tears of gratitude secretly fell and moistened the lapels of my gown. The reason was that when I had read the *Āgama Sūtras* previously I had noticed passages about humbly receiving the o-kesa upon the head, but I had not clarified the standards for this as a practice and had not understood it very well. Seeing it done now, before my very eyes, I was overjoyed.

The inner side of the rakusu is inscribed by the teacher or preceptor with the Dharma name of the newly committed student, which, in the Diamond Sangha, the teacher and student decide upon together. Over the years one accumulates multiple Dharma names in the various ceremonies that involve taking refuge. I have three at this point. Each of them expresses an ideal for my path. The teacher might also inscribe a saying or a poem from Zen literature that inspires and encourages. The pattern on the outer side of the rakusu is derived from a story in oral tradition:

> When the Buddha was walking with his disciples, they came to a promontory overlooking paddies of rice, and remarked, "Let's make these fields the pattern of our robes."

To this day the kesa and rakusu are sewn of little rectangular scraps of cloth that present the beauty, scope, and fecundity of rice fields. This metaphor emphasizes once again that we are not so much taken up with old Shākyamuni, the personality, or the many Indian and Chinese personages who followed him. What did they say? What did they do? Therein lie the teachings. In this story of the origin of the kesa, Shākyamuni pointed to the rice fields, indicating that it is the fields themselves that present the Tao. Wearing our rakusu here in our place in the Dharma world, we make visible the teachings of the rice fields, and express our gratitude and homage to the Buddha for pointing them out to us. I suggest that the fields are not merely figures of speech. We actually wear and make manifest the rice fields of long-ago India and modern-day California, as we wear the sun, the moon, the stars, and the great Earth—the clouds, the rain, and the wind, and all the beings of the Earth, each of them coming forth as the Tathāgata, our teachers of the perennial Dharma. Kikaku, prominent disciple of Bashō, wrote:

> The beggar:
> he wears heaven and earth
> as summer clothes.[25]

Kikaku was not particularly a student of Zen, but here he is unwittingly a Zen teacher. In blessed poverty of spirit, all of us wear heaven and earth as our summer and winter clothes.

In this poverty of spirit, the postulants face the preceptor, usually the Zen master, and begin their Jukai or Tokudō ceremony with the Three Vows of Refuge in the Buddha, Dharma, and Sangha—realization, the teachings, and the community of all beings. "I take refuge in the Buddha; I take refuge in the Dharma; I take refuge in the Sangha." These are the vows of all Buddhists everywhere and the Refuge Ceremony is their initiation into the religion. They are repeated at the outset of all sūtra services in monasteries and lay Zen centers, and thus the student is initiated anew at each ceremonial gathering.

In the formal ceremony, students are then offered the Three Pure Precepts: to maintain the moral code (the Ten Grave Precepts), to practice all good Dharmas, and to save the many beings. In the first of these Three Pure Precepts, my vow is to follow the way of not killing, not stealing, and so on. Here I find the hard light of clear definition, the sharp navigational beam of noble speech and conduct. In the second of the Pure Precepts, to practice all good Dharmas, all good ways, my vow is to express my love. Placing these two Pure Precepts one after the other, I am reminded that the negative and the positive express the same vow. *Ahimsā* is *Karunā; Karunā* is *Ahimsā*. Non-harming is love; love is non-harming.

Finally, the Third Pure Precept, to save the many beings, sets forth the function of the first two. It gives specific direction to my way of non-harming and love. Thus I turn the Wheel of the Dharma with all people, animals, and plants. These Three Pure Precepts are likewise repeated as vows at the outset of all sūtra services in the Mahāyāna tradition.

Ten Grave Precepts then arise from the Three Pure Precepts and clarify the Buddha Dharma. They are examined as kōans at the end of formal study in the Rinzai tradition as a kind of recap of earlier work. After you have seen clearly into the total absence of self, soul, and essence in your own body and in the bodies of all others; after you have realized the precious, unique nature of individual people, animals, plants, stones, and stars; and after you have realized their intimate interrelationships, you can integrate and authenticate your views. "Present your vow!" I demand for each precept in turn. I don't ask for a mere echo of the words. Let me see it!

1) I TAKE UP THE WAY OF NOT KILLING. This first precept balances our primary vow to save the many beings. "Save" is a term we associate with missionizing. Here the etymology is something like, "I vow to let them cross over" (to the other shore of realization). On the one hand, I vow to set up the bridge for you. On the other, I vow not to harm you, and thus prevent you from crossing over. With these vows, and with the personal peace that comes with conscientious zazen, the difficult questions we face in our lives—from how to deal with vermin to how to deal with unwanted pregnancy—become clearer.

Thus the teaching and formal practice integrate with daily exigencies. We find that an absolute position, say, of never harming the roaches in the kitchen, will probably lead to harm in our families. But on the other hand, ruthlessly and endlessly exterminating roaches to protect the health of our children can lead to a wishy-washy kind of relativism. The solution is, of course, for the family to keep the kitchen as clean as a Zen temple, so that the roaches must do their scavenging elsewhere. Then the occasional roach can be escorted outside.

Questions about unwanted pregnancy are not as easy. Again, one would hope that a quiet mind and the Buddha's teaching of non-harming can help the woman work through her crisis. Abortion is killing, but what are the implications of non-harming as an absolute commandment in each specific case? How about the mother, who might be so burdened by an extra child that all her children are harmed?—indeed, that society generally is harmed, that the very Earth is harmed? The woman is feeling her place in the endless stream of procreation, finding her body responding positively to its role, dreaming of her infant at her breast. Men and even other women do not share her particular dilemma. It is our duty to stand by her in her predicament, support her decision, and offer her our help, if she should ask for it. We should also organize for a universal way of compassion and care that will keep such terrible predicaments to the smallest number possible.

On a larger scale, we must as responsible citizens of the world deal with issues of war and the destruction of the planet. Incredibly murderous engines are ready to destroy all human life and almost all animal and plant life. So-called conventional weapons destroy entire societies year by year, and weapons of mass destruction (read "nuclear bombs") are set to extinguish the planet.

No less dangerous is the biological disaster suffered by forests, meadows, wetlands, lakes, rivers, seas, and the air, threatening the life of literally everything. How should one resist ruinous technology while supporting a family? This is the conundrum one carries day and night. I vow to cultivate my love and to apply it in my daily life, at home and in the larger community. I vow to moderate my lifestyle for the protection of all beings. I vow to speak out decisively with like-minded friends.

2) I TAKE UP THE WAY OF NOT STEALING. The integrity of others is violated by stealing. There is, moreover, a certain order of things, a certain harmony. The Sambhogakāya, the Buddha's "Body of Bliss," is the interbeing of mountains, rivers, animals, towers, people—and it functions in people by morality. We attend this moral order by following the precepts. The books of my friends, for example, are their bodies, as much as their fin-

gers and toes. I cannot steal a library book without violating this harmony. Then what about the order that is imposed from greed, and deprives people, animals, and plants of their right to live out their lives? Like questions of abortion, the easy resolutions are elusive. I vow to find within myself the ground of respect for the integrity of each being and of each collective of beings.

3) I TAKE UP THE WAY OF NOT MISUSING SEX. It seems that Classical Buddhism limited this precept to a careful exposition of where, when, and with whom sexual intercourse might be appropriate. But beyond such rules, the misuse of sexual intercourse is the lie of giving, when the act is really taking. With such a lie, the entire relationship is a lie. And there are other ways to misuse sex than just in the sexual act. A relationship that involves dominance, exploitation, and passive aggression is an ongoing violation of this precept. The drive to tear the other down can be so overtly violent that the malefactor lands in criminal court, but each of us can find this Māra, this Destroyer, lurking in our motives and responses. Honest sex, the easy joyous act and relationship, is *dāna*, the gift that brings happiness to the world and to the family.

4) I TAKE UP THE WAY OF NOT SPEAKING FALSELY. Like the other precepts, not speaking falsely is simply a particular aspect of not killing. Here the vow is not to kill the Dharma, the truth of how things are. I lie to defend my false notion of a fixed entity—a self-image, a concept, or an institution. The situation becomes confused and the reality that the Buddha revealed becomes obscured. Sometimes, however, I feel that I must lie to protect someone else or large numbers of others. Am I lying to myself? It is all too easy. I vow to find the big picture and then to be true to that discovery.

5) I TAKE UP THE WAY OF NOT GIVING OR TAKING DRINK OR DRUGS. This was originally an injunction against wine. My teacher, Yamada Kōun Rōshi, would refuse a social drink of saké. If his host insisted, he would accept a tiny amount, touch it to his lips, and put it down again. At his level of Japanese society

such conduct bordered on rudeness, but he was not one to neglect his vows. I am not as strict, and take a small glass of wine
with my evening meal. Each of us draws an individual line.

By extension today, of course, the precept also refers to drugs.
I have heard friends take a righteous position about cocaine: "It
makes my mind more alert and helps me to communicate better." Maybe so, in occasional instances and in the very short run,
but cocaine is empirically provable to be confusing over time
and harmful to personal and social health. The same is true of
alcohol. By indulging you encourage others to indulge. Don't
take drugs and don't give them to others. Don't cloud your mind
or encourage others to cloud theirs.

6) I TAKE UP THE WAY OF NOT DISCUSSING THE FAULTS OF
OTHERS. Sometimes I think that more people get hurt by gossip than by guns. The point is that nobody has a fixed character.
Everyone has traits, tools of character to be used or misused. If
I have a tendency to be accommodating to other people, I can
misuse this trait in a self-centered way as a means for personal
protection. On the other hand, I can accommodate people in a
manner that is clearly beneficial to them. Character transformation is not a matter of changing traits. It is rather taking my innate configurations and making the most and best of them. I
vow to understand and encourage the fundamental qualities of
my character and of others.

7) I TAKE UP THE WAY OF NOT PRAISING MYSELF WHILE ABUS-
ING OTHERS. The reason I praise myself and abuse others is
that I seek to justify and defend myself as a superior being.
Actually, I am not superior or inferior. The Buddha himself is
not superior and Māra, the Destroyer, is not inferior. "Comparisons are odious." If I am authoritarian and put myself up
and others down, then I am not meeting their need to grow and
mature. I am not meeting my own need to listen and learn. The
world is multi-centered and we're all in it together. I vow to follow the way of modesty and to take joy in the liberation and at-
tainments of others.

8) I TAKE UP THE WAY OF NOT SPARING THE DHARMA ASSETS.
The Dharma assets are phenomena in their precious uniqueness,

the perfect harmony of their interdependence and their absence of any abiding self. When I am not stingy, then I conduct myself and say things that enhance my function as an avatar of the Buddha and I enhance that same function in others. My family members, friends, and everyone and everything are heartened on their path of perfection. My act of sparing the Dharma assets, withholding teaching, money, goods, help, and ordinary decent responses, leads to pain and grief across the world. I vow to be generous.

9) I TAKE UP THE WAY OF NOT INDULGING IN ANGER. Those of us who have attended religious retreats have had the experience of bathing in anger. Something unreasonably tiny, perhaps something we don't even notice, punctures a nasty bubble of angry gas and we sit there on our zazen pads playing out scenarios of retribution. However, this condition fades and the experience reveals the power of anger and its possibilities. William Blake says, "The tygers of wrath are wiser than the horses of instruction." Kuan-yin hurls a thunderbolt of anger from time to time. I vow to find the place of equanimity where my anger can come forth when appropriate to save everybody and everything.

10) I TAKE UP THE WAY OF NOT SLANDERING THE THREE TREASURES. Slander of the Three Treasures is Wrong Views, denial that there can be such a thing as liberation from anguish, denial that practice is a virtue, and denial of friendship. This is the ultimate destruction of the Buddha Dharma and of happiness in the world. Conceptualizing the Three Treasures and making them into a kind of structure that can only be admired from outside is another way of slandering them. I vow to practice Right Views as I stand up, sit down, and greet my family members and friends.

Sometimes I hear the expression "to break the precepts," as though they were laws. The way of Shīla and its precepts is morality beyond formal regulation. It is the way of Ahimsā that arises from an ultimate kind of intimacy with all beings. Without it the Buddha

Dharma does not apply and is not relevant. Sūtras and commentaries are isolated and cold. With the lights of Ahimsā, however, Karunā finds a way.

The vows of Jukai, the equivalent vows in ordination ceremonies, and the follow-through expected of Zen students, lay and clerical, are natural developments from both the Classical Eightfold Path and from Ta-hui's account, and similar Mahāyāna accounts of the Buddha's words at his great attainment: "All the many beings are endowed with the wisdom and virtue of the Tathāgata, yet simply because of their delusions and preoccupations, they cannot bear witness to their endowment." Sixteen specific ways of practice to make the Way personal set the scene for realizing what has been true from the beginning. Such a life can include zazen in brief intervals, and can also include keeping in touch with the teacher, perhaps by phone, a practice that we in the Diamond Sangha formalize as though it were an encounter between teacher and student in the inner room of the Zen center. I don't ever promise a rose garden, but it seems to me that the young mother and the busy bureaucrat really can practice authentically like the rest of us, every day, all day, whatever happens. Authentic practice is not compartmentalized into sesshin.

Authentic practice is also a rhythm. Commonly you hear the criticism that American Buddhism is weekend monasticism. But monastic training itself has intense and moderate periods in sequence. In the entry to a Rinzai Zen monastery, you will see a board inscribed with a single ideograph, *dai* or *sho*. *Dai* is "great," *sho* is "small." During the great period, there is a sesshin every month, and there are long periods of zazen every day. Nobody goes out, except for *takuhatsu*, the time to chant in the streets of a nearby town or village and accept alms.

On the other hand, during the small period there are no sesshin. Periods of zazen are short, and many of the monks leave to help out at home. Only when money or food runs low will there be *takuhatsu*. The temple atmosphere is noticeably relaxed.

Our American lay practice follows this natural model, and the householder who attends a weekend sesshin is a true descendant of monks and nuns who wandered during most of the year, and only gathered with confreres and consoeurs during the rainy season. Yet we today live harried lives, and sesshin is often the respite. The ancient pattern of intense practice followed by a kind of vacation is turned upside down. Sesshin becomes the vacation.

We are reinventing the Way, and it seems to me that we can only do this through authentic practice—unremitting activity, zazen, or cooking supper with a baby on one's hip. Our family, job, and community practice can be every bit as rough, every bit as irregular, even every bit as life-threatening as Bashō's footsore journeys. "Without bitterest cold that penetrates to the very bone, how can plum blossoms send forth their fragrance all over the whole world?" These are Dōgen Zenji's words in the *Eihei Kōroku*, and they can never be used up. Please persevere.

Really, authentically, there is no sequence, no *dai* followed by *sho*, no practice followed by realization, no realization followed by application, but only unremitting activity on the path—perhaps, of course, with incidental milestones.

Right Effort is the key. Vows, beginning with the Three Vows of Refuge, the Three Pure Precepts, and the Ten Grave Precepts, are the *upāya*, or appropriate means, that fuel authentic practice. Vows make metaphysics personal and experience even more intimate. Without vows, there can be no practice, all day, every day.

Zen students and teachers who fail conspicuously to live up to ordinary ethical standards, or who allow themselves to be swayed unduly by the spirit and culture of their times, have failed to live up to their vows. I think of the xenophobic and anti-Semitic expressions by Yasutani Rōshi and other Japanese masters during World War II, which have been brought forcefully to our attention recently.[26] When I studied with Yasutani a quarter-century after the war, I found no indication that his ideals were anything but harmonious.[27] I have learned, however, that a residue of his old views continued to appear in his writings. I am saddened by this. Culture is profoundly influential, yet the jewel of the Dharma can shine through the mist. Go thou and avoid doing likewise—the mist will lift and the jewel will shine with its original brightness.

I am profoundly grateful to my teachers, including Yasutani Rōshi, and to their ancestors. None of them were autodidacts, not even the Buddha. What nonsense would I be talking now (if indeed I were still alive) without their exacting guidance in authentic practice!

What about the future? At eighty-six, with my teaching career behind me for the most part, I am gratified that teachers with better eyes than mine show clear promise that the Way of the Buddha will flourish. Moreover Zen students are beginning to study the old texts in the original languages. The teishō of Dōgen, the dialogues of Chao-chou, and the sayings and doings of shadowy figures like Kuei-tsung and P'an-shan are coming alive for us in translations that are cogent and incisive.

Zen has returned in a new hemisphere. It is not only clarified by translations and commentaries, it is informed by psychology, Vipassanā Buddhism, and Christianity—the way Ch'an and Zen were informed by Confucianism, Pure Land Buddhism, and Shinto in earlier centuries. There is a subtle line between informing and blending, however, and a number of eclectic admixtures play out their respective streams to this day.

Confucianism influenced by Zen maintains a presence in modern Japan in various forms. Pure Land Buddhism is really the substance of popular Ch'an in the Chinese diaspora. The samurai who used Zen discipline under Sung expatriate masters in Japan, and then under early Japanese Zen teachers, are still around, flourishing their swords, East and West. Certain Zen centers rework the Dharma from Jungian perspectives, complete with psychological counseling —often in conjunction with a simplified kind of *vipassanā* practice of examining thoughts and emotions. Some Christian-Zen masters replace *shunyatā*, the void, with a kind of "oversoul." These ways of picking and choosing among options for teaching pervade the discipline and ritual, degrading ancient rhythms into popular tunes. Chao-chou and Dōgen hang their heads.

This is, of course, not to deny the virtue of influence or the richness that other views contribute. Zen students find that the Confucian orientation to family and community rather than to the self tends to confirm the Buddhist teaching of mutually dependent arising. Pure Land Buddhists inspire us with their serenity and good-will. Samurai can teach us courage and grace. Lessons from psychology fill gaps in Zen teaching, giving terms like "transference" to certain phenomena that were known to the old teachers, but perhaps never understood very well. And certainly Christians can model the way of compassion for Buddhists whose vows to save the many beings are not always honored in the real world of family and community.

Zen is changing as it moves eastward across the Pacific Ocean. Indian Dhyāna Buddhism changed as it became Chinese Ch'an. Likewise Ch'an as it became Japanese Zen. By lights of the new culture, the extraneous is chipped off, and the fundamentals are burnished. I am convinced that we are arriving at a twenty-first-century Western version of Zen that is authentic, a Zen that Chao-chou or Dōgen would recognize. Authentic is authentic, for all the differences in time, place, and culture. Violets continue to appear each spring. The Buddha indicated that the rice fields conveyed his teaching,

> And hark! how sweet the throstle sings!
> He, too, is no mean preacher:
> Come forth into the light of things.
> Let Nature be your teacher.

Wordsworth hints at how one comes forth into the light of things ("with a wise passiveness," et cetera), but the old Zen masters were far more specific and confident. Sōen Rōshi used to quote Chao-chou, saying, "If you follow my instructions for twenty years and don't realize anything, you may dig up my skull and use it as a night soil dipper!"

The Basics

First Steps

I beg to urge you, everyone:
life-and-death is a grave matter,
all things pass quickly away;
each of you must be completely alert:
never neglectful, never indulgent.

This is the evening message of sesshin, the time of seclusion of the community, called out by a senior member just before lights-out. It expresses three concerns of the Zen student: first, being alive is an important responsibility; second, we have little time to fulfill that responsibility; and third, rigorous practice is necessary for fulfillment.

Our model is Shākyamuni Buddha. Known as the founder of Buddhism, he lived in India more than 2,500 years ago—but religion is fundamentally not a matter of history. I recall a course in Buddhism given by Dr. D. T. Suzuki at the University of Hawai'i a long time ago. He began the course by telling the story of Shākyamuni. He did not tell it as history or biography, but as the story of Everyone—the story of you and me.

The Buddha was born a prince and it was predicted that he would become either a great religious leader or a great emperor. His father, the king, preferred to see his boy become a great emperor, so he had him trained in the arts of the warrior and the statesman. He also provided the comforts and entertainment appropriate to the station of a young prince—fine food and clothing, and the rest of it.

This is your story and mine. When we are young, we are all little princes and princesses. We are each of us the center of the universe. In fact, our mouths are the center, and everything enters therein. We are guided by our parents toward a sense of responsibility, but despite the program set up about us, we emerge, each in our own way, as individual inquirers.

The Buddha's program of power and ease palled for him before he was thirty. It is said that despite his father's efforts to protect him from the realities of suffering, he was witness to sickness, old age, and death. Once, he glimpsed the figure of a monk in the palace compound and asked about him. Pondering deeply, he questioned his purpose in the world. Finally he left his little family in care of his father to seek his spiritual fortune in the forest.

You can imagine the difficulty of this decision. Everything that anyone might hold dear, a beautiful spouse, a baby son, a career as a beneficent ruler—all given up in a search that could well lead nowhere. His decision was rooted in profound concern for all beings. Why should there be suffering in the world? Why should there be the weakness of old age? Why should there be death? And what in the life of a monk might resolve such doubts? These questions plagued the young Gautama. He recognized that unless he resolved his doubts, his leadership could not truly bring fulfillment to others.

Our childish pursuit of gratification palls and we too sense that something we do not understand lies within all our hectic coming and going. Our selfish ways become unsatisfying. Perhaps it is when we attempt to find a sexual mate that we become especially aware of our difficulties. For all its promise of peace and wholeness, the partnership can turn out to be very hard work. It becomes clear that the human path of maturity is rigorous and takes determination.

The Buddha's search led him to become a monk and to seek instruction in philosophy and the attainment of so-called higher states of consciousness. He studied with the leading yoga teachers of his time, but remained unsatisfied. Though he could control his mind, and though he gained a complete grasp of the abstruse and subtle philosophical formulations of his time, he could not resolve the question of suffering.

In our twentieth-century Western setting, religion is not so other-worldly. It is not necessary to leave one's family to search out good teachers and it is not necessary to become a monk or nun to receive good instruction. Like the Buddha, however, we can be relentless in our pursuit of the truth we sense from the beginning. "If not here, then somewhere else, somehow else."

The Buddha went on from philosophy and mystical studies to take up asceticism. He denied himself food, sleep, shelter, and clothing. For a long period he struggled with his desires and his feelings of attachment. But this way too turned out to be a dead end. For all his self-denial he could not find true peace.

Nakagawa Sōen Rōshi once said to me, "Zen is not asceticism." He said this by way of assuring me that I need not follow his example of swimming off the coast of Japan in February. But Zen is not indulgence either. The practice involves rigor and is not possible in a casual lifestyle. We need to find the Middle Way. The Buddha learned, and we learn also, that lengthy fasting and other kinds of excessive self-deprivation only weaken the body and spirit and make the practice more difficult. As the *Tsʼai-ken tʼan* tells us, "Water which is too pure has no fish."[1]

So the Buddha turned back to meditation, which he had undoubtedly learned from his teachers. He took his seat beneath a Bodhi tree, determined not to rise until he had resolved all his doubts. According to the Mahāyāna tradition, early one morning he happened to look up, saw the morning star, and cried out, "Oh, wonderful! wonderful! Now I see that all beings of the universe are the *Tathāgata*! It is only their delusions and preoccupations which keep them from acknowledging that fact."

Tathāgata is another name for Buddha. It means literally "thus come," or more fully "one who thus comes," and implies pure appearance—coming forth as the living fact. All beings are Buddha. All beings are the truth, just as they are. A great Tʼang-period teacher used the expression "Just this!" to present the heart of deepest experience (BS-49).

This deepest experience is not available to the casual onlooker. Delusions and attachments consisting of self-centered and conceptual thinking obscure the living fact. The Zen path is devoted to clearing away these obstructions and seeing into true nature.

This can be your path, the Middle Way of zazen, or seated practice. The Middle Way is not halfway between extremes, but a completely new path. It does not deny thought and it does not deny the
importance of self-control, but reason and restraint are not its main
points.

Dr. Suzuki used to say that Zen is noetic, by which I understand
him to mean that it originates in the mind. It is not intellectual, but
involves realization, the purest gnosis of "just this!" It also involves
application of such realization in the daily life of family, job, and
community service.

Making It Personal

In taking up Zen Buddhism, we find that the life of the Buddha is
our own life. Not only Shākyamuni's life, but the lives of all the succeeding teachers in our lineage are our own lives. As Wu-men Hui-
k'ai has said, in true Zen practice our very eyebrows are tangled with
those of our ancestral teachers, and we see with their eyes and hear
with their ears (GB-1). This is not because we copy them, or change
to be like them. I might explain Wu-men's words by saying that in
finding our own true nature, we find the true nature of all things,
which the old teachers so clearly showed in their words and actions.
But the authentic experience of identity is intimate beyond explanation. And it is not only with old teachers that we had complete intimacy. The Chinese thrush sings in my heart and gray clouds gather
in the empty sky of my mind. All things are my teacher.

On the Zen path, we seek for ourselves the experience of Shākyamuni. However, we do not owe fundamental allegiance to him, but
to ourselves and to our environment. If it could be shown that
Shākyamuni never lived, the myth of his life would be our guide. In
fact it is better to acknowledge at the outset that myths and religious
archetypes guide us, just as they do every religious person. The myth
of the Buddha is my own myth.

Thus, it is essential at the beginning of practice to acknowledge
that the path is personal and intimate. It is no good to examine it
from a distance as if it were someone else's. You must walk it for yourself. In this spirit, you invest yourself in your practice, confident of

your heritage, and train earnestly side by side with your sisters and brothers. It is this engagement that brings peace and realization.

Concentration

The first step on this way of personal engagement is concentration. Usually, we think of concentration as focusing on something with intense mental energy. This is not incorrect, but for the Zen student it is not complete. Even in ordinary experience, we transcend concentration. For example, what happens when you take a civil service test? If you are fully prepared, you sit down and write. Though your neighbor becomes restless, or it begins to rain outside, your attention doesn't swerve. Before you know it, you are finished. A relatively long time has passed. Suddenly you find that your back is stiff and your feet are asleep. You feel tired and you want to go home and rest. But during the course of the test, your stiffness and your tiredness did not distract you. You were absorbed in what you were doing. You became someone taking a test. You forgot yourself in your task.

Rebuilding an engine, nursing a child, watching a movie—all these acts may transcend concentration. Focusing on something involves two things, you and the object, but your everyday experience shows you that when you are truly absorbed the two melt away, and there is "not even one," as Yamada Rōshi liked to say.

Accepting the Self

The everyday experiences of forgetting the self in the act of, say, fixing a faucet, may be understood as a model for zazen, the meditation practice of the Zen student. But before any forgetting is possible, there must be a measure of confidence. The diver on the high board lets everything go with each dive, but could not do so without the development of confidence, a development that goes hand in hand with training. Such letting go is not random. The diver has become one with the practice of diving—free, yet at the same time highly disciplined.

Even champion divers, however, do not touch their deepest potential simply by working out on the high board. A more useful model may be found among the archetypes of zazen, such as Mañ-jushrī who occupies the central place on the altar of the zendō. He holds a scroll, representing wisdom, and a sword to cut off all your concepts. He is seated upon a recumbent lion, and both Mañjushrī and the lion look very comfortable. The lion power is still there, however, and when Mañjushrī speaks, it is with the voice of that lion. Completely free, and completely controlled! The new student must make friends with the lion and tame it before he or she can take the lion seat. This takes time and patience.

At first this inner creature seems more like a monkey than a lion, greedily snatching at bright-colored objects and jumping around from one thing to another. Many people blame themselves, even dis-like themselves, for their restless behavior. But if you reject yourself, you are rejecting the agent of realization. So you must make friends with yourself. Enjoy yourself. Take comfort in yourself. Smile at yourself. You are developing confidence.

Don't misunderstand. I am not directing you to the way of pride and selfishness. I point to the way of Bashō, who loved himself and his friends with no pride at all:

> At our moon-viewing party
> not a single
> beautiful face.

I commented on quoting this poem elsewhere: "What homely bas-tards we are, sitting here in the moonlight!"[2] This kind of humor-ous, deprecatory self-enjoyment is the true basis for responsibility, the act of being responsible. When you make a mistake, do you pun-ish yourself or can you shake your head with a smile and learn some-thing in the process? If you curse yourself, you are postponing your practice. If you simply tick off the error and resolve to do better the next time, then you are ready to practice.

If Shākyamuni Buddha had dwelled upon his own inadequacies rather than the question of suffering in the world, he would never have realized that everything is all right from the beginning. Zazen is not the practice of self-improvement, like a course in making friends and influencing people. With earnest zazen, character refinement does occur, but this is not a matter of ego-adjustment. It is forgetting the self.

Yamada Rōshi has said, "The practice of Zen is forgetting the self in the act of uniting with something." This does not mean that you should try to get rid of your self. That is not possible except by suicide, and suicide is the greatest pity, for you, like each other being of the universe, are unique, the Tathāgata coming forth in your particular form as essential nature.

Breath Counting

Zazen is a matter of just doing it. However, even for the advanced Zen student, work on the meditation cushions is always being refined. It is like learning to drive a car. At first everything is mechanical and awkward. You consciously depress the clutch and shift into low, then release the clutch gradually while depressing the gas pedal, steering to stay within the white lines and to avoid other cars. There are so many things to remember and to do all at once, that at first you make mistakes and perhaps even have an accident. But when you become one with the car, you are more confident. And you become a better and better driver with experience.

The preliminary method on the way of Zen is the process of counting the breaths, as it is for many other illuminative schools of Asian religion. Once, at our Koko An Zendo in Honolulu, we were hosts to a Theravāda Buddhist teacher from Sri Lanka. We asked him how he taught meditation to his disciples, and he proceeded to demonstrate to us the same techniques of counting the breaths that we had learned from our own Japanese Zen teacher. It is somehow the natural first step. The breath is both a spontaneous part of our physical system and, to some degree, under our control. In early days of our Western culture, breath was considered our very spirit, as our words "inspiration" and "expiration" show clearly. When we "expire," once and for all, we have ended our inspiration for this life.

In the next section, I will give a detailed exposition of Zen method. For now, it is sufficient simply to count your breaths. Sit with your back straight, and count "one" for the inhalation, "two" for the exhalation, "three" for the next inhalation, "four" for the next exhalation, and so on up to "ten," and repeat. Don't go above "ten" because it is too difficult to keep track of higher numbers. You are not exercising your thinking faculty in this practice; you are developing your power to invest in something.

Counting is the first mental exercise you learned as a child. It is the easiest of all formal, mental efforts, the closest to being second nature. I have seen people who have migrated to a new country and adjusted themselves fully to their adopted culture and language, still counting their bills at the bank with the numbers of their childhood: *un deux trois quatre, ichi ni san shi.*

But though breath counting is natural, you cannot dream at it and just let it happen. Truly to meet the challenge of your rampaging mind, you must devote all your attention just to "one," just to "two." When (not if!) you lose the count and you finally realize that you have lost it, come back to "one" and start over.

Many people can count to "ten" successfully the first few times they try, but no one who has not practiced can maintain the sequence for long. Though one needs a disciplined mind even for quite ordinary purposes, such as conducting business or teaching, few of us have the faculty of extended attention. I have had people tell me after trying zazen for twenty-five minutes, "You know, I never even got to 'one'!" Counting the breaths shows us that indeed, as a Chinese proverb says, the mind is like a monkey or a wild horse.

Breath counting is not the kindergarten of Zen. For many students it is a full and complete lifetime practice. But even with just a month of practice, a few minutes each day, you will be able to focus more clearly on your work or study and to give yourself more freely to conversation and recreation. You will have learned how to begin, at any rate, the task of keeping yourself undivided, for it is thinking of something other than the matter at hand that separates us from reality and dissipates our energies.

From *Taking the Path of Zen*

The Way

Zen Buddhism is one path among many. I have heard it said that all paths lead to the top of the same mountain. I doubt it. I think that one mountain may seem just a small hill from the top of another. Let one hundred mountains rise! Meanwhile you must find your own path, and your own mountain. You may have an experience of some kind that points the direction clearly, or you may have to explore for a while. But eventually you will have to settle on a particular way, with a particular teacher.

Trusting yourself to a specific path naturally involves risks. Unquestioning acceptance might lead you to blind belief in something quite unhealthy. You should be sure that a given path is worthy of your investment. The process of deciding "This is (or is not) the way for me" takes time. At any Zen center worthy of the name, no one will rush you. In a true *dōjō* (training center), evidence of worth will be found at every hand, and you will soon reach the point of trust.

Zazen as Experiment

The heart of Zen training is zazen. Without zazen, there is no Zen, no realization, and no application of the practice. It has its roots in earliest Vedic times and was well established by Shākyamuni's day. It has since been refined by trial and error in countless training centers through some ninety generations of Zen teachers. By now its form is well established.

Yet the mind remains vast and creative. Words of our ancestors in the Dharma turn out to be helpful, but the way itself is still guided by experiment.

We are concerned with realizing the nature of being, and zazen has proved empirically to be the practical way to settle down to the place where such realization is possible. This is not a way that is designed for Japanese, for intelligentsia, or for any particular class or category of individuals. The fact that zazen originates in India and China, and that it comes to us through Korea and Japan, is not so very important. As North and South Americans, Australians, Europeans we make it our own.

There is a further important point. Zazen is not merely a means, any more than eating, sleeping, or hugging your children is a means or method. Dōgen Kigen Zenji, founder of the Sōtō sect in Japan, said, "Zazen is itself enlightenment." This unity of ends and means, effect and cause, is the Tao of the Buddha, the practice of realization.

The Posture

I have heard that someone asked Sasaki Jōshū Rōshi, "What of Zen is necessary to preserve?" He replied, "Posture and the breathing." I think I might say simply, "Posture."

Posture is the form of zazen. To avoid fatigue and to permit consciousness to settle, legs, seat, and spine should support the body. If strain is thrown on the muscles and tendons of the back and neck, it will be impossible to continue the practice beyond a short period.

We may take our model from the posture of a one-year-old baby. The child sits bolt upright, with spine curving forward slightly at the waist, rather than completely straight up and down. The belly sticks out in front, while the rear end sticks out behind. Sitting with the spine completely straight at this age would be impossible, as the muscles are still undeveloped—too weak to hold the body erect. Curved forward, the vertebrae are locked into their strongest position, and the child can forget about staying erect.

When you take your seat on your cushions, or on a chair if your legs don't bend easily, your spine should curve forward slightly at the waist like the baby's. Your belt should be loose, and your stomach be allowed to hang out naturally, while your posterior is thrust back for solid support. Katsuki Sekida, former resident advisor to the Diamond Sangha, once sent out New Year cards with the greeting, "Belly forward, buttocks back." This is how we should greet the New Year, or the new day.

If the spine is correctly positioned, then all else follows naturally. Head is up, perhaps bent forward very slightly. Chin is in, ears are on line with the shoulders, and shoulders are on line with the hips.

The Legs

Legs are a problem. Few people, even children, even in Japan, are flexible enough to sit easily in a lotus position without painful practice. Our tendons and muscles need stretching over many months before we can be comfortable. Yet, in the long run, sitting with one or both feet in the lap is far superior to sitting in any other position. In that way you are locked into your practice and your organs are completely at ease. Sitting in a chair, however, may be the only option for one suffering from injury or arthritis.

Certain exercises are helpful in stretching for the lotus positions by sitting on a rug or pad:

1. Bring heels of both feet to the crotch, bend forward with your back straight, and touch your face to the floor, placing your hands on the floor just above your head. Knees also should touch the floor in this exercise and if they do not, rock them gently up and down, stretching the ligaments.
2. Bring your feet together with your legs outstretched, bend forward, and touch your hands to the floor by your feet, keeping your back and legs straight; if possible, touch your face to your knees.
3. Extend your legs as far apart as possible. Bend forward with your back and legs straight and touch your face to the floor, placing your hands on the floor, either outstretched or just above your head.

Makkōhō Position 1

Makkōhō Position 2

Makkōhō Position 3

Makkōhō Position 4

4. Double back one leg so that your foot is beside your seat, with your instep, shin, and knee resting on the rug or pad. Bend the other leg back in the same way. Now lie back on one elbow, then on both elbows, and finally lie back flat. At first you may have to lie back against a sofa cushion so that you are not completely flat, and perhaps have someone to help you. If you can manage to lie flat, raise your arms over your head until your hands touch the floor and then bring them to your side again.

Yasutani Rōshi did these exercises every morning before breakfast, well into his eighties. It may take you some time to become flexible enough to do them even partially. Maintain the effort and your zazen will be less demanding physically.

These four exercises are the core of *Makkōhō*, a Japanese system of physical conditioning. Don't push yourself too hard or you may strain a muscle or pull a ligament. At the limit of each stretch, breathe in and out three or four times and try to relax.[3]

Cushions

Correct zazen posture requires the use of a cushion and a pad. The pad is at least 28 inches square, stuffed with kapok or cotton batting so that it is about 1½ inches thick. The *zafu*, or cushion, completes the setup. It is spherical, stuffed with kapok or buckwheat hulls, 12 inches or more in diameter. It flattens out somewhat in use. Ordinary pillows may be substituted for it, but they are not as practical. Foam rubber is sometimes used to fill the pad, but it makes an unsteady seat. It cannot be used for the zafu.

The zafu elevates your rear end. This makes for correct posture without straining. I have known yogis who could take the full lotus position while standing on their heads, but few who could meditate for twenty-five minutes without a cushion.

Getting Seated

Bring the zafu to the back edge of the pad, sit on it, and rest both knees on the pad. For the lotus position, place your right foot on your left thigh, as high as possible, and then your left foot on your

Full Lotus

Half Lotus

Seiza

Burmese

right thigh. The half lotus is simply the left foot on the right thigh, while the right foot is drawn up under the left thigh. The full lotus is the most secure way to sit. The half lotus is adequate; it will distort the body slightly, but not enough to matter. It is all right to place the right foot on the left thigh by way of compensating for a spinal deviation or as relief during sesshin.

There are two other possibilities. One is the Burmese style, in which one leg is placed in front of the other, so that both ankles are resting on the pad. This position is not quite as steady as half lotus, but it is easier on the knees. As you get used to it, you may be able to start taking up half lotus for brief intervals at first, and then for longer periods.

The other option is the *seiza* position, which is something like kneeling, except that your rear end is supported by a zafu. Some people turn the zafu on edge before sitting on it. This keeps the legs closer together and is more comfortable. Your weight rests on your seat, knees, shins, and ankles. Like the Burmese position, seiza is not as secure as half lotus, but it may be used as a kind of intermediate practice while the legs are becoming more flexible through daily stretching exercises. It is also useful as a relief during sesshin.

The one most desperately uncomfortable position is the conventional cross-legged, or tailor fashion, of sitting. Both feet are under the thighs. The back is rounded; the belly is drawn in. The shin of one leg rests on the ankle of the other, and severe pain is inevitable. The lungs must labor to draw in their air and other organs seem cramped as well. Sitting in this way is probably not conducive to good health or to good practice.

The incomplete half lotus, in which the upper foot rests on the calf of the other leg, rather than upon the thigh, also may be painful after a while, not in the legs, but in the back. Somehow, it is difficult to be fully erect in this position, and one must strain in the effort.

All these suggestions about leg positions should be taken as guidelines, not as rules. Do the best you can, and no more will be asked. One of our members at the Maui Zendo did a full seven-day sesshin flat on her back. She had ruptured a disk, and could not even sit up without assistance. Daitō Kokushi, great master of early Japanese

Zen, had a withered leg and could not sit in any of the conventional
ways. It is said that he was only able to bring that leg to its correct
place on his thigh at the end of his life. "All my life I have been obey-
ing you," he said to his leg. "Now you obey me!" With a mighty
heave, he brought his leg into position, breaking it, and dying in the
same moment.

I recommend against such drastic practice, at least until you are
ready to die. The full lotus position is the most secure way to sit, but
it is also the one most likely to injure the overeager beginner. Your
legs should be fairly flexible before you attempt it, and even then,
don't sit in that way for long periods until you are fairly comfortable. You may "pop your knee," and this may result in permanent
damage.

A yoga teacher advised me that people should be careful to support their knees with their hands when placing their legs in position
for zazen, and when unfolding them at the end of a period. This is
cogent advice. The knees are comparatively weak joints.

Eyes and Hands

Your eyes should be about two-thirds closed, cast down, looking at
a point about three feet ahead of you. It should be remembered that
if your eyes are closed, you may become dreamy; if your eyes are
wide open, you will be too easily distracted. Also, don't try to keep
your eyes focused. After a while you will find that they naturally go
out of focus whenever you sit.

Place your hands in your lap in the meditation *mudrā*. Your left
hand should rest, palm upward, on the palm of your right hand, and
your thumbs should touch, forming an oval. (It is said, technically,
that it is the tips of your thumbnails that should touch.) Your hands
should rest in your lap, just touching your belly, and your elbows
should project a little. Some Zen teachers suggest that you imagine
you are holding a precious jewel in your hands; others suggest that
you place your attention there. In any case, the hand position is crit-
ically important, for it reflects the condition of your mind. If your
mind is taut, your thumbs will hold the oval; if your mind becomes

dull or strays into fantasy, your thumbs will tend to collapse. (Note that in the Rinzai school, the hands are sometimes merely clasped together, with the right hand holding the left thumb.)

Beginning Your Practice

When you sit down, place your feet in position, lean far forward, thrust your posterior back, and sit up. Next, take a deep silent breath and hold it. Then exhale slowly and silently, all the way out, and hold it. Breathe in deeply again and hold it, and all the way out once more. You may do this through the mouth, but note that at all other times you should breathe through the nose. These two deep inhalations and exhalations help to cut the continuity of your mental activity and to quiet the mind for zazen.

Now rock from side to side, widely at first, then in decreasing arcs. Lean forward and back in the same way, and you will find that you are well settled and ready to begin your breath counting. Follow the instructions I gave you earlier. Count "one" for the inhalation, "two" for the exhalation, and so on up to "ten," and repeat. After a few days, or a few weeks, you may begin to feel comfortable with this practice. Then try counting exhalations only, keeping your mind steady and quiet on the inhalations.

More on Breath Counting

You will find breath counting to be a useful means throughout your life of Zen training. Whatever your practice becomes later on, you should count your breaths from "one" to "ten," one or two sequences, at the start of each new period of zazen. It will help you to settle down, and will serve to remind you that you are not just sitting there, but sitting with a particular practice.

At best, you become one with your object in zazen, so if you merely sit with a focus, you tend to close off your potential. You and your object remain two things. Let yourself be receptive with each point, each number, in the sequence of counting. You and the count and the breath are all of a piece in this moment. Invest yourself in each number. There is only "one" in the whole universe, only "two" in the whole universe, just that single point. Everything else is dark.

It is not as important to reach "ten" as it is to become intimate with each point in the sequence. "Intimacy" is a synonym for "realization" in the old Zen texts. And the point, as you know from geometry, has no dimension, no magnitude. There is the great mystery itself, appearing with each new point.

At first, as a beginner, you will be conscious of each step in the procedure, but eventually you will become the procedure itself. The practice will do the practice. It takes time, and for months, perhaps, you will seem to spend your time dreaming rather than counting. This is normal. Your brain secretes thoughts as your stomach secretes pepsin. Don't condemn yourself for this normal condition.

Breath counting is only one of many devices you can use in your practice. Later I will discuss some others with you in detail.

From *Taking the Path of Zen*

Words in the Dōjō

Introduction

"Words in the Dōjō" are edited from extemporaneous homilies I offered in Diamond Sangha sesshins over the years, from about 1978 until the publication of this work in 1993. Sesshins are part of a traditional cycle of Zen training practiced in Far Eastern Buddhist monasteries, and have their origin in the monsoon retreats of early Buddhist and pre-Buddhist religious in India. Most of the year, the Indian monks (and a few nuns) wandered as mendicants, but when the rains came, they gathered at centers to renew their vows and deepen their understanding. In Japan today the cycle of practice is still keyed to the seasons, with sesshins embedded in longer training periods—which in turn alternate with intervals that include only maintenance work around the monastery and light training.

Lay Zen centers in the West follow this rhythm of practice in a general way. In the Diamond Sangha, for example, we have two training periods per year, each with a seven-day and a five-day sesshin. Between training periods the practice is less demanding, though we have frequent weekend sesshins. In addition, the special eight-day *Rōhatsu ō-zesshin* (Eight-Day Sesshin during Great Cold), from the evening of November 30 to the morning of December 8, is an extended celebration of the enlightenment of the Buddha Shākyamuni.

At the sesshins of most Zen Buddhist centers, students rise at 4:00 AM and practice zazen for twenty-five- to thirty-five-minute periods throughout the day until lights-out at 9:00 PM. This routine is broken by intervals of formal walking between the periods of zazen, and by formal meals, a sūtra service, two or three personal interviews per day, a talk by the rōshi (old teacher), and brief periods of rest. Cooking, cleaning, and leadership tasks are handled by the students themselves. There is no casual talking and just the natural kind of socializing that comes with living and working together with sisters and brothers in silent, common purpose.

I described earlier how to sit in zazen. The posture is such that it can be forgotten while the student devotes all possible energy into focused inquiry. For the most part, this practice is keyed to the breaths and can be the practice of counting them from one to ten, of shikantaza (sitting with no theme), or of kōan work (focus upon and attunement with a single matter)—usually beginning with the word "Mu," lifted from the well-known Zen story:

> A monk asked Chao-chou in all earnestness, "Has the dog
> Buddha-nature, or not?"
> Chao-chou said, "Mu."
>
> (GB-1)

"Mu" means "no" or "does not have," so the student faces a dilemma: Buddhist literature declares that all beings have Buddha-nature, yet here is Chao-chou, perhaps the greatest Chinese master, saying that the dog does not. But practice with Mu is not a matter of puzzling over this dilemma. Instead, the student sets logic aside, and musters body and mind to breathe Mu, just Mu, with inquiring spirit. It is a practice that has, down through the centuries, brought countless monks, nuns, laymen, and laywomen to a realization of their true nature. It is a perennial religious path and is naturally marked with occasional episodes of discouragement and despair. Many of the words in this section are intended to encourage an inquiry into Mu in such difficult circumstances.

My custom is to appear in the dōjō during the mid-morning block for zazen with the students, just before the first interviews of the day. I find something brief to say during that time, when the students are getting settled in for a period of zazen. I also come to the dōjō at the very end of the day, after the evening dokusan is over, to join the students for the closing ceremony. As the students stand, I again offer a few words. Thus some of the "Words in the Dōjō" in this collection were originally intended to help people find their way while they were on their cushions and some were intended for them to take along to bed.

I have arranged my pieces to reflect the various aspects of Zen practice, and added some comments. I removed the more distracting references to time and place, but have left in the natural allusions. Doves, cardinals, and thrushes sing, and geckos shout at the Koko An Zendo in suburban Honolulu. Bluebirds sing and turkeys gobble at the Ring of Bone Zendo in the Sierra foothills in California. Kookaburras create their diversions at Sydney and Perth. At a sesshin in Adelaide we were serenaded by bullfrogs, and the little stream by the old Maui Zendo murmurs its constant instruction. Zazen is not sensory deprivation—anything but! Birds and geckos and bullfrogs guide us. Be open to these natural teachers, wherever you may be practicing.

The First Night

Students gather for sesshin in the late afternoon the day before sesshin formally begins. They unpack, make their beds, and assemble for a work meeting. After a circle of self-introductions, sesshin jobs are assigned and explained. Newcomers are given orientation to mealtime procedures, and a supper follows. At 7:00 PM there is one period of zazen, then, followed by opening remarks from the rōshi, dōjō leaders summarize the sesshin procedures. There is then a brief period of zazen and a short sūtra, and at 9:00 the students retire.

I was reflecting as I unpacked my suitcase this evening that all of us bring baggage to sesshin. I want to unpack all of my baggage and put it away, and I urge you to put away your stuff too. When you forget yourself and are united with your task, *that* is your liberation. If there is a milestone of realization on the path, well and good, but it is in the continued practice of uniting with your work that you turn the Wheel of the Dharma for yourself, for the Sangha, and for the world.

We begin our sesshin tomorrow morning at four o'clock, and continue for seven days. It is like a dream, one that is repeated each month, and is repeated elsewhere as people gather for sesshin in many places and on many occasions. We sit in this dream with students from all over the world. It is a dream of the other as no other than myself, of all time as this time now, of every place as this very Bodhi seat. The whole universe musters itself and concentrates together in sesshin—the birds, the rain, the cicadas. The circumstances are ideal. All the sesshin arrangements are settled. Everything is settled. You can forget your ordinary concerns.

The word "sesshin" is an ambiguous term with three intimately related meanings: "to touch the mind, to receive the mind, to convey the mind."

To touch the mind is to touch that which is not born and does not die; it does not come or go, and is always at rest. It is infinite emptiness—empty infinity—the vast and fathomless Dharma which you have vowed to realize.

To receive the mind is to be open with all your senses to instruction. Someone coughs, a window squeaks, a gecko cries, cars on the freeway hum in the distance, the bell rings, the teacher makes a comment—these are instructive expressions of the mind.

Finally, you convey the mind by the utmost integrity which you present in your manner, as you stand, sit, eat, and lie down with settled dignity, composure, and recollection—as the Buddha himself or herself. You are the teacher of us all and of yourself.

You also convey the mind by containing your actions. In this way you will not distract yourself or others, and you will offer space for everyone to evolve. When I was in Japanese monasteries, I noticed that monks had a particular style of walking. There was almost no sound. You can apply this kind of care to opening the door, to eating and so on. Contain yourself, contain Mu, and in this way you will convey the mind.

We are lay disciples of the Buddha Shākyamuni. He felt that in order to meet the Tathāgata you must be a monk. But this idea is challenged by the lives of Vimalakīrti, the Layman P'ang, Dr. D. T. Suzuki, and the many wise tea women, nameless but not forgotten in Zen Buddhist history. Like those great laypeople in our lineage, we are challenged to fold the intensive practice of the monk into our daily lives. In a very real sense, we have an advantage over the monks. The world is in our face all day long, and even during sesshin we know it is only a telephone call away. That call can come at any moment. Use your time.

Coming Home

The old-fashioned word for a psychiatrist was "alienist," the one who treats aliens. Zen practice is rather different from psychiatry, but its purpose is the same. The alien suffers from duhkha, *the anguish of feeling displaced, and, as the Buddha said,* duhkha *is everywhere. It is the dis-ease we have in common.*

Walking from the cottage to the dōjō through the very light rain, I reflected how Hawaiian people regard rain as a blessing. Then hearing the dedication of our sūtra to the guardians of the Dharma and the protectors of our sacred hall, I reflected that while there are indeed unseen guardians and protectors, the rain is also our guardian, the wind in the Bodhi leaves and Sangha members too. In this protected place settle comfortably into your practice.

The World Does Zazen

The student of Zen Buddhism finds the light of inspiration in beings and incidents of the world. Thus, unlike the way of most meditative traditions, the light is not sought exclusively within. Fundamentally, however, inside and outside are not two.

The sound of the wind and the songs of birds are essential elements of zazen, just as essential as correct posture. When the sounds die down, the silence takes their place. But if sounds and silence are missing, then you are lost in thoughts and your practice is stalling. Let sounds and silence sustain you as you face your kōan.

An incident can be instructive or disruptive, depending largely on the attitude we bring to it. If you are walking through a familiar room in complete darkness, you might bump into a table or a chair.

With one kind of attitude you curse. With another you say, "Oh, there's the table—there's the chair—now I know the way." The song of the thrush and the cry of the gecko—the sounds of people coming in or going out—these can be instructive or disruptive, depending on how open you are to guidance. I hope you can respond, "Oh, now I know the way."

Hui-hai said, "The gate to the Dharma is relinquishment."[4] Give yourself over to breathing Mu. There is just a tiny step from distraction to attention. Take that step again and again. Maintain that step. Let yourself be reminded by the cardinal, the persistent prompting of the cardinal [a cardinal sings outside]-Mu-[the cardinal sings again]-Mu-[the cardinal sings again]-Mu.

Emptiness

The term "emptiness," in the Buddhist context, can be a problem for new students. It does not mean "vacuum," but rather it is the void that is full of potential. It has no bounds. At the first sesshin I attended in Japan, I was introduced to the monk who was to be a big brother for me during the seven days. He said, "How do you do? The world is very broad, don't you think?" I was quite charmed, but I had no idea what he meant. Yet, as Nan-ch'üan said to Chao-chou, "If you truly reach the genuine Tao, you will find it as vast and boundless as outer space."

(GB-19)

Dōgen Zenji described realization as the "body and mind dropped away." Yamada Rōshi called it "forgetting the self." Sesshin is a time when you practice this forgetting for a few days. You don't know if it is the second day or the fourth day, unless you are reminded. You hear the bells that end the period of zazen, and think, "Why! I just sat down!" Each moment is full and complete—the empty universe itself completely in focus—simply as Mu. This is the occasion of great promise.

Zazen is very difficult when you try to concentrate on Mu in the context of contending thoughts. In that realm, Mu seems just one option among many. It seems very limited in the presence of so many other engaging possibilities. Please don't make it hard for yourself in this way. Listen to the silence. Breathe Mu there. Persevere and you will find it is the only option—not limited at all, but including everything.

Condition

I hope you will not be preoccupied with difficulties. Thirty-five years ago, I was involved in therapy, and one day the therapist asked me, "Why did you want to catch a cold?" This made me angry, and I still think it was a poor question. I am ready to accept the fact that I placed myself here on purpose, and that I created my condition on purpose, but I am not ready to explore in detail all the minute reasons. I hope you will agree with me. You can practice in whatever condition you find yourself, healthy or sick, happy or sad.

This is the first or second sesshin for quite a number of you, and I know you are suffering a lot of pain. There are several things I can say about this matter, but the most important is that the purpose of sesshin is not to turn out crippled samurai. If you reach a certain point of pain, then you should sit on a bench or in a chair. If you were born lazy, I would say to you, "Sit through your pain," but I know you are not lazy. There are chairs in the alcove. Please use them. Sit there for one block of zazen and then, if you wish, return to your cushion for the next block. Or sit there for the rest of sesshin. I sat my first several sesshin in a chair—from beginning to end. You will not find quite the measure of stability on a bench or in a chair that you might on cushions, but there is a trade-off. Even in a chair you can touch the mind. Don't let pride get in your way.

Sometimes you might find that you are creating pain by avoiding it. If you try to lift yourself somehow to avoid the pain in your knees or ankles, you create tension that makes the pain much worse. When you settle into the pain, you can actually settle under it and the pain can disappear. Tomorrow, maybe you will get your second wind and will be able to relax naturally, and then the pain will go away.

In your zazen, you might encounter a feeling of unusual sensitivity or of unusual transparency. Or you might experience fear. Walk right through these conditions. They can be very promising, but not if you focus on them.

Take advantage of your condition. Use your condition. If you feel strange or weird, don't try to recover your common state of mind. Go straight along with Mu in that strange weird condition. It can be very promising. Breathe Mu, only Mu.

Preoccupation with condition is the *bête noire* of Zen, the black beast of practice, the bugaboo of true zazen. Don't give that animal a second glance or it will eat you up and take over. Let your condition go, let everything go, and simply face your kōan.

If you have the flu or a pinched nerve, you must lie down. If there's a fire, you must gather up Bodhidharma and go outside. But there is a vast range of conditions, inner and outer, that you can ignore. Katsuki Sekida told us a story which was current just after the great earthquake in 1922, when much of Tokyo was destroyed. An operation was in progress in a hospital. The doctor and staff carried it forward and completed it even though the lights went out and they were dependent on natural lighting from the windows. The building shook violently. It was only when the patient had been wheeled out that they looked at each other and said, "That was an earthquake."

The Single Point

During a sesshin in Japan, the rōshi will commonly speak about the development of the sesshin. Often, he will use the metaphor of a battle. He might say, "Now we are preparing for battle," or "Now we are drawing up our battle lines," or "Now we are meeting the enemy." It is not false to think of sesshin as development or confrontation. But there is another way. There is no time at all. No development, no ongoing practice. There is only this thought-moment, only this Mu-moment.

We probably measure time by the incidence of our thoughts. When there are no thoughts, there is no time. Key Mu to your breath. Let your Mu be breathy. In this way, there will be no room for thoughts and your Mu will be infinitely spacious.

In true zazen, or I may say, in ordinary zazen, there are no dimensions. There is no time at all and also no space: the drum and the bell sound in our hearts. The gecko calls from the very center of the mind. "Buddha nature pervades the whole universe, existing right here now."[5]

Carry Your Practice Lightly

When I first started zazen in earnest, I was in Japan. I felt isolated, and I worried about my personal problems and my inability to communicate. Then when I turned my attention to Mu, I was pretty grim about it. One day, my teacher, Sōen Rōshi, listened to my presentation in dokusan, and said, "Please carry your Mu lightly."
"How can I do that?" I wondered.

Sōen Rōshi used to say that sesshin is a symphony. At the end he would play a recording of the Fourth Movement of Beethoven's Ninth by way of celebration. There are many parts and movements and intervals in our sesshin symphony. Together we re-create Shākyamuni's composition. Individually we find fulfillment in our parts. Enjoy your playing. Enjoy your practice.

By now some of you may feel that Mu is a heavy burden. But, you know, Yamada Rōshi said, "To tell the truth, Mu has no meaning." Where could there be any weight? Carry Mu lightly, and all your other concerns will be light as well. Lighten up and Mu will become clear.

Perhaps you have a tendency to treat zazen rather glumly, especially during sesshin. But really it is a very interesting practice, with your strengths, your weaknesses, your physical qualities, your mental and emotional qualities—all of them at play. You seek intimacy with Mu. What an interesting challenge it is! Pursue that challenge with childlike enthusiasm, like a scientist. Regard the whole process objectively, knowing that your best is also the Buddha's best.

If you are glum about your Mu, then it will form a kind of heavy continuity, a hard shell, and there will be no place for the cicadas or the kookaburra to penetrate. When Chao-chou said "Mu," he was a tottering old priest and probably he said it very softly. This is a clue to how we should hold our Mu. With determination, of course, but the Mu itself is very soft. Essential nature itself is very soft. In fact, it has no substance at all.

Attention

How gratifying it is to sit in the dokusan room and have someone come and exclaim in a smile, "The tape in my head has switched off!" Attention to the point has brought this happy condition into being. Now attention can nurture the point and let it flower.

You might find that one problem in your practice is an anxiety to get on with it. You dwell upon time, and so your attention is diffused and your Mu is just a blur. Please resist this tendency. Make your Mu an interlude. Make your next Mu an interlude. Configure each Mu, each breath moment.

Coming and Going

In Far Eastern languages, many idioms link "coming" with "going." The polite way to bid goodbye to your household is to say, "I go and return." Coming and going, we are near or far, old or young, dying or being born, here in this "floating world." Yet the floating world can also be rooted, as we learn when we settle ourselves in zazen and then stand for the next ceremony.

When you think only in terms of sequence, you are like the one in the midst of water crying out in thirst. When you think just in terms of future attainment you are like the child of a wealthy home wandering among the poor. Let down your bucket where you are. The water is fresh right here.

Some teachers enjoin their students to penetrate Mu, to break into Mu. This is misleading, I think. Wu-men makes it clear that in practicing Mu you engage in a process, a ripening, and there are two things to be said about it. The first is that it is all right to be where you are in this process. And the second is, of course, that you enhance the ripening by breathing Mu with each breath.

Patience

Cheerless endurance is the ultimate kind of patience—at one end of the scale. But if your practice is bleak, then the upshot of your practice will be bleak. Zazen is not a means to an end. Means and ends are actually the same. Try cheerful patience. That's the other end of the scale.

It is natural to feel impatient during sesshin. "When will I ever get it?" But patience is the Tao of all the Buddhas. Patience is not endurance. It is loving acceptance, loving acceptance, breath by breath. And when you follow the way of patience you find your own best realization, not someone else's.

The Sacred Self

The self is simply a bundle of perceptions. Perceptions themselves, their organs, and things perceived are without substance, as the Heart Sūtra *tells us.[6] Yet at the same time, the self is the agent of realization and the setting of serious practice.*

You may feel, "Oh, I have these weaknesses and these faults and they are impeding my practice." But really faults and weaknesses are only pejorative words for qualities. They are points of growth, points of change. Your laziness is your patience and your anger is your sense of justice.

Becoming Settled

Each moment is eternity itself. How do you practice that? Come to a halt. Stay there. Settle there. Treat each breath as though it were your last. Someone asked me, "How should I treat each breath as though it were my last?"

I said, "Breathe. Settle into Mu. Sink into Mu. Put everything else to
one side. Let everything else go. Let there be only Mu. Let Mu breathe
Mu."

Consider for a moment that each of your exhalations, however long
or short it might be, is really a sigh. Let yourself down with each exhalation, as though it were a sigh. Our grandmothers knew that
when they sighed, they could let their worries go.

Switch Back to Mu

In his workshops, Thich Nhat Hanh says, "Your mind is like a TV. When
you want a busy channel, you switch to a busy channel. When you want
a quiet channel, you switch to a quiet channel."

The path of Mu is clearly marked, like a hiking trail with white
painted stones. Leaves in the wind, the calling of doves, the scolding
of mynahs are your teachers. Your thoughts themselves can be reminders. Their appearance is your signal.

Diligence

Zen teachers like to draw circles. Sometimes they draw them around
from right to left, sometimes around from left to right. These circles can
represent emptiness, fullness, or the moon. Or they can represent the prac-
tice. The circle that goes around from right to left—against the path of
the sun on the sundial—represents the hard way of practice before any
glimmer of understanding appears. When it goes around from left to
right, following the path of the sun, it represents the easier way of prac-
tice after a glimmer opens the Way. But both before and after the glim-
mer, the practice requires investment and conscientious diligence.

We have a tendency to think, "Oh, there's always next sesshin," just
as in daily life we think, "There's always tomorrow." Don't bet on it.
This is the last breath of the last block of sitting of the last sesshin.
Tomorrow just isn't in the contract. I was recalling as I made my
bows just now that the person who made this bowing mat and this

zafu died after she sent them and before they reached us by parcel post. We are all of us at risk, and the tendency to postpone can be a pernicious trap. Where will you be next November, or even at the time of our next sesshin? You can't say. The time of true life is this very thought frame.

Some of you have asked me how you can control your thoughts. Who is in charge here? When you breathe in and then breathe out, are there any thoughts there? Focus scrupulously on breathing in and breathing out.

The Dark Night

Sometimes you find yourself in a desert-like place where there is not a drop of water, not a blade of grass, not a bit of sustenance. Everything is dry and dreary. This is not a condition that is peculiar to the Zen path— it is described as the "sick soul" by William James in his Varieties of Religious Experience. *It is a condition of great promise. You are walk-ing the path with all your ancestors in the Dharma, and all earnest pil-grims of religion everywhere.*

Discouragement is no more than a condition. You ask yourself, "What in heaven's name am I doing here, counting my breaths, or repeating a meaningless syllable!" Ah, yes! Remember your vows. Don't be managed by your condition.

Simple and Clear

There is no magic involved in Zen practice. You do not pursue stale prac-tice and then suddenly find everything pure and clear. Practice Mu as purely and clearly as you can. That is the nature of your Mu, with or without realization.

Nan-ch'üan said: "Among students of the Way, fools and dullards are hard to come by."[7] Fortunately, there have been a few, after all.

Afterword

*When I come into the dōjō for the ceremony at the end of sesshin, I some-
times recall the story I heard at Ryūtakuji about monks long ago at the
end of a sesshin. They were filled with enthusiasm and elected to sit on
for another seven days. I know the feeling, and I think most students
have experienced it. All that effort to concentrate and get settled on Mu
is at last beginning to pay off—and now ironically the sesshin is coming
to an end. "Shall we sit another seven days?" After the most minute hesi-
tation everyone will say, "Well, no, not this time. Let's move on." The
cycle of intensive work is phasing out, and now we must find ways to
apply our good work.*

Intimacy is the quality of our practice and of our realization. Please
remember this as you return to your home and job.

You have survived on zazen during these many days, and you are
probably more tired than you feel. Allow yourself to come down
naturally. Make rest your practice now, and avoid talk that is ex-
cessively analytical. Keep yourself simple, as the Buddha mind is
simple.

From *Encouraging Words: Zen Buddhist
Teachings for Western Students*

Commentaries

The Old Pond

The old pond;
a frog jumps in—
the sound of the water.[1]

Furu ike ya Old pond!
kawazu tobikomu frog jumps in
mizu no oto water's sound

The Form

Ya is a cutting word that separates and yet joins the expressions before and after. It is punctuation that marks a transition—a particle of anticipation.

 Thus there is a pause in meaning at the end of the first segment, but the next two segments have no pause between them. In the original, the words of the second and third parts build steadily to the final word *oto*. This has penetrating impact—"frog jumps in water's sound." Haiku poets commonly play with their base of the three parts, running the meaning past the end of one segment into the next, playing with their form, as all artists do variations on the form they are working with. Actually, the word "haiku" means "play verse."

Comment

This is probably the most famous poem in Japan, and after three hundred years and more of repetition, it has, understandably, become a little stale for Japanese people. Thus, as English readers, we may have something of an edge in any effort to see it freshly. The first line is simply "The old pond." This sets the scene—a large, perhaps overgrown lily pond in a garden somewhere. We may imagine that the edges are quite mossy and probably rather broken down. With the frog as our cue, we guess that it is twilight in late spring.

This setting of time and place needs to be established, but there is more. "Old" is a cue word of another sort. For a poet such as Bashō, an evening beside a mossy pond is ancient indeed. Bashō presents his own mind as this timeless, endless pond, serene and potent—a condition familiar to mature Zen students.

In one of his first talks in Hawai'i, Yamada Rōshi said: "When your consciousness has become ripe by true zazen—pure like clear water, like a serene mountain lake, not moved by any wind—then anything may serve as a medium for enlightenment."

D. T. Suzuki once said that the condition of the Buddha's mind while he was sitting under the Bodhi tree was that of *sagara mudrā samādhi* ("ocean-seal absorption"). In this instance, "mudrā" is translated as "seal," as in "notary seal." We seal our zazen with our zazen mudrā left hand over the right, thumbs touching. Our minds are sealed with the serenity and depth of the great ocean in true zazen.

There is more, I think. Persistent inquiry casts that profound serenity. The entire teaching of Zen is framed by questions. It is the story of men and women who were open to agonizing uncertainties about ultimate purpose and meaning. Tradition tells us that the Buddha was preoccupied with questions about suffering. Profound doubts placed him under the Bodhi tree, and his exacting focus brought him to the serene inner setting where the simple incident of noticing the morning star could suddenly disclose the ultimate Way.

In Bashō's haiku, a frog appears. To Japanese of sensitivity, frogs are dear little creatures, and Westerners may at least appreciate this animal's energy and immediacy. Plop!

"Plop" is onomatopoeic, as is *oto* in this instance. Onomatopoeia is the presentation of an action by its sound, or at least that is its definition in literary criticism. The poet might prefer to say that she herself becomes that sound. Thus the parody by Sengai is very instructive:

The old pond!
Bashō jumps in,
The sound of the water![2]

Hsiang-yen became profoundly attuned to a sound while cleaning the grave of Chung, the National Teacher. His broom caught a
little stone which sailed through the air and hit a stalk of bamboo.
Tock! He had been working on the kōan "My original face before
my parents were born," and with that sound his body and mind
dropped away completely. There was only that *tock!*[3] Of course,
Hsiang-yen was ready for this experience. He was deep in the
samādhi of sweeping leaves and twigs from the grave of an old master, just as Bashō was lost in the *samādhi* of an old pond, and just as
the Buddha was deep in the *samādhi* of the great ocean.

"*Samādhi*" means "absorption," but fundamentally it is unity with
the whole universe. When you devote yourself to what you are
doing, moment by moment—to your kōan when on your cushion
in zazen, to your work, study, conversation, or whatever in daily
life—that is *samādhi*. Do not suppose that *samādhi* is exclusively
Zen Buddhist. Everything and everybody are in *samādhi*, even bugs,
even people in mental hospitals.

Absorption is not the final step in the Way of the Buddha.
Hsiang-yen changed with that *tock*. When he heard that tiny sound,
he began a new life. He found himself at last, and could then greet
his master confidently and lay a career of teaching whose effect is
still felt today. After this experience, he wrote:

One stroke has made me forget all my previous knowledge.
No artificial discipline is at all needed;
In every movement I uphold the ancient way
And never fall into the rut of mere quietism;
Wherever I walk no traces are left,
And my senses are not fettered by rules of conduct;
Everywhere those who have attained to the truth
All declare this to be of the highest order.[4]

The Buddha changed with noticing the morning star—and after a
week or so he arose from beneath the tree and began his lifetime of
pilgrimage and teaching. Similarly, Bashō changed with that *plop*.
The some 650 haiku that he wrote during his remaining eight years

point surely and boldly to the fact of essential nature. A before-and-after comparison may be illustrative of this change. For example, let us examine his much-admired "Crow on a Withered Branch."

> On a withered branch
> a crow is perched:
> an autumn evening.

Kare eda ni	Withered branch on
karasu no tomari keri	crow's perched:
aki no kure	autumn's evening.

The Japanese language uses postpositions rather than prepositions, so phrases like the first segment of this haiku read literally "Withered branch on" and become "On (a) withered branch." Unlike English, Japanese allows use of the past participle (or its equivalent) as a kind of noun, so in this haiku we have the "perchedness" of the crow, an effect that is emphasized by the postposition *keri,* which implies completion.

Bashō wrote this haiku six years before he composed "The Old Pond," and some scholars assign it to the milestone position that is more commonly given the later poem.[5] I think, however, that on looking into the heart of "Crow on a Withered Branch" we may see a certain immaturity. For one thing, I sense an implication that the crow somehow represents or evokes the autumn evening, a precious kind of device that I don't find in Bashō's later verse. But more fundamentally, this haiku is a presentation of quietism, the trap Hsiang-yen and all other great teachers of Zen warn us to avoid. *Sagara mudrā samādhi* is not adequate; remaining indefinitely under the Bodhi tree will not do; to muse without emerging is to be unfulfilled.

Ch'ang-sha made reference to this incompleteness in his criticism of a brother monk who was lost in quietism:

> You who sit on the top of a hundred-foot pole,
> although you have entered the Way, it is not yet genuine;
> take a step from the top of the pole
> and worlds of the ten directions will be your entire body.
>
> (BS-79)

The student of Zen who is stuck in the vast, serene condition of nondiscrimination must take another step to become mature.

Bashō's haiku about the crow would be an expression of the "first principle," essential nature, emptiness all by itself—separated from the world of sights and sounds, coming and going. This is the ageless pond without the frog. The poet then took that one step from the top of the pole into the dynamic world of reality, where frogs play freely in the pond and thoughts play freely in the mind.

> The old pond has no walls;
> a frog just jumps in;
> who is hearing that sound?

From *A Zen Wave:*
Bashō's Haiku and Zen

The Mountain Path

In scent of plum blossoms
pop! the sun appears—
the mountain path.

Ume ga ka ni	Plum scent in
notto hi no deru	pop sun's appearance
yama ji kana	mountain path

The Form

The single word *ume* refers to plum blossoms. In English, the word "plum" refers to the fruit, and we must use two words to speak of the blossoms. In Japanese and Chinese, it is quite the other way. One must use at least two words to speak of the fruit. *Ga* is used as a possessive postposition like *no,* but it indicates a much more tightly linked expression, like "plum-blossom scent." *Ni* (in) establishes the aroma of plum blossoms as the environment of the entire poem.

The second segment of the poem begins with *notto,* a phonaestheme, that is, a figure of speech which has some suggestion of meaning by its sound, as in "scurry," "tip-top," or "helter-skelter." It is often, though not always, onomatopoeic. It is poetical rather than discursive. *Notto!* presents the popping up of the sun.

Hi no deru (the sun's appearance), following immediately thereafter, is in apposition to *notto.* Apposition has common usage in such phrases as "my brother the musician," and it is the same here, though one might miss it at first: "Pop!" *is* the sun's appearance. This second segment modifies the third, so that one might discursively translate the two together: "The mountain path as the sun comes popping up." But the *kana* at the very end of the verse is a cutting word that serves to emphasize the poem's final noun. As in "The Old Pond," the momentum here builds steadily to the end: "mountain path" is the ultimate subject of the poem.

Comment

This poem is dated 1694, the year Bashō died. It shows him on pilgrimage, up before dawn, picking his way along a mountain path in the dim light. On the slopes of the mountain, groves of plum trees are in fragrant blossom, and this is a seasonal cue for the earliest spring—it is bitterly cold. Sometimes plum trees hold snow as well as blossoms.

The scent of plum blossoms in the cold of early spring has been a favorite theme of Japanese and Chinese poets from ancient times. It is also a model for emergence to realization from the difficult passage that necessarily precedes it—the valley of the shadow of death. In the *Eihei Kōroku*, Dōgen Zenji asks: "Without bitterest cold that penetrates to the very bone, how can plum blossoms send forth their fragrance all over the world?" Bashō is trudging along in the freezing, early morning, lost in the pervasive scent of plum blossoms, ready at last in the depths of his psyche for the sun—and *notto!*—it appears. *Pop!* he realizes it.

Notto! The Japanese language is full of phonaesthemes, mostly onomatopoeia, in keeping with the intimate (rather than abstract) nature of Japanese expression. In English, such words are largely confined to children's language, as in "bang-bang," "grr-woof," "clop-clop," and the like, but they are common in Japanese adult language, adding lightness and humor to daily discourse. The photographer will say *Niko-niko* to evoke a sparkle of teeth and a feeling of delight, and everyone will smile in response to the expression's intimate appeal.

The expression *notto* is rather rare, however. My Japanese-English dictionary cites only this poem, using R. H. Blyth's translation, "on a sudden, the rising sun!" as an example.[6] Professor Blyth translated the term "suddenly" in another rendering of the haiku. But "on a sudden" and "suddenly" are both descriptive terms. *Notto* and "pop" are the action itself—from the inside. Bashō's experience of nature was more than observation, more than commingling: the sun, as Bashō, went *notto!*

Professor Blyth's discursive translations do point up one very significant aspect of Bashō's expression: the immediacy implicit in *notto*. Yamada Rōshi often said that true realization will invariably be sudden—shallow, perhaps; slight, perhaps; but never gradual. With that *notto,* Bashō emerged from utter absorption in plum-blossom scent into the world of path, pack, and staff.

Zen practice follows the same pattern, through concentration, realization, and personalization (English terms of Yamada Rōshi). These are the three fundamental Ox-Herding Pictures, one might say, and none of us can afford to stop short of the third step.[7] We can see quite clearly Bashō's experience of all three in this haiku: first he is lost in fragrance only; then he pops up as the sun; and finally he pushes along in his personalization of the Way. "The Old Pond" built simply toward the experience of *oto,* from *samādhi* to realization, but nothing of their application is even implied in the poem itself. In this later haiku, however, the movement builds through a sudden experience to personal integration of that experience and the world of coming and going. Concentration permits realization, but to reach maturity, one must take another step.

When Hakuin was very old, he had a marvelous reputation all over Japan, and hundreds of students came to study with him. But he had just a little house for a temple. When I visited that temple in Hara in 1951, it still had no separate zendō, and in Hakuin's time, by no means could all of the monks crowd into the main hall, so some sat in the graveyard, and some found space under pine trees on the beach nearby. Hakuin, then in his middle eighties, tottered amongst these students, weeping because he no longer had the strength to urge them on with his stick. This was Hakuin's personalization of the Way.[8]

What about the Priest Chü-chih? He had practiced zazen very rigorously before he met T'ien-lung. T'ien-lung held up a finger and

Chü-chih abruptly saw it in the context of vast, empty reaches of countless universes. For the rest of his life, Chü-chih embodied the Tao of the Buddha and of all succeeding Buddhist teachers down to his own master. Whenever he was asked about the Buddha Dharma, he always held up one finger. True maturity. When he was about to die, he said to his assembled monks: "I received this one-finger Zen from T'ien-lung. I've used it all my life, but have never used it up." Having said this, he entered into his eternal rest. This was Chü-chih's personalization of the Way (GB-3).

Seeing one finger, hearing a frog jump into the water, experiencing the sunrise, washing one's face in the early morning—anything will serve as a medium of realization if the mind is serene and clear through earnest zazen.

Bashō embodied the Tao, hiking through the mountains and writing haiku. Chü-chih presented the same true nature, with one finger, as did Hakuin, lost in his tears. Standing up, sitting down—the Great Way is none other than that.

> Appearing completely,
> the sun and plum blossoms,
> Bashō, you, and I.

From *A Zen Wave:*
Bashō's Haiku and Zen

Quail

Now, as soon as eyes
of the hawk, too, darken,
quail chirp.

Taka no me mo   Hawk's eyes too
imaya kurenu to   now as-soon-as darken when
naku uzura   cry quail

The Form

Bashō used a number of postpositions and other particles to convey his meaning in this haiku. *No* means "of," while *mo* is "also" or "too." *Ya* carries its implication as a cutting word, but here it also means "as soon as." *Nu*, as the ending of the verb *kurenu*, indicates "definitely," or "completed," and *to* means "when." "Eyes of the hawk too are darkened" means that everything has become dark. When the hawk can no longer see, the quail begin chirping in the bushes.

Comment

This verse reflects Bashō's sensitivity to the interplay of life. The quail hides during the day in prudent respect for the hawk. The hawk preys upon quail, the quail upon insects, the insects upon smaller things. Yet each is pursuing its own life quite independently.

But this is only an overtone of the verse. More fundamentally, it points up the epoch of sunset, which, like sunrise, is a point of great change. It is not only the beauty of sun and clouds that affects us at such times. We and the world are transformed and become new. I am reminded of the first of T. S. Eliot's "Preludes":

> The winter evening settles down
> With smell of steaks in passageways.
> Six o'clock,
> The burnt-out ends of smokey days.
> And now a gusty shower wraps
> The grimy scraps
> Of withered leaves about your feet
> And newspapers from vacant lots;
> The showers beat
> On broken blinds and chimney-pots,
> And at the corner of the street
> A lonely cab-horse steams and stamps.
>
> And then the lighting of the lamps.[9]

When I taught this poem in high school, one of my students wrote a paper on the continuation of day into night that is implied in the line "And then the lighting of the lamps." The dreariness of the day in the London slum becomes the dreariness of evening. Yet there is still some magic remaining. Even today, the small child gets a thrill from turning on the electric light at evening. The day is past; the night begins. The light of the sun becomes that of the lamp. My boyhood visits to relatives who had no electricity were enhanced at evening when the kerosene lamps and candles were lit.

Sitting in the dōjō and allowing it gradually to become dark before turning on the lights is an important device in our practice. Leaders in Rinzai Zen monasteries make the most of it. At sunset, monks gather in the zendō while one of their brothers strikes the great temple bell to punctuate his reading of the *Kannon Gyō (Avalokiteshvara Sūtra)*. Then as it gradually gets darker, they sit silently in zazen, and when the head monk can no longer discern the lines in the palm of his hand, he signals for *kinhin*, formal walking in line around the dōjō, which begins the evening program.

As the sun changes to the lamp, zazen changes to *kinhin*, the eyes of the hawk change to the chirping of the quail. Step by minute step, the universe changes. Now light, now dark, now hawk, now quail, now sea, now land. It is at the edge of transition that we find experience.

On Guam there is a fish that climbs trees—well, little bushes, anyway. When you walk near them, the fish scatter hurriedly and plunge back into their original element. These first amphibia, far older than the earliest human, yet still at the very point of transition from the sea, evoke the experience of immediacy at the hinge of evolution.

What is the substance of that very point? What is the substance of turning on the lamp? What is the substance of the first chirp of the quail? What is the substance of the fish crawling up the branch? In minutely subtle ways, there is transformation through time, space, and agent. With each kōan, your practice changes, and as the penetrating vitality of the hawk becomes the contented chirping of quail, the substance of no-quality is felt anew.

Here is another of Bashō's haiku about change at evening:

> The temple bell fades
> and the scent of cherry blossoms
> rise in the evening

Kane kiete	Bell fades
hana ka wa tsuku	flower scent strikes
yūbe kana	evening!

The movement of this poem is carried by the verb *tsuku,* which means "strike" or "ring." The cherry blossoms ring their scent. *Kane* is "bell," but always "temple bell" when used alone. *Kane* and *tsuku* have (in this instance) the same phonetic element in their ideographs, providing an intimate link between hearing and scenting. Harold G. Henderson translates:

> As the bell tone fades,
> blossom scents take up the ringing—
> evening shade.[10]

I think this fails as an English verse, but it is a valiant attempt to render Bashō's tightly laced intention.

It is sunset time, and as the sound of the temple bell fades with the light, cherry blossoms are sensed, and it is evening. Wu-men says you must hear with your eye (GB-16). Bashō is saying you must hear with your nose. But that is a bit off the main point of this poem. The sound of the bell rises in the scent of the cherry blossoms in the mind of Bashō in his haiku in English in my words in your mind in your vows in your bows in your laughter with your friends.

Step by step you are in tune with karma, the law of the universe. When you are truly stuck on Mu, then you pass Mu. When you pass Mu, then you pass the source of Mu. When you pass the source of Mu, then you stop the sound of that distant temple bell. So it goes. So it remains.

> Drink earth and sunshine
> deep tonight;
> a toast to new life past.

From *A Zen Wave:
Bashō's Haiku and Zen*

The Shepherd's Purse

When I look carefully—
nazuna is blooming
beneath the hedge.

Yoku mireba	Carefully looking when—
nazuna hana saku	*nazuna* flower blooms
kakine kana	hedge!

The Form

This is a unified haiku that builds toward the final cutting word, *kana.* The entire poem is an exclamation, but an exclamation mark in English would be too heavy. The *ba* ending of *mireba* indicates "if" or "when."

Comment

A rather ordinary-seeming verse, but one that is widely appreciated in Japan. The *nazuna,* a small plant called "Shepherd's Purse" in English, bears tiny white flowers with four petals. Even Bashō might be tempted to pass it by, but he does not. He is attracted by flecks of white beneath the hedge and pauses to look closely. There are nazuna flowers, blooming with full spirit. Seeing the nazuna flowers evokes an "Ah!" of appreciation for the living things.

In his essay "The Morning Glory," D. T. Suzuki comments on this verse. "Once off human standards which are valid only on the plane of relativity, nazuna weeds match well with the peonies and roses, the dahlias and chrysanthemums."[11] Bashō of course did not reason like this; he was a poet, and he intuited all this and simply stated: "When closely seen it is the nazuna plant blooming."

Professor Suzuki then takes up the social implications of our inability to notice the nazuna:

> We are always ready to destroy anything, including ourselves. We never hesitate to slaughter one another and give this reason: there is one ideology that is absolutely true, and anything and anybody, any group or any individual who opposes this particular ideology deserves total annihilation. We are blatantly given up to the demonstration of self-conceit, self-delusion, and unashamed arrogance. We do not seem nowadays to cherish any such feelings as inspired Bashō to notice the flowering nazuna plant. . . . We trample [such flowers] underfoot and feel no compunction whatever. Is religion no longer needed by modern man?

Quite an outburst from our kindly Sensei. One may feel that it is hardly upheld by the slight nature of the haiku—a quaint old Japanese poet gazing upon a weed three hundred years ago. Can we balance the peace movement, say, on such a delicate base? And how can Professor Suzuki justify bringing religion to the discussion?

I think it is possible to show how Bashō is teaching us religion with his nazuna haiku, and how the denial of the nazuna is "self-conceit, self-delusion, and unashamed arrogance." The first step in Bashō's teaching is to remove us from the "human standards which are valid only on the plane of relativity." These standards place peonies, roses, dahlias, and chrysanthemums on the level of beautiful flowers, and the nazuna on the level of weeds. When you're truly removed from that point of view, then unsalted food is unsalted, and salty food is salty—that's all. Then Koreans are Koreans; Japanese are Japanese—that's all. Neither can be ennobled; neither can be denigrated. Each can be enjoyed: the rose in the White House garden, the nazuna under the hedge. Projecting relative standards upon the nazuna is projecting conceit and arrogance. Only a weed! If we permit such a relative base of judgment to remain intact for the nazuna, then that same base will provide affection for Koreans and hatred for Japanese, or the reverse. We will be unable to see things, animals, and people as they are.

To continue on with Professor Suzuki:

> When beauty is expressed in terms of Buddhism, it is a form of self-enjoyment of the suchness of things. Flowers are flowers, mountains are mountains, I sit here, you stand there, and the world goes from eternity to eternity; this is the suchness of things. A state of self-awareness here constitutes enlightenment, and a state of self-enjoyment here constitutes beauty.

Upon seeing the flower, Bashō realized *this! This!* On seeing the flower, he enjoyed it. And on seeing the flower, he wrote the haiku. Professor Suzuki puts these three elements into philosophical categories as follows:

> Enlightenment is the noetic aspect of prajñā-intuition, beauty is its affective aspect, and the great compassionate heart is its conative aspect. In this way we can probably understand what is meant by the doctrine of suchness.

This remarkable passage sums up the unity of realization, aesthetic experience, and love. Noetic pertains to the mind, affective to emotion, and conative to desire or will. "Suchness" is such a dry word, and prajñā is only a sound from a dead language, but contained in them is this living trinity of experience: just that nazuna flower, just that beautiful nazuna flower, let me present you that nazuna flower. This is the trinity of seeing, appreciating, and sharing. True seeing is appreciating; true appreciation is motivating. Thus the Buddha saw the morning star, enjoyed the morning star, and walked the length and breadth of India teaching his experience. These are the Three Bodies of the Buddha, the *Dharmakāya, the Sambhogakāya,* and the *Nirmānakāya*—the Body of Enlightenment, the Body of Bliss, and the Body of Manifestation.

Professor Suzuki's essay "The Morning Glory" is constructed around a haiku by Fukuda Chiyo-Ni, one of Japan's greatest poets:

> The well bucket
> taken by the morning glory;
> I beg for water.

Asagao ni	Morning glory by
tsurube torarete	well bucket taken
morai mizu	beg water

The poet came out for water in the early morning and found the morning glory vine twined about the well bucket, so she was moved to beg water from the neighbors rather than to disturb the vine.

Some critics find this poem too precious, but Professor Suzuki points out that one of Chiyo-Ni's variants for the version usually cited uses *ya* rather than *ni* at the end of the first segment. The *ya* serves to cut the verse at that point, and to express the "Ah!" experience of the poet, lost in just that morning glory. So Professor Suzuki translates the haiku:

> Oh, morning glory!
> The bucket taken captive,
> Water begged for.

And he comments: "At the time, the poetess was not conscious of herself or of the morning glory standing against her. Her mind was filled with the flower, the whole world turned into the flower, she was the flower itself. When she regained her consciousness, the only words she could utter were, 'Oh, morning glory,' in which all that she experienced found its vent." This is the meaning of Sōen Rōshi's words, "Enjoy your Mu." Emerging from this enjoyment is the great compassionate heart, to beg for water rather than to disturb the vine. Emerging from this enjoyment we greet one another; we take care of each other's children; we resist inhumanity and injustice. Emerging from his appreciation of the nazuna haiku, Professor Suzuki berates the war psychology of nations and the self-centered arrogance of individuals.

I find that students who seek out the zendō as a sanctuary from social pressures may tend to object to the emphasis on compassion in Zen practice. I believe this reveals the self-centered nature of their original motive for doing zazen. Unless this self-concern is turned about, there can be no maturity.

Compassion takes practice, like any other kind of fulfillment. I am often told that compassion should flow naturally. This is true. Also, Mozart should flow naturally from your fingers when you sit at the piano. It is important and essential to understand that Zen is not simply a matter of spontaneity. It is also practice. By practicing zazen, you do zazen. By sitting with a half-smile, you practice enjoyment. By smiling at your friends, you practice the great compassionate heart. The act is the practice. The practice is the act. Sitting when you do not feel like it—that is zazen, that is the rare *udumbara* flower of Buddha-hood. Smiling at your friends when you do not feel like it—that is compassion, annihilating greed, hatred, and folly, and giving life to the healing spirit of Kanzeon.

I have been told that practice of compassion is dishonest when one does not feel compassionate. This argument makes my blood boil. To what are you being honest? Nothing but a whim! You do not belong here.

If you say this is all didactic, I have no objection. The haiku master and the Zen master are teachers. Bashō's purpose was not merely self-expression. With his great compassionate heart, he was saying, "Go thou and do likewise." He even wrote some haiku that were didactic in content. One such verse which fits our purposes neatly in this chapter is unfortunately only ascribed to Bashō.

> For one who says,
> "I am tired my children,"
> there are no flowers.

ko ni aku to	"Children of tire"
mosu hito ni wa	says person for
hana mo nashi	flowers even none

This verse is titled "Shown to a Student," marking it as an occasional verse not originally composed for general education. *Hana* refers to cherry blossoms, and appreciation for the ephemeral beauty of cherry flowers marks a capacity to appreciate the best of human culture.

Bashō, or whoever wrote this verse, is saying that your realization, enjoyment, and love cannot be separated. When love is absent, cherry flowers go unappreciated, and the suchness of nazuna is unknown. Apparently the inspiration for this haiku is a poem in the *Manyōshū* that warns there would be no memorial service for a mother who had a reluctant spirit in caring for her children.[12] The *re*-creation of this idea by the haiku poet is deeper and more immediate than the original. There are no nazuna for such a parent. There is no realization of the Dharmakāya.

Ta-lung Chih-hung presents the final verse for us this time. A monk said to him: "The body of color perishes. What is the eternal Dharma body (Dharmakāya)?" Ta-lung said:

> The mountain flowers bloom like brocade;
> The river between the hills is blue as indigo.
> (BCR-82)

From *A Zen Wave:*
Bashō's Haiku and Zen

The Ten Verse Kannon Sūtra for Timeless Life

Kanzeon	Kanzeon!
namu butsu	I venerate the Buddha,
yo butsu u in	with the Buddha I have my source,
yo butsu u en	with the Buddha I have affinity—
buppō sō en	affinity with Buddha, Dharma, Sangha,
jō raku ga jō	constancy, ease, assurance, purity.
chō nen kanzeon	Mornings my thought is Kanzeon,
bo nen kanzeon	evenings my thought is Kanzeon,
nen-nen jū shin ki	thought-after-thought arises in mind,
nen nen fu ri shin	thought after thought is not separate from mind

This is the sūtra *Enmei Jikku Kannon Gyō*. In the Diamond Sangha we recite it in Sino-Japanese, though we tried out an English translation in the early days of the Maui Zendō. That experiment lasted two days as I recall, and was firmly put down.

Yamada Rōshi once remarked that the *Enmei Jikku Kannon Gyō* is really a kind of *dhāranī*. I think he was right, offering a clue, perhaps, to the reason my English translation didn't work. Far Eastern *dhāranī* are not translations, but transliterations of Sanskrit. Original texts are lost for the most part. Their rhythmic forms have been recited for 1,500 years, and we sense how they are empowered with the devotions of thousands of monks, nuns, and laypeople over the centuries.

The *Enmei Jikku Kannon Gyō* was, however, composed in Chinese originally, not in Sanskrit. It has the rhythm and the empowerment of a *dhāranī*, but it also has meaning that is open to explication.

To begin at the beginning: The term *enmei* (sometimes *emmei* with the "n" elided to "m") is usually interpreted to mean "prolonging" life. *Jikku* (or *jukku*) means "ten verses" or "ten lines." *Gyō* (elided from *kyō*) is "sūtra."

Zen teachers including Hakuin Ekaku are fond of recounting folk stories about the miraculous effects of the Sūtra as a lifesaver. It is important, however, to see into other implications of *enmei* and such related terms as *kotobuki* ("long life") and *furui* ("ancient"). The ultimately ancient is the timeless, a reference to the essential nature which is not born and does not die. It is timeless—not eternal and not ephemeral. The morning star presented the timeless to the Buddha Shākyamuni, and distant peach blossoms presented the timeless to Ling-yün.[13] The *Enmei Jikku Kannon Gyō* extends life for the believer, and it brings the Buddha's own experience of timelessness in this moment to the rest of us.

The first line evokes Kanzeon (Kuan-shih-yin), the full name of Kannon, "The One Who Perceives the Sounds of the World." Kanzeon evolved from the male figure Avalokiteshvara in the earlier Indian Buddhist pantheon, and is worshipped as the "Goddess of Mercy" in Far Eastern folk religion.

As the Goddess of Mercy, Kanzeon saves people from drowning, injury, injustice, evil spirits, and bandits. She releases prisoners whether they are innocent or guilty, and gives pregnant women their choice of a male or a female child. If you are pushed off the top of Mt. Sumeru and call out Kanzeon's name, you will be suspended in the air like the sun—or so we are assured by the *Lotus Sūtra*.[14]

I honor this deep faith. It is a comforting bulwark that sustains countless people who might otherwise be miserable and feel hopeless. You will even find Kanzeon worshipers among Zen students. But Harada Dai'un Rōshi would ask, "How old is Kanzeon?" If the student replied, "Ageless," the Rōshi would ring his little bell. "Back to your cushions for more work!" Kanzeon may be a goddess in the sky who manipulates karma for the true believer, but *she* can also be *he*—looking out through very ordinary eyes, hearing with very ordinary ears, using very ordinary tools like a wok or a word processor.

Indeed, sometimes Kanzeon is represented holding a thousand tools in a thousand hands. Sometimes she stands with a compassionate expression, holding a jar of ambrosia and a lotus. Sometimes she is just sitting there, altogether comfortable in her Mudrā of Royal Ease. Her presence alone serves as a teaching. With many mudrās, she teaches in many ways—for example: "Time for supper!"

When Mother or Father calls from the kitchen, "Time for supper!" the children cry out, "Time for supper!" This echo is not just Kanzeon's announcement bouncing about, but the children's confirmation that they have internalized the message and have made it their own.

Wu-men Hui-k'ai, the Lin-chi master who later compiled the *Wu-men kuan,* heard the sound of the drum announcing the noon meal, and found himself to be on the Peak of Wonder, dancing at the center of paradise. He then announced himself in turn with a great career of teaching that set generations of subsequent teachers dancing. This is the function of Kanzeon.

"Ripeness is all," so of course the function of Kanzeon is also to study and practice—to prepare for the drum or the morning star. The drum and the morning star too had to prepare for their announcements. This is not a pathetic fallacy. The timpanist plays upon a living being. The stars are bursting with their messages. Turn to a child for the star's announcement.

Enlightening, being enlightened, calling and responding, the birds and stars as Kanzeon save us, as they as themselves save us, and as Kanzeon the figure "up there in the sky" saves us. At the same time, it is important not to cling to archetypes, as meaningful as they may be. Individuation on the Buddha Way is the triumph of selfless practice—and the unspoken acknowledged triumph of forgetting triumph, and forgetting that you have forgotten. It is the endless process of realizing Yün-men's caution that it is better to have nothing than to have something good (BCR 86). Stopping at any one point is Kanzeon denying herself her process of fulfilling.

Kanzeon is not the one who perceives the sounds of the world, as the *Diamond Sūtra* might say if it addressed the matter—therefore we call her "Kanzeon." Therefore we begin the *Enmei Jikku Kannon Gyō* by calling her name: "Kanzeon!"

This is an evocation, it seems to me, like old Western poets calling upon their muse to inspire their lyrics. We call upon Kanzeon to inspire our Sūtra and our lives. We call upon ourselves as Kanzeon. We call upon ourselves to inspire Kanzeon.

With this evocation, the Sūtra sets forth the foundation of Kanzeon's being: *Namu butsu. Namu* is transliterated from the Sanskrit *namah,* and means literally "to submit to," "to make obeisance to." With our understanding of obeisance we can translate it, "I cast everything away in the presence of the Buddha." As Dōgen Zenji says in the *Kyōjūkaimon,* the ocean of essential nature is the most important matter. "It is beyond explanation. We can only accept it with respect and gratitude."[15]

Butsu is Buddha—"the Enlightened One," Shākyamuni, and each of his wise and compassionate successors—a name empowered even more than the Sūtra itself with the devotions of countless disciples. The Buddha is also the wisdom and compassion that comes forth as you and me. It is the name we give to enlightenment and its potential, and to the mystery that comes forth as beings and their universe.

Acceptance is Kanzeon, hearing the sounds of the world. She perceives the distress and pain everywhere, and is realized by the announcements of geckos and children. The compassionate action of Kanzeon arises from the empty place of grateful receiving. With *namu butsu* I venerate the great power for the Way which is generated by this profound act of opening myself: "I bow in the presence of the Buddha."

Yo butsu u in / yo butsu u en. These two lines present my relationship with the Buddha, and yours—our relationship with this great power for the Way. An incomplete translation of the two lines would be, "With the Buddha we have *in*; / with the Buddha we have *en.*" *In* and *en* are Classical Buddhist terms that mean "direct or inner cause" and "indirect or environmental cause."

Every action occurs in the harmony of *in* and *en,* and the two terms are often combined to reflect this unity as *innen.* The tree grows from its seed—the direct cause, and with the influences of earth, water, air, and sun—the indirect causes.

Like Kanzeon, as Kanzeon—you and I have *in*, direct cause, with the Buddha. We form the cause of Buddha. "This very body is the Buddha."[16] This transitory, imperfect frame is the Tathāgata, the Buddha who comes forth *thus*, no less than Shākyamuni himself.

How to translate *in* is the question. I choose "source," the best I can do, but it is a tautological rendering. It is like saying the body is the source of the body. The Buddha is the source of the Buddha. But sometimes tautology can be instructive as an agent of emphasis, to bring the matter home.

You and I also have *en*, indirect cause, with the Buddha. *En* is a very important word in the Japanese language. *Fushigi na en*, "mysterious affinity," is an intimate expression frequently used to confirm a relationship between teacher and student, or between friends or lovers. "Affinity" is a word we can use to describe how molecules come together to form a cell—how cells come together to form the organs of a fetus. The dynamics of the plenum are the dance of affinity and separation. It is affinity with the Buddha that brings the affinity in the Sangha. Sangha affinity realizes the Buddha.

Buppō sō en—affinity with Buddha, Dharma, Sangha—the Three Treasures. Affinity with the Buddha is repeated here; it cannot be repeated too often. But be careful. The old teachers used the name to refer to the historical Buddha, of course, but also to "this very mind," "this very body," "the absolutely concrete," and so on, including the ambiguous scattershot. Dōgen says in the *Gyōbutsu-yuigi*, "Unless you are the active Buddha, you will never be free from the bonds of Buddha."

"Dharma" has many meanings, more than forty I am told, but for our purposes there are two, "the teaching" and "the practice." The teaching has three main elements:

1. Beings and the universe itself have no identifiable substance, either in form or in essence.
2. Each being affects all other beings, each act influences all other actions, in the dynamic web of the universe.
3. All beings exist uniquely and as elements of each other, diversely and harmoniously.

The practice too has three main elements:

1. Following the guidance of a good teacher and the writings and examples of good teachers of the past.
2. Following the guidance of friends, family members, and all beings.
3. Following the guidance of personal inspiration.

The teaching without sound practice is abstract and ultimately meaningless. Practice that is not based on sound teaching can be self-centered and capricious. Bracing the union of teaching and practice is the clear sense of responsibility which we inherit directly from the Buddha, and bracing this sense of responsibility is *bodhichitta,* the imperative for realization and compassion. Without this organic chain of inner directives, the Dharma is neglected, and society and its habitat slide into corruption.

Finally, we have affinity with the Sangha. "Sangha" comes from the Sanskrit root meaning "aggregate," and has been used traditionally to refer to the Buddhist priesthood. In the Mahāyāna, however, it refers to all beings and their symbiosis—their interbeing. In the Sūtra, "Sangha" is the "Buddha Sangha," the kinship of students who practice together, the only mode of realizing the Buddha Way. There are Buddhist hermits, of course, but these are men and women who choose solitude after long years of practicing with sisters and brothers, and essentially are still practicing with them and with all beings. They are firmly grounded in their realization of intimacy and containment. Note also that Sangha is the harmony of the Buddha and the Dharma, the practice and realization of evanescence, intimacy and diversity in my life and yours, and in our lives together.

We have our source in, and our affinity with, the Buddha; we find affinity with the Three Treasures of Buddha, Dharma, and Sangha; and—like Kanzeon, as Kanzeon—with this affinity we have *jō raku ga jō,* "constancy, ease, assurance, purity." These are the four attributes of nirvana—freedom from time, distress, bondage, and delusion.

Nirvana is freedom, but not anything antinomian. Freedom is play. By "play," I mean enjoyment, of course, but also scope for movement—flexibility. You and I are not irrevocably linked to a re-lentless sequence of events, and therefore we can find timelessness in the moment. We do not feel doomed, and therefore "Every day is a good day" (BCR-6). We must feed, clothe, shelter, and medicate ourselves, but we can also devote ourselves selflessly to family, community, and the world. We can enjoy the world without exploiting it, and we need not isolate ourselves.

Jō, the first of the four attributes of nirvana, is a translation of a Sanskrit term meaning "constant" or "eternal," but it also means "normal" or "ordinary." The timeless is the ordinary. The changeless is the everyday.

> Chao-chou asked Nan-ch'üan: "What is the Tao?"
> Nan-ch'üan said, "Ordinary mind is the Tao."
> (GB-19)

After further conversation, Nan-ch'üan goes on to say, "If you have truly realized the Tao beyond doubt, you will find it is as vast and boundless as outer space." Just like the sky! How ordinary! How everyday!

Vast as outer space—the Tao is not created and not extinguished. It is the unmoving void, charged with inconceivably dynamic potential, bursting through with Chao-chou's realization, or standing up when guests enter the room, making greetings in the most cordial and hospitable manner. *Jō* is Kanzeon, like smoke that is neither empty nor substantial—timeless essential nature passing around the cookies and juice.

Raku, the second attribute, is comfort or ease, as in Kanzeon's Mudrā of Royal Ease.[17] I am always quoting Nakagawa Sōen Rōshi: "Enjoy your Mu." This seems difficult when legs hurt and anxiety comes up, but the Rōshi is reminding us that practice is enlightenment—the nature of training is the nature of realization. At the beginning, zazen is commonly stressful, but it mellows into something quite comfortable before realization appears. Practice before and after that experience is Kanzeon herself, comfortably sitting there, with mind and body at rest. This is not, of course, to encourage indulgence. Have a look at Hakuin's portrait of Kanzeon sitting comfortably in zazen. She is not neglectful.

I translate *ga,* the third attribute, as "assurance," but literally the ideograph means "self." As the Dalai Lama is always saying, assurance and equanimity are the same thing. Equanimity is the quality of mind that comes with realizing to the very bottom that everything including the self is empty, and that this emptiness is truly all right.

In terms of karma and science, selves are made up of the Five Skandhas, perceptions and things perceived, which in turn arise from genes and early influences that are ultimately untraceable. Science leads once again to a dead end, perhaps leaving one ready for understanding that the skandhas are themselves empty, and the genes and environmental influences are reducible to formless, ultimately unidentifiable tendencies.

Nonetheless, here I am! Here is the Buddha! Here are the many beings! The equitable self is the presentation of the equitable universe, potent with confidence as the plenum itself is confident.

We are creatures of the great forest of the cosmos. We are born, grow through childhood and youth into maturity, and pass through old age and death, leaving our remains to compost the vitality that continues to pulse and burgeon. My role and yours is to produce the richest compost we can, not only for the future, but as an ongoing product of the many small deaths of our lives. Small deaths, the Great Death of realization, and physical death—these are all a matter of relinquishment, of forgetting the self. It is the self forgotten that is equitable, assured, realized.

> Tao-hsin made his bows before Seng-ts'an and said, "I beg the compassion of Your Reverence. Please teach me the Dharma Way of emancipation."
> Seng-ts'an said, "Who is binding you?"
> Tao-hsin said, "No one is binding me."
> Seng-ts'an said, "Then why should you search for emancipation?"
> Hearing this, Tao-hsin had great realization.
>
> (TL-31)

The delusion that he was bound was the bondage of Tao-hsin. Freedom from that bondage was Tao-hsin realized. It sounds simple, but better men and women than any of us have sweat blood to make this great transition from the self-center to the multi-center, from the *me* world to the compassionate world of Kanzeon.

Jō, the final attribute of nirvana, is different from *jō,* the first word. There are scores of words pronounced *jō* in Japanese, all of them with different graphs. This *jō* means "purity," including the ordinary sense of "clean."

Some people are preoccupied with purity, and this is their defilement. In the old days of the New Age, I met many of them, dying of fruitarianism, breaking out in boils they regarded as drains for their impurities. Thank heaven we are past that phase! Hui-kʻo, Bodhidharmaʼs successor, helped Seng-tsʻan through his preoccupation with purity:

> Seng-tsʻan said, "Your disciple is suffering from a fatal illness
> [probably leprosy]. I beg Your Reverence to release me from my
> sins."
> Hui-kʻo said, "Bring me your sins and I will release them for
> you."
> Seng-tsʻan said, "I cannot find my sins, in spite of all my efforts."
> Hui-kʻo said, "I have already released your sins for you. From now
> on, live by the Buddha, Dharma, and Sangha."
>
> (TL-30)

With this Seng-tsʻan found liberation, perhaps not from his physical symptoms but from his tenacious preoccupations, and in turn he was able to help Tao-hsin to find freedom from his—in the remarkably similar exchange quoted earlier. In East Asia, leprosy was, and still is, widely believed to be the result of bad karma, and Seng-tsʻan shared this impure idea. Actually, however, karma is not some kind of judge out there waiting to condemn us. When Seng-tsʻan looked closely, he couldnʼt find his bad karma. Hui-kʻo confirmed his freedom from such delusions, and cautioned him about practicing his realization in daily life by maintaining the Buddha Way.

All this is not to deny the effects of oneʼs conduct. If Seng-tsʻan had lived in poverty in a district where leprosy was prevalent, then he was probably more vulnerable to the disease than other people might have been. It would, however, be a crude oversimplification to suppose that he contracted the disease because, say, he threw a stone at a leper when he was a little boy in an earlier incarnation.

Of course, an act of throwing a stone at a leper becomes part of the subtly complex network of affinities relating to leprosy that pervade the universe. But to draw a direct causal connection from throwing the stone to catching the disease is like other deterministic ideas about karma—for example, that a little white thing escapes from the body at death and goes cruising around looking for a couple making love to find its rebirth. Such notions reduce to crude materialism the untraceable, infinitely dynamic streams that come together to form the infant, and so we say they are superstitious. At the same time, Seng-ts'an, you, and I are responsible for our cruel conduct. When people get hurt, our atonement will not mend bones, but it can transmute anger, revenge, and self-condemnation. At the beginning of our sūtra service we recite:

> All the evil karma, ever created by me since of old,
> on account of our beginningless greed, hatred and ignorance
> born of our conduct, speech, and thought
> I now confess, openly and fully.

Chō nen kanzeon / bo nen kanzeon. Chō is morning and *bo* is evening. "Mornings my thought is Kanzeon, evenings my thought is Kanzeon." (English is such a discursive language! See how succinctly the lines read in Sino-Japanese: "Morning thought Kanzeon, evening thought Kanzeon.") Of course, "thought" doesn't mean "musing upon." If the line is rendered "Mornings I think of Kanzeon," that would place Kanzeon back on the altar. It is rather, "Mornings my thought is no other than Kanzeon herself or himself."

The ideograph for *nen*, "thought," is made up of two parts: the top is "present" or "now"; the bottom part is "mind." Together they are the vast mind coming forth in this moment, framed by this particular personality and situation.

The "vast mind" is a discovery of the Mahāyāna, and does not appear in Classical Buddhism, where "mind," however subtle and powerful, is the human mind and nothing more.[18] The Mahāyāna vision is a paradigm shift, a discernment of mind as void of attributes or fixed nature, yet the nature of everything, "whether sentient beings or as Buddhas, as rivers and mountains of the world"[19]—and, of course as *nen*, as thoughts.

Coming forth, the *nen* is a pulse or a frame, and the topic is supplied by past circumstances, often immediately past. Here the Sūtra says that every moment, morning and night, my thought is itself the Bodhisattva enlightened, enlightening the self, and enlightening all beings.

Like our gāthās and our vows, the *Enmei Jikku Kannon Gyō* sets forth a light for our path. My best person is Kanzeon each moment of perceiving a bulbul, of listening to complaints about my failings, of speaking out against injustice and cruelty, of breathing Mu on my cushions.

Nen-nen jū shin ki / nen nen fu ri shin. "Thought-after-thought arise in mind; thought after thought are not separate from mind." This final couplet sets forth the human talent of thinking, and its function as an expression of mind.

On translating the first of these lines, I render *nen-nen* with hyphens—"thought-after-thought"—to reflect the use of a repeat or ditto mark for the second *nen* in the original. "Thought-repeat-repeat-repeat-. . ." would be the implication. In the second of these lines, the graph for *nen* is simply given again. "Thought, then thought, then thought, then thought . . ." would be the implication. Interestingly, the Sōtō sūtra books show this distinction, but the Rinzai sūtra books do not. I choose the Sōtō version because it clarifies the two very different kinds of thought sequence which arise in the human mind.

The first line sets forth the audiotape of chatter that orbits the self—*me* this and *me* that. It charges around in the head during zazen, exhausting the student physically, and can induce the most profound despair. Notice how debilitated mentally ill people become. A huge amount of their energy is taken up with the sole self. Their eyes are on the ground, but they don't see the grass. Yet even the most sane of us can be taken up with stories, memories, fantasies, conjecturing, and fears while sitting on our cushions, while the thrush sings on to deaf ears.

Once I envisioned this phenomenon of thought-after-thought as I sat in zazen. I found myself facing a large, very soft, organic-looking mass that was pulsing with life. There was a little aperture in this mass like a mouth or a vagina, and tiny beings were escaping from the aperture one after another in very rapid succession. I knew these tiny beings were my thoughts, and somehow this perception helped me to deepen my practice, but I can now link it to the wisdom of my betters, Yen-t'ou, for one:

> Luo-shan asked Yen-t'ou, "What about when arising and vanishing continue without ceasing?"
> Yen-t'ou shouted, "Whose arising and vanishing?"
>
> (BS-43)

When I worked on this case with Yamada Rōshi, he translated Luo-shan's question, "What about when thoughts rise and fall without ceasing?" Luo-shan was concerned about the incessant chatter in his head. But can you own the thoughts as they appear—one thought, then the next one—as they arise in the mind? Luo-shan! Fred! Linda! This was the turning point for Luo-shan; the great, intimate realization of owning suddenly sprang up.

The second line, "Thought after thought is not separate from mind," is not expressive of repetition, but rather of process. A new thought follows the old thought and builds upon it. Paul Shepard writes, "There is a difference between thinking about something, and the use of that something as a means of further thought."[20] That further thought can be realization. Thoreau wrote in *A Week on the Concord and Merrimack Rivers*:

> There are perturbations in our orbits produced by the influence of outlying spheres, and no astronomer has ever yet calculated the elements of that undiscovered world which produces them. I perceive in the common train of my thoughts a natural and uninterrupted sequence, each implying the next, or, if an interruption occurs it is occasioned by a new object being presented to my senses. But a steep, and sudden, and by these means unaccountable transition, is that from a comparatively narrow and partial, what is called common sense view of things, to an infinitely expanded and liberating one.[21]

Here is Yün-men offering his disciple Tung-shan Shou-ch'u a steep and unaccountable transition from his usual, uninterrupted sequence:

Tung-shan came to see Yün-men. Yün-men asked him, "Where were you most recently?"

Tung-shan said, "At Ch'a-tu."

Yün-men said, "Where were you during the summer?"

Tung-shan said, "At Pao-tzu Monastery in Hu-nan."

Yün-men said, "When did you leave there?"

Tung-shan said, "August 25th."

Yün-men said, "I spare you sixty blows."

Next day, Tung-shan came again and said, "Yesterday you said you spared me sixty blows. I don't know where I was at fault."

Yün-men said, "You rice bag! Do you go about in such a way, now west of the river, now south of the lake!"

With this, Tung-shan had great realization.

(GB-15)

The natural sequence of responses to Yün-men's everyday kind of questions and Tung-shan's matter-of-fact kind of responses continued until Yün-men presented a steep and sudden interruption. Nothing happened. Wu-men comments:

All night, in the ocean of yes-and-no, Tung-shan struggled to the ultimate. As soon as dawn broke, he went again to Yün-men, who explained everything in detail. Even though Tung-shan had realization, he was not yet brilliant.

Without Yün-men's accord with his student and his exquisite sense of timing, Tung-shan would have been left in the dark. This is the beauty of the Zen way. One cannot depend on the chance of a fortuitous realization. A good Zen teacher can set the scene for the accident of sudden understanding, and then help the student to polish that understanding to true brilliance.

This final couplet of the Sūtra can be traced to *The Awakening of Faith in the Mahāyāna,* a succinct summation of doctrine that probably originated in China in the sixth century. In Yoshito S. Haketa's translation we read:

Though it is said that there is [an inception of] the rising of [deluded] thoughts in the mind, there is no inception as such that can be known [as being independent of Mind].[22]

The interpolations are those of the translator, and in the setting of the text, I would judge them to be accurate. The notion of a universal yet empty mind arose with the Mahāyāna. By the sixth century it could be formulated quite clearly in *The Awakening of Faith.* Thoughts were earlier considered to be irrevocably delusive, but now they could be seen as the mind unfolding. Still later this formulation was internalized by Zen Buddhist monks. Bassui addressed his assembly and said:

> This mind is originally pure. It was not born with this body, and it does not die with its extinction. What's more, it cannot be distinguished as male or female, or shaped as good or bad. It is beyond comparison, so we call it Buddha-nature. Moreover, like waves from the ocean, the many thoughts arise out of this original nature.[23]

If thoughts arise like waves in the ocean, they also follow the same path as light, in particles of waves—in waves of particles. Thoughts are the photons of the mind. They rise and fall endlessly, but if we focus only upon the flow, the continuum becomes simply a timeline, ending finally for us when interventions in the hospital fail. Too bad.

In the experience set forth by this Sūtra, each thought, ever so brief, is Kanzeon herself, turning the Dharma Wheel. I am reminded of the image of Kuya Shōnin at Rokuharamitsuji in Kyoto. Kuya was an early Pure Land teacher who went about the country calling out the mantrā of his faith, *Namu Amida Butsu,* "Veneration to Amitābha Buddha." The sculptor renders him as a pilgrim walking slightly bent over, with a row of little Amitābha Buddhas coming out of his mouth on a wire, representing a thread, which, after all, is the root meaning of "sūtra."[24]

All those little Buddhas coming from Kuya's mouth look exactly the same, but the many Kanzeon thoughts that emerge as the mind are different. Some praise, some are critical; some are jolly, some are sad. Some say, "Let me help you." Some say, "You must do it yourself." Moreover, as William James makes clear, each thought qualifies one's previous thought, and also qualifies one's environment and personality and worldview as well as the environment as it is changing with the thoughts expressed by others.[25]

In my vision of thoughts appearing from a little aperture, I could identify the large, living mass as my own mind. I have had other visions I could identify as my mind, particularly as a structure of diaphanous cells greatly enlarged and distantly removed like very high clouds, as though I were viewing them from the inside, as the transparent ceiling of the sky. These visions help to verify the message of the Sūtra—the mind is the source of thoughts, and the brain of the individual human being is not the only reference. George Meredith said that stars are the brain of heaven.[26] Would people and birds be the brain of Earth? To respond, one must begin with fundamentals. P'an-shan Pao-chi, who taught early in the ninth century, is recorded as challenging his students, "In the Three Worlds there is no Dharma. Where shall we search for the mind?" (BCR-37).

No teaching, no phenomena. I understand P'an-shan to be suggesting that in the Three Worlds of past, present, future, and all dimensions, there is nothing at all to be called mind or anything else, including realization.

> Yün-men said to his assembly, "Hearing a sound, awakening to
> the way; seeing a form, understanding the mind. This is like the
> Bodhisattva Kuan-shih-yin [Kanzeon] buying a cheap cake with
> her penny. Casting it down, she gets a jelly-doughnut.
>
> (BS-82)

The implication is that the jelly-doughnut is nicer. Even a great realization-thought is a cheap cake, though at the moment it seems delicious. Rather than allowing yourself to be used by the thought process, switch over to using it, and a more delectable pastry appears. Abusing the process, neurotic obsessions build upon each other. Allowing it to play, the mind reveals itself more and more richly.

Kumarajiva and his colleagues who translated Indian texts into Chinese early in the fifth century chose the Chinese word meaning "sky" to translate *shunyāta*, or "emptiness." The saying, "The nature of my mind is the empty sky" is proverbial in Zen communities. The empty sky and the sky within my skull are the same sky. Flitting across, idea-birds connect with this twig and that branch and endow us with wisdom. In Paul Shepard's words, "A bird flying across the sky is an idea coming from the unseen of the preconscious and disappearing again into the realm of dreams."[27]

Indeed, beneath the airy ceiling of my great skull I find many thoughts that sing of speckled eggs and ropes and things, not to mention Robert Louis Stevenson. The tiny beings I saw emerging from the unknown aperture of my living flesh *re*-present trees, towers, animals, and people of a landscape that changes from Australia to Hawai'i to California, though it is always intimately familiar.

Yamada Rōshi used to say, "The mind is empty infinity, infinite emptiness, full of possibilities," which themselves are the empty mind, of course. For human beings these possibilities can be ignorant or imbued with song, but it is the singing *nen* that changes the world. Children understand this in their own way very well, and resonate to Stevenson's "Singing":

Of speckled eggs the birdie sings
And nests among the trees;
The sailor sings of ropes and things
In ships upon the seas.

The children sing in far Japan,
The children sing in Spain;
The organ with the organ man
Is singing in the rain.

Hui-neng says that with an enlightened thought, you compensate for a thousand years of evil and destruction.[28] This is the potency of what we call provisionally the great mind, brought forth in a single pulse. Wu-men says the one moment-*nen* perceives eternity (GB-47), but the *Enmei Jikku Kannon Gyō* deals finally away with perception. One tiny thought is itself the mind of the mountains, the rivers, the great Earth, the sun, the moon, and the stars, to use one of Dōgen Zenji's favorite expressions. Realizing this is *com*-passion, living, suffering, and dealing with exigencies together with everyone and every thing.

It is Kanzeon's realization, her light on my path, and though there is no way I can consistently be the Kanzeon as drawn by Hakuin or carved by Mokujiki or set forth in the *Enmei Jikku Kannon Gyō,* I can find her as myself in peak moments—as you can—and in other moments we can be our own best Kanzeon, open to songs and flowers, showing peace in a troubled world.

Kanzeon! Namu Butsu!

From *Original Dwelling Place: Zen Buddhist Essays*

Hui-neng's "Think Neither Good nor Evil"

The Story

The Sixth Ancestral Teacher was pursued by Ming the Senior Monk, as far as Ta-yü Peak. The Teacher, seeing Ming coming, laid the robe and bowl on a rock and said, "This robe represents the Dharma. There should be no fighting over it. You may take it back with you."

Ming tried to lift it up, but it was as immovable as a mountain. Shivering and trembling, he said, "I came for the Dharma, not for the robe. I beg you, Lay Brother, please open the Way for me."

The Teacher said, "Don't think good; don't think evil. At this very moment, what is the original face of Ming the Senior Monk?"

In that instant Ming had great satori. Sweat ran from his entire body. In tears he made his bows, saying, "Besides these secret words and secret meanings, is there anything of further significance?"

The Teacher said, "What I have just conveyed to you is not secret. If you reflect upon your own face, you will find whatever is secret right there with you."

Ming said, "Though I practiced under Hung-jen with the assembly, I could not truly realize my original face. Now thanks to your pointed instruction, I am like someone who drinks water and knows personally whether it is cold or warm. Lay Brother, you are now my teacher."

The Teacher said, "If you can say that, then let us both emulate Hung-jen. Maintain your realization carefully."

Wu-men's Comment

It must be said that the Sixth Ancestor forgets himself completely in taking action here. He is like a kindly grandmother who peels a fresh lychee, removes the seed, and puts it into your mouth. Then you only need to swallow it down.

Wu-men's Verse

It can't be described; it can't be pictured.
It can't be praised enough; stop groping for it.
The original face has nowhere to hide.
When the world is destroyed, it is not destroyed.

(GB-23)

Comment

Hui-neng is called the Sixth Ancestor because he was sixth in succession from Bodhidharma, who brought the seeds of Zen Buddhism to China. He was born in 638, the son of a civil servant who lost his position and then died young, leaving the young boy and his mother penniless. It is said that Hui-neng had no schooling, and that as a child and youth he worked as a peddler of firewood to support himself and his mother.

One day, while delivering wood to a customer, he heard a monk reciting the *Diamond Sūtra;* his mind opened and he experienced deep realization. The young Hui-neng approached the monk and asked who his teacher might be. The monk said his teacher was the Fifth Ancestor, Hung-jen, who lived a thousand or more miles away at the temple of Huang-mei in North China. Hui-neng resolved to go there and study. A neighbor kindly agreed to support his mother, and Hui-neng set out like the young Shākyamuni to seek his spiritual fortune. Arriving finally at Huang-mei, so the story goes, he was shown into Hung-jen's presence. Hung-jen asked him:

"Where are you from, that you come to this mountain making obeisance to me? What is it that you seek here?"

Hui-neng said, "I come from Ling-nan in the South. I have come this long distance seeking no particular thing, only the Buddha Dharma."

Hung-jen said, "If you are from Ling-nan, then you are a barbarian. How can you become a Buddha?"

Hui-neng said, "Though people from the North and the South are different, there is no north or south in the Dharma, or in Buddha-nature. Though my barbarian's body and your body are not the same, what difference is there in our Buddha nature?"

Hung-jen recognized the worth of his new student, but assigned him to the harvesting shed to husk rice, no doubt awaiting developments.

A few months passed and Hung-jen felt the need to name a successor. He announced a contest for this purpose, saying, "Whoever believes that he is worthy of transmission should submit a poem showing his understanding of the Way, and I will acknowledge the writer of the most cogent poem as next master in our line." All monks felt that the leader of the assembly, Shen-hsiu, had the clearest insight of all, so none of them wrote anything. Shen-hsiu, however, wasn't sure of his own attainment. Instead of turning in a poem, he inscribed one anonymously on a wall that was being prepared for a mural. If it were approved, he could step forward and announce his authorship. If it were disapproved, he could just keep quiet. So he wrote:

> The body is the Bodhi Tree;
> the mind is like a clear mirror;
> moment by moment, wipe the mirror carefully;
> let there be no dust upon it.

Hung-jen praised this poem very much, and he had all his monks commit it to memory and recite it. However, he said nothing about making its author his successor. Hui-neng heard a monk reciting the poem and recognized immediately the limitation of its author's realization. Learning of the contest for the first time, he dictated his own poem to a monk who wrote it on the wall beneath that of Shen-hsiu:

Bodhi really has no tree;
the mirror too has no stand;
there is nothing at all from the beginning;
where can any dust alight?

Although everyone was impressed with this second poem, there was quite a disturbance when it was rumored that the nondescript layman in the harvest shed had dictated it. Hung-jen recognized the worth of the poem, but he prudently rubbed it out with his slipper, saying it was of no value. That night, however, he summoned Hui-neng to his room and preached to him on the *Diamond Sūtra*. Hui-neng grasped the inner sense of the sūtra at once, and thereupon Hung-jen conveyed the robe and bowl of Bodhidharma to him as symbols of transmission. Warning him that out of jealousy some monks would seek to do him harm if he remained at the monastery, the teacher personally rowed Hui-neng across the river and advised him to polish his realization secretly for some time before emerging as a teacher. Next day, Hung-jen told his monks what had happened, and they became agitated, as they felt sure that their old teacher had made a mistake in choosing the young layman as his successor. They set out in pursuit of Hui-neng in order to bring back the precious symbols of transmission. The Senior Monk Ming, a former general who was powerful in body and will, soon outdistanced all the others in the pursuit.[29] The story in the present case picks up here.

Is it a true story? From very early times, Buddhist history has been retold to present archetypal themes clearly. For example, on examining the internal evidence, most scholars believe that Hui-neng could not have been illiterate. In fact, the historical validity of the entire *Sūtra of Hui-neng* is doubtful. Never mind. Scholars seek the historical facts, Zen students seek religious themes. My own view is that where scholarship helps to clarify the themes, it can be very useful. The rest can distract the student of religion from resolving life-and-death questions.

Such chronicles as this should be read for their value as folk stories, and from that perspective, what a fine story it is! It is especially important for us to see the mythic import of Hui-neng's illiteracy, his lay status, and the defeat of Shen-hsiu. Such elements support the Tao that is not established on words, that is transmitted outside tradition, and that is not concerned just with wiping away dusty thoughts. Other items of interest include the act of Hung-jen rowing his successor to the "other shore," a metaphor common to all world religions, the dangers of the kind of gossip and malice that distracted the monks at Huang-mei, and the importance of allowing one's realization to mature, and not seeking to teach too soon. The whole case is an adult fairy story that orients our deepest consciousness to the Way.

As a senior monk, Ming must have had some understanding of the Dharma, yet he allowed himself to be carried away by group perceptions. This is all too human. With the drop of a hat, incautious Zen students including you and me will get drawn into group excitement and neglect the Buddha Way.

But as Ming ran, he appeared to have left anger behind. There was nothing else in his mind—just running after Hui-neng. The Sixth Ancestor, seeing him coming, laid the robe and bowl on a rock, and said, "This robe represents the Dharma. There should be no fighting over it. You may take it back with you." These words must have been very startling to Ming. He tried to lift up the robe, but it was immovable as a mountain. Ah! There you see the state of his mind! Suddenly he was in touch with the profound and subtle law of the Tathāgata: the Dharma cannot be transmitted by outward symbols, and it is vain to chase after them.

I am reminded of Frederick Franck's story of his conversion to vegetarianism. As a small child during World War I, he lived with his family in Holland, then a neutral country, less than a mile from the Belgian border, and so witnessed "the incomprehensible horror of seeing living human flesh in the tatters of German, Belgian, and French uniforms coming across the border on pushcarts and other improvised ambulances. It sensitized me against all forms of physical violence." During those childhood years, Franck was forced against his will to eat fish and meat, and was preoccupied with a homegrown kōan: whether it was more evil to eat whole sardines than a slice of cod. Finally, one day his doubts were resolved: "It happened in a restaurant when a fragrant *fillet de sole amandine* was put in front of me. I took my fork, but it refused to touch the fish; I ate the *pommes duchesse* and never knowingly ate animal flesh again."[30] The fork would not touch the fish, just as the robe would not budge for Senior Monk Ming. Now Ming had to take another step. Shivering and trembling, he said, "I come for the Dharma, not for the robe." He wasn't just making a defensive excuse, but had suddenly realized his own true intention. "I beg you, Lay Brother, please open the Way for me." Thus he opened himself sincerely.

Hui-neng said, "Don't think good; don't think evil." This is an essential preamble to true realization. In the *Hsin-hsin ming* we read, "To set up what you like against what you dislike—this is the disease of the mind."[31] "Comparisons are odious." I hear grown-up people say, "I don't like so-and-so." Such prejudice limits one's understanding of the Buddha-nature of the world and its beings.

Rather than setting up "good and evil" in the mind, set up right views, the first step of the Eightfold Path. These are the views that are in keeping with the interdependence of things and their essential emptiness. "Don't think good; don't think evil" means really, "Find the silent place of essential harmony in your mind, and be ready for what might come."

Hui-neng goes on to say, "At this very moment, what is the original face of Ming the Senior Monk?" This challenge is the source of the kōan "What is your original face before your parents were born?" For Ming it was a fresh, new, existential question, and he had great realization. Sweat ran from his entire body. In tears he asked, "Besides these secret words and secret meanings, is there anything of further significance?"

Hui-neng answered, "What I have just conveyed to you is not secret. If you reflect upon your own face, you will find whatever is secret right there with you."

Ming said, "Though I practiced under Hung-jen with the assembly, I could not truly realize my original face." No problem with Huang-mei, but Ming's pursuit and Hui-neng's words give him a perspective that is altogether changed.

"Now, thanks to your pointed instruction, I am like one who

drinks water and knows personally whether it is cold or warm." At last it is intimate. "Lay Brother, you are now my teacher." Ming was ready to follow his new guide.

Hui-neng said, "If you can say that, then let us both emulate Hung-jen." Hui-neng had Hung-jen's caution in mind, and was saying, in effect, "I must deepen my realization for a while. I cannot be your teacher at this time. You had best return to Huang-mei and bring peace to the monastery there."

First, Hung-jen's monastery was apparently a center of jealousy and distrust. The monks were upset that a mere layman had written a fine poem—and then that he had been selected as Hung-jen's successor. If there is no harmony in the Buddha's temple, how can its residents bring harmony to the world and fulfill their vows? Another way to understand Hui-neng's final injunction is that the monks were rightfully upset that their teacher had chosen someone who had only a slight experience of Dharma training. How could such a fellow receive Dharma transmission? Scandal! In any case it was important that Ming return to the monastery and help everybody to settle down and become true disciples.

Finally, Hui-neng cautioned the Senior Monk Ming, "Maintain your realization carefully." This is advice for us all. Practice certainly does not end with realization.

Wu-men comments: "It must be said that the Sixth Ancestor forgets himself completely in taking action here." His body and mind drop away, in fact—and the needs of the Senior Monk Ming stand paramount.

"He is like a kindly grandmother who peels a fresh lychee, removes the seed, and puts it into your mouth. Then you only need to swallow it down." Wu-men is not saying that Hui-neng explains everything discursively, but that his teaching is so effective that you only need to be present to understand it.

Wu-men's verse reads: "It can't be described, it can't be pictured; / it can't be praised enough, stop groping for it." *It* is your original face. *It* can be presented but it is beyond praise, and it can't be described. One can't generalize about it. It most assuredly is not something confined in a robe or a bowl, as Hui-neng understood very well. He wisely hid them away, and the practice of numbering the ancestors stopped with him.

"The Original Face has nowhere to hide." It is not secret at all. There are no boundaries at all. "When the world is destroyed, *it* is not destroyed." Why not?

From *The Gateless Barrier: The Wu-men kuan (Mumonkan)*

Yang-shan's Sermon from the Third Seat

The Story

Yang-shan dreamed he went to Maitreya's realm and was led to the third seat. A senior monk struck the stand with a gavel and announced, "Today, the one in the third seat will preach."

Yang-shan arose, struck the stand with the gavel, and said, "The truth of the Mahāyāna is beyond the Four Propositions and transcends the One Hundred Negations. Listen, listen."

Wu-men's Comment

Tell me, did he preach, or not? If you open your mouth, you are astray. If you cannot speak, then it seems you are stumped. If you neither open your mouth nor keep it closed, you are one hundred and eight thousand miles off.

Wu-men's Verse

> In broad daylight, under the blue sky,
> he preached a dream within a dream.

Absurd! Absurd!
He deceived the entire assembly.
(GB-25)

Comment

Yang-shan was an early T'ang master, a cousin of Lin-chi in the
Dharma. He lived in the ninth century and is revered as the founder,
with his master Kuei-shan, of the Kuei-yang school of T'ang Zen.
This is the school remembered for harmony rather than for confrontation in its dialogues. From *The Transmission of the Lamp:*

> Yang-shan went with Kuei-shan to the fields to help him with
> plowing. He said, "How is it that this side is so low and the other
> side is so high?"
> Kuei-shan said, "Water can level all things; let the water be the
> leveler."
> Yang-shan said, "Water is not reliable. It is just that the high
> places are high and the low places are low."
> Kuei-shan said, "Oh, that's true."

Student and teacher are in perfect accord. Equality and variety are
in perfect harmony.

Yang-shan was known to his contemporaries as Little Shākya, a
name we might render as "Shākyamuni Junior," and he certainly was
a true son of the Buddha himself. He acquired this name through a
fabulous story:

> A magician flew in from India one day. Yang-shan asked him,
> "When did you leave India?"
> The magician said, "This morning."
> Yang-shan said, "What took you so long?"
> The magician said, "Oh, I went sight-seeing here and there
> on the way."
> Yang-shan said, "You obviously have occult power but you
> haven't yet dreamed of the great occult power of the Buddha
> Dharma."
> The magician returned to India and told his followers, "I went
> to China to find Mañjushrī [the incarnation of wisdom]. Instead
> I found Little Shākyamuni."[32]

It is interesting that a teacher who scorned ordinary occult accomplishments such as flying through the air would also be remembered for his dream of going to Maitreya's mythological realm. Maitreya is the Buddha still to be born, due to appear a very long time from now. He is waiting in the Tushita Heaven in deep *samādhi*, gradually evolving with all beings toward his ultimate role as world teacher.

Yang-shan dreamed he went to Maitreya's realm, the Tushita Heaven. This seems to have the quality of *makyō*, "uncanny realm," the vision or other sense distortion that is experienced during zazen. It is a term that is related to the name of Māra, the Evil One. The Chinese *Shūrangama Sūtra* sets forth fifty kinds of makyō, some of which are clearly milestones on the path, but it warns that preoccupation with these positive symptoms can lead one astray. Here is one example:

> Suddenly you will see Vairocana seated on a radiant throne surrounded by thousands of Buddhas, with hundreds of *lacs* of countries and of lotus flowers . . . This is the effect of being awakened by your mind's spirituality, the light of which penetrates and shines on all the worlds. This temporary achievement does not mean you are a saint. If you do not regard it as such, you are in an excellent progressive stage, but if you do, you will succumb to demons.[33]

I am reminded of a story that John Wu told in his class on Christian mysticism at the University of Hawai'i many years ago. A priest had a vision of the Virgin Mary at a young age, and then spent the rest of his life painting, rubbing out, and repainting his vision on the wall of his cell. He treated a sign of promise as its fulfillment, and remained there. A cautionary tale.

Zen teachers tend to be scrupulous in their concern that makyō can be delusive. Yet they will acknowledge that a makyō will commonly precede deep realization, and can even occur as a confirmation of that realization.

A makyō shows where a Zen student stands both in practice and in life. You may find yourself appearing as the central figure in a ritual that confirms you on the path, much as Yang-shan was confirmed as a teacher. No bluff is possible here. Some of my students have found themselves to be Buddhist figures, covered with gold leaf, or with gold light. It is an experience that transcends sexual identity—women might find themselves to be Shākyamuni, men to be Kuan-yin. There is a sense of the very old, or of the timeless, and a strong feeling of encouragement will follow.

Distinguish such a makyō from the ordinary sensory distortion that appears commonly in zazen. Colored lights, a feeling of transparency, bells when there are no bells—these are symptoms that you have reached a place that is deeper than ordinary thinking, and you can take heart. Your practice is going well. There is no drama, however. You have not yet reached the timeless place that can promise realization before long. Likewise the ordinary dream may have some significance, but if it does not include a strong sense of the timeless, it is not true makyō.

Although it is not identified as such, Case 35 of *The Blue Cliff Record* is surely a makyō. Wu-cho visits Mt. Wu-t'ai, believed to be the abode of Mañjushrī, the mythological incarnation of wisdom. In very wild and rough terrain, Mañjushrī conjures up a temple where Wu-cho could spend the night. They have quite a remarkable dialogue, and next day when it is time for Wu-cho to go, Mañjushrī orders his servant boy to see him to the gate. Wu-cho asks the boy, "What temple is this?" and when the boy points, he turns his head. The temple and the boy too have vanished completely. A dream— and the dialogue of that dream is one of the toughest kōans we face:

> Wu-cho asked Mañjushrī, "How is the Buddha Dharma being maintained here?"
> Mañjushrī said, "Sages and ordinary people are living together. Dragons and snakes are mixed."
> Wu-cho asked, "How many are there?"
> Mañjushrī said, "Front three three, back three three."

That's the kind of wild nonsense that appears with complete coherence in a makyō or in a deep dream.

When Yang-shan told his teacher Kuei-shan about his dream, Kuei-shan remarked, "You have reached the level of sage."[34] What do you suppose he meant by that? Yamada Rōshi once remarked to me, "It is possible to be enlightened without being a sage," using "enlightened" in the rather technical sense of having a glimpse of essential nature. And, of course, it is possible to be a sage without being enlightened in that narrow sense. Kuei-shan is saying, however, "You are an enlightened sage." High praise indeed.

What is a sage? A mature human being, I would say. Yang-shan could dream that he went to the Tushita Heaven and was led in to sit at the third seat because that was his seat, just below those of Maitreya and Shākyamuni. He had matured to that level. He really was Little Shākya.

The seating arrangement in Yang-shan's dream should be seen in the context of Asian society. We don't pay much attention to the hierarchy of seating in Western culture, but in the Far East the most honored guest sits nearest the altar—or in Japan, nearest the *tokonoma*, the alcove which is the center of the household. The next most honored seat is the next one, and so on down. I have seen a number of polite arguments about who should sit in the high seat, the gist of them being that *you* not *I* should occupy the high place. Sometimes tempers become ruffled, faces flush, voices rise, and even brief wrestling matches may erupt. These confrontations commonly occur when two individuals are fairly equal in status. If the pecking order is better established, there may be polite murmurs of protest but that is all. Yang-shan's place was clear to all those present, and to himself.

I have not read that Yang-shan's dream of going to the Tushita Heaven was a makyō. I think the old teachers must have recognized it as such—a makyō that goes beyond promise and presents the essential world itself. There in the presence of the Buddhas, Yang-shan confidently arose, struck the stand with a gavel, and said, "The truth of the Mahāyāna is beyond the Four Propositions and transcends the One Hundred Negations. Listen, listen."

The Four Propositions are the one, the many, being, and nonbeing. The One Hundred Negations are made up with four negatives for each of the propositions—not, not not, neither not nor not not, and both not and not not—making sixteen. Then each of these sixteen is found in the past, present, and future. That makes forty-eight. These have either appeared, or have not yet appeared, so that makes ninety-six. Negate the original four and you get the One Hundred Negations. "Out! out!" cries Kuei-shan. "Erase! erase!" The truth of the Mahāyāna has nothing whatever to do with such intellection. It is found, as the Buddha pointed out in the beginning, beyond the realm of words, yet even with the word "beyond" perhaps some kind of image appears.

> The Emperor Wu of Liang invited the Mahāsattva Fu to speak on the *Diamond Sūtra*. Fu took the high seat, shook the lectern once, and descended. The Emperor was astonished.
> Chih-kung asked, "Your Majesty, do you understand?"
> The Emperor said, "I don't understand."
> Chih-kung said, "The Mahāsattva Fu has expounded the Sūtra."
>   (BCR-67)

The Mahāsattva Fu was a contemporary of Bodhidharma, though perhaps they never met. He is not a part of our lineage, formally speaking, but is one of the great personages who appeared from the potent matrix of Chinese Buddhist culture in those early, pre-T'ang times.

Yang-shan rapped the gavel—just as Fu shook the lectern. Then he added words of explication, ending with a cautionary "Listen, listen!" Pay attention! Who is hearing that sound? Don't neglect this point.

Wu-men comments: "Tell me, did he preach, or not? If you open your mouth, you are astray. If you cannot speak, you are astray. If you cannot speak, then it seems you are stumped. If you neither open your mouth nor keep it closed, you are one hundred and eight thousand miles off." You will have to wait around for Maitreya, as Wu-men remarks in his comment to Case 5 of his *Wu-men kuan*, and ask him about it. Wu-men is simply echoing Yang-shan. Cut through the miasma and listen.

"Did Yang-shan preach or not?" It is popularly said in Zen that the Buddha Shākyamuni did not preach a word throughout his life. The Zen Buddhist sermon, the teishō, is a "presentation of the shout," and the shout is that of a peacock or a coyote or the mallet striking the wooden drum. At its heart, the teishō at its best has no trace of meaning, and, like the other shouts, it is the very quality of wisdom. Listen! listen!

Wu-men's verse reads: "In broad daylight, under the blue sky, / he preached a dream within a dream." That's how it is. Like Shakespeare's play within the play of *Hamlet*, which is all play, the dream is within the dream of broad daylight and blue sky, where the Buddha Dharma and the Dharma of trees and birds are completely clear. All life is a dream, as the *Diamond Sūtra* and other sūtras say.

"Absurd! Absurd!" Wu-men's verse continues. "He deceived the entire assembly." Zenkei Shibayama points out that another version of the story ends with the words "The monks dispersed," presumably with joy at Yang-shan's teaching.[35] Maybe they thought that the truth of the Mahāyāna is simply a matter of transcending the Four Propositions and the One Hundred Negations. If so, they didn't really listen.

From *The Gateless Barrier: Wu-men kuan (Mumonkan)*

The Five Modes
of Tung-shan

The Phenomenon and the Universal

Mode I

THE PHENOMENON WITHIN THE UNIVERSAL

When the third watch begins, before the moon rises,
don't think it strange to meet and not recognize the other,
yet still somehow recall the elegance of ancient days.

Mode II

THE UNIVERSAL WITHIN THE PHENOMENON

An old woman, oversleeping at daybreak, meets the ancient mirror,
and clearly sees a face that is no other than her own.
Don't wander in your head and validate shadows any more.

Mode III

EMERGING WITHIN THE UNIVERSAL

Within nothingness the road is free of dust.

If you can simply avoid mentioning the emperor's name,
you will surpass the eloquence of the Sui dynasty poet.

Mode IV

PROCEEDING WITHIN PHENOMENA

Like two crossed swords, neither permitting retreat;
dexterously wielded, like the lotus in the midst of fire—
a natural imperative to assail heaven itself.

Mode V

ARRIVING WITHIN TOGETHER

Not falling into being or non-being—who can be in accord with this?
Everyone longs to leave the eternal flux,
not just to live in harmony, but to return and sit by the charcoal fire.

Honor and Virtue

Mode I

As the sacred master, make the way of Yao your own:
he governed with propriety, and bent the dragon waist;
when he passed through a market, he found culture flourishing—
and the august dynasty celebrated everywhere.

Mode II

For whom do you bathe and make yourself presentable?
The voice of the cuckoo urges you to come home;
hundreds of flowers fall, yet the voice is not stilled;
even deep in jumbled peaks, it is calling clearly.

Mode III

Flowers bloom on a withered tree in a spring beyond kalpas;
you ride a jade elephant backwards, chasing a winged dragon-deer;
now as you hide far beyond innumerable peaks—
the white moon, a cool breeze, the dawn of a fortunate day.

Mode IV

Ordinary beings and Buddhas have no interchange;

mountains are high of themselves; waters are deep of themselves.
What do the myriad distinctions and differences reveal?
Where the partridge calls, many flowers are blooming.

Mode V

When head and horns peep out, it no longer endures;
if you arouse your mind to seek Buddha, it's time for compunction;
in the Kalpa of Emptiness, there is no one who knows;
why go to the South to interview fifty-three sages?

Comment

Mode I

THE PHENOMENON WITHIN THE UNIVERSAL

When the third watch begins, before the moon rises,
don't think it strange to meet and not recognize the other,
yet still somehow recall the elegance of ancient days.

Tung-shan Liang-chieh was a ninth-century Zen teacher in the line of Ch'ing-yüan, and is venerated as the founder of the Ts'ao-tung (Sōtō) Sect. His gāthā about the third watch is the first in his cycle of five poems about understanding the Dharma entitled "The Five Modes of the Phenomenon and the Universal."[36] It is a cycle that relates to the substance of Zen Buddhist practice, and is closely related to his "Cycle of Honor and Virtue," which relates to the manner of practice. I discuss the two cycles together in these essays. "Five Ranks" and "Five Degrees" are usual translations of the ideographs I render here as "Five Modes," if only to de-emphasize the progression. Each mode is complete in itself, but I find also a step-by-step development from one mode to the next.

In this first mode, the phenomenon is you yourself after you have become well settled in your practice. You reach midnight, the third watch in Chinese horology, and find yourself suddenly facing the most profound darkness and silence, the vast and fathomless void. Your discriminating mind is altogether quiet. You have entered the place beyond thought and words, where the ice has melted and the old house has collapsed. There is nothing at all there. At the same time you have a strong sense of encouragement and a feeling of endearing intimacy with the most ancient wellsprings. You are enjoying your Mu.

Notice that Tung-shan does not begin with the first watch. He does not begin with advice, like Wu-men, to take up Mu and settle into this single word of a single syllable. He does not caution us not to speculate on interpretations. He skips ahead and begins at a point equivalent to the middle of Wu-men's comment on "Chao-chou's Dog": "Inside and outside become one, and you are like a mute person who has had a dream. You know it for yourself alone" (GB-1).

As Hakuin Ekaku says, this is a most important step—the Great Perfect Wisdom Mirror is completely revealed, but strange to say, it is like black lacquer.[37] You cannot see what it is, and if you try to express it, you cannot help falling into error. Some people regard this mode as the be-all and end-all of Zen practice, and error is too weak a term for their position. They loll complacently in self-absorption, declaring everything to be void. "Nothing special," said the monk Hui. That won't do, as Ch'ang-sha said (BS-79). "The light of things" is hidden in the void, yet it is plain to be seen, plain to be known intimately:

> A monk asked Yün-men, "What is the pure and clear body of
> the Dharma?"
> Yün-men replied, "Flowery hedge."
>
> (BCR-39)

Such an inclusive realization of the omnipresent worlds of the Dharma is still to come, however. In this first mode, things are completely dark. The other is there, but you can't make out the lineaments. You have an encouraging sense of beginningless, ancient times, but you can't put it into words. Don't think this strange, that is, don't preoccupy yourself with your inability. You are in process and there is more to go. The question remains, what is the other?

> Wu-tsu said, "Shākyamuni and Maitreya are servants of another.
> Tell me, who is that other?"
>
> (GB-45)

Zen teachers are forever speaking of that other. Lin-chi said:

On your lump of red flesh, there is a true person of no rank who is
constantly going in and out of your face. Those of you who have
not yet confirmed that one, look! look!

(BS-38)

Shākyamuni, Maitreya, and all ancestral teachers, including Lin-chi
himself, are servants of this true person of no rank who goes in and
out of the face of each of us. "Look! look!" You cannot afford to stay
in the complacent mode of "nothing special," for when malice appears, you will be at a loss, and you will retreat or lash out in response, making everything much worse. Maintain your practice and
your understanding will deepen. The green pear hangs in the sunshine, and the farmer says confidently, "Not yet!"

How should one proceed with this ripening process? Here is the
path, set forth in the first gāthā of Tung-shan's "The Five Modes of
Honor and Virtue":

> As the sacred master, make the way of Yao your own:
> he governed with propriety, and bent the dragon waist;
> when he passed through a market, he found culture flourishing—
> and the august dynasty celebrated everywhere.

The Emperor Yao was a king of legend and folklore from misty be-
ginnings where personal nobility was the highest order of human
attainment. The metaphor is Confucian, a natural image for a Chinese master, but the point is Buddhist: "You yourself are the sacred
master. You yourself are the Buddha. Begin there. Live up to your
sacred nature. Live up to your Buddha-hood!"

If Confucian and Buddhist metaphors seem removed from the
standards of our modern acquisitive society, the point is that any
ideal of dignity and honor and integrity will stand out vividly in
contrast to the conspiracies and conflicts of class and race and
nation-state that endanger humanity—and in contrast to anthro-
pocentric conspiracies and conflicts that endanger the Earth and its
many beings. Tung-shan presents for us a model of personal dignity
and honor and integrity for our difficult task of practice within the
predatory systems that surround us and infuse our lives.

Like other masters of the past and present, Tung-shan speaks to
you and me with the utmost respect. The Buddha himself used the

highest honorifics in addressing his followers. We are indeed all members of the sacred community of Bodhisattvas. This is a much deeper acknowledgment than simple acceptance of the self.

"He governed with propriety, and bent the dragon waist." The mythological Yao is your attendant spirit and mine, as we govern ourselves and engage with our family, colleagues, and community. "The dragon waist" is the imperial midsection, the belt-line of the Buddha, yielding with a bow in the give-and-take of communal decision making.

Confucianism stresses the natural influence of the one with inner harmony to bring harmony to the world. Buddhism stresses mutually dependent arising. This is harmonious, as that is harmonious. Governing with propriety and bending the dragon waist, Yao finds the culture of a harmonious society celebrated everywhere.

This is a matter of bringing forth what is already there. We are Buddhas from the beginning, and in temporal terms this means from birth. We are guided by parents and teachers to respond from our innate nobility, and very early we can identify that nobility as our own, and begin to express it as ourselves. Step by step we cultivate flexibility and honor through the daily exigencies, and our words and conduct resonate far beyond the burning of the soup or the repair of a skinned knee.

"When he passed through a market, he found culture flourishing." Here the sacred master enters the city with bliss-bestowing hands. This is the ultimate scene of the Ten Ox-Herding Pictures, the Future Buddha (you and me) arrived, mingling with publicans and prostitutes and enlightening them all. The culture flourishes with the encouragement of each Buddha, each center, fulfilling herself and himself and all beings in our multi-centered universe.

Tung-shan links generous nobility and judicious governance with culture, for indeed Yao and his spiritual descendants encourage the culture that is inherent and potential in the human being: music and dance and drama and poetry and storytelling and metaphysics and architecture and sculpture and painting. They encourage the enjoyment of rivers and mountains and flowers and trees and clouds. They encourage a bountiful and dynamic spirit of serving and trading among individuals and groups with specialized talents.

"And the august dynasty celebrated everywhere." This is pride of community, taking joy in common nobility and turning the Wheel of the Dharma. The inner working of the universe—the ultimate harmony of mutual interdependence—is actualized. The Hua-yen literature presents a model of this celebration called the "Net of Indra," where every point is a jewel that perfectly reflects and indeed contains every other point. The dynasty, the epoch, is august because its many queens and kings behind counters in trade; in classrooms with children; in studios, gymnasiums, factories, farms, homes, and offices, take pride in living up to their noble heritage. (In Tung-shan's ideal, everyone has work and a home.) They celebrate each other as they say "Good morning; how are you?" They celebrate the world in their particular bioregions, cherishing configurations and interrelationships.

Tung-shan's vision arises from an experience that kindles the Buddha's own nobility. We can sense its potential at every juncture through our delusions and preoccupations. How can we bring it forth from beneath our own Bodhi tree?

Thus Tung-shan establishes the tone of practice. It is a holy path, and you accept yourself with the utmost veneration as a pilgrim who takes the ancient teachings as your own. You have a sacred responsibility to yourself, to your ancestors, and to all beings, to fulfill your noble heritage.

Indeed you inherit the royal crown of the Blue Planet itself and its earth—each clod of clay, as William Blake says in the *Book of Thel*:

> My bosom of itself is cold, and of itself is dark,
> And he that loves the lowly pours his oil upon my head,
> And kisses me, and binds his nuptial bands around my breast,
> And says, "Thou mother of my children, I have loved thee,
> And I have given thee a crown that none can take away."

I frequently say that you share the nature of Shākyamuni Buddha. Tung-shan says, in effect, you share the nature of the Emperor Yao. It is also true that you share the nature of the royal clod of clay, the mother of everyone and everything. Live up to your nobility!

When you govern yourself with propriety and take up the noble practice of breathing Mu—letting Mu breathe Mu—the old house collapses, and you are free to know the ancient joy of the vast and fathomless Dharma. All modes of Zen practice depend upon this first step, and are included within it.

Mode II

THE UNIVERSAL WITHIN THE PHENOMENON

An old woman, oversleeping at daybreak, meets the ancient mirror,
and clearly sees a face that is no other than her own.
Don't wander in your head and validate shadows any more.

Several terms in Chinese can be translated "old woman," and this one implies a muddlehead. Tung-shan is here taking an ordinary, sexist metaphor of his time and using it to present the feminine talent of both women and men to forget the self.

Katsuki Sekida once told us a story of attending sesshin with a friend, an older man. On the last morning after breakfast they sat silently together on the narrow balcony of the zendō, watching the sunrise. "Oh," said the old man vacantly and slowly, "the sun is coming up." Mr. Sekida recognized the potent stupidity of this mundane remark, and urged his friend to see the rōshi at his next opportunity. There the old man encountered the ancient mirror.

In the interval between waking and sleeping, between sleeping and waking, and when life flickers in the last moments before death, the "certain certainties" of food, sex, and money fade away, and deeply instilled coordinates of purpose and memory disappear. This is the condition that Mr. Sekida's friend found in his practice. People in this state feel lost, they drop things, fall down, and weep inexplicably. They appear before the rōshi unable to speak, yet they are clearly simmering. Wonderful!

When this existential stupidity is fully ripened, the ancient mirror finally drops its dark veneer. The morning star has a chance. The gecko has a chance. "Here I am," calls the bell; "Here I am," shouts the thrush. In his comment on this second mode, Hakuin quotes Dōgen's contrast of self-centered pursuits with the act of perceiving the bell and the star: "That the myriad things advance and confirm the self is enlightenment. That the self advances and confirms the myriad things is called delusion."[38] Dōgen here warns us against ordinary acquisitiveness—the Faustian dream, Mode Zero, so to speak, a phase that precedes the Way of the Buddha:

> Shall I make spirits fetch me what I please,
> Resolve me of all ambiguities,
> Perform what desperate enterprise I will?
> I'll have them fly to India for gold,
> Ransack the ocean for orient pearl,
> And search all corners of the new-found world
> For pleasant fruits and princely delicates.

Christopher Marlowe's magnificent language evokes the admirable energy of Faust, and we are seduced by a lawn party of lords and ladies, their elegant appointments, their splendid food and drink, and their gracious servants—the whole affair ransacked from ocean, forest, and the labor of the poor. Resources are depleted; entire nations are ruined.

> I'll have them read me strange philosophy
> And tell the secrets of all foreign kings;
> I'll have them wall all Germany with brass,
>
> ♦♦♦
>
> And reign sole king of all the provinces;
> Yea, stranger engines for the brunt of war
> Than was the fiery keel at Antwerp's bridge,
> I'll make my servile spirits to invent.

The confident men who laugh so intimately among their peers at the lawn party are gathering intelligence and making contingency plans. The creative leadership of Yao has shifted and the genius of the nation has been subverted to a mindless escalation of protection and aggression. The brass ring about the country becomes Star Wars, and the technology that developed a clever bomb under a bridge brings forth the pure ugliness of nuclear conflict and planetary devastation.

We and our fathers have created civilizations and prepared their destruction with the pursuit of authority as personal fulfillment. Our mothers have participated as well, but Faust was not a woman, and like Gretchen our mothers have for the most part been drawn along in complicity with the masculine forces that governed their lives.

Having said all this, I must acknowledge also the virtue of confirming and naming the myriad things. We would not be human without our disinterested quest of knowledge and our joy in recreating forms and experiences with art, music, and literature. These pursuits are not errors, however, the sort Dōgen had in mind. The delusion is self-aggrandizement, the confirmation of the importance of others for our greed, power, and acquisition that have no bounds.

Dōgen taught zazen and realization as a process of individuation within his specific sociocultural and historical context. He lived in safer times, but you should not permit the sense of urgency you feel in our dangerous world to divert you from his guidance. He and Tung-shan and Hakuin and their ancestors and successors stood on ground you and I can stand upon and deal with the prospect of nuclear winter and biological holocaust.

The ground of our ancestors is under your feet, but it takes great effort to realize it. If this is merely a personal effort to reach something, it is called delusion, Dōgen says. In fact, it is Māra, The Destroyer. However, when you join the mountains, rivers, trees, animals, and other people in the universal pursuit of understanding, then at a ripened moment the morning star or the thrush or a word from a friend comes forward and actualizes your true nature. You are then the Bodhisattva Kuan-yin, hearing the sounds of the world.

Inside and outside are one in this experience; male and female are one in the practice. When you muster your masculine élan to seek out your essential nature, you are at the same time readying your feminine sanctuary. Your senses are open. The sound of the wind and the *crack!* of the kyōsaku pass right through your body. Eventually you find yourself in the vast and fathomless darkness of nothing at all, and it is then that you awaken at last and encounter the ancient mirror. The myriad things stand forth vividly and call out bravely. You hear the gecko as if for the first time, "*Chi! Chi! Chichichichi!*"

In a single cry
the pheasant has swallowed
the fields of spring.[39]

Like the Buddha's experience of the morning star, this was a momentary realization. Thereafter, Tung-shan warns us, "Don't wander in your head and validate shadows any more." Indeed. Even if all appearances become the jeweled mirror of your own house—even if you yourself become the jeweled mirror of all houses, your practice continues, and your jeweled mirror and those of others become more and more clear. The cry of the gecko or the song of the thrush can open the gate—it is up to you to walk through and maintain your Way.

This ongoing practice is set forth in Tung-shan's second gāthā in his cycle of Honor and Virtue:

> *For whom do you bathe and make yourself presentable?*
> *The voice of the cuckoo urges you to come home;*
> *hundreds of flowers fall, yet the voice is not stilled;*
> *even deep in jumbled peaks, it is calling clearly.*

"Service" is the title of this gāthā, meaning service to your noble potential. "Lord and Vassal" is the subtitle Tung-shan used for his "Five Modes of the Phenomenon and the Universal." We serve our most honored nature by forgetting ourselves in our service, casting off body and mind, reflecting all things as ourselves.

"For whom do you bathe and make yourself presentable?" Tung-shan is reminding us of the noble nature we serve. We purify ourselves, "eliminating mistaken knowledge and attitudes held from the past" (GB-1). And as Dōgen says in the *Genjōkōan*, this casting away is continued endlessly.

"The voice of the cuckoo urges you to come home." The voice of the cuckoo is true nature itself, but from the vantage of practice, it is a wonderful reminder. One of my first teachers, Asahina Sōgen Rōshi, used to say in his Sunday talks to lay members of Enkakuji, "When someone comes in, Mu. When someone goes out, Mu. When someone coughs, Mu. When you walk down the hall, Mu. When you open the door, Mu. Let everything that happens remind you of Mu." Not only do you return to Mu, you return all the more strongly there each time, with all the more determination, and all the more modesty about what you might have attained so far.

"Hundreds of flowers fall, yet the voice is not stilled." Your delusions have dropped away, your concepts of sage and ordinary person, delusion and realization, subject and object, have been forgotten, yet this is not enough. The bell continues its reminder, the gecko cries, the neighbors raise their voices, the helicopter drones and rattles overhead. Come back to your home. Come back to Mu!

"Even deep in jumbled peaks, it is calling clearly." Even in the most difficult circumstances, when you feel isolated by the malice of people on the job and misunderstandings with your family members, when injustice is everywhere and the world is in crisis—the thrush sings magnificently in the hibiscus hedge. Come back to your home, come back to your place of rest. When you come forth from there, you come forth appropriately.

Mode III

EMERGING WITHIN THE UNIVERSAL

Within nothingness the road is free of dust.
If you can simply avoid mentioning the emperor's name,
you will surpass the eloquence of the Sui dynasty poet.

Nothingness (*k'ung* in Chinese, *kū* in Japanese, literally "sky") is the environmental equivalent of Mu, so to speak. The road of *k'ung* is the Tao of the Buddha, completely free of dust—that is, completely free of compulsions, anxieties, and preoccupations. Mode III is the darkness and emptiness of Mode I revisited, but now there are no obstacles:

> A monk asked Tung-shan, "When cold and heat come along, how can I avoid them?"
> Tung-shan said, "Why not go where there is neither cold nor heat?"
> The monk asked, "Where is there neither cold nor heat?"
> Tung-shan said, "When it is cold, let the cold kill you. When it is hot, let the heat kill you."

Preoccupation with unpleasant weather, with the advance of old age, with the imminence of death, with the danger of nuclear war—this is a dusty path. Why not go where there is no old age and death? Why not go where there is no danger?

Where is there such a place? Right here in nirvana. When it is hot, is there anything but heat? When it is cold, is there anything but cold? In times of bereavement or danger let your situation enter you fully.

How about the situation of comfort or pleasure? Well, that's like the reststop on a climb. Time for rebandaging the blisters and offering water to a dry throat. Time for an interlude of sharing with good companions. Then on we go.

All along one deals with the challenging and difficult factors of one's life. The *Heart Sūtra* promises freedom from anguish, not freedom from afflictions. The path is one of suffering the afflictions of life—allowing them, as Tung-shan says. If you allow the afflictions to advance and confirm yourself, your body and mind disappear, and the thrush can take over.

This is the Great Death, for which physical death is an imperfect analogy. When Imogen in Shakespeare's *Cymbeline* dies, her half-brother Guiderius sings:

> Fear no more the heat o' the sun,
> Nor the furious winter's rages,
> Thou thy worldly task has done,
> Home art gone, and ta'en thy wages.

Guiderius is addressing his sister's body, now released from fear of heat and cold. With the Great Death, however, we escape *into* heat or cold. Altogether intimate with the flaming sun of summer or the freezing blizzards of winter, we return to our original home free of worry, and we continue our practice of freedom from worry.

Remember that the old teachers were never talking about a state, always about an experience, a peak experience that opens a door. If the experience comes too soon, the door may not be evident. People often complain to me that they have been practicing for a long time without anything happening. "Count your blessings," I want to say. You will have real cause for complaint if Mu becomes evident when you first sit down. "Is this all?" you will ask. The peak experience earned with arduous climbing will reveal further peaks, and broader vistas.

This continuing practice, the Great Life, is a matter of being careful about the name of the emperor. In old times in East Asia and even today in Japan, one does not mention the august name of the current ruler. He is known as "His Imperial Majesty, the Present Emperor." The analogy here is, of course, that you do not give your deepest understanding or the object of your deepest understanding a name. Like the pious Jew who will not pronounce the name of God, like Bodhidharma responding to the Son of Heaven, we conscientiously avoid concepts of our liberation.

> Emperor Wu of Liang asked Bodhidharma, "What is the first principle of the holy teaching?"
> Bodhidharma said, "Vast emptiness, nothing holy."
> The Emperor said, "Who is this, standing here before me?"
> Bodhidharma said, "I don't know."
>
> (BCR-1)

"Who are you?" the Emperor asks. "I don't know who I am," Bodhidharma replies. "I don't know where I came from; I don't know where I am going." Bodhidharma not only avoids mentioning the Emperor's name, he declines to identify his own august nature.

Dwelling there, you come forth with eloquence that surpasses a legendary Sui-dynasty poet and orator whose coherent words silenced all competitors in speech contests. The point here is, of course, not to defeat others, but to bring forth the mind of the fathomless void and present the appropriate topic clearly, or take the appropriate action decisively. It is the search of Mode I, the Phenomenon within the Universal, brought to fulfillment.

The appropriate topic is the Dharmakāya itself, the pure body of the Dharma that is altogether empty—the nature of all phenomena. This is the Way that is free of dust, but it is along the dusty roads of the Ganges Valley that the Buddha turned the Wheel of the Dharma—his appropriate action. Not everybody preaches, some will rite, some will create music or art, some will take in abandoned children, some will volunteer in cooperatives, some will organize against exploitation. Some will do all of these, and more. As Hakuin comments:

> In this rank, the Mahāyāna bodhisattva does not rest in the realm
> of attainment, but from the sea of no-effort lets great uncaused

compassion shine forth. Standing on the four pure and great
Universal Vows he lashes forward the Dharma Wheel.[40]

It is a Way that is creative and free, and so can offer encounters and
activities that are quite remarkable and funny, though the upshot is
peaceful. Here is Tung-shan's gāthā for the third mode of his cycle
of Honor and Virtue:

> Flowers bloom on a withered tree in a spring beyond kalpas;
> you ride a jade elephant backwards, chasing a winged dragon-deer;
> now as you hide far beyond innumerable peaks—
> the white moon, a cool breeze, the dawn of a fortunate day.

This gāthā is entitled "Achievement," partly in a congratulatory
sense, and also as a milestone marking a new beginning, the way a
graduation ceremony is called "Commencement." Other meanings
of the original term are "merit" and "good results." You have indeed
attained profound equanimity. The end, however, is not yet.

"Flowers bloom on a withered tree in a spring beyond kalpas"—
this is the path, the Tao of the Buddha, free of dust, the road beyond
time and space. The tree does not come or go, and is completely at
rest, yet it blooms with the marvelous skin tones of Rembrandt and
the joyous celebrations of Mozart. It comes forth with the eloquence
of all great poets. "Dwell nowhere, and bring forth that mind," as
the *Diamond Sūtra* says.[41] After supper, you take up dishcloth and
dishes. After breakfast, you step from your house to the corner to
catch the bus.

"You ride a jade elephant backwards, chasing a winged dragon-
deer." The winged dragon-deer is the *ch'i lin,* the mythological
mount of beings who inhabit the air. This is the realm of Dharmakāya Kōans:[42]

> Lifting my leg, I kick the Scented Ocean upside down;
> lowering my head, I view the Four Dhyāna Heavens.
>   (GB-20)

The Scented Ocean surrounds the Peak of Wonder, and from its
summit you can view the Four Dhyāna heavens of Hua-yen cosmol-
ogy below you. Yet, like flowers blooming on a withered tree, this is
ordinary, daily life, though it is not the daily life of anxieties and

compulsions. It is the supernatural world of this world. In the realization poem he submitted to his teacher Shih-t'ou, the Layman P'ang wrote:

> My supernatural power and marvelous activity:
> Drawing water and carrying firewood.[43]

"Now as you hide far beyond innumerable peaks"—the innumerable peaks are all about, and you are not somewhere else. Like the Buddha Shākyamuni you have left your palace of indulgence. You are hidden away from your old categories of delusion and enlightenment, worldly people and sages, but there you are in the midst of greed, hatred, and ignorance.

From Shākyamuni's time to the present, the Buddhist monk has been called the "home-leaver." That is, the monk leaves family, friends, and worldly career to come back to the origin. The traditional layperson could not do this. The home was not sacred, and the temple was not profane. As modern laypeople we hide ourselves in our own families, among our own friends, at our own workplace. We leave home without leaving home. We find our home where we are.

Commonly we say in Zen, "There is nothing to attain." This is a subtle metaphor, open like all traditional wisdom to radical misunderstanding. "Ordinary mind is the Tao." This is not the ordinary mind of looking out for number one. It is rather "the white moon, a cool breeze, the dawn of a fortunate day." It points clearly to the practice of all the Buddhas. As Yün-men said, every day is a fortunate day (BCR-6).

Mode IV

PROCEEDING WITHIN PHENOMENA

> *Like two crossed swords, neither permitting retreat;*
> *dexterously wielded, like the lotus in the midst of fire—*
> *a natural imperative to assail heaven itself.*

Self and other are provisionally separate; emptiness is provisionally forgotten. Your aspiration for realization—and your aspiration that all beings be realized—encounters people, animals, and things of the world, including your own thoughts and feelings. You muster your body and mind and center yourself upon a single matter like the kōan Mu, the task at hand, or a friend in conversation. These are beings of the ancient mirror, and you take up the sword of Kuan-yin to challenge them.

The Buddha seated under the Bodhi tree was completely centered on his question about suffering. "Why should there be suffering?" Everyone and everything likewise became centered, engaging the Buddha in Dharma combat. Neither side could advance or retreat.

Suddenly the tension vanished, and the morning star prevailed. Both sides realized their wisdom and virtue to their own best under-standing—the Buddha as Buddha, the morning star as the morning star. But this is the mode of returning home, a mode yet to come in our sequence. The Dharma encounter presented in this fourth mode of Proceeding within Phenomena is subtle confrontation of Mu, for example, continuing on and on.

Holding Mu firmly, you find everything else is Mu, holding you firmly. This is called the *samādhi* condition of "Silver Mountain, Iron Cliff." It is Bodhidharma, facing the wall of his cave for the last nine years of his long life. It is the wall facing Bodhidharma and holding him. It is the Buddha holding fast to his question of suffer-ing, and finding it holding him as well.

The vow to maintain the tension of this mode, whatever happens, opens the way to practice to the end of one's life and beyond, even if there is no resolution. Pain and inconvenience hold us on course, malice and misunderstandings hold us, family members and friends and their love hold us, the mutual practice of working with sisters and brothers in the Sangha holds us, the calls of doves and cardinals hold us.

This is "the lotus in the midst of fire" in Tung-shan's usage, a metaphor from the *Vimalakīrti Sūtra* that originally referred to aspi-ration in the midst of desires.[44] Tung-shan broadens the metaphor to mean "aspiration in the midst of samsāra"—all the phenomena of the world.

The two are joined. The athlete knows about this creative ten-sion. Skiers and surfers press ahead, the snow or sea presses back, and away they go, released. The artist, musician, poet, and indeed all of us—homemakers, bureaucrats, merchants, teachers—all know the tension and its fulfilling possibilities.

In traditional mondō, inside and outside are joined in what is really confrontation with oneself. With each breath of zazen, and indeed in every conversation and every kind of encounter, the engagement without surrender can lead to syntheses that would otherwise not be possible. This from the record of Lin-chi:

> Ma-yü came to see Lin-chi. He spread his mat and asked, "Which is the true face of the twelve-faced Kuan-yin?"
>
> Getting down from the rope-bottomed chair, the Master seized the mat with one hand and with the other grabbed hold of Ma-yü. "Where has the twelve-faced Kuan-yin gone?" he asked.
>
> Ma-yü jerked himself free and tried to sit on the chair.
>
> The Master picked up his stick and hit at him. Ma-yü seized the stick, and holding it between them, they entered the Master's room.

The spirit of "holding it between them, they entered the Master's room" is like that of "two crossed swords, neither permitting retreat . . . to assail heaven itself." We dramatized this in a Dharma encounter at the Koko An Zendō. The student and I ended up grasping my little staff and exiting together up the stairs, as everybody clapped. This is the joyous tussle of children and baby animals; it is the delight of sexual love; it can be the dynamic of family and community interaction. It is corrupted in confrontations where Māra the destroyer presides—in dark passages of communal, corporate, and international warfare.

The nineteenth-century statesman and warrior Yamaoka Tesshū narrowed Tung-shan's metaphor of two crossed swords to the literal, and reduced the poetry to swordsmanship. The master Tekisui Gibōku had given him the fourth mode about the two crossed swords as a kōan:

> Every minute for the next three years, Tesshū butted his head against this kōan. During breaks in conversation, Tesshū would cross two pipes, trying to figure out the problem, while eating he would put his chopsticks together like two swords. Tesshū always kept a pair of wooden swords near his bed. If a possible solution presented itself at night, Tesshū would jump out of bed and ask his wife to grab a sword and confront him.[45]

Finally, it was in zazen that the swords crumbled. He announced that "final awakening had come, like dew reflecting the world in total clarity."

I think that the metaphor itself holds the sword, as all the kōan metaphors do, as all true poems do, as the challenges of daily life do from moment to moment. To take metaphor literally and to persist there playing with pipes and chopsticks and wooden swords might enable the fool to become wise, as in Blake's proverb, but I am sorry that Tesshū could not confront the likes of Chia-shan to check his "final awakening."

> A monk asked Chia-shan, "What if one sweeps away the dust and sees the Buddha?"
> Chia-shan said, "You must brandish your sword."
>
> (BS-68)

Not yet! Not enough! Not enough yet! Even when the dew naturally reflects the world, the true master will keep his sword handy for any thought of finality.

This is the natural virtue of continual engagement, using virtue in its neutral meaning of "quality," and is rooted in the fact of uniqueness among all beings. Though there are important milestones— very important milestones—like the fifth mode to come, the final awakening remains unmentionable. It is like a negative number, existing in somebody's head, while the Wizard of Oz turns out to be a little man working the levers of power in the governor's office in Kansas.

Tung-shan brings us back to the poetry of differences that Tesshū tried to work out with his left chopstick and right chopstick. Here is Tung-shan's gāthā called "Virtue and Virtue," the fourth in his cycle of "Honor and Virtue":

> *Ordinary beings and Buddhas have no interchange;*
> *mountains are high of themselves; waters are deep of themselves.*
> *What do the myriad distinctions and differences reveal?*
> *Where the partridge calls, many flowers are blooming.*

This is the Nirmānakāya, the Buddha body of infinite variety. Every dewdrop glistens in the sun, and even a dead ant is altogether precious:

Go bring him home to his people.
Lay him in state on a sepal.
Wrap him for shroud in a petal.
Embalm him with ichor of nettle.
This is the word of your Queen.[46]

Unless it is clear to you that Buddhas and ordinary beings, and indeed each particular thing, are uniquely themselves, you become abstract and careless. In learning to pay attention, the Japanese term *mottainai* is very instructive. Literally meaning "irreverent" or "sacrilegious," it is commonly used to mean "wasteful." An ordinary usage would be "It is sacrilegious to use so much paper." Nuclear war and biological holocaust are the natural upshot of ignoring *mottainai*.

All this is not to deny oneness and emptiness. Oneness and emptiness on the one side complement uniqueness on the other. As Wumen wrote:

Moon and clouds are the same,
valleys and mountains are different.
(GB-35)

It is pleasant to retreat into the universe of oneness and emptiness. One finds there a cool nirvana, with no distinctions—and no responsibilities, for there is no one to be saved. But, as Ch'ang-sha said, "a spring mood is better than the autumn dew falling on the lotus flowers" (BCR-36). In the spring mood, or mode, mountains are high of themselves, seas are deep of themselves. Joy comes and we take delight, sorrow comes and we weep. The *Hibiscus brackenridgei* and its varieties, *kauaiana, mokuleiana, molokaiana,* all of them gladden our hearts, and each *Hibiscus brackenridgei*, variety *kauaiana,* comes forth personally as itself. Each flower, each leaf has its own particular configuration, and its own particular challenge.

What do all these distinctions and differences reveal? Tung-shan answers his own question: "Where the partridge calls, many flowers are blooming." I am reluctant to offer my own comment, and prefer to follow my first teacher, R. H. Blyth, and quote the poem he loved more than all others:

Swiftly the years beyond recall,
Solemn the stillness of this fair morning.
I will clothe myself in spring-clothing,
And visit the slopes of the Eastern Hill.
By the mountain-stream a mist hovers,
Hovers a moment, then scatters.
There comes a wind blowing from the south
That brushes the fields of new corn.[47]

Mode V
ARRIVING WITHIN TOGETHER

Not falling into being or non-being—who can be in accord with this?
Everyone longs to leave the eternal flux,
not just to live in harmony, but to return and sit by the charcoal fire.

Fundamentally, of course, everyone is in complete accord with the complementarity of being and non-being: every person, every animal, every plant. Standing up, sitting down, eating, drinking—there is no separation in this ultimate unity.

Realizing this in daily life is another matter. Not falling into being is not becoming preoccupied with technology and fashion or pursuing fame. Philosophically, it is not confining yourself to the world of fullness, oneness, uniqueness, and variety. The Buddha cannot find a home in such one-sided notions.

Not falling into non-being is avoiding the Cave of Satan, a vacuous echo chamber, where nothing matters and there is nothing special. It is the exclusive place of purity and clarity, emptiness, the vast and fathomless void, where no Bodhisattva can survive for even a moment.

Avoiding these two perils of being and non-being was a challenge to Shākyamuni and Tung-shan. It is our challenge, our field of practice.

Fluctuations in the practice of Shākyamuni Buddha were probably very tiny and our deviations are broad, but once we enter the path, our lives are practice, whatever our condition might be. One of my Zen friends likens practice to the radar beam that guides the airplane to its destination. This beam does not lock the airplane into a fixed path. It does not create a constant condition. It is only a beam, and when the airplane strays and its mechanism senses the beam becoming fainter, then built-in corrective devices bring it back to the proper direction, only to have it stray again. So long as the mechanism functions, the airplane swings back and forth across the beam, unerringly on its true path.

Keizan offers a poetical mechanism to help us stay on the beam:

> Though we find clear waters surging to the vast blue sky in autumn,
> how can it compare with the hazy moon on a spring night?
> Most people want to have it pure white,
> but sweep as you will, you cannot empty the mind.
>
> (TL-6)

Do you incline toward the full, complete, Sambhogakāya of the great ocean, surging to the heavens? The hazy moon, the misty rains in Mānoa Valley are a good reminder that harmony is a vast net of interbeing, and not merely a projection of human expectations. It is in interbeing that we take our pleasure here, not just the interbeing of people, animals, and plants, but of form and emptiness, life and death. Bashō knew this lesson well:

> The day when Fuji
> is obscured by misty rain—
> that's interesting.

Do you incline toward the pure and clear Dharmakāya, the vast sky with not a bit of cloud? In Asian languages, "pure white" means "colorless," and "colorless" means "formless." "Most people want to live without any blemish," Keizan says in effect, and indeed this is our ideal. The life of practice set forth by the earliest Zen teachers in the vow we repeat at every gathering:

> Greed, hatred, and ignorance rise endlessly,
> I vow to abandon them.

The Three Poisons rise endlessly, and sweep as we will, we cannot empty our minds of them. Nonetheless, we vow to eliminate them completely. Joyously we sweep and sweep under the hazy moon.

"Everyone longs to leave the eternal flux." The other day someone spoke of a recent personal tragedy, saying that her grief had taught her how to "get off the train." She explained that at last she was not caught up by the continuity of work and "driving on to the next task," and that for the first time she could enjoy the greenness of leaves and the redness of hibiscus flowers. Their beautiful colors became intimately her own. She was no longer wasting her powers in the world of achievement. I see this change continuing to unfold in her life as she consciously applies her deeper understanding.

In getting off the train, one comes home. William F. Powell translates Tung-shan's last line: "But after bending and fitting, in the end still return to sit in the warmth of the coals."[48] We try to accommodate ourselves, we try to live in accord with circumstances, to harmonize, to go on to the next task—but ultimately we long for the mood of Kuan-yin, sitting in royal ease, one knee upraised.

My friend who described the experience that came with her tragedy continues her professional work, her Zen practice, and her family life. The warm coals could be her metaphor, however, as it can be ours, home fires that sustain us late and soon, as we get and spend. The Mudrā of Royal Ease we love in images of Kuan-yin can be the seal of our own consciousness as we wait in the gridlock of morning traffic. Tung-shan sets forth this practice, this home, this Mudrā of Royal Ease, in the final gāthā of his cycle of Honor and Virtue, called "Virtue upon Virtue":

> *When head and horns peep out, it no longer endures;*
> *if you arouse your mind to seek Buddha, it's time for compunction;*
> *in the Kalpa of Emptiness, there is no one who knows;*
> *why go to the South to interview fifty-three sages?*

What is the antecedent of "it" in the first line—"it endures no more"? In a note relating to this poem, Powell quotes a dialogue between Nan-ch'üan and Tao-wu:

> Nan-ch'üan asked, "What can you say about the place where knowledge does not reach?"
> Tao-wu said, "One should absolutely avoid talking about that."
> Nan-ch'üan said, "Truly, as soon as one explains, horns sprout on one's head, and one becomes a beast."[49]

There is nothing wrong with being a goat or a water buffalo, but a goat-woman or a buffalo-man is not truly human. Tao-wu and Nan-ch'üan were both correct, but I can't help noticing suspicious bulges on the foreheads of both of them, not to mention my own. Earlier, Tung-shan cautioned us about avoiding the name of the emperor. That was a lesson in cultivating creativity in expounding the Dharma. Here he is concerned not with our maturity in teaching, but with our very purpose and motive.

Even when you feel an aspiration for Buddha-hood, you correct yourself, Tung-shan says. Such aspiration is *bodhichitta,* the fundamental imperative of all great teachers—but it can also be an addiction and a pose. As Paul warned the Corinthians, "Let him that thinketh he standeth take heed lest he fall." Paul is concerned about keeping the faith. Tung-shan suggests that faith itself can bring us down. It is time to take stock. There is nothing at all to be called Buddha-hood. Be easy!

The Kalpa of Emptiness is an incredibly long interval in the measurement of vast reaches of time that Indian philosophers devised, and here it is a metaphor—the mind of not-knowing, the mind of Bodhidharma standing before the Emperor of China, and the mind of his many wonderful heirs, including Ma-tsu: "not mind, not Buddha" (GB-33). In the final chapter of the Hua-yen literature, the pilgrim Sudhana traveled to the South to interview fifty-three great teachers, and his last teachers were Maitreya and Samantabhadra. There is no need to follow Sudhana's path. Maitreya is not the future Buddha, after all.

From *Avaloka: A Journal of Traditional Religion and Culture*

Hsüan-sha's
Drainage Ditch

The Story

Ching-ch'ing said to Hsüan-sha, "I have just arrived at this monastery. I ask the master to point out the entry to the teaching."

Hsüan-sha said, "Do you hear the sound of the water in the drainage ditch?"

Ching-ch'ing said, "I hear it."

Hsüan-sha said, "Enter there."

Hearing these words, Ching-ch'ing had great satori.[50]

Personae

Hsüan-sha Shih-pei was a Dharma heir of Hsüeh-feng, and a brother monk of Yün-men and the many other worthies in Hsüeh-feng's assembly. He was grandfather in the Dharma of Fa-yen Wen-i, the founder of the last great tradition of T'ang Ch'an or Zen Buddhism. The Ching-ch'ing in this story is an otherwise unknown young monk, a generation younger than Ching-ch'ing Tao-fu, who was another successor of Hsüeh-feng.

The Second Story

In an interview with Hsien-yen An, a scholar repeated the story of Hsüan-sha's advice to Ching-ch'ing and asked, "What if Ching-ch'ing had said that he couldn't hear the sound of the water in the drainage ditch?"

An said, "Professor!"
The scholar said, "Yes."
An said, "Enter there."
The scholar said nothing further.[51]

Personae

Hsien-yen An was a grandson in the Dharma of Fa-yen, which makes him a great-great-grandson of Hsüan-sha. The story of the drainage ditch was still an important topic after four generations.

Comment

Natural sounds and sounds of the human voice are vital elements of Zen practice. Yün-men asks, "The world is so vast and wide, why do you put on your seven-piece robe at the sound of the bell?" Commenting on Yün-men's challenge, Wu-men asks: "Does the sound come to the ear, or the ear go to the sound?" (GB-16). When the sound comes to the ear, you are hearing. When the ear goes to the sound, you are listening. If you are thinking something or feeling something, the sounds still come through, but maybe not as clearly. You can be sure that Ching-ch'ing was completely alert to Hsüan-sha's words as to the water in the drainage ditch. Even more, he was completely filled, first with the murmur of the water, and then with his teacher's words of instruction. Here at Kaimu, you are filled with the call of the cardinal, the cooing of doves, the sound of the surf on the shore. Enter there.

Dōgen Zenji said in the *Genjōkōan* that the self advancing and confirming the myriad things is called delusion. That is the act of listening and recapping. When the myriad things advance and confirm the self on *hearing,* that is realization. We can be seduced by notions of directionality, that it is wrong to direct oneself to things and name them, and right to be named by things. Of course it is human to name things. It is naming things that makes us human. The haiku poet Teiji wrote,

Hearing its name,
I looked again
at the flower.[52]

Adam's first responsibility was to name the beings around him. He directed himself to the myriad things. Wu-men's question remains, however. Does the sound go to the ear or the ear go to the sound? The Buddha's basic teaching is dependent co-arising, implying that without the ear, there would be no sound. Without the sound, there would be no ear. Alertness is all.

We take our kōan, "Who is hearing that sound?" from the teishōs of Bassui Tokushō, who holds forth the model of Kuan-yin, or Kannon, enlightened through her practice of hearing sounds. The Buddha named her "The one who hears the sounds of the world," and she became the incarnation of mercy in Far Eastern folk religion. To hear the sounds of the world is a blessed power, Bassui says, a limitless power that ordinary human beings share, and is nothing supernatural. He warns:

If you were to conclude that it is the mind, nature, Buddha, or the Way; if you were to call it the principle, the matter, the nontransmitted teachings of the Buddhas and patriarchs . . . [and so on for quite a list of metaphysical options], you would still be mixed up people who haven't left the path of reason.[53]

You cannot fulfill the Buddha's teaching by being preoccupied intellectually with philosophical possibilities. The scholar wasn't open to the words of Hsien-yen An, and had to subside. He was in a lonely place, one all too familiar to most of us. The way out is the Mahāyāna, the great vehicle of birds and trees, people and towers, mountains and rivers, all practicing together, all doing zazen together in mutual interdependence, all creating together. Allow yourself to be open and vacant and empty from the beginning, just breathing in and out. The songs of the dove pass right through, the chattering of the mynah passes right through, the faraway sound of the airplane, the car going by, all pass right through. Not only do they pass right through. You yourself are passing through the dove, through the mynah, through the airplane. You yourself chant with the universe. Who is hearing that sound? Bassui relates a story about Ching-ch'ing Tao-fu, the other Ching-ch'ing, Hsüan-sha's Dharma brother:

> Ching-ch'ing asked a monk, "What is that sound outside?"
> The monk said, "The voice of a dove."
> Ching-ch'ing said, "If you want to avoid falling into hell, never slander the true Dharma Wheel of the Tathāgata."[54]

"How is this so?" Bassui asks. "Look closely with your eyes focused." Allow yourself to hear with your ears focused. Bassui then goes on to quote the more familiar story of that same Ching-ch'ing asking the same question:

> Ching-ch'ing asked a monk, "What is that sound outside?"
> The monk said, "The sound of rain dripping."
> Ching-ch'ing said, "Ordinary people are upside down, falling into delusion about themselves and pursuing outside objects."
> (BCR-46)

The identical trap! They fall into hell, in other words. Naming! Naming! The first thing you learn in a foreign country is the word for "toilet." You can poke around and find a restaurant, a hotel, and a taxi without asking anybody where they are. But "Where is the toilet?" If you can't ask that question you are doomed. You fall into hell, for sure.

Thus you fall into hell by not naming, as well as by naming. Hobson's choice. Adam named the beasts and birds to gain dominion. That is "called" delusion. But as Wu-men asks, "Don't you know that the true Zen student can ride sounds and veil forms? He or she sees all and sundry, and clearly handles each and everything deftly" (GB-16). That is the other kind of dominion, the realm of Maitreya's pagoda, of pagodas within pagodas within pagodas without end, where the Bodhisattva Kanzeon takes delight in hearing the water in the drainage ditch because it is not a sound to hear from the edge to the center, for it is all middle to begin with. That's the center of responsibility, mine and yours.

From *News from Kaimu*

Giving

"Giving," or *dāna*, is the first of the Six (or Ten) *Pāramitās*, or Perfections, which evolved with the advent of Mahāyāna Buddhism some two thousand years ago. They were derived from the three-part teaching of Classical Buddhism: *Shīla*, *Samādhi*, and *Prajñā*—morality, absorption, and wisdom.[55] These Perfections manifest the love of categories and classifications that distinguishes the culture of India. Though at first such lists can seem tedious, with unpacking they produce the treasures I seek to burnish here.

The dictionary definition of dāna is charity or almsgiving—of goods, money, or the teaching. More generally, dāna is the spirit and act of generosity. Its salutary effects are endless, and they multiply beyond measure at each point of renewal.

Thus dāna is intimately tied in with karma—cause and effect—and its neglect too has inevitable consequences. As Lewis Hyde says in his landmark book *The Gift,* "When property is hoarded, thieves and beggars begin to be born to rich men's wives."[56]

It is with the Dāna Pāramitā that the Buddha's teaching of universal harmony is put into practice. Mutual interdependence becomes mutual intersupport. It is practice that is not only Buddhist, but perennial as well. The Earth itself flourishes by what Emerson calls the endless circulation of the divine charity: "The wind sows the seed, the sun evaporates the sea, the wind blows the vapor to the field . . . the rain feeds the plant, the plant feeds the animal."[57] The very stars hold themselves on course through a mutual interchange of energy.

In keeping with this natural charity, ancient customs of gift giving and circulating the gift kept primal human society healthy. The Native Americans who greeted the Puritans in Massachusetts understood this well, though their guests, it seems, did not, for they scornfully called the customs "Indian giving." In its uncorrupted form, the potlatch ceremony of northwestern America was usually a grand ritual of giving away precious possessions by the tribe on the occasion of naming a new chief. "Giving ennobles."[58] In dedicating our sūtras to Ancestral Teachers we turn the virtue of the recitation back to Buddhas and Ancestral Teachers in gratitude for their guidance. We are constantly receiving that teaching, constantly sending it around again.

In Classical Buddhism there were several categories of dāna. One category was dual, the pure charity that looks for no reward and the sullied "charity" whose object is personal benefit. Another formulation was triple: charity with goods, doctrine, and services. Still other formulations make it clear that dāna was traditionally considered to be preaching by monks, support of temples and monks, and gifts to the poor by laypeople, and donations of clothing and medicine to the poor by the temples themselves.

With the development of the Mahāyāna, the Sangha became universal, and was no longer centered upon monks and nuns and their temples. Dāna became the open door to realization, showing clearly what had been there from the beginning, for by any name and in any practice, dāna is the hallmark of human maturity. The gift itself is food—often in fact, always by analogy. Its virtue is absorbed and its substance is passed on to nurture all beings.

Yamada Rōshi, used to say, "I wish to become like a great tree, shading all beings." The Dāna Pāramitā was his ideal and I am grateful that he could put it into words so gracefully. Earlier Zen Buddhist expressions of dāna are also heartening:

> A monk asked Hui-hai, "How can the gateway of our school be entered?"

Hui-hai said, "By means of the Dāna Pāramitā."

The monk said, "According to the Buddha, the Bodhisattva Path comprises six Pāramitās. Why have you mentioned only the one? Please explain why this one alone provides a sufficient means for us to enter."

Hui-hai said, "Deluded people fail to understand that the other five all proceed from the Dāna Pāramitā and that by its practice all the others are fulfilled."

The monk asked, "Why is it called the Dāna Pāramitā?"

Hui-hai said, "'Dāna' means 'relinquishment.'"

The monk asked, "Relinquishment of what?"

Hui-hai said, "Relinquishment of the dualism of opposites, which means relinquishment of ideas as to the dual nature of good and bad, being and non-being, void and non-void, pure and impure, and so on."[59]

Hui-hai does not include the dualism of self and other in his list of dichotomies we must relinquish, but it is clear that he intends that it be included, for he goes on to say,

By a single act of relinquishment, everything is relinquished . . . I exhort you students to practice the way of relinquishment and nothing else, for it brings to perfection not only the other five Pāramitās but also myriads of other [practices].

This total relinquishment is the self forgotten, the dropped-away body and mind. The self is still a center, but it is outflowing. The food and housing and clothing and money it requires to function are metabolized as giving—we eat to be able to serve, in other words. The ordinary way of receiving in order to receive even more becomes transformed to a way of sustaining the self in order to practice Buddha's teaching of wisdom and compassion.

Yet "eating to serve" has a slightly righteous tone. If the self is outflowing, what is the stuff that flows out? Is it simply obligation? I hope not. Is it self-sacrifice? Perhaps it is, when viewed from outside. From a personal perspective, however, you will find that it is easier and more natural than the word "sacrifice" implies. Also, it is important to take care of the one who gives, otherwise the flow dries up. Recreation, re-creation, is important for the Bodhisattva.

Finally, is it compassion? Yes, but a specific kind of compassion that arises with gratitude. The English word "gratitude" is related to "grace." It is the enjoyment of receiving as expressed in giving. It is a living, vivid mirror, in which giving and receiving form a dynamic practice of interaction. For receiving, too, is a practice. Look at the word *arigatō,* Japanese for "thank you." It means literally "I have difficulty." In other words, "Your kindness makes it hard for me to respond with equal grace." Yet the practice of gift giving lies at the heart of Japanese culture. The word *arigatō* expresses the practice of receiving.

Finally, giving is the fulfillment of one's first vow, to save the many beings. The many beings are not "out there," but are right in here, within your boundless skull. When you give, you enhance the great organism of your own body. When you evade a chance to give, you impoverish that very same person.

Dāna brightens and clarifies the Dharma, the Buddha Way, and with continued unfolding it brings natural authority for more brightening and clarifying. You see its power in those who are acknowledged as leaders in traditional societies. In American history, it is the authority of John Quincy Adams, who served as president for a single term, and then selflessly in the House of Representatives for the last seventeen years of his long life. In Buddhist history, it is Tou-shuai relinquishing his role of master and returning to practice as a monk. In relinquishing conventional power, Adams and Tou-shuai found the authority of the timeless. They pass it on to us, and with each gift of empowerment the strength of dāna in the world is enhanced. The Wheel of the Dharma turns accordingly.

Mu-chou, an elder brother of Lin-chi in the assembly of Huang-po, was a monk of great moral authority. In *The Blue Cliff Record,* he appears in an interesting story:

> Mu-chou asked a monk, "Where have you just come from?"
> The monk gave a shout.
> Mu-chou said, "That's a shout on me." The monk shouted again.
> Mu-chou said, "Three shouts, four shouts, what then?"
> The monk said nothing.
> Mu-chou gave him a blow and said, "You thieving phoney!"
>
> (BCR-10)

At this time, Mu-chou lived quietly in a little hut near a highway where monks would call on him for instruction. When the monk in this story approached Mu-chou, he was undoubtedly psyched up for the occasion, ready for the deepest possible experience. It wasn't going to be an ordinary conversation at all. Mu-chou had a great reputation as a severe teacher. After all, it was he who broke Yün-men's leg in the course of enlightening him.

So Mu-chou says, "Where have you just come from?" The monk gives a shout. That first shout was pretty good. "Where do I come from? Come on!"—the monk seems to be saying—"Give me a break! That's really a smelly question."

"Oh," says Mu-chou gently. "You have shouted me down. You have beaten me at my own game. You are the sage and I am the ordinary fellow." You see dāna functioning here. By temporizing, Mu-chou gives the monk free play. I can imagine how he fixed his eyes on the monk—can he step into the opening?

The monk shouted again. What do you make of that second shout? Mu-chou is disappointed and hardens his line just a little. "When you run out of shouts, what happens next?" There's another great chance, monk! I give you this space for a response. What do you say?

But he couldn't say anything. Stuck in the mud!—and Mu-chou gives his last great compassionate effort. *Whack!* "You faker!" There are many other examples of this kind of dāna in Zen Buddhism. Lin-chi would shout at his dense monks, "You shithead!"—or words to that effect.

What happened to the monk when Mu-chou hit him and yelled insults at him? Nothing, probably. But it wasn't for want of Mu-chou's effort. In those sacred circumstances, where presumably the monk had mustered his body and mind in preparation for the deepest possible experience, Mu-chou was filling a Bodhisattva role as best he could, though he would have denied it such a label. His great concern for the monk extends to countless beings. Suppose you were that monk, sitting before Mu-chou. How would you respond to his question, "Three shouts, four shouts, what then?" Thus you can receive his dāna as your own redemption. You can then take yourself in hand in similar situations and convey it to friends and family members.

Yet Mu-chou did not spend all his time in formal teaching. Between visitors, he occupied himself with making straw sandals of the kind worn by monks on pilgrimage. Such sandals are carefully crafted, but they wear out. So Mu-chou would weave them in various sizes and put them beside the highway. Monks would come along, say, "Oh, look at those nice sandals. I wonder where they came from? Let's see now, here's my size." And they would go on, with feelings of great gratitude. For a long time nobody knew who was making the sandals until finally Mu-chou was found out and became known as the "Venerable Sandal."

Mu-chou practiced in his hut by the road, teaching and crafting sandals—and we practice in our own circumstances. Dāna is simply remembering what we are, avatars of the Buddha, and practicing our giving where we are. There is no need to call it Dāna Pāramitā. You and I are perfecting our outflowing selves, saving the many beings as we greet one another and encourage one another.

Dōgen Zenji said in the *Bodaisatta Shishōbō* that giving a single phrase or verse of the teaching becomes a good seed in this life and other lives:

> One should give even a single coin or a single blade of grass of resources—it causes roots of goodness in this age and other ages to sprout. Teaching too is treasure, material resources are teaching. It must depend on the will and aspiration.

◆◆◆

> When one learns well, being born and dying are both giving. All productive labor is fundamentally giving. Entrusting flowers to the wind, birds to the season, also must be meritorious acts of giving. ... It is not only a matter of exerting physical effort; one should not miss the right opportunity.[60]

◆◆◆

> Giving is to ... transform the mind of living beings.... One should not calculate the greatness or smallness of the mind, nor the greatness or smallness of the thing. Nevertheless, there is a time when the mind transforms things, and there is giving in which things transform the mind.

Birth and death are both ultimate forms of giving, but the key to the practice of dāna is Dōgen's observation that will and aspiration are its roots. *Bodhichitta,* the endeavor and hope for Buddha-hood, is the fundamental motive. This is not merely endeavor and hope for personal realization. I return so often to the words of Hui-neng about the first of the "Great Vows for All," the Four Bodhisattva Vows: "The many beings are numberless; I vow to save them." This, Hui-neng said, is a matter of saving them in my own mind. I vow to cultivate an attitude of saving, which is no other than the attitude of giving. This can be far more than charity. It can be the gift of body and mind, the experience of "Great Death" in Zen Buddhist terms.

Yet there is no need to wait for any kind of experience. You and I can practice the dāna of trust and respect just as we are, *as if* it were perfected—and thus it is indeed perfected. With our own personalities and character traits, wearing our clothes and eating our meals, Shākyamuni and Kanzeon practice *as if* we were Buddhas and Bodhisattvas—in our smallest acts of catching the bus and answering the telephone. The will to practice is the only requisite.

From *The Practice of Perfection: The Pāramitās
from a Zen Buddhist Perspective*

Reflections

Words from the Rōshi

Introduction

"Words from the Rōshi" are little essays I composed for newsletters of the Diamond Sangha, first at the Maui Zendō, beginning about 1977, and then from 1984 onward at the Koko An Zendō in Honolulu. They were intended as pieces for particular times and places, and in a serial collection they show changes in Western Zen Buddhism and in my own views. Some reflect steps in our centers toward establishing a moral code that is based upon clearly enunciated but relatively undeveloped principles found in the tradition. Others are concerned more generally with our task of establishing our religion in the West and in fulfilling our vow to save the many beings.

My original inspiration in Zen Buddhism was R. H. Blyth's *Zen in English Literature and Oriental Classics,* and I am still inclined to explore those elements of Western culture that seem to touch depths where Zen Buddhism too can be discerned. Thus a number of the essays touch on European or American ideas that I find related to my Zen path.

Finally, still other essays reflect my concern that we keep in touch with the ancient. We turn the Wheel of the Dharma in our time and place in the most relevant manner possible, but the Wheel itself is the teaching of the Buddha and his Asian successors.

Finally, we must find the Middle Way, which is neither a matter of stiffly retaining nor carelessly abandoning. The very heart of the great matter is the Middle Way. Making that heart our own, and keeping in touch with our friends, we can express our gratitude with the utmost cogency.

The Middle Way
1990

Early in this century, physicists began using the word "complementarity" to show how light can be discussed in terms of both waves and particles, even though these two descriptions seem to contradict each other. "Complementarity" can also be used when speaking about many other apparent contradictions in our own study—being and non-being, for example.

The nature of the self is another complementarity—ego and non-ego. It can be explained mathematically, so to speak, but in our lives the subject of research is not "out there," and is, in fact, the observer herself or himself. The burden of proof is not upon research instruments, but upon the conduct of the self. If the observer behaves egotistically, then the teaching of ego as non-ego is mocked.

This teaching is not, however, a denial of ego, any more than emptiness is a denial of form. "Form is exactly emptiness; / emptiness is exactly form," as the *Heart Sūtra* says. Ego is exactly non-ego; non-ego exactly ego. You and I are each of us unique, with potentials that are yours and mine to fulfill. At the same time, there is no abiding self; nothing to be called "soul" that is fixed during life and goes prowling around after death to search for new parents. The qualities that come together by mysterious affinities to form you or me or the guava bush form selves that are insubstantial, yet here we are!

The challenge of our practice on our cushions is to realize this most intimate complementarity by experience. The challenge of our practice in daily life is to present this same complementarity while, for example, we gradually give our children independence. No thing abides; substance is only a dream. We dance as Shiva the mystery and joy of the Buddha Sangha—the trackless wilderness and the planets on their course.

1991

Some people consider Zen Buddhism to be anti-intellectual. But the Buddha, Te-shan, Hsiang-yen, and many others among our ancestors were accomplished philosophers before they took up the practice of zazen—and when they became teachers, their powerful intellects gave marvelous articulation to their enlightenment. The Middle Way is the path of integrating knowledge and experience, wisdom and compassion.

1991

Time and no time, substance and the void, existence and non-existence—these are the traditional dyads of the human program. With zazen we find the Middle Way, and the hoary concepts of dimension drop away.

Using the Self

1981

In the *Ts'ai-ken t'an,* a seventeenth-century Chinese book of brief essays and fables, we find this passage:

> The wind blows through a bamboo grove, and the trunks clatter together. When it has passed, the grove is silent once more. Geese crossing the sky are reflected in a cold, deep pool. When they are gone, no trace remains. For the sage, when something comes, it appears in the mind. When it goes, the mind returns to the void.[1]

We can test our practice with these metaphors. "What is it that does not die down in my mind?" Ask yourself that. It will probably turn out to be something that centers on your self.

1982

When I was a teacher of creative writing, I had a hard time persuading my students to treat their first drafts as something preliminary.

They thought of them as something sacred that should not be touched. With this emotional investment, they were unable to finish their work.

We all have this problem. When we do something, we feel obliged to defend our action. When we say something, we will then argue from those words as though they formed an irrefutable premise. Yet our teacher Shākyamuni is still doing zazen and really is only halfway to complete enlightenment. Keep yourself open to correction, open to change. This is the Buddha Tao.

Ordinary Mind Is the Tao

1991

Our teachers are not limited to Chao-chou, Yün-men, and others. Recently I have had occasion to look again at the work of Frederick Franck, disciple of Albert Schweitzer, Pope John, Daisetz T. Suzuki, and his own genius. Franck's writing and his art instruct our practice, on our cushions and in our daily life. He writes:

> It has often been said that the word "religion" derives from the Latin *religare,* to bind together. Reflecting on what this "binding together" might mean, I concluded that . . . the term "religion" refers to a picking up of the pieces—to a gluing together of what was broken and fragmented—to re-storing the shards of my fragmented existence in order to attain, what? To attain my wholeness as a person. But more than that: to bring about my integration into the greater wholeness of the human community, and from there into that of the biosphere of our Earth.[2]

What is the process by which one picks up the pieces and restores wholeness? In a catalog of Franck's recent paintings and drawings, the critic Frans Boenders wrote that Franck's drawing is an act that brings the latent into the open: "He helps it being born, as if he were a midwife . . . tenderly respecting its intactness, its dignity, one might even say its sacredness."[3]

I am reminded of John Donne's "The Crosse":

Carvers do not faces make,
But that away, which hid them there, do take.

Boenders continues: "One wonders what the artist gains from these in-scapes, and can only conclude that it must be the satisfaction of a work well done, a process brought to its conclusion. Ultimately, however, it may be his way to liberation, to a kind of salvation."

In other words, Frederick Franck's painting and drawing bring forth all he meets and thus his art brings forth himself. He inspires people, animals, plants, landscapes, seas, and clouds to become truly themselves. He fulfills the first Bodhisattva Vow, to save the many beings as his own self-realization. There are, of course, many other ways to save the many beings and oneself, but all can be guided by this marvelous octogenarian, whose message is many-layered, yet ultimately simple: "No one ever becomes adult," he wrote, but "becomes either delightfully childlike or pitifully juvenile."[4]

Cycles and Stages
1991

Some students of religion postpone their lives and then wake up one day and say, "Wait a minute, here I am forty years old and I don't have a spouse or a career. What am I going to do when I grow up?" They have let things back up as they wait to be enlightened, or to be settled in mind. This shows a misunderstanding of the nature of practice.

Right Practice, the ninth step of the Eightfold Path, does not involve waiting for the psyche to ripen. The clock is ticking. Right Practice is taking yourself in hand. For the lay student, it can include college, a career, and a family. It is to get on with living. The confidence and maturity that come with a productive life will enhance zazen and deepen satori.

The Moral Path
1985

Antinomianism is the doctrine that true faith gives one freedom from morality. Its expression might be "Since I am saved, anything goes." This is a heresy that developed early in Christian history, and is particularly associated with the Anabaptists of the sixteenth century.

There is Buddhist antinomianism too. Its expression is "When I am hungry, I eat; when I am tired, I sleep." Yet those same words can voice the great mind itself. Could "anything goes" express salvation? Yes, if you contain that "anything."

Dreams and Archetypes
1980

Reading Virginia Woolf's *The Waves* recently, I came across the following:

> [Bernard speaking] "Everything is strange. Things are huge and very small. The stalks of flowers are thick as oak trees. We are giants lying here, who can make forests quiver."[5]

I am reminded of a game I would play in bed when I was very small. I would scratch the sheet, and the sound would be at once tiny and far away, and very loud, close at hand. In zazen, this uncanny condition arises naturally. Your eyes naturally go out of focus and the lens of your cortex likewise goes out of focus. If you give your full attention to Mu in that context, then you are walking near the palace.

1982

Recently I have been reading *The Japanese Letters of Lafcadio Hearn*, edited by Elizabeth Bisland. Hearn was a storyteller who was born on the Ionian island of Leucadia in 1850. After working as a journalist and freelance essayist in the United States, he ultimately settled in rural Japan in 1890, where he lived until his death in 1904. His principal correspondent in this collection is Basil Hall Chamberlain, who was professor of Japanese at Tokyo Imperial University in the same general period. Here is Hearn describing his life with his Japanese wife and their family:

> However intolerable anything else is, at home I enter into my little smiling world of old ways and thoughts and courtesies where all is

soft and gentle as something seen in sleep. It is so soft, so intangibly
gentle and lovable and artless, that sometimes it seems a dream
only; and then a fear comes that it might vanish away. It becomes
Me. When I am pleased, it laughs; when I don't feel jolly, everything
is silent. Thus, light and vapory as its force seems, it is a moral force,
perpetually appealing to conscience.[6]

What is the appeal to conscience? To belong to the other, as the other
belongs to Me. To take my turn and laugh when the other is pleased,
and fall silent when appropriate. To have a role in the vapory, mutual, moral force that is our true home.

1986

Transference is the act of entrusting one's process of growth to another person to some degree. It can be the investment of a lover in a
loved one, a student in a teacher, a client in a psychologist, a disciple in a priest. It is an important step in the process of becoming
settled in a relationship, becoming educated, and becoming morally
and spiritually self-reliant. It has two rules.

The first rule is that each party understand what is happening.
Transference is a temporary condition and can lead to a profound
relationship that still includes elements of guiding and being guided.

It changes and, with understanding, neither party will give way
to the feelings of regret that inevitably accompany the ending of one
phase and the beginning of the other. If both parties know in advance that this period will be difficult, then perhaps it can be met
with tolerance and good humor.

The second rule is that neither party betray the process.
Responsibility for keeping this rule lies particularly with the one
who is trusted, but the one who invests trust also has something to
practice. Respect the bond for what it is, and don't try to make it
something else. In other words, you must not be literal with your
affection. I am not really your father; you are not really my children.
Transference is a mysterious force. I dream about you, my students
—and you dream about me. Transference gone bad has the anguish
of divorce and its hatreds. It can destroy lives. Let's be mindful and
tender with each other.

1988

Enjoy a *samādhi* of frolic and play on the sidewalk of birth and death
on your way to the temple. Bow in the dōjō with Maitreya and
friends and read sūtras from maps and calendars. In our midst the
Buddha points above and below, announcing his sacred nature and
the sacred nature of all beings.

Creation and destruction, form and emptiness, the many and the
one: these are the complementarities of the dream. With delight to
the depth of tears, we dance our dream.

Time does not pass, but we pass through the evanescent phases
of youth, maturity, and old age. If this passage is in the realm of "certain certainties," then the light is hard and glaring. Mu is a device,
and realization is reduced to a knack. "I" is either affirmed or denied, and the Dharma remains a convolution of intellectual para-
doxes. Finally death is abrupt and agonizing. The dream's the thing,
as well as the play, wherein we'll catch the conscience of the king.

1990

Lately I have been reading *Nature in Asian Traditions of Thought:
Essays in Environmental Philosophy.*[7] This is a mixed bag of papers,
some of them, it seems, almost deliberately difficult, some of them
brilliant. I especially enjoyed the overview "Pacific Shift," by William
Irwin Thompson.

With the "Pacific Shift" Professor Thompson tells us that we enter
an era in which the individual is brought back to involvement with
the ecology of the whole. Religion itself becomes holistic—nothing
new for Asians, but for the rest of us on the other side of the Pacific,
something very new indeed. Truth can no longer be expressed in an
ideology, whether that ideology is capitalist, Marxist, Buddhist, or
Islamic. Truth is something unnameable that is above or beyond ideology. Technology, which has established the global village, has
inadvertently, perhaps, clarified this truth—for one thing, our intimacy with old enemies. We move around with them just as organ-
elles exist symbiotically within the cell.

We are awakening to the great communal world tentatively, still
clinging to a substantive psyche, misconstruing our experiences. We

isolate ourselves and exploit our environment. The "Pacific Shift" helps us to understand that human maturity is not the individual in control but rather is fundamental harmony made real.

Thompson quotes Paul Shepard, author of *Thinking Animals,* to suggest that human thought evolved to express a taxonomical array of animals and plants, giving richness of metaphor to the human mind. Thus when species die out, and when indigenous languages disappear, metaphors die with them and no longer inhabit the mind. Our children become deprived and our species becomes impoverished. Protecting the environment and saving plants and animals accomplish more than just conserving biodiversity and ecosystems. These actions also preserve human sensibility and the sensibility of the world.

1991

Philip Yampolsky and other scholars are unassailable when they debunk the historicity of the *Platform Sūtra* and the Zen Buddhist transmission tables. Bodhidharma, it is clear, never uttered the famous Four Principles, and the Buddha did not twirl a flower before his assembled disciples. All of these are dreams, folk stories, mythology.

Our kōan study is intentionally full of non-historical stories, from Pai-chang's dialogue with his unevolved self about a fox to Wu-cho's conversation with Mañjushrī about dragons and snakes (BCR-2, 35). When Yang-shan shared his dream of going to the Tushita Heaven with his teacher Kuei-shan, he received his teacher's confirmation and confirmation by all the Buddhas (GB-25).

Transmission is dreamed again when Wu-men reminds us that we "walk hand in hand with all the ancestral teachers in our lineage, seeing with the same eyes, hearing with the same ears" (GB-1). It is dreamed still again when Hsüan-sha says, "The Buddha Shākyamuni and I studied together."[8] And still again in our own transmission and jukai ceremonies.

It is all a dream. In zazen, the thrush confirms Mu for you on your cushions. In kinhin, our formal walk in the dōjō, Zen Buddhist students everywhere, past, present, and future, walk mindfully together with us in our dōjō. In sūtra services we chant with the Buddha and his disciples down through the ages. When bowing in the dokusan room, you cast everything away as Yamada Rōshi bows before Yasutani Rōshi, as Yasutani Rōshi bows before Harada Rōshi, and so on back—and to come. Interacting in the Sangha, you cultivate your treasure of mutual love and consideration to make this the best possible place to practice. And in your daily life, you recall upon each occasion that all beings are one family, and everyone is infinitely precious.

Zen practice is altogether dreary unless it is a celebration of the Buddhas of the Three Worlds and their celebration of us. Postmodernists remind us of relevance—good point!—but when we toss the bath water, Dōgen Zenji remains at the podium. Chao-chou stays too. The Buddha stays. The celebration, difficult and never perfect, is continued endlessly.

1991

One of my colleagues remarked recently, "All is metaphor." It seems to me that this message is the very heart of the Buddha's teaching. When I listen closely to this heart of hearts, I find that I can distinguish three rhythms.

The first rhythm is the natural entropy of human words, concepts, and archetypes. They self-destruct at once because they have no essence. As the *Diamond Sūtra* says, "The Buddha does not have the thirty-two distinguishing marks of a Buddha."[9] There is nothing to believe, there is no ground of faith, the great void itself lies at the heart of expression.

The second rhythm is the power of human words, concepts, and archetypes, despite their ephemerality. The single word "Mu" has set countless pilgrims on the path of Right Views. "Everyday language is the whole universe," Dōgen Zenji says in *Jippō*. "You rice bag!" shouted Yün-men at Tung-shan, and Tung-shan was profoundly enlightened and all beings were enlightened (GB-15). This is the ultimate disclosure, the opening to the universe of the universe.

The third rhythm is the power of notions, concepts, and archetypes expressed by beings of the non-human world, with the crack of the clappers at the end of zazen, with the yellow of a field of mustard, with the subtle touch of the wind on wet skin. "When you endeavor in right practice," Dōgen said in *Keisei Sanshoku,* "The voices and figures of streams and the sounds and shapes of mountains, together with you, bounteously deliver eighty-four thousand gāthās."

All is metaphor, indeed.

The Lay Sangha
1991

Recently I asked Sulak Sivaraksa, the Thai Buddhist activist, "Generally in the United States these days, husband and wife both work. They are tired when they get home and must look after their children and their house. They scarcely have energy for coming to a Buddhist meeting, much less for engagement in the community. What suggestions do you have for this dilemma?"

He answered graciously and gently, acknowledging the problem, pointing out that it is not just a matter of budgeting time and energy. It is, he said in effect, a matter of lifestyle.

In other words, the nice house and nice car and the private school are the problem. They need protection and maintenance. They focus our attention upon the unit, rather than upon the whole. Society itself, as we have structured it, needs protection and maintenance too; the cost is felt by everyone and ordinary folks must exhaust themselves just to put food on the table.

This is Wrong Effort, somehow. Right Effort, on the other hand, is Right Lifestyle, and indeed this is the Chinese understanding of the term: the Way of the Sage, living on the plainest of food in the plainest of accommodations.

Yet following the Way of the Sage individually would itself be isolating. Somehow we must conspire, breathe together, in networks to build the Buddha's Way of interdependence within and beside the acquisitive system that is all about us, using the tools and lines of communication that are already in place for our own global purposes. Otherwise we are maintaining a steady course of using up ourselves and the world.

Kōan Study and Its Implications
1991

One of the participants at the recent conference on Dōgen Zenji at Tassajara was Hee-Jin Kim, professor of religion at the University of Oregon. Author of the cogent, scholarly *Dōgen Kigen: Mystical Realist*, Dr. Kim read a paper called "Method and Realization: Dōgen's Use of the Kōan Language."[10] In this paper he casts a critical eye on D. T. Suzuki's treatment of kōan language as a means rather than as a presentation.

Dr. Suzuki regarded the kōan as a paradox that entices the student to seek a solution. This search leads to a blank wall that must be broken through by sheer force of will and spirit.

On the other hand, Dōgen Zenji says, "Discriminating *is* words and phrases, and words and phrases *liberate* discriminating thought." Dr. Kim goes on to say, "In other words, the kōan language presents the workings of Buddha Nature."

A kōan is simply a matter to be made clear, as my betters remind me. The Tao is not a matter of deliberate frustration and release. It is a matter of becoming intimate with, say, Mu. Mu presents the workings of Buddha Nature. It is not a device to force you into a corner.

1988

What was called the self, growing up from childhood, turns out to be the skin of isolation. It sloughs off and is forgotten when the song of a cardinal emerges as one's own consciousness, when the laugh of a child emerges, when the pain of a friend emerges. Walt Whitman's "I am large—I contain multitudes" becomes clear, and then more clear, for me and for everyone. Each point in this clarification is a peak experience, and is only a glimpse at best. Even the Buddha's realization under the Bodhi tree was a glimpse, a very deep and broad glimpse, of course, but one that he could make more and more clear for himself and others thereafter through his long life of practice and teaching. Unless you take yourself in hand like the Buddha and take up the practice of clarifying more and more deeply the many implications of your realization, the cardinal singing with your own voice becomes no more than a memory, and the way opened by that realization is obscured.

These days, I am hearing that kōan study is framed in a cultural context that is far away and long ago, that it is not relevant to our times. The samurai in Kamakura made the same complaint to their Chinese teachers, so those teachers made very sincere efforts to Japanize the teaching. You can read about their work in Trevor Leggett's books full of kōans with a Japanese flavor.[11] Few of those acculturated kōans survived. Our own study is derived from Japanese teachers, but only "The Sea of Isé" remains from the effort to make the study familiar to Japanese students:

> In the Sea of Isé,
> ten thousand feet down,
> lies a single stone.
> I wish to pick up that stone
> without wetting my hands.

The one Japanese element here is the place-name. Likewise there are certain Chinese historical, geographical, and folkloric elements in kōan study, but these are easily explained. The kōans themselves arose in T'ang times, an extraordinary period of cultural efflorescence in which culture itself was transcended. These are family jewels and we reset them only with the utmost care.

1988

A correspondent recently asked me whether or not I believe in karma. I replied that I do not, any more than I believe in gravity. The question is faulty. It posits karma as a thing or maybe even as a kind of deity. "Karma" simply means "action," and the reason of action: affinity and causation.

The most profound fact described by the word "karma" is mutual inclusion—"interbeing," to use Thich Nhat Hanh's term. I include you and all beings; you include me and all beings. Each of us is unique and precious and we are individually the universe in a par-

ticular guise. Anything that happens to any of us happens to all. If I
resist this natural law, then I create disharmony throughout the limitless organism. When I work toward clarifying interbeing, then I
am turning the Wheel of the Dharma by whatever name.

The organism is the Sangha, the big Sangha of the fathomless
universe, the medium Sanghas of various dimensions, cosmic and
mundane, and tiny Sanghas made up of only a few members in the
most microscopic particle. The Buddha Sangha is one such organism. Mahāyāna, Theravāda, and Vajrayāna are akin and each of their
many branches has its own familial intimacy. Enhancing these affinities is our karma, our work.

Understanding karma, standing under the term and making it my
own, is to become its meaning and to give personal energy to the
great rotation. Be clear about this. Taking the Buddha's word into
ourselves so completely in daily life that there is no residue—this
fulfills his vows forever.

Integrity and Nobility

1982

One of our ancestors in the Dharma, not the Zen Buddhist Dharma
but the big Dharma, is Mahatma Gandhi. He lived by Satyagraha, a
word he coined from Hindi, which means "holding to the truth."
Gandhi held to the truth in his long campaign for personal, communal, and national honor—we can do the same in our own long
campaigns.

I don't know who it was that said, "Every man has his price."
Some forgettable person. Living by Satyagraha, you have no price.
Your integrity can't be compromised. You don't play games now so
that you can be straight later.

1988

In putting away my books the other day, I ran across a volume of
poetry with my grandmother's signature on the flyleaf: Jessie Louise
Thomas. It was dated 1879, when she was twelve years old. Above
her name, in faint pencil, she had written:

Better not be at all
Than not be noble.
        —Tennyson

Values like nobility, merit, and even morality have unfortunate over-
tones of hypocrisy these days, but this does not diminish their perennial virtue. My grandmother aspired to nobility from her Victorian
childhood, and she raised her own children and influenced her
grandchildren to be noble. She knew nothing of the Buddha, but
echoed his words: "Be upright in your views—in your thoughts, in
your speech. . . ."

Noble, upright speech arises from clear understanding that none
of us will be here very long, and it behooves us to be kind to one another while we can. It arises from knowing in our hearts that we
need each other and cannot survive alone. I vow to speak out of consideration for the frailty of my friends, and my own frailty, and out
of consideration for our intimate family relationship. I vow not to
speak as though the errors of others were ingrained or as though I
were separate.

I vow to live up to my grandmother's aspiration and to the Noble
Path of the Buddha.

1988

On reading Philip Sherrard's *The Eclipse of Man and Nature*,[12] I was
struck by his suggestion that every religious person is a priest. This
is in keeping with my injunction during sesshin that every partici-
pant is a leader, but my words simply refer to the manner of the student in the dōjō. Sherrard's point is deeper, and as a theme for the
Diamond Sangha it is particularly interesting.

In our dōjō, every person is lay. In a sense this is the same as "every
person is a priest." We do not have a hierarchy of ordained over non-
ordained. But just as "everyone is a leader" encourages people to take
responsibility for sesshin, so "every person is a priest" deepens my
awareness and yours of the religious responsibility implicit in our
status. Religious responsibility will be different for each individual,
but the Sixteen Bodhisattva Precepts are excellent guidelines.

The Net of Indra

1982

When Gary Snyder read his poetry in San Francisco recently, he began by asking members of the audience to enjoy their breathing, and then he said, "Thich Nhat Hanh taught me that." Thich Nhat Hanh was next on the program and before he read his poems he said to the audience, "Enjoy your breathing." Then he added, "Gary Snyder taught me that." The audience enjoyed a good laugh, but I wonder if everybody truly saw the point of the joke. In our con-spiracy, we enjoy our breathing together, mutually interacting—and really, is there anyone who is not a teacher? Anyone who is not a student?

1981

Practice is twofold. The first part is training; the second is the act itself. And these are not two things: when you train, the act itself is happening; when you are the act itself, your training is deepened.

Practice is to work "as if." The lawyer practices as if she or he were an attorney. The doctor practices as if she or he were a physician. Doing and learning are one and the same. It is just as though you were trying to play the piano with Mozart's hands. At first such action "as if" is awkward, but with practice your music becomes your own best creation. In the same way, your zazen becomes your own best inspiration, and your interaction with others expresses the love which has been in your heart from the very beginning.

1982

In the *Paradiso*, Dante and Beatrice visit various levels of heaven and interview inhabitants there. The first level is the Moon, where they meet souls of priests and nuns who sinned grievously and were forgiven. It is very cool there, and the souls don't smile much. It is nonetheless heaven, just as higher reaches where souls are ecstatic are also heaven. One of the souls explains that all souls are receptacles, and in heaven all are filled. My first teacher R. H. Blyth commented, "Some are barrels and some are thimbles."

As Zen students, we can understand this allegory to mean that one experience is slight and another is deep, but each is insight into essential nature. One may bring a smile, another a laugh, but each in its own way is joyous.

The allegory falls apart at this point, for the Zen student does not stop with one experience. But can go on to deeper and clearer understanding.

1988

Most Western people consider Confucianism to be moral philosophy, but it is more. It is, in fact, one of the parents of Zen Buddhism. In a recent essay, "The Continuity of Being: Chinese Visions of Nature,"[14] Professor Tu Wei-ming sets forth the Confucian view of the universe as a single body whose moving power is *ch'i,* pure and penetrating, yet not discernable in form. This cosmic function is impersonal and impartial. Each being is its modality in a particular form and activity. All modalities are made of *ch'i,* and thus human beings are organically related to rocks, trees, and animals. Professor Tu calls this view "moral ecology," and quotes the Confucian writer Chang Tsai: "All people are my brothers and sisters, and all things are my companions."

Ch'i runs creatively through sisters, brothers, and companions that makeup the universe. Exchange and interplay among the many forms andspecies are altogether possible, and this transformative option has an important place in Chinese literature. In *Monkey,* the hero is born from a piece of agate, and in *The Dream of the Red Chamber,* Pao-yü is transformed from a piece of jade. The heroine of the *Romance of theWhite Snake* develops the power to transfigure herself into a human being in the course of several hundred years of self-cultivation.

There are profound implications for zazen here. The word *ch'i* can enrich our understanding of Essential Nature, a term that sometimes seems rather static. In everyday Chinese, *ch'i* is the word for "breath," a word whose English etymology is "welling up." Life welling up is, for the Chinese, life in constant transformation. Thus your breath is no other than the transformative power of the universe. Let Mu breathe Mu, and you are putting yourself in harmony with your sisters and brothers as they evolve themselves, and with your companions the moon, the planets, and the stars in their awesome, unknown destiny.

Non-Violence Within the Dōjō and Outside
1982

Takuhatsu is the term for the practice of monks and nuns walking the streets of cities and towns, chanting sūtras and accepting offers of money or rice for temple support.

When I see takuhatsu on the streets of Kamakura or Tokyo, I have a strong sense of the ancient. Ragged monks in archaic bamboo hats thread their way through well-dressed commuters in a setting of trains, trucks, buses, taxis, and commercial buildings. I am reminded not of some hidden truth, but of something lost, or almost lost, in the passage of time.

What is our takuhatsu as Western Zen students? The Zen journal is an obvious analogy: teaching and—we hope—raising money. There are other analogies, such as orientation programs and the occasional university class presentation. The Buddha Sangha also has a role in the larger Sangha, with Christian, Jewish, and humanist friends, to encourage social justice, peace, and the protection of animals and plants.

Zen Buddhism has declined in Japan, probably because it has remained within the monastery, emerging for the most part only in activities that accord with government and business policies. It seems to me that our journals and our appearances as Zen Buddhists outside the Zendō must be in support of our temple Earth, as well as our place of formal practice.

What, sensible people may ask, are you doing sitting there on your butt in the presence of some 3,000 nuclear weapons stored just a few miles away? Our practice will be organic when it nourishes peace in that dimension as well as within the dōjō.

1989

I had the pleasure of meeting with Joanna Macy recently, and she shared with me a communication she had sent to colleagues in preparation for a panel discussion being planned around the forthcoming visit of the Dalai Lama to the San Francisco Bay Area. Here are ideas I have lifted from that communication.

Joanna points out that we live in a world that can die. Whole species and life-support systems are already dying, and massive want, hunger, oppression, disease, and conflict assail a growing proportion of the planet's beings. We can do something about it and yet we tend to act as if we don't believe what is happening. She asks, "How can we become simply *present* to what is going on and let it become real to us? Great adventures await us; what is it that erodes our will, our creativity, our solidarity?"

Joanna finds that many people (especially those drawn to Eastern paths) have developed notions about spirituality that hinder them from realizing their power to effect change. Among the "spiritual traps" that cut the nerve of compassionate action are these:

1. That the phenomenal world of beings is not real. With this view the pain of others and the demands on us that are implicit in that pain are less tangible than the pleasures or aloofness we can find in transcending them.
2. That any pain we may experience in beholding the world derives from our own cravings and attachments. With this view, the ideal way to deal with suffering becomes nonattachment to the fate of all beings, not just nonattachment to matters of the ego.
3. That we are constantly creating our world unilaterally through our subjective thoughts. Confrontation is considered negative thinking, acceptance is positive. Therefore it is concluded that when we confront the injustice and dangers of our world we are simply creating more conflict and misunderstanding.
4. And the corollary, that the world is already perfect when we view it spiritually. We feel so peaceful that the world itself will become peaceful without our need to act.

Shackles and traps drop away in such lucid exposition of Wrong Views. Our responsibilities stand forth clearly.

About Practice

1977

Question: "I got your tape today and found it most interesting. However, as I am in prison, I have no funds to pay for books. Is there a way you can help me?"

"I find the breath counting very relaxing. I have had no problem with this as yet, except when I sit with my legs in my lap for a long time. I have trouble walking afterwards. Is there something I am doing wrong? I'll close for now. Peace be with you."

Response: "I'm sending you my collection of orientation talks. I hope you find it useful. About your practice—it is good that you can find breath counting to be relaxing. This shows that you are doing it correctly. Sink into the count. Melt into the count. On the first breath, there is the first thought. Let that breath and that thought be "one." On the next breath there is the next thought. Let that breath and that thought be "two." Not two things, just the number "two." Then the next breath and thought is "three" and so on up to "ten," and up to "ten" again, and again. But don't be too concerned about reaching "ten." Let there be only the number, and all around it there is nothing, just silence and space. Only "one," only "two," only "three," and so on. In this way you find true rest, true peace.

"It is natural that your legs go to sleep. If you limit your periods of sitting to twenty-five minutes, then you cannot harm yourself by sitting in half lotus, unless you are unusually stiff, or already have an injury or have some other physical handicap such as arthritis. Be sure, however, that you are quite flexible before attempting full lotus (both feet in the lap). It is definitely possible to injure your knee or your hip by attempting full lotus too soon, so go easy and do just a little at a time.

"Do stretching exercises as well as zazen. Stretch muscles and tendons in your groin, thighs, knees, and ankles. When you do zazen, your two knees and your rear end form a triangle. Your rear end should be elevated a few inches above the level of your knees. In this way you can keep your back comfortably straight. Keep your head up and your eyes lowered. When it comes time to stand, take it easy. Take hold of your ankle and knee, lift your leg, and let it down to the mat. Stand slowly with your feet on a hard surface and wait a bit before you step out. Your circulation will soon return.

"All of us here join in sending you loving good wishes for peaceful and fruitful zazen. Take good care of yourself physically—your health is very important. Some teachers say you should ignore the self, but your self is the agent of peace and realization. Please be careful with it."

1987

Spoofs are an important part of any religious tradition for they add new perspectives. Where they are excluded as sacrilegious the tradition suffers. This is especially true when the spoof is in touch with the mystery in its own way. Thus *Monkey*, the great spoof of Chinese religion, is a fine teacher.

In presenting their new perspectives, however, spoofs are by their nature hard on the old ones. Kabir, for example:

> Qazi, what book are you lecturing on?
> Yak yak yak, day and night.
> You never had an original thought.
> Feeling your power, you circumcise—
> I can't go along with that, brother.
> If your God favored circumcision,
> Why didn't you come out cut?[15]

"Blasphemy!" cry the Mullahs, as they did in response to Salman Rushdie's *Satanic Verses*.

1990

In her essay "Reflections on the Right Use of School Studies," Simone Weil cites an Eskimo story about the origin of light: "In the eternal darkness, the crow, unable to find any food, longed for light, and the Earth was illuminated." She goes on to say, "If there is a real desire, if the thing desired is really light, then the desire for light produces it. There is a real desire when there is an effort of attention."[16]

In Buddhist terms it is *bodhichitta*, the desire for enlightenment that fuels our patient attention. There is more. Weil goes on to suggest that while desire is one aspect of attention, the acknowledgment of one's own mediocrity is the other.

This acknowledgment, which Weil describes as a sense of one's stupidity, can be rendered in our context as openness. If you establish a set of values and standards for the practice, then you obscure the light, no matter how cogent your values and standards may be. But with humility, poverty of spirit, you are open to the light in its full brilliance.

Dōgen Zenji urges us to "muster body and mind," and this is the power of *bodhichitta*. In the *Keisei Sanshoku* he cites the poet Su

Tung-p'o, who was enlightened by the sound of the brook in the middle of the night. Ripened in his authentic practice, he was receptive to the sound of the water, as Te-shan was receptive to the sudden darkness when Lung-t'an blew out the candle, as the Head Monk Ming was receptive to Hui-neng's question about his original face (GB-23, 28).

Sometimes people express doubts about their faith, and I would anticipate hearing similar doubts about attention. But just as you would be fully enlightened with total faith, so every event would confirm your being if you mustered fully receptive attention. Nobody's perfect and we're all on the path.

Death and the Afterlife
1990

Consider a healthy plant that is growing from its top. It will have buds lower down on the stem but they will just sit there without developing. If you nip off the top of the plant, however, then all the buds on the stem will suddenly sprout and you will soon have a plant with many branches. The whole world is a plant like this. Living beings are the growing tip of essential nature, and if you cut this tip, then the force that brought forth oxygen, lichen, grasses, and all the trees, animals, birds, and fishes of the world will break out somewhere else in the world, or somewhere else in the universe, perhaps in very different forms.

If human beings die out, then the buds of language and speculation among primates and cetaceans will surely burst forth, or if they don't survive either, among some other beings after a time. I am sure of this. It's not mere hope but is the way things are in this vast Milky Way and beyond.

It's hard to accept the possibility of humanity dying, with our many kinds of learning and art and music, with the hopes of countless mothers and fathers who brought forth children with trust in the future. It's even harder to accept the possibility of the Earth itself dying, with its millions of years of gradual evolution through countless species of plants and insects and animals and birds in rich diversity. It is our responsibility to devote ourselves to save the Earth and its beings, and this we vow in our sūtra services to do every day: "The many beings are numberless, I vow to save them." And in the work of fulfilling our vows, we are supporting the incredible creativity of empty universal nature—ready to burst forth with living beings wherever there is a chance for them. It is this incredible potency that gives hope to our work.

From *Encouraging Words: Zen Buddhist Teachings for Western Students*

The Morning Star

When the Buddha exclaimed that all beings have the wisdom and virtue of the Tathāgata, he had just looked up and noticed the morning star. What connection does Venus in the eastern sky just before dawn have with his pronouncement? What are the implications of that connection for us as Buddhists?

Most people regard Zen practice as a process of purifying the human mind in order to reach a certain condition where a sense experience, such as seeing or hearing a stone strike a stalk of bamboo, will trigger realization. This process of purifying involves zazen and the rest of the Eightfold Path—Right Views, Right Resolve, Right Action, and so on. When you are ready, some little thing will happen, and then everything will be clear.

It is possible to get such an impression of the Zen process from reading Wu-men's comment on Case 1 of the *Wu-men kuan*. You devote all your energy to Mu, inside and outside become one, and then a single spark lights your Dharma candle (GB-1). Hakuin Zenji's "Song of Zazen" sets forth the process without mentioning the sense experience. There's a turning about, a fulfillment of your own merit, and you find that singing and dancing are the voice of the Law.[17]

But what is it that turns you about? I suggest that we tend to be self-centered in our attitude toward kenshō, and to regard it entirely as the culmination of a human process. We view this process in a psychological way, as though Buddha-nature were coterminous with human nature, and our task is simply to deepen ourselves to the point where we are in touch with our pure essence. Then at that point we are able to acknowledge all kinds of new and interesting things about the universe.

There is enough truth in this self-centered view of the practice to convince the Zen student that it sums up the Buddha Tao. However, it is something like a child's view of procreation. All the facts are in line, but the adult can only smile at the simplistic and mechanical picture they present. The love and the fun and the fulfillment and the mystery are all absent. What is missing in the mechanical view of Zen practice? The star is missing.

What is the star? It is a being, and like other beings it comes forth with the wisdom and virtue of the Tathāgata. And like other beings its beauty and mystery are obscured by our self-imposed human limitations. In *The Merchant of Venice*, Lorenzo says to Jessica:

Look, how the floor of heaven
Is thick inlaid with patines of bright gold.
There's not the smallest orb which thou behold'st
But in his motion like an angel sings,
Still quiring to the young-ey'd cherubins;
Such harmony is in immortal souls;
But whilst this muddy vesture of decay
Doth grossly close it in, we cannot hear it.

Lorenzo implies that while we are mortal (self-centered?), we cannot hear the harmony of the spheres, but how does he know that? As one of my friends remarked, he obviously does know it and his lines sing with his knowledge.

When I was eleven and twelve years old, I lived with my grandparents on Mt. Hamilton, where my grandfather was an astronomer at Lick Observatory. On Saturday evenings, the public was invited to drive up from San Jose and nearby areas to look through the two refracting telescopes, the big Thirty-six Inch and the smaller Twelve Inch. On a given Saturday night, the Thirty-six Inch might have been focused on Saturn, and the Twelve Inch on the moon. An astronomer would be on duty to explain scientific matters.

I too would be a part of the viewing public. I would listen carefully to the scientific explanations, but my real motive was to get that brief glimpse through the telescope of Saturn, or the moon, or some other heavenly body. I never told anybody what happened on those occasions. I don't think I even mused to myself about finding myself out there in space—I only knew that I loved those momentary experiences, and lived for them from week to week.

It was only when I grew up and read Dante that I found that other people also heard music when they looked at the stars. When I found George Meredith referring to stars as the brain of heaven, I recalled vividly the awe I felt as a half-grown child looking through the eyepiece of a great telescope aimed at the night sky.

You might say, using Zen language, that I experienced "just that planet," or "just that moon landscape." However, though I was focused on what I was seeing, the experience itself was expansive and liberating. I had a sense of vastness. I was lost in the universe.

This is a hint of the mature experience of the star, of the flower, of rain on the tin roof. When the Buddha twirled a flower before his assembly, Mahākāshyapa smiled. Sometimes in the dokusan room, a student will say that Mahākāshyapa experienced just that flower. This is all right as far as it goes, but it doesn't go far enough. Wumen comments in his verse attached to this case:

> Holding up a flower
> the snake shows its tail.
> (GB-6)

Or, as Hsüeh-tou remarked, "When you see horns over a hedge, you know an ox is there" (BCR-1). Experiencing the thing in itself, star, flower, tail, horns, is realization of mind. This mind is the myriad things and beings of the universe, and when a single thing advances and actualizes the self, all things are realized, and the self is liberated accordingly.

Why is this? "Self nature contains the myriad things," as Hui-neng said.[18] Self-nature is your own true nature. It is the great empti-ness that is neither inside nor outside, both inside and outside—none other than people, buildings, bushes, animals, birds, and so on.

Actualized by the morning star, the Buddha found himself in his original, expansive home, as that home. How do you see Shākya-muni here? What is the wisdom of the Tathāgata? Your task as a Zen student is to demythologize the lofty claims for the Buddha's wis-dom, and present it as it is, with all its truly miraculous power, as your own body. What is the virtue of the Tathāgata? Again, it is important to clarify the marvelous qualities of the Buddha on the verandah of your own house.

Demythologizing does not mean you should reduce your prac-tice to a manipulation of yourself and your environment. The me-chanical view of Zen that places the entire function of Prajñā within the human being is closely related to the self-centered and anthropo-centric view of the universe which gives rise to the destruction of the wilderness, the extermination of plant and animal species, the suppression and exploitation of peoples, and the horrible possibili-ties of nuclear war. When we are preoccupied with ourselves, we are out of touch with things as they are, with the marvels of stars and the grass, and we vent our greed upon the world until our isolation becomes a way of life. Then we can even consider abandoning our Earth home and colonizing space, as some of our ancestors colo-nized the New World.

When I was a little boy learning to read, I was fascinated by a dreadful book that told the story of the colonization of Australia and Southeast Asia, a book that had been my mother's when she was a little girl. It presented a conventional, bloodthirsty, turn-of-the-century view of the White Man's Burden. There were engravings of natives with fearsome weapons butchering innocent missionaries, and these pictures aroused prurient excitement in me as I pored over them. I can also remember feeling a twinge of sorrow at a picture of English colonists pursuing the natives of Tasmania. I learned either from the text or from my father, who knew about such things, that almost all the Tasmanian natives were eventually killed off, and that now the island is populated almost entirely of people of English and other European ancestry.

I remember thinking that I would not want to live in a place where there were no natives. I was too young to reflect upon the implications of this thought—the fact that I lacked native consciousness and so sought this consciousness in others. I sensed vaguely that when native consciousness is completely eliminated from the land, then everyone is alienated. I did not at that time understand that the traditional people in my own Hawai'i were suppressed and exploited, and that many nations in my own United States had been wiped out, while many of the others had been reduced to an ultimate kind of indignity.

We residents of Hawai'i and North America live in a kind of space colony because we cannot acknowledge the star, the hila-hila grass, or the deer. We have forgotten (if we ever knew them) the teachings of the Peacemaker, revered as founder of the Iroquois Confederacy, and the traditions within which he arose:

> We are shown that our life exists with the tree life, that our well-being depends on the well-being of the vegetable life, that we are close relatives of the four-legged beings. In our ways, spiritual consciousness is the highest form of politics. . . . We believe that all living things are spiritual beings. Spirits can be expressed as energy forms manifested in matter. A blade of grass is an energy form manifested in matter-grass matter. The spirit of the grass is that unseen force which produces the species of grass, and it is manifest to us in the form of real grass.[19]

This passage is part of the "Haudenosaunee Address to the Western World," presented to the United Nations at Geneva in 1977, and is startlingly similar to the Buddhist position. In Dōgen Zenji's writings we read that all existences are Buddha-nature, and in Yamada Rōshi's teishōs we hear the same fact from the opposite perspective, that Buddha-nature is empty infinity that is at once charged with infinite possibilities.

Notice that the Haudenosaunee statement begins with the words "We are shown." How are we shown? By the grass itself, by the star itself. Of course the Native American has ways to prepare for such an experience. As Zen Buddhists we have zazen, dokusan, teishō, and the life of the precepts. Learning to focus and to cultivate an experience of attunement is profoundly important. But the experience itself is not merely an isolated act of personal human adjustment. After zazen we should step out and look up at the sky. Dōgen Zenji makes this process clear in a celebrated passage in his *Genjōkōan:*

> To study the Buddha Way is to study the self. To study the self
> is to forget the self. To forget the self is to be confirmed by the
> myriad things.

It is the myriad things of the universe that confirm you and me. The fundamental substance is Buddha-nature. Native Americans use the term "Good Mind" for what they perceive to be fundamental. For both Buddhists and Native Americans, essential nature pervades all phenomena, here with the energy form to be a blade of grass, there with the energy form to be a star.

The Native American finds oneness with the world through fasting, isolation, and dreams. The Zen student sits in the Zen hall practicing concentration and serenity. Differences between the two paths and their expressions are clear and distinct. But both acknowledge the experience of the myriad things advancing and actualizing the human self.

Modern Native Americans have built on their tradition and can acknowledge that spiritual consciousness is the highest form of politics. Modern Zen Buddhists are only beginning to move outside their monastery walls to acknowledge the social power of their convictions. In this process, we Buddhists can learn from the Peacemaker:

> "Righteousness" refers to something akin to the shared ideology of
> the people using their purest and most unselfish minds. It occurs
> when the people put their minds and emotions in harmony with
> the flow of the universe and the intentions of the Good Mind. . . .
> The principles of Righteousness demand that all thoughts of preju-
> dice, privilege, or superiority be swept away and that recognition be

given to the reality that the creation is intended for the benefit of all
equally—even the birds and animals, the trees and the insects, as
well as the humans.[20]

This is a part of a summary of the Peacemaker's principles that forms
the Constitution of the Iroquois Confederation. I am reminded of
the admonitions on the subject of equality that Yamada Rōshi often
repeated to us: we must rid ourselves of invidious concepts of high
and low, sage and ordinary person, male and female. I am reminded
of Gary Snyder's words in "Buddhism and the Coming Revolution":

> Avatamsaka [Hua-yen] Buddhist philosophy sees the world as a vast
> interrelated network in which all objects and creatures are necessary
> and illuminated. From one standpoint, governments, wars, or all
> that we consider "evil" are uncompromisingly contained in this
> totalistic realm. The hawk, the swoop, and the hare are one. From
> the "human" standpoint we cannot live in those terms unless all
> beings see with the same enlightened eye. The Bodhisattva lives by
> the sufferer's standard, and . . . must be effective in aiding those
> who suffer.[21]

Gary Snyder goes on to point out that the "mercy of the West has
been social revolution; the mercy of the East has been individual insight into the basic self/void," and adds, "We need both." Indeed.
We need also the teaching of science, for example, the wisdom of
Lewis Thomas, who makes it clear that all of us, trees, waters, animals, people, worms, and nettles, are intimately interconnected in
universal symbiosis.

Nothing is static, and today we face the possibility that we live
in the end-time. We seem to be carried along by mass karma, yet I
believe that it will only take a single leap in consciousness for the
human race to change its dangerously exploitive ways. One individual life of integrity reminds us all that truth is the only possible
Tao. One small group of people truly dedicated to reinhabiting the
Earth with native, enlightened consciousness can convince the
nations.

We have the human talent of Shākyamuni, of the Peacemaker,
and of the patriarchs and matriarchs in the past who have been

shown by a star, by a coyote, or by a shout in the sacred hall that "the earth and I are of one mind," in Chief Joseph's legendary words. All of us hold in our hearts the archetype of hard practice and its application, the Tao of Samantabhadra, the Bodhisattva of Great Action. Let us put our minds and emotions together in righteousness.

From *The Mind of Clover: Essays in Zen Buddhist Ethics*

A Garland of Haiku

Internment, 1942–1945

In 1940–1941, I worked for the Pacific Naval Air Base Contractors, helping to build an airbase on Midway Island, and then a submarine base on Guam. The war came, and I was caught and taken for internment in Kobe, Japan. With little to do besides camp maintenance, my fellow internees and I spent our time reviving old interests with the aid of a good library. I found a copy of Miyamori's *An Anthology of Haiku: Ancient and Modern,* which I had studied in prewar days, and was inspired to try my hand at writing haiku in English.

Our first camp was on the waterfront, and our second was located in the foreign section of the city, with a tall wooden fence across the front of the property and a view of the street from the second floor. Occasionally, I would spend time at the window, watching the residents walking by.

> People moving
> through the steady rain
> within themselves

It was the season, probably June, 1943, when "the rain it raineth every day." My verse is less in keeping with the tradition of Bashō than with the humanist haiku poet Shiki, who lived at the end of the nineteenth century. When I showed this verse later to R. H. Blyth, he said that it seemed it was raining within the people, as well as outside. That was an interesting interpretation, and more Zen-like than I could appreciate at the time. I had meant simply that now, deep in the war, the rain induced a retreat by people into an inner world. A comma after rain, in other words.

It was not a completely successful verse, but it was the only haiku from that middle period of my internment that I brought along with me when we moved to our last camp, in the hills above the city. I also brought along Blyth's *Zen in English Literature and Oriental Classics*, which I had recently obtained and read and reread many times. Here in the new camp I met Professor Blyth himself, and studied the Japanese language and the poetics of haiku with him. Looking back I marvel at the confluence of circumstances that made our meeting possible.

Though the war raged on, and the city below us was destroyed in napalm raids, it was a peaceful, sylvan environment.

> The mountains darken
> with the chirping
> of a nearby cricket

This is a little different from Bashō's "Quail" upon which I spun comments earlier: "Now, as soon as eyes / of the hawk, too, darken, / quail chirp." His theme was transition, whereas mine was (unknowingly) mutually dependent arising. However, one can turn almost anywhere in Bashō to find even more vivid expressions of accord. This from his last years:

> The voice of the cuckoo
> and the five-foot
> irises

It is not that Bashō created a link between the cuckoo and the irises, rather the intimacy was there for him to notice and set forth. Similarly, one summer afternoon, probably July or August of 1944, I stretched out in a little grove of pine trees, and suddenly found I could trace an established freeway in a borough unknown to human beings:

> The branches move
> from tree to tree
> with a squirrel

That same summer, I set forth a slight verse that a different preposition would have deepened:

> The sun glitters
> on the path
> of a snail

The Japanese poet will send verses to a friend with the request *Naoshite kudasai,* "Please correct." From almost sixty years past, from the other side of the world, I receive that message from myself. If "on the path" could be "from the path," then it would be true to ancestors I had not yet encountered. Dōgen says in his *Genjōkōan,* "The whole moon and the sky in its entirety come to rest in a single dewdrop on a grass tip." Similarly, the sun shines brightly from the depths of a puddle, and from the slime of a snail's path.

> The hawk hovers
> in the wind
> above the waves of grass

Technically, the bird is a kite, but, without a lot of explanation, that wouldn't be clear. Wind is a marker for autumn, when I wrote this verse and those that follow, in 1944. The wind is invisible, but manifest in both the steadiness of the large bird and the movement of the grass. Stevenson wrote of this wonder in *A Child's Garden of Verses:*

> I saw the different things you did,
> But always you yourself you hid.
> I felt you push, I heard you call,
> I could not see yourself at all—
> O wind, a-blowing all day long,
> O wind that sings so loud a song!

Another verse about steadiness, not of a sturdy bird of prey, but of the most ephemeral of flyers, the butterflies:

> Butterflies float
> through the hanging
> cedar branches

The cedar branches float as well, resting on the air itself as they extend far from their trunk in the silence and warmth of an autumn afternoon.

> Something coming
> through the dry
> bamboo grass

As I lie in weeds on the warm earth, inviting my soul like Walt Whitman, hidden beings will not let me be alone. A little scary, as when Macbeth approached:

> By the prickling of my thumbs,
> Something wicked this way comes.

Similarly:

> With a cry
> a shadow crossed
> the mountain path

The unknown world again, yet the unknown world is this world—constant, at least for now:

> The caterpillar
> was still moving
> through the grass.

And the final constant:

> Silently
> the ridges fade
> into the mist

Ryūtakuji, 1951

In the fall of 1950, I returned to Japan on a fellowship to study haiku and Zen. With the help of Professor Blyth I rented a tea hut on the compound of Kenchōji, a monastery in Kamakura, and signed up for sesshin at Enkakuji, a neighboring monastery, led by Asahina Sōgen Rōshi. I found Zen practice in a Japanese monastery to be too difficult. I had practiced in Los Angeles with Senzaki Nyogen Sensei, but we just sat in chairs during evening meetings twice a week. The rigors of long periods of formal zazen at Enkakuji were too much for my sedentary knees. I had heard from Senzaki Sensei about his friend, Nakagawa Sōen Oshō (he was not yet a rōshi), so I wrote to him at his monastery in Mishima, south of Tokyo, and asked if I could visit for a consultation. At the end of my letter, I wrote out a haiku:

> *Kisha bue to onaji neiro ya aki no kane*
> The train whistle
> the same tone
> autumn bell

I had written "temple bell" as the last line, but after we met, Sōen Oshō, who in those days was far better known as a haiku poet than as a Zen elder, suggested that "autumn bell" would be better, as "bell" in haiku implies "temple bell," and "autumn" is necessary to mark the season. Anyway, he responded directly with a haiku by telegram. That bit of paper got lost over the years, but I think I can reconstruct the verse from memory:

> *Yamadera no momiji no shita ni matte oru*
> Beneath red maple leaves
> at our mountain temple
> I await you

I was profoundly impressed by Sōen Oshō, and by the temple, and asked if I could practice there with him. Arrangements were made, and I moved in that following January. The schedule and the zazen were no easier than they were at Enkakuji, but with kind support I survived until my twelve-month grant expired the following August.

I practiced with the monks and, with the encouragement of Sōen Oshō, I wrote the occasional haiku. In my honor, a scroll inscribed with a verse of Bashō's hung in the alcove of my room. On one occasion camellias were arranged beside it.

> *Tsubaki ochi Bashō no jiku wa chito yureru*
> A camellia falls
> the Bashō scroll
> moves a little

Camellias are relatively heavy flowers, and they fall with a little "plunk." I felt at the time that this haiku was a little precious, and I still think so, but Sōen Oshō liked it, and submitted it with a few of my other efforts to the haiku journal *Shinsetsu* (*New Snow*), which duly published them.

Early in the spring of 1951, I accompanied Sōen Oshō on a trip to Kyoto, where he visited important priests in the Myōshinji line of Rinzai Zen to offer gifts and pay his respects in connection with his forthcoming installation as abbot of Ryūtakuji. Those were days before the bullet train, and the trip was leisurely, with many stops.

> *Yūeki ya idezu hairazu haru no kaze*
> The station at evening
> no one gets off or on
> spring breeze

In Kyoto, we made the duty visits and were plied with ceremonial tea. One day I counted nine bowls. I was buzzing on a caffeine high, exhausted from running around, living on my nerves. But we took time to visit the important cultural treasures of Kyoto and Nara, and the understated beauty of the Katsura Detached Palace in particular put me back in touch with myself. The teahouse on the Palace compound is placed in harmony with the garden and the main Palace building, and in contrast with the studied severity of the Palace, is rural in feeling, almost like a miniature farmhouse, reminding one of the marriage of culture and utility that brought forth the best in old Japan.

> *Haru gasumi shōkintei to na mo shizuka*
> Spring mist

> Pine Harp Pavilion
> the name too is peaceful

Pines in Japan are descendants of the trees of earliest times, setting the scene for the lives of Zen students and their practice, and for artists, musicians, and poets as well. In a single name, the genius of the Katsura evoked the voice of the most ancient, the ultimate communiqué of peace.

On our return to Ryūtakuji, we walked with our bags by the light of a full moon up the *sandō,* the "path of devotion" from the Sawaji road to the monastery. There at the foot of the stone steps leading to the temple gate a little grove of plum trees had come into full bloom in our absence.

> *Sandō ni ochitsuite iru tsuki to ume*
> On the path to the temple
> completely composed
> the moon and plum flowers

The monastery became a scene of busy preparation for the forthcoming ceremony that would install Sōen Oshō as abbot. When my tasks were done, I sometimes took a trail that led from the main buildings up the hill to a tiny shrine. Along the trail stood stone images of arhats, disciples of Shākyamuni Buddha, each carved with distinctive features and expressions. Sometime over the centuries one of them had lost his head:

> *Atama nashi no rakan ni chōchō tomari keri*
> On a headless arhat
> a butterfly
> alights

"Ah, wonderful!" Sōen Rōshi exclaimed, "Someday you will value your own poem." Perceptions of the same event do indeed tend to change, not that they replace one another in a sequence, but rather each adds a new dimension and the poem is thus enriched. There is the unique juxtaposition of stone and butterfly, then the mutilated figure is seen restored by the butterfly, and at last there is stone-hard sensibility fallen away in the presence of a beautiful, ephemeral being.

Sometimes, I would take a trail that led to the ancient path from the town of Mishima to Mt. Hakone and beyond to Tokyo. The intersection of the two paths is on a ridge that overlooks a wide valley, with Mt. Fuji rising in the distance. In the spring, Fuji seems to float in the misty air.

> *Haru no fuji kumo no gotoku ni kumo no kage*
> Fuji in spring
> like a cloud
> the shadow of a cloud

Ryūtakuji stands on the side of a hill, overlooking the village of Sawaji, which at that time was a scattering of houses in rice fields. A farmworker in Sawaji who had helped maintain the temple grounds lost his sanity, and was fixated on his old workplace.

> *Kyōjin ya wakaba no naka ni ware wo miru*
> The madman
> within the new leaves
> watches me

In the silence of the temple compound, suddenly I glimpse a half-hidden face with the twisted expression of a hardened schizophrenic, disclosing a being who lived apart from the sacred dimension of practice, and apart from the ordinary world of coming and going as well. I am a stranger to the one he sees.

The day of the ceremony came, and it poured rain. Undismayed, hundreds of guests in their best suits and dresses, and in their most ornate brocade robes, arrived and crowded into the main hall for solemn sūtras and ancient pageantry.

> *Uguisu to take bue mazare yama no shiki*
> The bush warbler
> and the bamboo flute mingle
> mountain ceremony

Behind the main hall of Ryūtakuji lies a little graveyard for prominent masters of the temple that is enclosed by a low stone wall. Just outside the wall stands a plum tree, now fully grown, but then just a slip. It was the same season of rains in June when, eight years and a lifetime before, I had composed my verse about people walking through the streets of Kobe within themselves. It was the plum tree now that was within itself.

Shikkari to usukōbai ya ame no naka
Steadfastly
the thin plum tree
in the rain

The Dance of Affinity

Students come to practice Zen Buddhism with questions, basically "Why?"—and this is a question that relates to karma. Originally, the word "karma" meant "action," but it evolved to mean "cause-and-effect" and "affinity."

"Why" can be the door to affinity, the Buddha's own joy in identity. According to the Mahāyāna tradition, he announced his reconciliation of his question "Why should there be suffering?" with the exclamation: "Wonderful! Wonderful! Now I see that all beings are the Tathāgata." That is, all beings are fully realized as they are. "Only," he went on to say, "their delusions and preoccupations keep them from realizing that fact."

Why should there be suffering? Why should there be illness? Why should there be old age? Why should there be death? These questions arise from our desire for permanence, and are thus rooted in delusion and preoccupation. Yet they led to the Buddha's realization and can lead to ours. Blake wrote: "If the fool would persist in his folly he would become wise."

The question must be correctly focused, however. If the focus is upon the fact that one has the question, or that it is difficult or depressing, then nothing comes of it except more suffering. Unlike bushes and grasses and zebras and mongooses, we are blessed and cursed with self-consciousness. We are all of us nonetheless Buddhas, and by the fact that we are self-conscious, we can, even with the most profound modesty, become aware of our own wisdom and compassion.

The Buddha's first sermon, devoted to the Four Noble Truths, shows the way to a reconciliation of our questions. The fourth truth is the Eightfold Path, which teaches us how to follow his guidance to maturity. From Right Views of the self and the world, to Right Meditation, the eight milestones mark the way of selflessness and love. We follow these simple stones with the same longing that drew the young Gautama from his father's house to the forest and ultimately to the tree of realization. The world is unfolding with the power of longing—the Buddha for all his completeness is nonetheless unfolding with the power of longing of each being.

Unfolding is the moment-by-moment course of particular beings, in keeping with their individual nature—that is, by their affinities, drawing upon some things more than others. It is no accident that you appeared, and at the same time there is no gentleman with a white beard up there in the sky who decided you should come forth. Nor were you determined by an impersonal fate outside yourself. Rather it was formless tendencies to become your body and personality that came together—the *you*-aspect of the universe, so to speak, coalescing to become what you are.

Physics and its mathematics track tendencies. Aristotle observed that things tend to fall down. His scientific descendants are now more refined in their understanding of how objects in motion relate to each other, but their conclusions are still couched in terms of tendency. The Law of Karma is simply the Buddhist account of the tendency of things to relate to each other. Moreover it traces tendencies of tendencies. The great harmonious body of tendencies tends to coalesce in unique ways. They coalesced as you and continue to coalesce as you.

When I say that your particular tendencies came together and continue to come together, I mean they are yours only in that they make you up. And when I say "they" make you up, I am not using the right pronoun. It is *you*—the plural *you,* infinitely plural, including birdsong and rain. There are countless plural *you*'s, each one unique and particular. And of course, when the plural *you* loses cohesion, then you as a person will die. What happens then? The elements that came together from such disparate sources dissipate into earth, water, fire, and air. Your karma continues to become the parent, the uncle or aunt, the cousin, the grandparent, great-grandparent, and so on, for innumerable beings. It continues in every being you have touched, and all the beings they have touched. Will there be a time for your elements to coalesce again?

Add that to your question box. In any case, before the final irrevocable option at the end of your present mind, you tend to follow a certain path among many that offer themselves. Just as you are ready to take a certain step at a certain time in your life, so before you were born, the vastly disparate elements that were you and not yet together were ready at a certain moment to conceive. The same history can be traced for all beings. Modern physics and psychology have developed a term to describe this step of coming together—"non-causal synchronicity"—and Buddhists have their terminology: *fushigi na en,* "mysterious affinity."

What is it that brought us here together today? Just within our own memories, we can sense that each of us has been preparing for this moment throughout our lives. Looking back we can see that everything you and I did and experienced from the time we were very little, each small decision, each encounter, each incident, directed us inexorably to this place at this time.

Moreover, we can trace the conspiracy of our parents, grandparents, and on back to the first appearance of our ancestral human beings, and before that to our ancestral lichen and our ancestral gases, and even before that—all breathing together to bring us here. In each generation, in each moment, birdsong in the trees, stones in the fields, and clouds on the mountains inspired and expired together to bring us here. All the accidents and incidents in the lives of our ancestors—and in the lives of the many other beings in the great hemisphere of our multi-dimensional past—line up on hindsight to make this meeting possible. The mystery of this conjunction is the "why," the "what," the "how."

What is it that caused your great-grandmother on her meeting with your great-grandfather to recognize him as her future mate and the future father of her children? You can call it a mystery, but it is a mystery that does not imply doubt. We can presume she felt something definite. She felt affinity.

"Affinity" identifies the attraction that brought our great-grandparents together, our grandparents together, our parents together, and our own feelings when we join with our mates. It also identifies the attraction that brought all the elements of your body and personality together, and all other bodies and personalities. The many ancestors and sisters and brothers that made you up felt something definite in their own way, and came together to become a particular liver, heart, brain, and quality of intelligence, creativity, spirituality, and overall personality, all of them in keeping with the qualities of your other parts. This conjunction sets the tone of your life.

Affinity, affinity. All beings are made up by affinity. The whole universe, through every dimension, forms a vast net of affinity that is all of a piece—a multi-dimensional web. With any movement within the web, everything moves. Each gesture, each blink brings a new kind of equilibrium and new kinds of interplay throughout the net. This is a never-ending process from the unknown past to the unknown future, and through all other dimensions including the eternal present. Touches that bring joy and harmony bring new interplay and new equilibrium. Touches that cause suffering and death bring new interplay and new equilibrium as well.

Touches that bring joy and harmony are choices for the present and future; touches that cause suffering and death play out the past. Touches for the present and future arise from consciousness, that is to say conscience, for as the *Oxford English Dictionary* tells us, consciousness and conscience have the same definition. To be human in the deepest sense is to be at once aware and concerned. Thus the Buddha responded to the urging of the gods, and arose from beneath the tree to share his realization, first of all with his five disciples in Benares. The world changed radically, but each touch by each being brings joy or sorrow, and everyone and everything adjust. It is a panoramic interplay. The countless adjustments in turn generate the process of constant change in both the objective and the subjective worlds, and this process is never-ending.

My birth and yours were unique, each birth is unique, and every incident across the world and across the great nebulae is unique—and every event unfolds the universe. When I stop to take a drink of water, everyone and everything is at that moment refreshed. My spirit is renewed, my words are clearer in diction and meaning. All beings are thereby more deeply enlightened, and the effects of this deeper enlightenment are felt at once, and they will play themselves out endlessly.

That drink of water came from the kitchen tap, but the tap is, of course, not the source of the water. Countless trees, shrubs, grasses, rivers, lakes, oceans, rocks; various kinds of soil, clouds, wind, the sun, the moon; and many other beings all brought the water to the tap, and the cycle does not end with me.

Each incident in your life and mine, and in all lives, is the interplay of all beings, and this interplay is not only in the objective world, nor is it only in the subjective world. The footstep I hear in the corridor in the early morning is myself, and so is the song of the thrush and the scent of the *puakenikeni*. The sun is my heart, as other teachers have said; the atmosphere is my breath—and this is true for you too, and for the cushions in this hall.

Chance and destiny are not adequate concepts for explaining karma. It's really a dance, isn't it!—a dance of sisters and brothers who come together by mysterious likeness and attraction. Their dances in turn come together with all the dances across the world. For some this can be joyless, even the dance of exploitation and murder, but for the Bodhisattva it is the great cotillion of intimacy.

When you are intimate with any being, you live through what that being lives through. This is a release from preoccupation with yourself, sometimes joyous, sometimes heartrending. It is the Tao of intimacy. Sometimes it is joyous *muditā*, the third of the classical Four Noble Abodes, boundless joy in the liberation of others. Sometimes it is compassionate, which by etymology is suffering with others. Either way, it is Buddha's own release from self, the heart of his teaching and practice.

Intimacy is not passive, and it is not confined to the human world. The song of the thrush recasts you, and in your response you recast the thrush and all beings. If you whistle back, you are creating more consciousness of intimacy, as you will notice by the way she flits closer and sings again. You are constantly being created and you are constantly creating others. When you are open and responsive in this way, then you are turning the Wheel of the Dharma with all beings.

What if you don't know how to whistle? What if you are schooled to ignore the bird or even to kill it? How do you handle a complex of affinities that provide, say, a weakness for alcohol, or an inordinate sex drive? If you find yourself with these tendencies, are you responsible for them? Yes, indeed. Negative tendencies are either rooted in the poisons of self-centeredness, or they lie in the human imperative for union and are somehow twisted up. Prune the poisonous stuff and let the plant grow appropriately to your vow to save the many beings.

How about the complex of affinities that bring you to a bank just as a robber comes in? Are you responsible for this situation? Lots of incidents led up to it, and once their results are in train, you might have no control. There is such a thing as world karma. I as the world am responsible, but there might be no way for me as an individual to help once the crisis has become acute.

Thornton Wilder's novel *The Bridge of San Luis Rey* is the story of people who appear from completely different circumstances to die together when a bridge collapses. It is a lesson in fate by hindsight. After all, what is fate but something in the past, in memory! The novelist takes us back into the lives of members of the disparate group that came to the bridge just before it fails, and shows how inevitable it seems that they should arrive together for their deaths.

The travelers had no control over the collapse of the bridge, and it is a sense of this lack of control that brings to human consciousness the "quiet desperation" of which Thoreau speaks. The arid soil of family misery might smother the spirit of its members for their entire lives—even though they longed from the beginning to work their way through it. The bundle of affinities that is you might not make it through your next financial crisis, or your next psychological depression. Without blaming yourself, however, you can still accept your fundamental responsibility. Terrifying death was the only option for the travelers at the moment the Bridge of San Luis Rey fell into the gorge. In less lethal circumstances you can use your experience of affinity to loosen particular karmic bonds, build upon what has happened, and thus maintain your Bodhisattva path. You might be struggling in a threatening situation, but there you are.

The French mathematician and astronomer Pierre-Simon Laplace, who lived at the end of the eighteenth century and the beginning of the nineteenth century, suggested that the atoms that came together in 1756 to form Mozart's brain did so in an altogether predetermined way. Even when they were merely dust during the aeons before the solar system came into being, they were programmed, Laplace declared, to produce *Don Giovanni* in Prague in 1787.[22] I am not suggesting anything so hopelessly fatalistic. Everything builds anew upon what has gone before, but there are diverse options at every step. You and I and everything and everyone move according to our affinities at each turn, at every moment. Looking back, we can see the mystery of inevitability. Looking ahead we can only hope and trust.

Everything we do from here is our step-by-step practice, using what support we have at hand. It is possible to transmute dependency upon alcohol to action based on a clear sense of mutual interdependence. It is possible to transmute an inordinate sex drive to the path of infinite compassion. It is possible to transmute self-centeredness to a realization of the multi-centered universe. It is possible to transmute a preoccupation with the material world into insight into its ephemeral, and indeed into its potent, yet empty nature.

With this shift you are open. You let sounds enter your body, and they recast you, kill you really, and transform you to a new being who integrates those sounds. You model more and more clearly the character of the universe in your particular Bodhisattva mold.

Of course, in being open to the world you pass off many things, just as you eliminate most of the food you eat. But your excreta don't look like broccoli and carrots anymore. They have been transformed by your process of absorbing what you have an affinity for, and disposing of what is left over. Sometimes you eat inappropriate food, and get sick. So it is important to eat appropriate food.

Toxic sense experiences can make you sick too. It is important to place yourself in a healthful setting when you can, if only by arranging plants in your home. "Sounds of the valley stream wash your ears clean; / the canopy of pine trees touches your eyes green."[23] Yet even the sounds of traffic and the squabble of neighbors can be good reminders to persevere. Nothing is static. When you persevere you unfold. Unfolding is the Buddha Way.

From *International Journal of Transpersonal Studies*

Verses for Zen Buddhist Practice

Waking up in the morning
   I vow with all beings
to listen to those whom I love,
especially to things they don't say.

Watching the sky before dawn
   I vow with all beings
to open those flawless eyes
that welcomed the morning star.

Lighting a candle for Buddha
   I vow with all beings
to honor your clear affirmation:
"Forget yourself and you're free."

Turning for refuge in Buddha
   I vow with all beings
to walk past pure and impure
straight down the Middle Way.

Turning for refuge in Dharma
    I vow with all beings
to oil and sharpen my tools
and fashion a home of the Tao.

Turning for refuge in Sangha
    I vow with all beings
to open myself to the geckos
and the strange behavior of friends.

Holding hands in a ring
    I vow with all beings
to ease the pain in the ring
of breath around the world.

When someone close to me dies
    I vow with all beings
to settle in ultimate closeness
and continue our dialogue there.

Facing my imminent death
    I vow with all beings
to go with the natural process,
at peace with whatever comes.

When I turn into somebody nasty
    I vow with all beings
to reflect on how it all happened
and acknowledge my long-hidden tail.

When everything loses its meaning
    I vow with all beings
to honor this intimate teaching
that clears my dependence away.

When I stroll around in the city
    I vow with all beings

to notice how lichen and grasses
never give up in despair.

Watching a spider at work
    I vow with all beings
to cherish the web of the universe:
touch one point and everything moves.

Hearing the crickets at night
    I vow with all beings
to find my place in the harmony
crickets enjoy with the stars.

When a car goes by late at night
    I vow with all beings
to remember the lonely bakers
who secretly nurture us all.

When a train rattles by at the crossing
    I vow with all beings
to remember my mother and father
and imagine their thoughts in the night.

When the racket can't be avoided
    I vow with all beings
to close my eyes for a moment
and find my treasure right there.

Accepting the fault of another
    I vow with all beings
to encourage the original talent
that endeavors to make itself known.

When people talk about war
    I vow with all beings
to raise my voice in the chorus
and speak of original peace.

If the bomb goes up after all
    I vow with all beings
to remember my mother's assurance:
"Never you mind, it's all right."

If the bomb goes up at last
    I vow with all beings
to relinquish even the Earth
to the unborn there all along.

Regarding national interest
    I vow with all beings
to show how conventional wisdom
is not always common sense.

With jungles and oceans in danger
    I vow with all beings
to return to my zazen practice
and settle there right in the Way.

With jungles and oceans in danger
    I vow with all beings
to suggest that interdependence
is the Way, as the Buddha maintained.

With tropical forests in danger
    I vow with all beings
to raise hell with the people responsible
and slash my consumption of trees.

Watching gardeners label their plants
    I vow with all beings
to practice the old horticulture
and let plants identify me.

On reading the words of Ta-hui
    I vow with all beings

not to diminish my betters
who lived to the point long ago.

On reading the words of Thoreau
    I vow with all beings
to cherish our home-grown sages
who discern the perennial Way.

Falling asleep at last
    I vow with all beings
to enjoy the dark and the silence
and rest in the vast unknown.

From *The Dragon Who Never Sleeps:*
Verses for Zen Buddhist Practice

"Do You Remember?"

A BUDDHIST REFLECTION

Ordinary memory is affected by the meditation practiced in Zen Buddhism, and perhaps in other Buddhist traditions as well. As you sit on your meditation cushions, you forget everything that would otherwise press on your consciousness, and focus exclusively on counting your breaths, on facing your kōan, or on the practice of sitting in pure vacancy.

After it is imprinted, the theme of your practice in the meditation hall comes up naturally as you pursue workaday affairs. Schedules and obligations tend to fade—to the extent that "Zen memory" is good-humored slang among practitioners for their tendency to forget important matters. Thus I learned early on to carry a notebook in my shirt pocket. (The phenomenon is not so severe, however, that I forget to take out my notebook and look in it from time to time!)

The inconvenience of carrying a notebook is offset by the delight of realizing, at least to some extent, "why the sea is boiling hot, and whether pigs have wings." An insight into existence and non-existence and their complementarity, and other similarly deep realizations, can be liberating, and I treat my notebook as simply part of a larger practice.

Other experiences possible in Buddhist practice include what Mircea Eliade called the "eternal return." Past times, hundreds, even thousands, of years past, are recalled to the personal present. For example, in Case 1 of *The Gateless Barrier*, a monk asks Chao-chou, "Has the dog Buddha-nature?" Chao-chou responds, "Mu" ("Doesn't have it"). When you realize the hard nut of Chao-chou's response, then, Wu-men says,

> You will not only interview Chao-chou intimately, you will walk
> hand in hand with all the ancestors in the successive generations
> of our lineage, the hair of your eyebrows entangled with theirs,
> seeing with the same eyes, hearing with the same ears. Won't
> that be joyous!

This is a model of sacred memory, a peak experience. It is kept alive in the dedication of sūtras to past ancestors and teachers, but it should not be considered to be a be-all and end-all kind of realization, but rather a temporary condition called *makyō,* "uncanny realm," a phase of practice which simply affirms that you are on the true path. It is not experienced exclusively in the context of Zen Buddhism. Recollection is essential in Pure Land schools in the practice of the *Nien-fo* (*Nembutsu*—"Recalling Buddha"). The practitioner chants *"Na Mi-to Fo"* (*"Namu Amida Butsu,"* "Veneration to Amitābha Buddha"). At the temple Rokuharamitsu in Kyoto, you can see the image of Kūya Shōnin, an early Pure Land teacher who went about the country calling out *"Namu Amida Butsu."* The sculptor renders him as a young pilgrim walking slightly bent over, with a row of little Amitābha Buddhas coming out of his mouth on a wire, representing the thread and content of his devotions.[24] Kūya Shōnin's every breath is Amitābha Buddha. He is *re-membering* Amitābha Buddha. D. T. Suzuki quotes a certain Myōkōnin, a Pure Land mystic:

> How grateful I am now! *Namu Amida Butsu.* I was utterly blind
> and did not know it. How shameful to have thought I was all
> right. I thought the *Nembutsu* was my own, but it was not. It
> was Amida's call.[25]

Another aspect of this "eternal return" kind of recollection relates to karma. "Karma" is the Buddhist term that is usually understood to mean "cause and effect," but it also refers to the mystery of affinity:

> The master Punyamitra said to Prajñātāra, "Do you remember events of the past?"
>
> Prajñātāra said, "I remember in a distant *kalpa* I was living in the same place as you; you were expounding the great wisdom and I was reciting the most profound scripture. This event today is in conformity with past cause."
>
> (TL-27)

Kalpa is sometimes translated as "eon"—inadequately, I think. It is a notion that rises from the boundless imagination of the mind of India, and is surely one of the Buddhist terms that is best left untranslated. It is explicated in a number of artful ways, for example, the length of time it would take a cube of iron, one hundred miles on a side, to be worn completely away by a celestial maiden who descends once every hundred years and brushes the top with her ethereal garments. Such a past is so far in the past that it transcends past—yet, Prajñātāra says, by our affinity, I recall its presence. We are together again.

If you are not mature, however, karma can evoke an "eternal return" very negatively. Here, for instance, is the remarkable story of the return of an edible fungus, also from *The Transmission of the Light:*

> When Kānadeva was traveling around teaching, he came to Kapilavastu and visited a rich man in whose garden grew a fungus on a tree. It was like a mushroom, with an exceedingly fine flavor. Only the man and his second son Rāhulata partook of it. After they ate it, it regrew, and when they ate it again, it sprouted again. Other members of the family could not find it.
>
> The rich man asked Kānadeva about this and he replied, "Once in the past, you gave offerings of food to a monk, and that monk's perception of the Way was not clear. He could not receive alms without feeling obliged to you, and so he became a tree fungus to repay you. Since just you and your second son provided offerings with pure sincerity, you are the ones who have been able to partake of it."

In attendance upon Kānadeva, on hearing about past cause,
Rāhulata experienced enlightenment.

(TL-16)

Dante himself could not have imagined worse retribution or a more
vivid metaphor for this poor monk's failure in his life to find liberation from his deeply held sense that he was unworthy of kindness.
After his death, his feeling of inadequacy is recollected in the edible
fungus, to be eaten again and again for all time. Keizan Jōkin, com-
piler of *The Transmission of the Light*, comments on this case in a
poem:

How sad that his eye of the Way was not clear;
astray within, compensating others for his lack;
the cycle of karma has not yet come to an end.

So it seems to me that memory, in its deepest, most sacred sense for
the Buddhist, comes with emancipation from self-concern. You are
then in touch with the eternal, the place where giving and receiving
are interactions within the same personal container, where Kānadeva
can crack my lectern with his gavel.

What might be the significance of the "eternal return" for North
Americans? Many traditional peoples, including Native Hawaiians
and Alaskans, still recall the eternal, though of course their expression differs from people to people. Contemporary Hawaiians are re-
constructing their religion by the place-names of their land, by the
names of subtly different kinds of meteorological phenomena, and
by names of plants, trees, birds, insects, animals, and fish. The rest
of us tend to float in our bioregions, and indeed in our families, ca-
reers, and temples of religion, more or less oblivious of inner histo-
ries and their implications. We even mock our Asian sisters and
brothers for lighting incense before photographs of their ancestors,
and thus we expose our own inability to recollect with gratitude.

When I visited Wendell Berry in Port Royal, Kentucky, he took
me into town to visit his great-grandfather's grave. How many of us
can do that! How many of us live in the same town as our parents,
much less our great-grandparents! How many of us can even name
our eight great-grandparents!

As a teacher of Buddhism, I find myself offering a reconstruction of the old Buddhist models of mercy, noble action, and enlightenment. We recall our profound humanity through their images: Avalokiteshvara, Samantabhadra, Shākyamuni. We live up to ourselves as those marvelous ancient archetypes, as well as we can, and find ourselves rooted and enriched in their perennial teachings.

Incidentally, this dimension of memory is also the place of compassion, as distinguished from mercy, for in our recollection of those old teachers as ourselves we suffer with them, and all other beings as well—but that is another story.

From Kenyon Review

About Money

In the Buddhist tradition, money is both clean and dirty. It is dāna, the gift, which supports the temple and its monks and nuns. But it is handled very ritualistically, enclosed in white paper, often conveyed on a tray. It must be purified somehow.

Money is the fodder of Māra, The Destroyer, who becomes fatter and fatter with each financial deal at the expense of the many beings. However, money can also be a device for Kuan-yin, the incarnation of mercy, whose thousand hands hold a thousand tools for rescuing those same beings.

Both Kuan-yin and Māra function as the Net of Indra. Each point of the Net perfectly reflects each other point. Each point is a hologram. Māra says, "All of you are me." Kuan-yin says, "I am all of you." It's the very same thing, except in attitude. Attitude poisons or nurtures the interbeing.

Ta-sui announced that you and I perish along with the universe in the Kalpa Fire (BCR-29). Joyous news! Joyous news! Money disappears. Suffering disappears. Even Māra and Kuan-yin disappear in the laughter of Ta-sui. How to find Ta-sui's joy is the question. The path is eightfold, the Buddha said: Right Views, Right Resolve, Right Speech, Right Action, Right Livelihood, Right Effort, Right Recollection, and Right Samādhi.

Māra hates Ta-sui for he confirms the demon's worst fears and

seems to exult in them. How can he joke about the ultimate end!
How can he threaten the structure of power and the system of acquisition! Māra hates the Eightfold Path because it undermines the
ramparts of his firehouse. The firehouse becomes a hostel and his
champion firemen become nurses. Who will put out the Kalpa Fire?

Meanwhile Kuan-yin reposes on her comfortable rock by the
waterfall, shaded by a willow tree. People say they don't like bowing
to Kuan-yin because she is just an icon or an idol. Of course it's nonsense to bow to an idol. Kuan-yin doesn't think of herself as an idol.
Her idol is her imperative, her imperative is her Right Views, her
Right Views are her blood and guts.

Kuan-yin's practice is elemental too. It is embodied everywhere—
as the Earth, for example, exchanging energy with Uranus and
Jupiter and Mercury and the others together with the Sun as they
plunge on course through the plenum. It is embodied as the plenum
itself with its incredible dynamics of nebulae and measureless, empty
spaces. You will find the dāna of Kuan-yin in tiny systems of mutual
support as well—as the termite, for example, nurturing parasites
who digest our foundations in exchange for a dark wet place to live.

Primal society also embodies the dāna of Kuan-yin, circulating
the gift that nurtures its families and clans. At a single festival, a
necklace of precious shells becomes two dozen precious pendants.
At a single market holiday, a knife becomes salt and salt becomes a
colt. The honor of a new chief is spread by blankets far and wide.

Of course, Māra blows his smoke through these exchanges. Did
the primal peoples know Māra from Kuan-yin? They never heard of
either, of course, but they knew greed and pride when they saw them
and so do we.

Māra isn't an icon either, yet he is bowing to himself all day long.
He hates the notion of circulating the gift. Instead he circulates the
folks. He maneuvers them, lines them up before his machinery, and
then offers them their products for their money. He circulates the
animals and their products, the grasses and their products, the trees
and their products. Broken glass set in cement on the tops of high
stone walls protects his treasure from those whose diligence pro-
duced it. Gates and armed guards and police dogs protect his children and judges protect his bookkeepers. With his ardent practice

the poor get so poor that he must give a little back to keep the arrangement functioning. He is ennobled and great institutions of benevolence bear his name. Bits of nature are conserved. Peruvian musicians are recorded. Yet the karma of wealth can be inspired by Kuan-yin. The wealthy are stewards named Kuan-yin.

All the while Kuan-yin herself sustains the poor. They are her teacher. She doesn't circulate the folks or their products; she leaves them be; she leaves the birds and the fish and the animals be, the stones and trees and clouds be—and does not move them around. The walls with their broken glass and guarded gates hold her in her place, outside. Out there, if she keeps the folks entertained, she might even get a grant. You can have a grant and do your thing, or you can go to jail. It's up to you, Kuan-yin.

It isn't easy for Māra to manipulate people and things. He practices so diligently that he forgoes golf and the theater sometimes. Kuan-yin forgoes golf and the theater too as she sits in Royal Ease, delighting in the birds as they dip in and out of the spray. But Māra never finds ease of any kind, not even in the middle of the night. His prostate gives him hell and he sweats with fear.

This is the uneasy, primordial mind, arising from the muck, as reptilian as any dinosaur. It is much older than Kuan-yin. How old is Kuan-yin? Don't say ageless. You are just letting Māra do his dirty work unchallenged. Don't say she is the moment. That is Māra's view as well, pouring out the drinks at his villa on Majorca.

Māra can be your fall-back mind and mine as well, always there. Kuan-yin, on the other hand, is eternally fresh and new. She can come into our time and go out of it freely, a trick Māra never learned. We cannot fall back on Kuan-yin; we have to remember her. With a single Māra-thought we are in his reins, giddiyup horsie! With a single Kuan-yin thought, we are laughing at the puppies. Namo Avalokiteshvara Mahāsattva! Namu Kanzeon Makasatsu! Veneration to the Great Being Who Perceives the Sounds of the World!

Māra and Kuan-yin create and cultivate many nets within the Net of Indra. Like the stars, the points in these lesser nets survive by exchanging energy, called money by Māra, called money by Kuan-yin sometimes. There are industries and collectives, golf clubs and base communities. In the lesser nets, Māra dominates, Kuan-yin

subverts. Māra co-opts the subversion. Kuan-yin chooses to counter
with her money sometimes, if it will keep the waterfall abundant
and the birds happy. Sometimes Kuan-yin runs an industry. Sometimes Māra runs a collective. Sometimes there are base communities within golf clubs. Sometimes there are golf clubs within base
communities.

It is possible to play endlessly with archetypes and metaphors.
Māra as the reptile mind can be called the id. Kuan-yin can be called
the superego. When the id is boss the forests burn in Revelations'
self-fulfilling prophecy. When the superego is boss the fires of love
are extinguished. But Māra and Kuan-yin are not Māra and Kuan-
yin; therefore we give them such names. Wipe away the terminology! Wipe away the archetypes! Let Māra and Kuan-yin disappear!

The anguish of nations and families arises from an anxiety to
prove oneself—or oneself together with kin and compatriots. The
vow to save everybody and everything can bring fun to the dinner
table and to international festivals. But proving yourself is the Way
of the Buddha, bringing forth your latent pantheon of Mañjushrī,
Samantabhadra, and the others as the self. (The archetypes keep
popping up anyway!) The vow to save everybody and everything can
be the imperative to bring Mother Hubbards to heathen Hawaiians.

Checks, bills, bonds—the tokens of power—transport solutions
of sugar and salt to rescue infants from dysentery. They prime the
pump of life and order eggplant parmesan at Auntie Pasto's Restaurant. They build the dam of energy. Moose and beavers and primal
people die. Checks, bills, and bonds dance to the music of attitude.
Māra has his music, Kuan-yin hers.

We're all in this great mess together. You can't hide out and drink
from streams and eat from trees. Or if you do you are languishing
at the top of a hundred-foot pole. Ch'ang-sha will kick you off
(BS-79). The culture we treasure does not exist apart. The munici-
pal symphony, museums, galleries, theaters, bookshops, even our
practice centers are intimately integrated into the acquisitive system. We have to work with this fact somehow. It is not clear to me,
as it may not be clear to you, how to go about this. As you go along,
the qualms can get worse. You can find yourself in a truly dark night,
with many misgivings about the Way and doubts about how to deal

with the terrible ethical problems that confront everyone—teachers, social workers, managers, homemakers, plumbers, receptionists.

The Japanese had one way to deal with guilt about money. In Kamakura, there is a shrine dedicated to purifying money called Zeniarai Benten, "the Benzaiten Shrine for Washing Money." It is still active, tucked away in the hills north of the city. Benten, or Benzaiten, is a figure derived from the Hindu deity Sarasvatī, venerated originally as the patron of music and poetry. According to Japanese folk religious beliefs, she also helps her followers acquire wealth by honorable means. If the means are not honorable, that's okay. At Zeniarai Benten, you can purify such money by washing it in the Benten's holy spring. Originally, of course, it was coins that were washed, but now the purification ritual includes drying paper money in the sunshine, under Benten's watchful eyes.

The rituals of Zeniarai Benten don't really work at levels of, say, international banking. In fact, they don't work anywhere in our society, for all money is tainted, and it is not at all clear what to do about it. I suggest that the way to deal with a lack of clarity is to accept it. It's all right not to be clear. The practice is to clarify. Moreover, you're working always with your ego. You never get rid of your ego. Your ego is just your self-image. Burnish your ego down to its basic configurations. Then it will shine forth. You can forget yourself as your vows take over your practice, like the birds in the spray of the waterfall.

From *Original Dwelling Place: Zen Buddhist Essays*

Envisioning the Future

"Small is beautiful," E. F. Schumacher said, but it was not merely size that concerned him. "Buddhist economics must be very different from the economics of modern materialism," he said. "The Buddhist sees the essence of civilization not in a multiplication of wants but in the purification of human character."[26]

Schumacher evokes the etymology of "civilization" as the process of civilizing, of becoming and making civil. Many neglect this ancient wisdom of words in their pursuit of acquisition and consumption, and those with some civility of mind find themselves caught in the dominant order by requirements of time and energy to feed their families. As the acquisitive system burgeons, its collapse is foreshadowed by epidemics, famine, war, and the despoliation of the Earth and its forests, waters, and air.

I envision a growing crisis across the world as managers and their multinational systems continue to deplete finite human and natural resources. Great corporations, underwritten by equally great financial institutions, flush away the human habitat and the habitat of thousands of other species far more ruthlessly and on a far greater scale than gold miners who once hosed down mountains in California. International consortia rule sovereign over all other political authority. Presidents and parliaments and the United Nations itself are delegating decision-making powers and oversight that enable faceless and increasingly unaccountable corporations to plunder resources and pillage economies.

Citizens of goodwill everywhere despair of the political process. The old enthusiasm to turn out on election day has drastically waned. In the United States, commonly fewer than 50 percent of those eligible cast a ballot. It has become clear that political parties are ineffectual—whether Republican or Democrat, Conservative or Labor—and that practical alternatives must be found.

We can begin our task of developing such alternatives by meeting in informal groups within our larger Sanghas to examine politics and economics from a Buddhist perspective. It will be apparent that traditional teachings of interdependence bring into direct question the rationale of accumulating wealth and of governing by hierarchical authority. What, then, is to be done?

Something, certainly. Our practice of the Brahma Vihāras—kindliness, compassion, goodwill, and equanimity—would be meaningless if it excluded people, animals, and plants outside our formal Sangha. Nothing in the teachings justifies us as a cult that ignores the world. We are not survivalists. On the contrary, it is clear that we're in it together with all beings.

The time has surely come when we must speak out as Buddhists, with firm views of harmony as the Tao. I suggest that it is also time for us to take ourselves in hand. We ourselves can establish and engage in the very policies and programs of social and ecological protection and respect that we have heretofore so futilely demanded from authorities. This would be engaged Buddhism, where the Sangha is not merely parallel to the forms of conventional society and not merely metaphysical in its universality.

This greater Sangha is, moreover, not merely Buddhist. It is possible to identify an eclectic religious evolution that is already under way, one to which we can lend our energies. It can be traced to the beginning of this century, when Tolstoy, Ruskin, Thoreau, and the New Testament fertilized the *Bhagavad Gita* and other Indian texts in the mind and life of M. K. Gandhi. The Southern Buddhist leaders A. T. Ariyaratne and Sulak Sivaraksa and their followers in Sri Lanka and Thailand have adapted Gandhi's "Independence for the Masses" to their own national needs and established programs of

self-help and community self-reliance that offer regenerative cells of
fulfilling life within their materialist societies.

Mahāyāna has lagged behind these developments in South and
Southeast Asia. In the past, a few Far Eastern monks like Gyōgi
Bosatsu devoted themselves to good works, another few like Hakuin
Zenji raised their voices to the lords of their provinces about the
poverty of common people, and still others in Korea and China organized peasant rebellions, but today we do not see widespread
movements in traditional Mahāyāna countries akin to the village
self-help programs of Ariyaratne in Sri Lanka, or empowerment networks similar to those established by Sulak in Thailand.

"Self-help" is an inadequate translation of *swaraj*, the term Gandhi
used to designate his program of personal and village independence.
He was a great social thinker who identified profound human imperatives and natural social potentials. He discerned how significant
changes arise from people themselves, rather than from efforts on
the part of governments to fine-tune the system.

South Africa and Eastern Europe are two modern examples of
change from the bottom up. Perceptions shift, the old notions
cannot hold—and down come the state and its ideology. Similar
changes are brewing, despite repressions, in Central America. In the
United States, the economy appears to be holding up by force of
habit and inertia in the face of unimaginable debt, while city governments break down and tens of thousands of families sleep in
makeshift shelters.

Not without protest. In the United States, tireless voices of cogent dissidents remind us and our legislators and judges that our
so-called civilization is using up the world. Such spokespeople for
conservation, social justice, and peace help to organize opposition
to benighted powers and their policies and thus divert the most out-
rageous programs to less flagrant alternatives.

Like Ariyaratne and Sulak in their social contexts, we as Western
Buddhists also modify the activist role to reflect our culture as well
as our spiritual heritage. But surely the Dharmic fundamentals
would remain. Right Action is part of the Eightfold Path that begins and ends with Right Samādhi. Formal practice could also in-

volve study, reciting the ancient texts together, Dharma discussion, religious festivals, and sharing for mutual support.

In our workaday lives, practice would be less formal, and could include farming and protecting forests. In the United States, some of our leading intellectuals cultivate the ground. The distinguished poet W. S. Merwin has through his own labor created an arboretum of native Hawaiian plants at his home on Maui. He is thus restoring an important aspect of Hawaiian culture, in gentle opposition to the monocultures of pineapple, sugar, and macadamia nut trees around him. Another progressive intellectual, Wendell Berry, author of some thirty books of poetry, essays, and fiction, is also a small farmer. In Kansas, still another reformative intellectual and prominent essayist, Wes Jackson, conducts a successful and practical research institute for small farmers. Networking is an important feature of Jackson's teaching. He follows the Amish adage that at least seven cooperating families must live near each other in order for their small individual farms to succeed.[27]

All such enterprise takes hard work and character practice. The two go together. Character, Schumacher says, "is formed primarily by a man's work. And work, properly conducted in conditions of human dignity and freedom, blesses ourselves and equally our products."[28] With dignity and freedom we can collaborate, labor together, on small farms and in cooperatives of all kinds—savings and loan societies, social agencies, clinics, galleries, theaters, markets, and schools—forming networks of decent and dignified modes of life alongside and even within the frames of conventional power. I visualize our humane network having more and more appeal as the power structure continues to fall apart.

This collaboration in networks of mutual aid would follow from our experience of pratītya-samutpāda, mutually dependent arising. All beings arise in systems of biological affinity, whether or not they are even "alive" in a narrow sense. We are born in a world in which all things nurture us. As we mature in our understanding of the Dharma, we take responsibility for pratītya-samutpāda and continually divert our infantile expectations of being nurtured to an adult responsibility for nurturing others.

Buddhadāsa Bhikkhu says:

> The entire cosmos is a cooperative. The sun, the moon, and the
> stars live together as a cooperative. The same is true for humans
> and animals, trees and soil. Our bodily parts function as a coopera-
> tive. When we realize that the world is a mutual, interdependent,
> cooperative enterprise, that human beings are all mutual friends in
> the process of birth, old age, suffering and death, then we can build
> a noble, even heavenly environment. If our lives are not based in
> this truth, then we shall all perish.[29]

Returning to this original track is the path of individuation that
transforms childish self-centeredness to mature views and conduct.
With careful, constant discipline on the Eightfold Noble Path of the
Dharma, greed becomes dāna, exploitation becomes networking.
The root-brain of the newborn becomes the compassionate, religious mind of the elder. Outwardly the elder does not differ from
other members; her or his needs for food, clothing, shelter, medicine, sleep, and affection are the same as anyone else's. But the elder's
smile is startlingly generous.

It is a smile that rises from the Buddha's own experience. Pratītya-
samutpāda is not just a theory but the profound realization that I
arise with all beings and all beings arise with me. I suffer with all beings; all beings suffer with me. The path to this fulfillment is long
and sometimes hard; it involves restraint and disengagement from
ordinary concerns. It is a path that advances over plateaus on its way,
and it is important not to camp too long on any one plateau. That
plateau is not yet your true home.

Dharmic society begins and prevails with individuals walking this
path of compassionate understanding, discerning the noble option
at each moment and allowing the other options to drop away. It is a
society that looks familiar, with cash registers and merchandise, fire-
fighters and police, theaters and festivals, but the inner flavor is completely different. Like a Chinese restaurant in Madras: the decor is
familiar, but the curry is surprising.

In the United States of America, the notion of compassion as the
touchstone of conduct and livelihood is discouraged by the culture.
Yet here and there one can find Catholic Workers feeding the poor,

religious builders creating housing for the homeless, traditional people returning to their old ways of agriculture.

Small is the watchword. Huge is ugly, as James Hillman has pointed out.[30] Huge welfare goes awry, huge housing projects become slums worse than the ones they replace, huge environmental organizations compromise with their own principles in order to survive, huge sovereignty movements fall apart with internal dissension. The point is that huge *anything* collapses, including governments, banks, multinational corporations, and the global economy itself—because all things collapse. Small can be fluid, ready to change.

The problem is that the huge might not collapse until it brings everything else down with it. Time may not be on the side of the small. Our awareness of this unprecedented danger impels us to take stock and do what we can with our vision of a Dharmic society.

The traditional Sangha serves as a model for enterprise in this vision. A like-minded group of five can be a Sangha. It can grow to a modest size, split into autonomous groups, and then network. As autonomous lay Buddhist associations, these little communities will not be Sanghas in the traditional sense but will be inheritors of the name and of many of the original intentions. They will also be inheritors of the Base Community movements in Latin America and the Philippines—Catholic networks that are inspired by traditional religion, and also by nineteenth-century anarchism. Catholic Base Communities serve primarily as worship groups, study groups, moral support societies, and nuclei for social action. They can also form the staff and support structure of small enterprises.

The Catholic Base Community is grounded in Bible study and discussions. In these meetings, one realizes for oneself that Jesus is an ally of those who would liberate the poor and oppressed. This is Liberation Theology of the heart and gut. It is an internal transformation that releases one's power to labor intimately with others to do God's work.

The Buddhist counterpart of Bible study would be the contemplation and realization of pratītya-samutpāda, of the unity of such intellectual opposites as the one and the many found in Zen practice, and the interdependence presented in the sacred texts, such as the *Hua-yen ching*. Without a literal God as an ally, one is thrown back on one's own resources to find the original track, and there one finds the ever-shifting universe with its recurrent metaphors of interbeing to be the constant ally.

There are other lessons from Liberation Theology. We learn that we need not quit our jobs to form autonomous lay Sanghas. Most Base Communities in Latin America and the Philippines are simply groups that have weekly meetings. In Buddhist countries, coworkers in the same institution can come together for mutual aid and religious practice. In the largest American corporations, such as IBM, there will surely be a number of Buddhists who could form similar groups. Or we can organize cohousing arrangements that provide for the sharing of home maintenance, childcare, and transportation and thus can free up individuals for their turns at meditation, study, and social action. Buddhist Peace Fellowship chapters might consider how the Base Community design and ideal could help to define and enhance their purposes and programs.

Thus it wouldn't be necessary for the people who work in corporations or government agencies to resign when they start to meet in Buddhist Base Communities. They can remain within their corporation or government agency and encourage the evolution and networking of communities, not necessarily Buddhist, among other corporations and agencies. Of course, the future is obscure, but I find myself relating to the revolutionary mythology of the Industrial Workers of the World (the famous "Wobblies" of the early twentieth century) that as the old forms collapse, the new networks can flourish.

Of course, the collapse, if any, is not going to happen tomorrow. We must not underestimate the staying power of capitalism. Moreover, the complex, dynamic process of networking cannot be put abruptly into place. In studying Mondragón, the prototype of a large, dynamic cooperative enterprise in the three Basque counties of northern Spain, William and Kathleen Whyte counted more than a hundred worker cooperatives and supporting organizations with 19,500 workers in 1988. These are small—even tiny—enterprises, linked by very little more than simple goodwill and a profound sense of the common good. Together they form a vast complex of banking, industry, and education that evolved slowly, if steadily, from a single class for manual training set up in 1943.[31]

We must begin with our own training classes. Mondragón is worth our study, as are the worker-owned industries closer to home —for example, the plywood companies in the Pacific Northwest. In 1972 Carl Bellas studied twenty-one companies whose inner structures consisted of motivated committees devoted to the many aspects of production and whose managers were responsible to a general assembly.[32] Reconciliation and harmony are not abstract concepts.

In the course of our training classes, it is also essential that we examine the mechanism of the dominant economy. Usury and its engines have built our civilization. The word "usury" has an old meaning and a modern one. In the spirit of the old meaning of usury—lending money at interest—the banks of the world, large and small, have provided a way for masses of people for many generations across the world to own homes and to operate farms and businesses. In the spirit of the modern meaning of usury, however— the lending of money at *excessive* interest—a number of these banks have become gigantic, ultimately enabling corporations almost as huge to squeeze small farmers from their lands, small shopkeepers from their stores, and to burden homeowners with car and appliance payments and lifetime mortgages.

For over 1,800 years, the Catholic Church had a clear and consistent doctrine on the sin of usury in the old sense of simply lending money at interest. Nearly thirty official church documents were published over the centuries to condemn it.

Out of the other side of the Vatican, however, came an unspoken tolerance for usury so long as it was practiced by Jews. The Church blossomed as the Medici family of bankers underwrote the Renaissance, but at the same time, pogroms were all but sanctioned. The moral integrity of the Church was compromised. Finally, early in the nineteenth century, this kind of hypocrisy was abandoned—too late in some ways, for the seeds of the Holocaust had already been planted. Today the Pope apologizes to the Jews, and even the Vatican has its bank. Usury in both old and modern implications is standard operating procedure in contemporary world culture.

Like the Medicis, however, modern bankers can be philanthropic. In almost every city in the United States, bankers and their institutions are active in support of museums, symphony orchestras, clinics, and schools. Banks have almost the same social function as traditional Asian temples: looking after the poor and promoting cultural activities. This is genuine beneficence, and it is also very good public relations.

In the subdivisions of some American cities, such as the Westwood suburb of Los Angeles, the banks even look like temples. They are indeed the temples of our socioeconomic system. The banker's manner is friendly yet his interest in us is, on the bottom line, limited to the interest he extracts from us.

One of the banks in Hawai'i has the motto "We say 'Yes' to you," meaning "We are eager for your money." Their motto is sung interminably on the radio and TV, and when it appears in newspapers and magazines we find ourselves humming the tune. Similar lightweight yet insidious persuasions are used with Third World governments to generate more lending profit through the construction of freeways and hydroelectric dams and skyscrapers.

Governments and developers in the Third World are, in fact, the dupes of the World Bank and the International Monetary Fund (IMF):

> It is important to note that IMF programs are not designed to increase the welfare of the population. They are designed to bring the external payments account into balance. . . . The IMF is the ultimate guardian of the interests of capitalists and bankers doing international business.

These are observations of the economist Kari Polyani Levitt, quoted as the epigraph of a study entitled *Banking on Poverty*.[33] The editor of this work concludes that policies of the IMF and the World Bank make severe intrusions upon the sovereign responsibilities of many governments of the Third World:

> These policies not only often entail major additional cuts in the living standards of the poorest sectors of Third World societies but are also unlikely to produce the economic results claimed on their behalf.[34]

Grand apartment buildings along the Bay of Bombay show that the First World with its wealth and leisure is alive and well among the prosperous classes of the old Third World. The Third World with its poverty and disease flares up in cities and farms of the old First World. In *The Prosperous Few and the Restless Many*, Noam Chomsky writes:

> In 1971, Nixon dismantled the Bretton Woods system, thereby deregulating currencies. That, and a number of other changes, tremendously expanded the amount of unregulated capital in the world and accelerated what's called the globalization of the economy. That's a fancy way of saying that you can export jobs to high-repression, low-wage areas.[35]

Factories in South Central Los Angeles moved to Eastern Europe, Mexico, and Indonesia, attracting workers from farms. In the meantime, victims in South Central Los Angeles and other depressed areas of the United States, including desolate rural towns, turn in large numbers to crime and drugs to relieve their seemingly hopeless poverty. In the mid-1990s, one million American citizens were in prison, with another two million or so on parole or probation. More than half of these had been convicted of drug-related offenses. It's going to get worse. Just as the citizens of Germany elected Hitler chancellor in 1932, opening the door to fascism quite voluntarily, so the citizens of the United States have elected a Congress that seems bent on creating a permanent underclass, with prison expansion to provide much of its housing.

Is there no hope? If big banks, multinational corporations, and cooperating governments maintain their strategy to keep the few prosperous and the many in poverty, then where can small farmers and shopkeepers and managers of clinics and social agencies turn for the money they need to start up their enterprises and to meet emergencies? In the United States, government aid to small businesses and farms, like grants to clinics and social agencies, is being cut back. Such aid is meager or non-existent in other parts of the world, with notable exceptions in northern Europe.

Revolving credit associations called *hui* in China, *kye* in Korea, and *tanamoshi* in Japan have for generations down to the present provided start-up money for farmers and owners of small businesses, as well as short-term loans for weddings, funerals, and tuition. In Siam there are rice banks and buffalo banks designed for sharing resources and production among the working poor. The Grameen banks of Bangladesh are established for the poor by the poor. Shares are tiny amounts, the equivalent of just a few dollars, but in quantity they are adequate for loans at very low interest to farmers and shopkeepers.

Similar traditional cooperatives exist in most other cultures. Such associations are made up of like-minded relatives, friends, neighbors, coworkers, or alumnae. Arrangements for borrowing and repayment among these associations differ, even within the particular cultures. In the United States, cooperatives have been set up outside the system, using scrip and labor credits, most notably, Ithaca Hours, involving 1,200 enterprises in the mid-1990s. The basic currency in the latter arrangement is equal to ten dollars, considered to be the hourly wage, subject to change with inflation. It is guaranteed by the promise of work by members of the system.

We can utilize such models and develop our own projects to fit our particular requirements and circumstances. We can stand on our own feet and help one another in systems that are designed to serve the many, rather than to aggrandize the wealth of the few.

Again, small is beautiful. Whereas large can be beautiful too, if it is a network of autonomous units, monolithic structures are problematic even when fueled by religious idealism. Islamic economists theorize about a national banking system that functions by investment rather than by a system of interest. However, they point out that such a structure can only work in a country where laws forbid lending at interest and where administrators follow up violations with prosecution.[36] So for those of us who do not dwell in certain Islamic countries that seek to take the Koran literally, such as Pakistan and some of the Gulf states, the macrocosmic concept of interest-free banking is probably not practical.

Of course, revolving credit associations have problems, as do all societies of human beings. There are defaults, but peer pressure among friends and relatives keeps these to a minimum. The discipline of Dharma practice would further minimize such problems in a Buddhist loan society. The meetings could be structured with ritual and Dharma talks to remind the members that they are practicing the virtues of the Buddha Dharma and bringing pratītya-samutpāda into play in their workaday lives. They are practicing trust, for all beings are the Buddha, as Hakuin Zenji and countless other teachers remind us. Surely only serious emergencies would occasion a delinquency, and contingency planning could allow for such situations.

Dharma practice could also play a role in the small Buddhist farm or business enterprise. In the 1970s, under the influence of Buddhists, the Honest Business movement arose in San Francisco. This was a network of small shops whose proprietors and assistants met from time to time to encourage one another. Their policy was to serve the public and to accept enough in return from their sales to support themselves, sustain their enterprises, and pay the rent. Their account books were on the sales counters, open to their customers.

Honest Business has evolved over the decades to sophisticated and organic programs that are inspired by progressive thinkers like Paul Hawken, whose book *Growing a Business* is one of more than a hundred books on the market whose titles echo his. The ideals of the old anarchists have taken root, blossomed, and borne fruit, and such enterprises as Patagonia, Ben and Jerry's Homemade Ice Cream, and the University National Bank of Palo Alto, California, prove that decency, service, and business are compatible.

The kitchen table is where it begins, and Kannon, Kuan-yin the entrepreneur with her thousand hands, can bring the enterprise into critical mass. Ordinary managers are motivated by the need to support their families and plan for tuition and retirement. They scrutinize every option and search out every niche for possible gain, and then follow through. Similarly, the manager of an organic enterprise —including clinics and social agencies and their networks—must be equally diligent. The picture of family and its welfare is infinitely broader—that's what makes the difference.

Those organizing to lobby for political and economic reforms must also be diligent in following through. The Base Communities throughout the archipelago that forms the Philippines helped to bring down the despot Ferdinand Marcos, but the new society wasn't ready to fly and was put down at once. The plateau was not the peak, and euphoria gave way to feelings of betrayal. However, you can be sure that many of those little communities are still intact. Their members have learned from their immediate history, and continue to struggle for justice.

A. J. Muste, the great Quaker organizer of the mid-twentieth century, is said to have remarked, "There is no way to peace; peace is the way." For our purposes, I would reword his pronouncement: "There is no way to a just society; our just societies are the way." Moreover, there is no plateau to rest upon, only the inner rest we feel in our work and in our formal practice.

This inner rest is so important. In the short history of the United States, there are many accounts of utopian societies. Almost all of them are gone—some of them lasted only a few weeks. I think we can find that many fell apart because they were never firmly established as religious communities. They were content to organize before they were truly organized.

Families fall apart almost as readily as intentional communities these days, and Dharma practice can play a role in the household as well as in the Sangha. As Sulak Sivaraksa has said, "When even one member of the household meditates, the entire family benefits."[37] Competition is channeled into the development of talents and skills; greed is channeled into the satisfaction of fulfillment in work. New things and new technology are used appropriately and are not allowed to divert time and energy from the path of individuation and compassion.

New things and new technology are very seductive. When I was a little boy, I lived for a time with my grandparents. These were the days before refrigerators, and we were too far from the city to obtain ice. So under an oak tree outside the kitchen door we had a cooler— a kind of cupboard made mostly of screen, covered with burlap that trailed into a pan of water. The burlap soaked up the water, and evaporation kept the contents of the cupboard cool, the milk fresh, and the butter firm. We didn't need a refrigerator. I can only assume that the reason my grandparents ultimately purchased one in later years was that they were persuaded by advertisements and by their friends.

We too can have coolers just outside the kitchen door or on the apartment veranda, saving the money the refrigerator would cost to help pay for the education of our children. Like our ancestors, we too can walk, bicycle, or take public transportation. We can come together like the Amish and build houses for one another. We can join with our friends and offer rites of passage to sons and daughters in their phase of experimenting and testing the limits of convention.

Our ancestors planned for their descendants, otherwise we might not be here. Our small lay Buddhist societies can provide a structure for Dharma practice, as well as precedent and flexible structures for our descendants to practice the Dharma in turn, for the next ten thousand years.

In formally sustaining the Dharma, we can also practice sustainable agriculture, sustainable tree farming, sustainable enterprise of all kinds. Our ancestors sustain us, we sustain our descendants. Our family members and fellow workers nurture us, and we nurture them —even as dāna, the gift, was circulated in ancient times.

Circulating the gift, the Buddhist monk traditionally offers the Dharma, as we offer him food, clothing, shelter, and medicine. But he also is a bachelor. Most of us cannot be itinerant mendicants. Yet as one who has left home, the monk challenges us to leave home as well—without leaving home. There are two meanings of "home" here. One could be the home of the family; the other may involve the family but is also the inner place of peace and rest, where devotion to the Buddha way of selflessness and affection is paramount. The monks and their system of dāna are, in fact, excellent models for us. The gift is circulated, enhancing character and dignity with each round. Festivals to celebrate the rounds bring joy to the children and satisfaction to the elders.

I don't suggest that the practice of circulating the gift will be all sweetness and light. The practice would also involve dealing with mean-spirited imperatives, in oneself and in others. The Buddha and his elder leaders made entries in their code of *vinaya* after instances of conduct that were viewed as inappropriate. Whether the Buddhist Base Community is simply a gathering of like-minded followers of the Dharma that meets for mutual support and study, whether it has organized to lobby for justice, or whether it conducts a business, manages a small farm, or operates a clinic, the guidelines must be clear. General agreements about what constitutes generous conduct and procedure will be valuable as references. Then, as seems appropriate, compassionate kinds of censure for departing from those standards could gradually be set into place. Guidelines should be set for conducting meetings, for carrying out the work, and for networking. There must be teaching, ritual, and sharing. All this comes with trial and error, with precedent as a guide but not a dictator.

Goodwill and perseverance can prevail. The rounds of circulating the gift are as long as ten thousand years, as brief as a moment. Each meeting of the little Sangha can be a renewal of practice; each work-day a renewal of practice, each encounter, each thought-flash. At each step of the way we remember that people and indeed the many beings of the world are more important than goods.

From *Original Dwelling Place: Zen Buddhist Essays*

Eating the Blame

One day, at the monastery of Fugai Ekun, a seventeenth-century
Sōtō master, ceremonies delayed preparation of the noon meal,
and when they were over, the cook took up his sickle and hurriedly
gathered vegetables from the garden. In his haste, he lopped off
part of a snake, and, unaware that he had done so, threw it into
the soup pot with the vegetables.

At the meal, the monks thought they had never tasted such
delicious soup, but the Rōshi himself found something remarkable
in his bowl. Summoning the cook, he held up the head of the
snake, and demanded, "What is this?"

The cook took the morsel, saying, "Oh, thank you, Rōshi,"
and immediately ate it.[38]

This is one of the many dialogues in Zen literature that teaches us
how to use a challenge, and not be used by it in the ordinary way.
What would an ordinary reply have been? "Oh, the ceremonies went
on so long I had to hurry to prepare dinner. I didn't notice that I
had part of a snake in the soup. Please excuse me."

A poor response, you will agree. But the cook in our story had
nothing to defend. He did not for one moment take the Rōshi's challenge as an accusation. He took the matter from there and gave
everyone a wonderful teishō.

How do you handle challenge? You have two options. One is to
defend, and the other is to dance. There are many kinds of defense:
to accuse the other, to excuse oneself, or simply to stand mute. In

any case, the defense is not a dance. There is no teishō; that is, there is no presentation, no teaching. The dance, too, is of many kinds. Sometimes there is an opportunity, as in this case, to make the whole matter disappear. Sometimes you can bundle it up neatly and toss it back. Sometimes a laugh is enough. Certainly we may be sure that this mondō ended with a laugh. Sometimes the dance can be a question, "What is your opinion?" or "How would you handle it?"

> Ching-ch'ing asked a monk, "What is that sound outside?" The monk said, "The sound of rain dripping." Ching-ch'ing said, "Ordinary people are upside down, falling into delusion about themselves, and pursuing outside objects."
>
> The monk said, "How would you handle it, Your Reverence?"
>
> Ching-ch'ing said, "I am on the brink of falling into delusion about myself."
>
> The monk said, "What do you mean, 'On the brink of falling into delusion about yourself'?"
>
> Ching-ch'ing said, "It's easy enough to explain, but to express the bare substance is hard."
>
> (BCR-46)

The monk had not the foggiest notion of what Ching-ch'ing was talking about but he danced very nicely, leading Ching-ch'ing on. Another person might have been intimidated and reacted protectively with Ching-ch'ing's first admonition, and we would have been deprived of the full teishō. The monk came back a second time too, you will notice. Yasutani Rōshi used to say, "You should always ask"—meaning, "Speak up when things are not clear, and get them clarified."

The readiness to dance is freedom from karma. Once when I was in doubt about what to tell people about my religion, I asked R. H. Blyth what he would say if someone asked him if he were a Buddhist. He said, "I would say, 'I am if you're not.'" Very witty, but also defensive, I think. The other person is defeated and that is not the purpose of the dance. Freedom from karma does not mean that I transcend cause and effect. It means I acknowledge that my perceptions are empty and I am no longer anxious to keep my ego bastion in good repair. Does a stranger walk through the ruined walls?

Welcome, stranger! How about a dance? The readiness to dance is the readiness to learn, the openness to growth.

> Tan-hsia asked a monk, "Where have you come from?"
> The monk said, "From the foot of the mountain."
> Tan-hsia asked, "Have you eaten your rice?"
> The monk said, "Yes, I have."
> Tan-hsia asked, "What sort of fellow would give you rice to eat? Did he have open eyes?"
> The monk said nothing.
> Later, Ch'ang-ching said to Pao-fu, "Surely it is one's role to repay Buddhas and Ancestral Teachers by giving people food. How is it that the one who served rice had no eyes?"
> Pao-fu said, "Server and receiver are both blind." Ch'ang-ching said, "Is the one who makes the utmost charitable effort nonetheless blind?"
> Pao-fu said, "Do you call me blind?"
>
> (BCR-76)

"Do you call me blind?" This is the kind of response we are forever giving in the face of challenge. What is it that gets in the way of the dance? Me! Me! Me! I have some eye after all. Do you still say I am blind?

After all, Pao-fu, all those skandhas are empty, you know. All those perceptions are vacant. Empty, yet not empty. What is the form of that emptiness? Well, that would be a dance in response to Ch'ang-ching's final question, "Is the one who makes the utmost charitable effort nonetheless blind?" What would you reply? Yüan-wu, editor of *The Blue Cliff Record*, offered his own response: "Blind!" said Yüan-wu. That's a good one. Pao-fu went on to become a great teacher, but it seems that at this point, he was still frozen in himself.

When I taught in the Upward Bound program at the University of Hawai'i, I tried to get the high school students to act out parts in the novel they were reading. Despite their assignment to prepare their parts, they stood at the front of the room, books in hand, and read aloud with no intonation at all, "'Where are you going,' he asked."

They had not learned to be free of themselves. They had not learned to unite with the matter at hand. Look at Marcel Marceau, the great French mime. There is no Marceau to be seen, only a kite flyer, only a butterfly catcher, only a prisoner with walls closing in. He dances with the circumstances, forgetting himself. Of course it is Marceau doing this. Forgetting the self is not some kind of mystical disappearance.

One of my colleagues remarked to me, "When I meet a student in dokusan, I am meeting my own master." What happens in dokusan? We both of us forget ourselves, I would hope. If you don't know, you say, "I don't know." If I don't know, I will say so. Sometimes students point out aspects of kōans I did not notice before. Sometimes people point out ways I could be more effective as a teacher, and this is very helpful. What do I have to protect?

Alas, the drama plays on and on: "He said this, and I said that. I should have said this other thing, and then he might have said— and then I would say. . . ." Bah! There is no end to it.

This is the problem with defensiveness. It has no end. Ultimately, however, in the oxygen tent, there is no defense. We know this deeply and are frightened of it. So we hold off the acknowledgment as long as possible. But really, there is nothing to defend. There is nothing to protect. There is nothing to depend upon.

This is the great joke of Zen. It is the great joke of the universe. There is no absolute at all, and that is the absolute. Enlightenment is practice, as Dōgen Zenji always said. And what is practice? Getting on with it. When you defend, you are blocking the practice. When you dance, you are getting on with it.

Lightness and heaviness form the contrast we find between those who can dance and those who are preoccupied with themselves. Lightness comes with the experience that one's center is the great void itself. This is the place of great peace. Like the Buddha emerging from beneath the Bodhi tree, you come forth from the experience of pure emptiness into the Sangha, into the dance of coming and going, appearing and disappearing.

Sangha is a treasure of the Buddha Tao, ranking with enlightenment and the truth. Singing and dancing are the voice of the Dharma;

cooking and gardening are the play of the Buddha. Sangha is the complementarity of unity and diversity, of emptiness and form. Sangha is the story of the Buddha, lived out in our work together.

The Sangha ideal is our guide through the complexities of people in combination. Everybody is different, and so misunderstandings arise. With our realization of pure emptiness, with our sense that nothing really matters, we find true devotion because we no longer worry about ourselves. The great potential of the Dharmakāya becomes our own unimpeded great action. Differences become configurations we can use and our collective energy can be focused on the task.

Let's get on with it.

From *Original Dwelling Place: Zen Buddhist Essays*

Sayings and Doings
of a Wise Bird

Searching for a Master

When Raven was living near Jackrabbit Rōshi, he visited him frequently to inquire about the Way. One day he asked, "I hear that the Buddha Shākyamuni looked up from beneath the Bodhi tree and saw the morning star and announced his realization. I get the feeling that something is missing from the story. What happened when he saw the star?"

Jackrabbit laid back his ears, closed his eyes, and said, "He realized the truth of mutually dependent arising."

"Well," thought Raven, "Jackrabbit Rōshi seems to know his Buddhism, but maybe I'm not a Buddhist." So he flew off to see Prairie Dog Rōshi. When he announced himself, Prairie Dog poked her head out of her burrow and blinked in the bright sunshine. Raven told her about his encounter with Jackrabbit Rōshi, and asked, "What happened when the Buddha saw the morning star?"

Prairie Dog crawled out and stood erect. She crossed her paws on her chest, scanned the horizon briefly, and said, "He realized the underlying fact of oneness."

"Well," thought Raven, "Prairie Dog Rōshi seems to know her metaphysics, but maybe I'm not a metaphysician." So he flew off to see Moose Rōshi and found him feeding on water-weed in the creek at Cedarford. Perching himself on a rock, he croaked for the Rōshi's attention. When Moose looked up, Raven told him about his encounters with Jackrabbit Rōshi and Prairie Dog Rōshi, and asked, "What happened when the Buddha saw the morning star?"

Moose dipped his face in the creek again and came up munching. "Delicious water-weed," he said.

"Well," thought Raven, "that sounds more natural." He sat on the rock a moment, but Moose said nothing further and just went on feeding. "Okay," thought Raven, "maybe I'll come back, but for now I think I'll continue this pilgrimage." So he flew off to see Brown Bear Rōshi.

Announcing himself, he stood and waited outside the den. Brown Bear eventually emerged and squatted silently on his haunches. Raven told him how Jackrabbit Rōshi had said the Buddha Shākyamuni realized the truth of mutually dependent arising, how Prairie Dog Rōshi had said he had realized the underlying fact of oneness, and how Moose Rōshi just said, "Delicious water-weed."

"What is your opinion, Rōshi?" asked Raven.

Brown Bear made a strange sound, and Raven couldn't tell whether it was a chuckle or a growl. Finally he spoke. "Something's still missing," he said. Raven waited respectfully, but the Rōshi remained silent.

"Well," thought Raven, "Brown Bear seems to know about something. Maybe I should stick around for instruction."

Metaphor

As they got better acquainted, Raven would ride on Brown Bear's back as he foraged for food. When they were setting out one day, Raven asked, "Do you teach exclusively with metaphor?"

Brown Bear said, "The robin sings in the oak tree; the finch sings in the madrone."

Raven asked, "What do they stand for?"

Brown Bear turned his head to look at Raven and asked, "The lark sings in the deep blue sky—what more can you ask?"

Raven asked, "What is this singing?"

Brown Bear turned back to the path and grunted, "We'll have auditions again tonight."

Faith

One morning after a round of zazen, Raven asked Brown Bear, "Does faith have a role in the practice?"

Brown Bear said, "Great faith."

Raven asked, "How should I direct it?"

Brown Bear said, "One, two, three."

The Unborn

Relaxing with Brown Bear under the night sky, Raven asked, "What is the unborn?"

Brown Bear said, "Awesome."

Raven asked, "Is it the same thing as the void?"

Brown Bear said, "Where does all this come from?"

Turning Points

Raven sat with Brown Bear at zazen early one morning, and afterwards he asked, "Why don't we study turning points that are relevant for the forest today?"

Brown Bear said, "Ask me a relevant question."

Raven asked, "Does the bear-hunter have Buddha-nature?"

Brown Bear growled, "Mu."

"There you go," Raven said. "'Mu' is an old Asian word."

Brown Bear said, "That's the difficulty."

Character

One evening, in a discussion of his personal problems, Raven asked Brown Bear, "What is the role of character in the practice?"

Brown Bear said, "I try to keep my promises."

Raven said, "I try to keep my promises too, but I'm easily distracted."

Brown Bear said, "The cold wind reminds me."

Birth and Death

One evening after chanting sūtras, Raven said, "Over at Jackrabbit Rōshi's community, we were taught that we should be free from birth and death. I've never known how to go about this."

Brown Bear said, "That's because it isn't possible."

Raven said, "There was a clear implication that it is."

Brown Bear lunged at Raven with a horrific snarl. Raven let out a croak and flew to a gray pine nearby.

Brown Bear looked up at him and asked, "What happened to make you croak?"

Raven hopped down to a lower perch and said, "I would rather ask the robin to explain."

Brown Bear sniffed and said, "Now the robin is taking over."

Raven said, "Only his beautiful song."

Brown Bear asked, "What happened to the stones and trees?"

Raven let out a croak.

Brown Bear asked, "Where did they go?"

Raven croaked and then croaked again.

Brown Bear nodded his big head slowly and showed his teeth at Raven. "The robin seems to have a bad cold this morning," he said finally, and both he and Raven laughed and laughed.

Thoroughgoing

Raven came to Brown Bear's den and walked right into his lair. "Time for me to be moving on," he announced.

Brown Bear asked, "What will you say about your study here?"

Raven said, "Brown Bear is quite thoroughgoing."

Brown Bear said, "Try camping out for a while."

The Dream

Raven took Brown Bear's instruction to heart. He wandered a long time, from forests to upland meadows to icy lakes. Finally, with pin-feathers under his beak getting sparse, he found an abandoned place in a tall spruce tree. He fixed it up, and students began to gather, in-cluding Porcupine, who had studied with Coyote Rōshi. Other early students were Woodpecker, Grouse, Badger, Owl, and Black Bear, who lived nearby. They would sit in a circle in the little meadow under the tall spruce. Raven would sit with them and afterward he would respond to their questions, and at more formal teaching times, he would take a perch in the outer branches of an oak tree close by—the Assembly Oak, as it came to be called. A stone out-cropping served as an altar. One fine day Raven took his perch and said to the assembly: "We are children in the dream of the Buddha Shākyamuni. He points to the center of our circle, and the King of the Gods sticks a blade of grass in the ground where he points. Our temple is established, and the Buddha smiles.[39] The bedrock heaved up from beneath the turf there on the far edge of our circle is his presence. We bow and chant his sūtras with his throngs of followers down through the ages. His incense fills the air. His teaching gives us pause. Stop here with him."

The circle was silent. Finally Owl called out, "Are you sure that's not just your dream?"

Raven bobbed his head. "It is my dream."

The Pivot

After zazen one evening Porcupine asked, "We examine turning points as our practice. What is the pivot on which this study turns?"

Raven said, "The large intestine."

Porcupine asked, "So it's all physical?"

Raven said, "All physical, all mental, all moral, all spiritual, all void, all material."

Porcupine thought about this and finally asked, "What's the up-shot?"

Raven said, "Trout in the pool, lilies on the bank."

Ego

During one of the early gatherings at Tallspruce, Badger asked Raven, "How can I get rid of my ego?"

Raven said, "It's not strong enough."

"But I'm greedy," Badger said insistently. "I'm self-centered and I tend to push other folks around."

Raven said, "Like I said."

The Spirit of the Practice

Relaxing with the others after zazen one evening, Owl asked, "What is the spirit of the practice?"

Raven said, "Inquiry."

Owl cocked his head and asked, "What do I inquire about?"

Raven said, "Good start."

Timid and Truthful

Woodpecker appeared in the circle one warm summer evening with a guest. "This is Mole," she said. "He has life questions, but is very timid about coming to meetings. He wants assurances that he is safe," and she cast a look at Badger and Owl.

Raven said, "Well, I'm a predator myself. It's good that we face this issue early." Addressing Mole, he said, "This is the Buddha's sacred temple, where his disciples from all over can feel safe together. You are safe here. Right, Owl? Right, Badger?"

"Safe here," they echoed.

Mole seemed to shiver, but he spoke up and said, "Thank you. I confess I still feel quite timid, but my questions make me stay. Funny situation, isn't it!"

Raven said, "Is there anything that isn't peculiar?"

Mole said nothing.

Raven said, "Anyway, do you want to ask something?"

Mole cleared his throat and asked, "Should I always tell the truth? Sometimes it does more harm than good."

Raven said, "Then it's not the truth." Mole sighed and was silent.

Owl spoke up and asked, "Then should I lie at such a time?"
Raven said, "Tell the truth."

Essential Nature

Early one morning, Woodpecker flew in for a special meeting with
Raven, and asked, "I've heard about essential nature, but I'm not
sure what it is. Is it something that can be destroyed?"

Raven said, "That's really a presumptuous question."

Woodpecker ruffled her feathers a little and asked, "You mean I
shouldn't question the matter?"

Raven said, "You presume there is one."

Bedrock Buddha

Once a disciple of Yogi Rhino sent Raven a message, saying, "You
just have a stone outcropping to represent the Buddha. You should
come over here and meet a living Buddha."

Raven mentioned this in a talk and said, "If that fellow stays on
with Yogi Rhino, he might realize that living Buddhas are all over
the place, and yet our bedrock stands forth alone."

Inspiration

Raven took his perch on the Assembly Oak and said, "Some folks
say that you must find your inspiration in your own heart. In a way
that's true; you must find the place of peace and rest and carry out
your life on that ground.

"It is also true that inspiration comes from somewhere else. The
Buddha looked up from his seat under the Bodhi tree and noticed
the morning star. With that he had his great realization. What did
he realize? That's what we have to get at.

"The Buddha also gave a broad hint about his new understanding when he said, 'Now I see that all beings are the Buddha.' All beings, all that exists, each and every thing, precious in itself, coming
forth saying 'Here I am!'"

Grouse muttered something, and Raven said, "Grouse, did you
have a question?"

Grouse said, "Here I am, but I don't think I'm so precious."
Raven said, "Cluck for us, Grouse." Grouse clucked.
Raven croaked.

Karma

One evening Gray Wolf appeared in the Tallspruce circle for the first time. After she had introduced herself, she said, "Is it all right to ask a question?"

Raven said, "Not only all right."

"Thank you," said Gray Wolf. "Maybe it's obvious to everyone else, but I don't understand the notion of karma. Could you explain it to me?"

Raven said, "Murder will out."

Gray Wolf said, "Sometimes crimes are never solved."

Raven said, "Help me not to live a lie."

Propinquity

Cougar also came by that evening for the first time. After Raven's final response to Gray Wolf, he asked, "Then is karma just cause and effect?"

Raven said, "Propinquity propinks."

Cougar shook his head vigorously and said, "Sometimes it makes me irritated."

Raven said, "Your great chance."

The Purpose of the Practice

Badger attended the circle irregularly because of family responsibilities. One evening he was able to come for zazen and questions. He asked, "What is the purpose of the practice after all?"

Raven asked, "Do you have an inkling?"

Badger hesitated. "I'm not sure," he said.

Raven said, "Doubts dig up the whole Blue Planet."

From *Zen Master Raven: Sayings and Doings of a Wise Bird*

Wallace Stevens and Zen

Like other American and European intellectuals of his time, Wallace Stevens was fond of Asian art and literature. During his career, he acquired Chinese paintings, half a dozen translations of Chinese poetry, and a Buddhist image a friend had sent from Sri Lanka, which he liked because it was "so simple and explicit."[40] Witter Bynner, later a popularizer of Chinese poetry and religion, was his classmate at Harvard (1897–1900). According to the scholar Patricia Willis, Bynner introduced Stevens to Zen Buddhist texts, though it must have been a superficial encounter, for almost no Zen material had been translated by then. He studied the writings of Nyanatiloka, a German Buddhist monk living in Sri Lanka, but seemed to prefer Chinese thought. In 1909 he was reading work by Okakura Kakuzo, probably *Ideals of the East,* and perhaps also his *The Book of Tea* with its chapter on "Taoism and Zenism," a very early account of Zen in English.[41]

It is not, however, in biography or history that the profound accord of Stevens and Zen Buddhism can be discerned. Its ground lies in his poetry itself, and Stevens's own "mind of winter," where there is no intellectual overlay to obscure things as they are:

One must have a mind of winter
To regard the frost and the boughs
Of the pine-trees crusted with snow;

And have been cold a long time
To behold the junipers shagged with ice,
The spruces rough in the distant glitter

Of the January sun; and not to think
Of any misery in the sound of the wind,
In the sound of a few leaves,

Which is the sound of the land
Full of the same wind
That is blowing in the same bare place

For the listener, who listens in the snow,
And, nothing himself, beholds
Nothing that is not there and the nothing that is.[42]

The title of this poem, "The Snow Man," refers not to a construction of snow with two pieces of coal for eyes, but rather to a man who has become snow. A snowman is a child's construction; a Snow Man is a unique human being with "a mind of winter," or, as Yasutani Rōshi used to say, "a mind of white paper." Many Zen stories point to this same mind. Look again at Tung-shan's "Cold and Heat":

A monk asked Tung-shan, "When cold and heat come along, how can I avoid them?"

Tung-shan said, "Why not go where there is neither cold nor heat?"

The monk asked, "Where is there neither cold nor heat?"

Tung-shan said, "When there is cold, let the cold kill you. When it is hot, let the heat kill you."

(BCR-43)

"Killed with cold" is to "have been cold a long time." That is the place where there is neither cold nor heat as a concept. When it is cold, one shivers. When it is hot, one sweats. There is just cold, or just heat, with no mental or emotional associations "in the sound of the wind, / In the sound of a few leaves."

The ultimate experience of perception of "pine-trees crusted with snow," or of "the sound of the wind," is the explicit sense that there is only that phenomenon in the whole universe; as Stevens expresses it: "the sound of the wind . . . is the sound of the land." This is the

nature of seeing or hearing for the Snow Man, perception by the self
which has been killed with cold. It is the mind of white paper that is
actualized by that sight, that sound. In *Genjōkōan,* Dōgen wrote,
"That the myriad things advance and actualize the self is enlightenment." In other words, it is that form, that sound, which makes up
my substance. In the words of Stevens: "I am what is around me"
(p. 86).

> Yün-men said to his assembly, "Each of you has your own light. If
> you try to see it, you cannot. The darkness is dark, dark. Now, what
> is your light?"
> Answering for his listeners, he said, "The storeroom, the gate."
>   (BCR-86)

In maintaining a mind of winter, Yün-men finds his light. There is
nothing to be called the self except the storeroom, the gate, and the
junipers shagged with ice. "The soul, he said, is composed / Of the
external world" (p. 51).

But when the mind is sicklied-over with concepts of the wind as
a howling human voice, then also clouds are faces, "Oak Leaves Are
Hands," and the self perversely advances and confirms the myriad
things. This is projection, the opposite of true perception, and is, as
Dōgen says, delusion—the fantasy of Lady Lowzen, "For whom
what is was other things" (p. 272). As Ching-ch'ing says, "Ordinary
people are upside down, falling into delusion about themselves, and
pursuing outside objects" (BCR-46). Presuming that our emotional
concerns are the center, we project ourselves onto the wind and the
leaves, smearing them with our feelings. We have not yet reached
the place where there is neither cold nor heat. We fall into delusion
about ourselves, and seek to enlarge that delusion by the pathetic
fallacy. Stevens had great fun mocking such self-centered fantasy:

> In the weed of summer comes this green sprout why.
> The sun aches and ails and then returns halloo
> Upon the horizon amid adult enfantillages.
>   (p. 462)

"Enfantillage" means child-play, or childishness. "Adult enfantil-
lages" I would understand to refer to the ascription of human qualities to non-human things, beginning with "why," the conceptual

weed which takes us furthest from realization of things as they are, and continuing with the projection of aches and other silly business upon the sun. The "why" of the child is complete in itself, however, as Stevens goes on to say in closing the same poem, "Questions Are Remarks":

> Hear him.
> He does not say, "Mother, my mother, who are you,"
> The way the drowsy, infant, old men do.

That would be the imagination which is not grounded in a mind of winter, and is thus infantile. Vital imagination has its roots in the bare place outside—which is "the same bare place / For the listener," a generative, not a nihilistic, place. Yamada Rōshi used to say, "The common denominator of all things is empty infinity, infinite emptiness. But this infinite emptiness is full of possibilities."

Empty infinity and great potential, the nature of all things as realized by the mature Zen Buddhist, are also the vision of the Snow Man, with his mind of winter and his capacity to perceive phenomena vividly. Indeed, the final line of "The Snow Man," "Nothing that is not there and the nothing that is," precisely evokes the heart of the *Heart Sūtra:*

> Form is no other than emptiness,
> Emptiness no other than form.[43]

This emptiness of all phenomena, including the self, is being uncovered in modern physics. What appears paradoxical emerges as the complementarity of the suchness and emptiness of all things. This the mind of winter perceives.

We find this complementarity in experiential terms expressed in the course of an exchange between Dōgen Kigen and his master, T'ien-t'ung Ju-ching:

> Body and mind dropped away!
> The dropped-away body and mind!
> (TL-51)

When body and mind drop away, the self is zero. The listener is "nothing himself" and thus experiences the "nothing that is not there," which is all things just as they are, with no associations—just "the junipers shagged with ice." This is a presentation of perennial religious experience as birth-and-death. With this profound realization, the great potential is fulfilled. Personalizing the empty ground, one finds all things are the self: "The dropped-away body and mind!" That is the self as white paper filled with the sound of the wind and the sound of a few leaves.

Bodhidharma, who brought Dhyāna Buddhism from India to China and is revered as the founding teacher of Zen, conveyed this same teaching in the often-told story:

> Emperor Wu of Liang asked Bodhidharma, "What is the first principle of the holy teaching?"
> Bodhidharma said, "Vast emptiness, nothing holy."
> The Emperor asked, "Who is this standing here before me?"
> Bodhidharma said, "I don't know."
>
> (BCR-1)

"Vast emptiness" is metaphysical description; "I don't know" is experience. And Bodhidharma went on from there to cultivate talented Chinese students, our ancestors in what is now Zen.

Emptiness is not only the common denominator of all things, it is itself all things, all space, all time together. Stevens wrote, in "Notes Toward a Supreme Fiction":

> There was a muddy centre before we breathed.
> There was a myth before the myth began,
> Venerable and articulate and complete.
>
> (p. 383)

This is as far as I can trace Stevens's credo as set forth in "The Snow Man." However, "Tea at the Palaz of Hoon," companion of "The Snow Man" at their publication in *Harmonium*, is, I feel, its fellow star in binary complementarity:

> Not less because in purple I descended
> The western day through what you called
> The loneliest air, not less was I myself.
> What was the ointment sprinkled on my beard?
> What were the hymns that buzzed beside my ears?
> What was the sea whose tide swept through me there?

Out of my mind the golden ointment rained,
And my ears made the blowing hymns they heard.
I was myself the compass of that sea:

I was the world in which I walked, and what I saw
Or heard or felt came not from myself;
And there I found myself more truly and more strange.

(p. 65)

Hoon's descent "in purple," like "Palaz" in the title of the poem, is redolent of royalty. It is the kinglike nature of one who emerges out of nothing at all, like the Buddha rising from his profound absorption under the Bodhi tree. He is the king whose domain includes the mountains of Lang and the rivers of Li:

A monk asked, "At the top of a hundred-foot pole, how do I step forward?"
Ch'ang-sha said, "Mountains of Lang, rivers of Li."
The monk said, "I don't understand."
Ch'ang-sha said, "The four seas and five lakes are all under the reign of the king."

(BS-79)

The top of the hundred-foot pole is the place of extremity in ordinary zazen, the place of undifferentiated oneness. There is another step. "How do I do that?" the monk asks. "Stand out of your way," Ch'ang-sha answers in effect. "You descend in purple as the compass of the four seas and five lakes."

Stevens would have appreciated D. T. Suzuki's translation of a line by Wu-men: "In royal solitude you walk the universe."[44] Professor Suzuki took liberties in using "royal" in this instance, for it does not appear in Wu-men's original Chinese. I feel sure that Suzuki was projecting his own experience of empty potency here, and that he shared the vision of "mountain-minded Hoon" (p. 121), descending "through what you called the loneliest air." Fully in accord with "the junipers shagged with ice" is to realize those junipers are none other than myself: "I was the world in which I walked." Actualized, Hoon walked the universe in royal solitude, "And there I found myself more truly and more strange." One is reminded of words attributed to the baby Buddha immediately after his birth, which Zen teachers are fond of quoting:

> Above the heavens, below the heavens,
> Only I, alone and revered.

I wonder if anyone has noticed that "Tea at the Palaz of Hoon" echoes Thomas Traherne's "Wonder":

> How like an Angel I came down!
> How bright were all things here!
> When first among His works I did appear
> O how their glory me did crown!
>
> The world resembled His eternity,
> In which my soul did walk;
> And everything that I did see
> Did with me talk.

Traherne was crowned by "His works"—actualized by the myriad things, as Hoon was anointed and sung with hymns, *as* the world in which he walked, finding himself "more truly and more strange." "And everything that I did see / Did with me talk"—like the vernal wood teaching Wordsworth his humanity, like the wild deer, wandering here and there, keeping the soul of Blake from care. I can't forgo citing Traherne once more, this time from his *Centuries of Meditation:*

> You never enjoy the world aright, til the Sea itself floweth in your
> veins, till you are clothed with the heavens, and crowned with the
> stars, and perceive yourself to be the sole heir of the whole world,
> and more than so, because men are in it who are every one sole heirs
> as well as you.[45]

Thus in different epochs and in different cultures, Wallace Stevens, Thomas Traherne and his successors, and Bodhidharma and his successors present the profound experience of forgetting the self to find actualization and confirmation by the world. I do not know how this could be, but there it is, perhaps no more remarkable than their having the same number of sense organs. But I think we have here something far more significant than human beings expressing common humanity. We are touching the connection between poetry and religion—something more than a connection—as R. H. Blyth insisted—they are, in fact, identical. The poet is a teacher of religion, the teacher of religion speaks in poetical metaphor. Zen teachers from the very beginning peppered their discourses with quotations from such poets as Tu Fu and Bashō, poets who had little or no formal connection with Zen. Of course, Zen was a part of the cultural atmosphere of T'ang China and Tokugawa Japan, but Tu Fu and Bashō were no more "Zen poets" than Stevens was. It is here that the "green sprout why" would take over our cultivation if we let it. I am content to acknowledge Stevens as one of the very few great poets who will be a source of endless inspiration for future generations of Western Zen students.

From *Original Dwelling Place: Zen Buddhist Essays*

Notes

Introduction

1. See David R. Loy, *A Buddhist History of the West: Studies in Lack* (Albany: State University of New York Press, 2002).

2. Bhikkhu Bodhi and Bhikkhu Ñāṇamoli, trans., *The Middle Length Discourses of the Buddha: A New Translation of the Majjhima Nikaya* (Boston: Wisdom Publications, 1995), p. 711.

3. Cited by Donald Swearer, "Three Legacies of Bhikkhu Buddhadāsa," *The Quest for a Just Society: The Legend and Challenge of Buddhadāsa Bhikkhu* (Bangkok: Santi Pracha Dhamma Institute, 1994), p. 17. Quoted also in "Envisioning the Future" in this collection.

4. Wallace Stevens, *Opus Posthumous* (New York: Vantage Books, 1957), p. 189.

5. Gudo Nishijima and Chodo Cross, *Master Dogen's Shobogenzo*, 4 vols. (Woking, Surrey/London: Windbell Publications, 1994–1999), Vol. III, p. 295.

6. Otobe Kaihō, *Kosoku Zenshū Kōan Taikan* (*A Complete Directory of Kōans of the Zen Sect*) (Tokyo: Kangyōsha, 1974), Case 128, p. 20.

7. Henry D. Thoreau, *Journal*, Volume 4: *1851–1852*, Leonard N. Neufeldt and Nancy Craig Simmons, eds. (Princeton, N.J.: Princeton University Press, 1992), p. 171. Alan D. Hodder, in his *Thoreau's*

Ecstatic Witness, guided me to this and other passages in Thoreau's writings (New Haven: Yale University Press, 2001).

8. Thomas Cleary, trans., *The Flower Ornament Scripture: A Translation of the Avatamsaka Sutra* (Boston: Shambhala Publications, 1984–1987), Vol. III, pp. 365–366.

9. John Masefield, *Poems: Complete in One Volume* (New York: Macmillan, 1928), p. 95.

10. Arthur Braverman, *Mud and Water: The Collected Teachings of Zen Master Bassui*, Revised and Expanded Edition (Boston: Wisdom Publications, 2002), p. 187.

11. From the *Wu-hui yüan*, cited by Thomas and J. C. Cleary, *The Blue Cliff Record* (Boston: Shambhala Publications, 1992), p. 605.

12. Braverman, *Mud and Water*, p. 105.

13. Yaichiro Isobe, *Musings of a Chinese Vegetarian* (Tokyo: Yuhodo, 1926), p. 199.

14. Thomas Merton, *The Wisdom of the Desert* (New York: New Directions, 1970), p. 62.

15. R. H. Blyth, *Zen in English Literature and Oriental Classics* (Tokyo: Hokuseido, 1942), p. 61.

16. Ibid., pp. 45–46.

17. Isshū Miura and Ruth Fuller Sasaki, *Zen Dust: The History of the Koan and Koan Study in Rinzai (Lin-chi) Zen* (New York: Harcourt, Brace & World, 1966), p. 259.

18. D. T. Suzuki, *Manual of Zen Buddhism* (New York: Grove Press, 1960), p. 13.

19. Po-Chü-i, *Haiku*, 4 vols., R. H. Blyth, trans. (Tokyo: Kamakura Bunko/Hokuseido, 1949–1952), Vol. I, p. 62.

20. David Hinton, trans., *The Selected Poems of T'ao Ch'ien* (Port Townsend, Wash.: Copper Canyon Press, 1993), p. 6.

21. Cf. Cleary and Cleary, *The Blue Cliff Record*, p. 566.

22. See "The Old Pond" and "The Mountain Path" in this collection.

23. Isobe, *Musings of a Chinese Vegetarian*, p. 4.

24. The following discussion of Shīla and the Sixteen Bodhisattva Precepts is adapted and enlarged from Robert Aitken, "Morality," *The Practice of Perfection: The Pāramitās from a Zen Buddhist Perspective* (New York: Pantheon Books, 1994), pp. 25–32.

25. Asatarō Miyamori, *An Anthology of Haiku: Ancient and Modern* (Tokyo: Maruzen, 1932), p. 252.

26. Brian Victoria, *Zen at War* (New York: Weatherhill, 1997), and *Zen War Stories* (New York and London: Routledge Curzon, 2003).

27. In the spring of 1962, Anne Aitken and I were part of Yasutani Rōshi's assembly when he hosted a pilgrim who was riding a bicycle from Kyushu to Hokkaido to advocate world peace. The Rōshi had the pilgrim address us about his mission, as he sat to one side, beaming his approval. Consider also the following, which Yasutani wrote in 1967, in *Flowers Fall: A Commentary on Zen Master Dogen's Genjokoan*, translated by Paul Jaffe (Boston: Shambhala Publications, 1996), p. 49:

> Unenlightened people have this karmic illness of considering whatever they attach themselves to to have a self. If they make a group, they consider the group to have a self. If they attach themselves to the nation, they consider the nation to have a self.

The Basics

FIRST STEPS

1. Isobe, *Musings of a Chinese Vegetarian*, p. 64.
2. Robert Aitken, *A Zen Wave: Bashō's Haiku and Zen* (New York: Weatherhill, 1978), p. 58.

THE WAY

3. Haruka Nagai, *Makkō-Hō: Five Minutes' Physical Fitness* (New York: Japan Publications, 1972).

WORDS IN THE DŌJŌ

4. John Blofeld, *The Zen Teachings of Instantaneous Awakening, Being the Teaching of the Zen Master Hui Hai, Known as the Great Pearl* (Leicester, England: Buddhist Publishing Group, 1974), pp. 25–26.
5. First words of a sūtra dedication. Robert Aitken, *Encouraging Words: Zen Buddhist Teachings for Western Students* (New York: Pantheon Books, 1991), p. 180.
6. Ibid., p. 173.
7. Cleary and Cleary, *The Blue Cliff Record*, p. 169.

Commentaries

THE OLD POND

1. The lead verse in this chapter and in the chapters following are by Matsuo Bashō, 1644–1694, the founder of the Bashō school of haiku poetry.
2. Daisetz T. Suzuki, *Sengai: The Zen Master* (Greenwich, Conn.: New York Graphic Society, 1971), p. 177.
3. Zenkai Shibayama, *The Gateless Barrier: Zen Comments on the Mumonkan* (Boston: Shambhala, 2000), pp. 54–55.
4. D. T. Suzuki, *Essays in Zen Buddhism: First Series* (York Beach, Maine: Samuel Weiser, 1985), p. 243.
5. See, for example, Kenneth Yasuda, *The Japanese Haiku* (Rutland, Vt.: Tuttle, 1957), p. 169.

THE MOUNTAIN PATH

6. Senkichiro Tachimata, ed., *Kenkyusha's New Japanese-English Dictionary* (Tokyo: Kenkyusha, 1954), p. 1249.
7. See Suzuki, *Essays in Zen Buddhism: First Series*, pp. 371–378.
8. Related by Nakagawa Sōen Rōshi, Hara, Japan, 1951.

QUAIL

9. T. S. Eliot, *Collected Poems 1909–1962* (New York: Harcourt Brace Jovanovich, 1963), p. 13.
10. Harold G. Henderson, *An Introduction to Haiku* (Garden City, N.Y.: Alfred A. Knopf, 1958), p. 48.

THE SHEPHERD'S PURSE

11. Daisetz T. Suzuki, "The Morning Glory," *The Way*, Vol. 2, no. 6, November 1950, and Vol. 3, no. 1, January 1951.
12. Hattori Kōseki, *Bashō Kushū Shinkō (New Studies in the Poetical Works of Bashō)*, 2 vols. (Tokyo: Shijō Shōbō, 1932), Vol. II, p. 704.

THE TEN VERSE KANNON SŪTRA FOR TIMELESS LIFE

13. Miura and Sasaki, *Zen Dust*, p. 292.
14. Burton Watson, *The Lotus Sutra* (New York: Columbia University Press, 1993), p. 304.
15. "Doctrine of Jukai." Not part of the *Shōbōgenzō*. Aitken, *Encouraging Words*, p. 194.

16. Hakuin Ekaku, "Song of Zazen." Ibid., p. 180.

17. Luis Frédéric, *Buddhism*, Flammarion Iconographic Guides (Paris/New York: Flammarion, 1995), pp. 158, 160.

18. "There are only three references to 'mind' in Theravāda Buddhism: (1) *Chitta*, thought; (2) *Mano*, mind (measuring and comparing); (3) *Vinna*, to know." From a conversation with Bhanté H. Gunaratana, Tucson, Ariz., October 3, 1994.

19. John Blofeld, *The Zen Teaching of Huang Po on the Transmission of Mind* (New York: Grove Press, 1958), p. 36.

20. Paul Shepard, *Thinking Animals: Animals and the Development of Human Intelligence* (New York: Viking, 1978), p. 47.

21. Henry D. Thoreau, *A Week on the Concord and Merrimack Rivers*, Carl F. Hovde et al., eds. (Princeton, N.J.: Princeton University Press, 1980), p. 386.

22. Yoshito S. Haketa, trans., *The Awakening of Faith: Attributed to Asvaghosha* (New York: Columbia University Press, 1967), p. 40.

23. Braverman, *Mud and Water*, p. 183.

24. Frédéric, *Buddhism*, p. 145. See "'Do You Remember?'" in this collection for further comments on this story.

25. William James, *The Principles of Psychology*, Volume 1 (New York: Henry Holt, 1918), pp. 224–248.

26. George Meredith, "Lucifer in Starlight."

27. Shepard, *Thinking Animals*, p. 35.

28. Philip B. Yampolsky, *The Platform Sutra of the Sixth Patriarch* (New York: Columbia University Press, 1967), p. 143.

HUI-NENG'S "THINK NEITHER GOOD NOR EVIL"

29. Ming's title was a token of his place of respect in the Sangha. There could have been other "senior monks" in the assembly. Shen-hsiu, on the other hand, held a singularly high position of leadership, junior only to Hung-jen himself.

30. Frederick Franck, "Notes on the Kōan," *Parabola*, Vol. 13, no. 3, p. 35.

31. Suzuki, *Manual of Zen Buddhism*, p. 76.

YANG-SHAN'S SERMON FROM THE THIRD SEAT

32. Kōun Yamada, *Gateless Gate: Newly Translated with Commentary* (Tucson: University of Arizona Press, 1990), pp. 132–133.

33. Charles Luk, trans., *The Śūrangama Sutra* (London: Rider, 1966), pp. 119–236.

34. See Shibayama, *The Gateless Barrier*, p. 183

35. Ibid., p. 186.

THE FIVE MODES OF TUNG-SHAN: THE VERSES

36. For an account of how the metaphysical rational of the Five Modes of the Phenomenal and the Universal evolved in Ch'an history see William Powell, *The Record of Tung-shan* (Honolulu: University of Hawai'i Press, 1986), pp. 63–65.

37. Miura and Sasaki, *Zen Dust*, p. 66.

38. Cf. Miura and Sasaki, *Zen Dust*, p. 69. Dōgen, however, disparaged Tung-shan's Five Modes and similar schemes in his *Butsudō*.

39. Yamei (Bashō School). Blyth, *Haiku*, Vol. II, (Tokyo: Hokuseido, 1950), p. 211.

40. Cf. Miura and Sasaki, *Zen Dust*, p. 70.

41. *Diamond Sūtra*, Chapter 10.

42. See Miura and Sasaki, *Zen Dust*, pp. 46–49, for a discussion of Dharmakāya kōans.

43. Ruth Fuller Sasaki et al., *The Recorded Sayings of Layman P'ang: A Ninth-Century Classic* (New York: Weatherhill, 1971), p. 46.

44. Robert A. F. Thurman, *The Holy Teachings of Vimalakīrti* (University Park: Pennsylvania State University Press, 1981), p. 70.

45. John Stevens, *The Sword of No-Sword: Life of the Master Warrior Tesshu* (Boulder: Shambhala Publications, 1984), pp. 17–18.

46. Robert Frost, "Departmental," *Complete Poems of Robert Frost* (New York: Henry Holt, 1949), pp. 272–273.

47. T'ao Ch'ien; Arthur Waley, *Translations from the Chinese* (New York: Alfred A. Knopf, 1941), p. 89.

48. Powell, *The Record of Tung-shan*, p. 62.

49. A quote from the *Tsu-t'ang chi* (*Ancestral Hall Collection*), ibid., note 174, p. 87.

HSÜAN-SHA'S DRAINAGE DITCH

50. Retold from Zenkei Shibayama, *A Flower Does Not Talk: Zen Essays* (Rutland, Vt.: Tuttle, 1970), p. 33.

51. Ibid.

52. Miyamori, *An Anthology of Haiku*, p. 396.

53. Braverman, *Mud and Water*, p. 158.
54. Ibid., p. 105.

GIVING

55. Richard H. Gard, ed., *Buddhism* (New York: George Braziller, 1962), p. 135.
56. Lewis Hyde, *The Gift: Imagination and the Erotic Life of Property* (New York: Vintage, 1983), p. 11.
57. Ralph Waldo Emerson, *Nature*, [and] Henry David Thoreau, *Walking* (Boston: Beacon Press, 1991), p. 11.
58. Hyde, *The Gift*, p. 28.
59. Cf. Blofeld, *The Zen Teaching of Instantaneous Awakening*, pp. 25–26.
60. Thomas Cleary, trans., *Shōbōgenzō: Zen Essays by Dōgen* (Honolulu: University of Hawai'i Press, 1986), pp. 117–118.

Reflections

WORDS FROM THE RŌSHI

1. Isobe, *Musings of a Chinese Vegetarian*, p. 69.
2. Frederick Franck, *Art as a Way: A Return to the Spiritual Roots* (New York: Crossroad Publishing, 1982), p. 24.
3. Franz Boenders, "Introduction," *Frederick Franck, Recent Paintings and Drawings* (Leiden: Galerie Amber, 1991), p. 2.
4. Franck, *Art as a Way*, epigraph.
5. Virginia Woolf, *Jacob's Room* and *The Waves* (New York: Harcourt, Brace & World, 1959), p. 90.
6. Elizabeth Bisland, ed., *The Japanese Letters of Lafcadio Hearn* (Boston: Houghton Mifflin, 1911), p. 40.
7. J. Baird Callicott and Roger T. Ames, *Nature in Asian Traditions of Thought: Essays in Environmental Philosophy* (Albany: State University of New York Press, 1989), pp. 25–36.
8. Quoted by Dōgen Kigen in his *Henzan*.
9. *Diamond Sūtra*, Chapter 13.
10. Hee-Jin Kim, "'The Reason of Words and Letters': Dōgen and Kōan Language," *Dōgen Studies*, William R. LaFleur, ed. (Honolulu: University of Hawai'i, 1985), pp. 54–82.
11. Trevor Leggett, *Zen and the Ways* (Boulder: Shambhala Publications, 1978), pp. 55–57.

12. Philip Sherrard, *The Eclipse of Man and Nature: An Inquiry into the Origins and Consequences of Modern Science* (West Stockbridge, Mass.: Lindisfarne Books, 1987), pp. 41–42.

13. Italo Calvino, *Six Memos for the Next Millennium* (Cambridge, Mass.: Harvard University Press, 1988), pp. 21–22.

14. Callicott and Ames, *Nature in Asian Traditions of Thought*, pp. 67–78.

15. Linda Hess and Shukdev Singh, *The Bījak of Kabir* (San Francisco: North Point Press, 1983), p. 69.

16. Simone Weil, *Waiting for God* (New York: Harper and Row, 1973), p. 107.

THE MORNING STAR

17. Hakuin Ekaku, "Song of Zazen." Aitken, *Encouraging Words*, p. 180.

18. Yampolsky, *The Platform Sutra of the Sixth Patriarch*, p. 146.

19. *Basic Call to Consciousness* (Mohawk Nation, via Rooseveltown, N.Y.: Akwesasne Notes, 1978), pp. 71–72.

20. *Basic Call to Consciousness*, p. 11.

21. Gary Snyder, *Earth House Hold* (New York: New Directions, 1969), pp. 91–92.

THE DANCE OF AFFINITY

22. David Lindley, *The End of Physics: The Myth of a Unified Theory* (New York: Basic Books, 1993), pp. 51–52.

23. Sōiku Shigematsu, *A Zen Forest: Sayings of the Masters* (New York: Weatherhill, 1981), p. 12.

"DO YOU REMEMBER?"

24. Frédéric, *Buddhism*, p. 145.

25. D. T. Suzuki, *Shin Buddhism* (New York: Harper and Row, 1970), p. 86.

ENVISIONING THE FUTURE

26. E. F. Schumacher, *Small Is Beautiful: Economics as If People Mattered* (New York: Harper and Row, 1975), p. 55.

27. Wes Jackson, *Altars of Unhewn Stone: Science and the Earth* (San Francisco: North Point Press, 1987), p. 126.

28. Schumacher, *Small Is Beautiful*, p. 55.

29. Swearer, "The Three Legacies of Bhikkhu Buddhadasa," p 17.

30. James Hillman, "And Huge Is Ugly," Tenth Annual E. F. Schumacher Memorial Lecture, Bristol, England, November 1988.

31. William Foote Whyte and Kathleen King Whyte, *Making Mondragón: The Growth and Dynamics of the Worker Cooperative Complex* (Ithaca, N.Y.: ILR Press, Cornell University, 1988), pp. 3, 30.

32. Carl J. Bellas, *Industrial Democracy and the Worker-Owned Firm: A Study of Twenty-One Plywood Companies in the Pacific Northwest* (New York: Praeger Publishers, 1972).

33. Jill Torrie, ed., *Banking on Poverty: The Global Impact of the IMF and World Bank* (Toronto: Between the Lines, 1983).

34. Ibid., p. 14.

35. Noam Chomsky, *The Prosperous Few and the Restless Many* (Berkeley, Calif.: Odonian Press, 1993), p. 6.

36. Nejatullah Siddiqui, *Banking Without Interest* (Delhi: Markazi Maktaba Islami, 1979), pp. x–xii.

37. Sulak Sivaraksa, *A Buddhist Vision for Renewing Society: Collected Articles by a Concerned Thai Intellectual* (Bangkok: Tienwan Publishing House, 1986), p. 108.

EATING THE BLAME

38. Retold from Nyogen Senzaki, "101 Zen Stories," in *Zen Flesh, Zen Bones: A Collection of Zen and Pre-Zen Writings*, compiled by Paul Reps (Rutland, Vt.: Tuttle, 1957), pp. 82–83.

SAYINGS AND DOINGS OF A WISE BIRD

39. Raven is echoing a Zen Buddhist folk story about the Buddha and Indra, King of the Gods: "When the Buddha was walking with his disciples, he pointed to the ground and said, 'This spot would be a good place to build a pagoda.' Indra took a blade of grass, stuck it into the ground, and said, 'The pagoda is built.' The Buddha smiled." (BS-4)

WALLACE STEVENS AND ZEN

40. Claudia Milstead, *The Zen of Modern Poetry: Reading Eliot, Stevens, and Williams in a Zen Context*, Doctoral Dissertation (University of Tennessee, Knoxville, 1988), p. 101; and Holly Stevens, ed., *Letters*

of Wallace Stevens (New York: Alfred A. Knopf, 1972), p. 328.

41. Milstead, ibid., pp. 101–104.

42. *The Collected Poems of Wallace Stevens* (New York: Alfred A. Knopf, 1954), p. 9. Quotations from Stevens's poetry are henceforth simply cited by the page number in *The Collected Poems of Wallace Stevens* (New York: Vantage Books, 1990).

43. Aitken, *Encouraging Words*, p. 173.

44. D. T. Suzuki, *Essays in Zen Buddhism: Second Series* (New York: Samuel Weiser, 1972), p. 248.

45. Thomas Traherne, *Centuries* (Wilton, Conn.: Morehouse-Barlow, 1986), p. 14.

Further Acknowledgments

The author gratefully acknowledges permission to reprint the following material:

"Preludes I" is quoted from *Collected Poems 1909–1962* by T. S. Eliot © 1936 by Harcourt Brace Jovanovich, Inc.; © 1963, 1964 by T. S. Eliot. Reprinted by permission of the publishers. The same poem, "Preludes I" is reprinted by permission of Faber and Faber Ltd. for reprinting in countries other than the U.S.A. Poems translated by R. H. Blyth in *Zen in English Literature and Oriental Classics* © 1942; in *Haiku*, Vol. I © 1949; and in *Haiku*, Vol. III © 1952, are reprinted by permission of Hokuseido Press. An eighty-five word excerpt from "Buddhism and the Coming Revolution" by Gary Snyder from *Earth House Hold* © 1969 by Gary Snyder is reprinted by permission of New Directions Publishing Corp. Passages from "Three Legacies of Bhikkhu Buddhadasa" by Donald Swearer in *The Quest for a Just Society: The Legacy and Challenge of Buddhadasa Bhikkhu*, edited by Sulak Sivaraksa © 1994, are reprinted by permission of The Thai Inter-Religious Commission for Development. Passages from *Dogen: Shobogenzo: Zen Essays by Dogen*, translated by Thomas Cleary © 1986 are reprinted by permission of the University of Hawai'i Press. A passage from *Master Dogen's Shobogenzo, Book 1*, translated by Gudo Nishjima and Chodo Cross © 1994, is reprinted by permission of Windbell Publications Ltd. Lines of translated verse from *The Middle Length Discourses of the*

Buddha: A Translation of the Majihima Nikaya © Bhikkhu Bodhi, 1995, 2001, are reprinted with permission of Wisdom Publications, 190 Elm Street, Somerville, MA 02144 U.S.A. www.wisdomspub.org. A passage from Henry David Thoreau's *A Week on the Concord and Merrimack Rivers* © 1980 by Princeton University Press, is reprinted by permission of Princeton University Press. A translated poem from *Appreciations of Japanese Culture* by Donald Keene, published by Kodansha International Ltd. © 1971 by Donald Keene. Reproduced by permission. All rights reserved.

Lines from *An Introduction to Haiku* by Harold G. Henderson, © 1958 by Harold G. Henderson is reprinted by permission of Doubleday Anchor. Lines from *Opus Posthumous* by Wallace Stevens © 1990 by Vintage Books and *The Collected Poems* by Wallace Stevens © 1982 by Vintage Books are reprinted by permission of Vintage Books.

Extract from *Essays in Zen Buddhism* by D. T. Suzuki published by Rider. Used by permission of The Random House Group Limited.

Every effort has been made to trace copyright material. In cases where this has not been possible, the publishers invite copyright holders to inform them so that due acknowledgement can be made in future printings of the book.